The Sex Life of My Aunt

MAVIS CHEEK

faber and faber

First published in 2002
by Faber and Faber Limited
3 Queen Square London WC1N 3AU

Typeset by Faber and Faber Ltd
Printed in England by Clays Ltd, St Ives plc

© Mavis Cheek, 2002

The right of Mavis Cheek to be identified as author
of this work has been asserted in accordance with Section 77
of the Copyright, Designs and Patents Act 1988

A CIP record for this book
is available from the British Library

ISBN 0–571–20508–9

2 4 6 8 10 9 7 5 3 1

Dedicated with love to my real Aunt,
Gladys Saunders,
last of the ten, whose sex life this most *definitely* is not

From the end of the earth will I cry unto thee, when my heart is overwhelmed: lead me to the rock that is higher than I.

Psalm LXI

I smiled to myself at the sight of this money. 'O drug!' said I aloud, 'what art thou good for, thou art not worth all the heap. I have no manner of use for thee, e'en remain where thou art, and go to the bottom as a creature whose life is not worth saving.'

However, upon second thoughts I took it away.

Daniel Defoe, Robinson Crusoe

In the Beginning Was Not the Word . . .

I'm no good at flirting. Never have been. My ploy as a teenager has never changed – if there are males in the vicinity, hold your head up high, stare straight ahead, walk casually. Deceive. If they call out, you ignore them. Walk on. If your eyes meet across the crowded tube, look down, away, up, anywhere but into theirs. Never smile. To smile is to be vulnerable. To meet their eyes and smile is to admit you are interested – and interested means *needy*. Save your smiles for children, kittens and the sunset over the sea . . .

But – if you do? If you risk it and return the enquiring look with a smile? Why then, they are as likely to say, 'Oh, but I was looking at the squirrels,' or 'I was admiring the tube map,' or 'Me? I was yearning for that *other* girl – over there. Oh, no, my dear – not *you* . . . Definitely not you.' God knows how many delicious, gorgeous, wonderful men I passed up in this fashion since I first put breast to brassiere. Hundreds? Thousands? Twenty or thirty at least.

Like many a girl of my time, I was taught from an early age to know my place. Which was a lowly one. Also, and unlike some girls, I was also taught not to put my head above the parapet, to expect little and be glad of what I got. Particularly in the matter of affection and certainly in the matter of that thing called love. That word leaves you wide, wide open. Love is need. Love, as soon as you enter it, is loss. Love. A strange and alien commodity in my growing-up world. Love was all right to be used about gob-stoppers – as in 'I'd love another one' – and all right to be used in 'Thank you, I'd love to come to your party,' but it was not a comfortable word otherwise. You certainly did not bandy it about in public, nor in private very much, towards things of a human nature. 'I love little pussy. Her coat is so warm . . .' was safe. I could say that in front of my mother and she would not blink. If I had asked her if she loved me, or declared that I loved her, she would probably have run a mile.

I did once have a go at sampling the word: when my older sister refused to speak to me for over a week, I went in tears to my mother and held on to her apron and cried into it and – aware that I was treading on dangerous ground – declared that I did not know what I had done and that I wished Ginny wouldn't behave like that because I *loved* her so much. I didn't, of course. That is to say I didn't know what it meant to love. But it seemed an appropriate way to impress my mother with how hard I took that silence. The love-word was all around of course – in films, on the radio, in magazines, in popular songs – but it was never used in our house, so far as I can remember, until then. Its use brought results. My normally laissez-faire mother roused herself, just for once, and stepped in and told my sister to get cracking with the verbiage or else. And though I never tried it again, it lingered in my mind that this love thing, this word, had tremendous power. Whatever it actually meant.

Nobody told me that they loved me until I was nineteen. Less a tragedy and more a family trait. If my mother, who had learned what a burden the word could be, might sprint a mile rather than use it, from what I gather so would her mother before her. If Grandmother Smart, who lived with us and held court in the two front rooms of the house, ever used it in her mothering days towards any of her ten children, none of them remembered it. Poverty and hard grind forbade either of those two women to speak of love when physical survival was all. Use the word love, and feel it, and you were lost. What those ten children did remember was that their father used the word to them. He it was who arrived at the corner of the street and flung open his arms for whichever was the first to arrive and be held. I learned this from my ancient and sole surviving aunt, Cora, the last time I saw her alive. He it was

2

who crooned the songs and stroked their hair and made life better with soft words and moments.

Of course, a father might also have supplied the missing word for me and meant it, but there wasn't one. Only an ephemeral shape, an absence, an ogre, the bogey man, a being read about in books, the live version of which was something only other children possessed. Almost all other children still had one in those early fifties days, and one that lived at home with them too. As far as I know, I never asked where mine was. Children learn not to tread where the family's bodies are buried. Which also teaches them, in later years, how to wound if they have a mind to. After all, to avoid the bodies you have to know where they are in the first place. So, as a child, although I wanted to, I never went up to my mother and said, 'Jennifer Lacey's mother holds her hand,' and 'Sally White's mother sits her on her lap to brush her hair' – I knew better. Such oblique commands would have made my mother withdraw from me even more. She was beyond it, unable to give, afraid of opening up any part of herself that the scar tissue caused by my father had sealed. I accepted it and got on with life. Some people had nice things and others did not – and that included being petted, a room of your own, and fathers. But it made for a very detached way of looking at things. If I don't venture then I can't be hurt.

I used to follow my sister around like an irritating insect. She would shake me off and I'd be back again in no time. But she was five years older than me, light years on in articulacy, and made it quite, quite clear that the fantasy brothers and sisters of our childhood fiction were not for us. The Famous Five, the Secret Seven, *Christmas at Blackberry Farm* – they were only books. In Enid Blyton a big brother ruffled a little sister's hair affectionately; in my house a big sister dragged me by mine and banged my head against the wall if I coughed too loudly. Ah, well. I accepted it. I was odious. I had no right to expect to be liked or wanted. I could be tolerated – but that, too, might change at any time.

3

So – anyway – you tend not to flirt, because flirting comes from confidence. It comes from knowing that if the other person says, 'Christ Almighty, what an appalling thought,' as you mistakenly wink and woggle at him, you can walk away laughing because you don't really care. His opinion counts for nought because – well – you have been loved all your life and so you love yourself. Not me. Inside, throughout my teens, I felt I was the female equivalent of Eliot's hollow men – stuffed, leaning against the next hollow human for dead-eyed support.

> We are the hollow men
> We are the stuffed men
> Leaning together . . .

At nineteen it all changed. The words 'I love you' were said for the very first time. And accepted. Even reiterated. This is the story of what I did when I confronted my own particular brand of 'Eyes I dare not meet in dreams . . .'. And of what I then did to the first person to ever say he loved me.

On Temple Meads Station I Sat Down and Wept

I believe I was around ten years old when I first realized that boys were more than just rivals for adult attention. And it was not much later that they began making it quite clear that they had realized it, too. I've been holding my nose up high in the air at the slightest flicker of interest across a dinner table ever since. Even as a respectably married woman. No – flirting was not in the blueprint. Indeed, I am so averse to it, so inept at it, so entirely and comprehensively unengaged by it, that when I went out for lunch with a woman friend and she suddenly went all peculiar around the eyeballs, I thought she was having an ocular aneurism. Worse – when I realized what she was doing eye-wise with the man at the table by the lavatories, I felt distinctly queasy. To the point where I couldn't finish the fish . . . To the point where, if the salmon was feeling a little on the seared side, it was nothing to my sudden transformation into St Lawrence with the griddle turned up . . . One of the stateliest and most intellectual of all the women I knew, transformed into some simpering, vulnerable missy from Kate Greenaway. It only needed the bonnet and the frilly pantaloons. Ogle, ogle, ogle, she went. I thought it was disgusting. Entirely disgusting. And wholly enviable. But I'm no good at it. No good at all. I would not have known where to begin.

All of which undoubtedly accounts for my marriage to Francis. The first person to tell me I was loved. And despite Carole's disapproval, my husband he would be.

Carole was my dearest friend. She was everything that I thought my sister should be and wasn't, and she *always* put her head above the parapet. She flirted as if it was a crusade. One in five, she reckoned, was a good pulling average. If they said they were only looking at the squirrels she just shrugged, smiled and walked away. Unscathed.

'Try it,' she used to urge. But I never did. Too risky by half. She thought Francis was too dull for me, and he was not afraid of her, but wary. Her life plan was fun now, love later, while I didn't have one, so Francis was very welcome. On meeting him for the first time, Carole said, 'Hi, Frankie!' To which he replied, very politely but very firmly, 'Francis.' Which wrong-footed both of them from the start. 'I'm *Dilly's* best friend,' she said defiantly. While everyone – family, friends, colleagues – called me Dilly, or Dill, Francis only ever called me Dilys. 'Dilys', he said simply, 'is a beautiful name.' When he asked me what it meant, and I said I didn't know, he took the trouble to find out. 'Dilys', he said, 'means the Perfect One. And that'll do me.' He meant it. Dilys, and only Dilys, would do. He was not being pompous – he was just himself. Perfectly and wholly Francis Edward Holmes.

He loved me with gratifying desperation and I thought, Well, that'll do me. In those early days I could read it in his eyes, see it as his hand shook, feel it blasting out of him like supersonic vapour. Than which, in matters of being wooed, there is no greater aphrodisiac. I caught some of the fall-out. He seemed the best thing ever to happen to me, and I think he was. When he said that he loved me, something fluttered and bumped against my ribs – stirring up the emptiness, apparently dispatching it. But what I did not know, not yet having read Flaubert on the subject, was the Big Truth behind 'In my heart there is a Royal Chamber that is forever sealed . . .'

So – Francis. To whom I was certain that I had given all of myself, and for ever. We met at the art gallery where I worked in the late sixties. Something had happened after 1960. Angela Carter blamed all that free milk and orange juice and cod liver oil which put a yeastiness in the air. Life fizzed. We took what was due to us and reserved the right to ask questions. It was a kind of democracy. Someone from my background could now enter the hallowed portals of the world of art just by answering an advertisement in a newspaper. In the past the job would have gone to a friend of a friend called the Hon. Priscilla de Vere Something. So there I was, hair like a pair of curtains, eyes weighed down with night-black mascara, in Bond Street, when Francis walked in to get himself some contemporary art.

He was a lawyer – just qualified – and he wanted a Hockney etching for his chambers. Indeed, at that point in the development of Arts into Investment, particularly in the City where he worked, *not* to have something by Scarfe on one wall and Hockney on the other was as bad for your image as turning up for a job interview at the GLC *sans Guardian* during the reign of Our Ken. It was the proper thing to have, and Francis was simply incapable of not conforming. But at least he liked contemporary art. At least he wanted to see it hanging on his walls or displayed on a plinth or table (he bought one or two pieces of sculpture, too) – which was not always the case. I had, in my time, sold Alan Davie lithographs to television executives, Dubuffet screenprints to bankers and Armitage bronzes to venture capitalists, only to find later that the sweet, unsuspecting items either hung upside down on their walls or were carefully placed the wrong way round and spotlit. On one occasion a complete set of big, gorgeous colourful Paolozzi screenprints was purchased, wrapped in strong brown paper and immediately placed in the vault of a bank. A good investment.

When Francis entered my life, I was nineteen and the only member of the sales staff present in the gallery that lunchtime (the current Hon. Priscilla de Vere Something had gone off to sort out her wedding list at the Army & Navy that day – a strange choice, I considered it, wondering what on earth, as newlyweds, they would want with military and naval artefacts and being unversed – then – in the erstwhile needs of Empire Wives). Of course, I was on safe ground, and of course our eyes met, though there was nothing daring or flirtatious about it. I just knew my ground, that was all. Besides,

7

there is absolutely no way you can sell someone a picture without meeting their eyes occasionally. Indeed, if you go through the spiel of 'Very small edition . . . this is an early one so the lines are sharper . . . something rather wonderfully Hogarthian about his narrative line', blah-de-blah, and you are staring at the ceiling throughout, you will never get to first base with the client's wallet. Besides, I was selling a picture, not selling myself, so it was always easy. I was also wearing a purple velvet quasi-Victorian frock from Laura Ashley – long skirt, buttons up the front, ruffles round the sleeves and hem – because I was going to an opening at the Tate that night. Odd as it may seem now, long, ruffled velvet frocks – and purple to boot – were considered stylish then. I was dressed to attract and it worked.

He smiled, I smiled, he bought. At first just the etching, but then, when it was framed and he came back to collect it, he also bought me. He took me to Rules, which was just round the corner, to 'celebrate the purchase', because Rules was the proper place to have lunch with a possible new girlfriend. Rules showed her you knew what was what, that you valued her enough to spend a decent amount of money, and it was proper enough to say My Intentions Are Perfectly Honourable. They also happened to offer those twin delights of the English Luncheon – oysters and game pie.

Well, if I was no good at flirting, I certainly knew what to do with oysters. There was no way you could get through life in the Cork Street circuit in the sixties and not know how to eat oysters, so I had learned. Oddly enough they never worried me – either in looks and feel, or luxurious price. My grandmother, who apparently suffered from quinsies (tonsillitis nowadays) throughout her childhood and who lived in the mean streets of Borough during the 1880s with a father who was a drayman and a mother who was a laundress, nevertheless was fed chopped oysters when she could swallow nothing else. They were – quite literally – ten a penny then. I grew up thinking of them – if I thought of them at all –

as very ordinary, so neither Rules, nor oysters, fazed me. But I also now knew about their suggestive qualities. I might not be able to flirt, but I certainly knew how to manipulate the props. The main thing for a bashful girl in those days was to appear not to know the effect she was having, while having it.

Not being able to flirt in an eyeball to eyeball manner meant that I tried harder with obliquer forms of attraction. It was the *sine qua non* of dating life, since the film of *Tom Jones* and the erotic, slavering eating scene, to try to turn your dining companion on by giving tongue to glistening morsels while appearing not to know you were doing so. I knew this was attractive, although – like quite a few of my girlfriends – I was unclear then what was so sexy about chewing, dribbling and slavering over meat and two veg while smiling like a drunken tart. But we did it anyway. Oral sex had not quite impacted on free love then. We knew something was out there, lurking, but we were not very clear what. Of course, it was Carole who told me eventually.

Anyway, I certainly gave good slaver to the oysters that day in Rules. I suppose the occasion was made the more erotic by the propriety of the place and its very name, both of which exude an air of correctness. The whole experience was undeniably sexy, I could see that – Francis was beside himself while attempting to continue normal conversation – and I – bathetically – enjoyed his company and appearing to be the centre of his world. Perhaps, after that lunch, just like the etching and its frame, he really did think that I was paid for too . . .

No, no – that is too cynical, too unfair. I am just looking back desperately to find causes, reasons, *justifications* for what has happened since. But it was the Hollow Woman – not Francis – who let it happen. In a way – yes – I was bought by him, but it was my choice. He was not like that. Not Francis. What he *was* – I should say *is* – like is, well, say the difference between Martin Luther King and Cassius Clay. Both good men, both dynamic men, but the one for ever honour-bound by his beliefs, the other set free by his achievement. Francis was wholly good, worthy, dedicated – but never going to punch anyone on the nose and reach for the stars. I don't even think he had a dream beyond the very normal ones of home comfort, hearth happiness, and high attainment in his profession. Honour was near the top of his list of required characteristics for both himself and the rest of the world, and even when he stumbled on the path, which was almost never, he quickly and genuinely repented.

When he asked me to marry him we were at Henley, another bit of *de rigueur* in those days and not yet metamorphosed into a businessman's bunfight. The Henley Regatta, then, was still a proper part of the Season, and any corporate hospitality was both expensive, discreet and restrained. Proper. We stood in the greeny shade of a willow watching the scullers, and he handed me a glass of champagne, looked me in the eye, raised his glass and said, 'To the next Mrs Holmes?' Which was very daring for Francis. I remember looking out over the water and watching the huge, gleaming muscular thighs of the men in boats and thinking 'Cor', and then Francis said, 'Penny for them?' And I was so anxious to avoid his guessing that I was actually wondering what it might be like to be had in the Biblical sense by one such as they that I said 'Yes' to his question immediately. 'I'm so happy,' he said, as I looked away from those pumping thews back at him. 'So am I,' I said firmly. And that little watery vignette of desire, which I had completely forgotten until recently, should never have been ignored.

The fact was that having been born into the opposite world from his, I observed the privileged classes at play, and while I was not seduced into pretending I was of them (and therefore becoming what my Grandmother Smart called being 'no better than she ought to be'), I was utterly and completely seduced by the elegance and the confidence and the trappings that went with it. In any case, in those heady democratic days of the sixties, it was a positive *plus* to come from the working class. This was our time, youth and a revolution that cut across all barriers. If I had put on a pound for every Hon. who adopted a Liverpool accent 'twixt '62 ('She Loves You') and '70 (bloody old Yoko) I'd be the size of Hampton Court. Social democracy was here to stay. We believed it. We had no idea it would last only approximately ten years. Having spent all my growing up in a hand-to-mouth existence in two suburban back rooms, I was ready for a combination of *La Dolce Vita* and the High Life. Being courted by Francis allowed me to open my arms to what money can buy and what old money, generally, already owns. Quality, elegance. The absolute quality and elegance that goes with wealth. Not twenty-nine shillings and eleven pence mock croc stilettos from Dolcis, but the real thing, caught in an Amazon swamp, fashioned by craftsmen and sold in Bond Street at three times the price of Russell & Brom, with handbag to match. I observed how certain things were done, and I learned on the hoof. By the time I was taken down to meet the parents-in-law-to-be in their West Sussex pile, I could pass muster as the right sort of gel (still necessary with them as the social revolution had not, quite, spread to the Raj generation) – if a little iffy on the family tree.

My accent, bearing, looks and job all fitted. When my future mother-in-law asked me what my father did, Francis very quickly stepped in and said, 'Army.' Which was true. He did not, of course, add that my father rose from humble Private in the RAMC to leave the war as Lieutenant, and was then stripped of his rank a few years later on account of a little embezzlement charge. Nor that my mother still worked in a factory. Nor that my father was a bigamist, which left my mother with two little bastards to support. Nor that she had learned to manage poverty at her mother's knee, my grandmother also having been abandoned, a mother of ten (abandoned in both senses, presumably, given that number of children) who exemplified another of her favourite slogans, 'Hard work never killed nobody', by going out cleaning offices in Gray's Inn, City Road, and surrounding areas. Curiously enough, she probably cleaned in the same building that housed Francis's first chambers by then. A possibility that we both found strange, though for quite different reasons.

Francis was easy with it all. When I took him home to meet my mother and he had to virtually climb over all the post-war furniture and tattiness that was home (she spread into the whole of the house she had shared with Grandmother Smart after she died), he made no comment about the telly remaining on, if low volume, and accepted the glass of sweet sherry with good manners. When she greeted him with the customary words of welcome to a man entering the house, 'Plenty of work?', he merely said, 'Yes, thanks,' instead of puzzling over it. His shrewd brain realized that to work was to live, quite literally, when you had grown up at the sharp end in the Depression. He did a very daring thing and, without being invited, began calling her by her Christian name, Nell. Later, in the kitchen, when I asked her if she minded, she said, 'No, of course not, it makes good sense.' It was as if I had asked her if she minded the Queen calling her Nell. Absurd. Francis was *quality*. He was also fair-haired.

My mother liked him, of course. She always did have a penchant – as she said afterwards – for fair men. Her first husband – well, her *only* husband, given my father's wife extant – was killed at the beginning of the war. No time to beget children. He was fair, I knew, from the photographs. Her constant preoccupation as she grew older was the cruelty of the Fate that took Fred from her and the even greater cruelty that let it lead her on its cloven hoofs towards my dad. If Fred had lived, she would never have met my dashing bastard of a father. Nor been taken in by his educated voice, his red-gold hair and blue eyes. The only photograph I had of him was black and white, their wedding day, and that was hidden well out of sight. But I knew his colouring, because I had it too. Grandmother Smart, who was always praising Virginia for being a Smart to the letter, was also very firm on the subject of my being physically my father's daughter. It was to my mother's credit that she never held it against me – for she hated him, and his memory, with a passion. 'If you get a good man, you hold on to him . . .' she said. With more feeling than I could ever remember. I was far too relieved to have got *any* man not to hold on to him very, very tightly. I'd begun thinking I was on the shelf at seventeen and a half. At nineteen, when I met Francis, I was convinced of it.

He and I were married six months after we met, four months after he proposed, at St Martin's, Holborn. And if my side of the family caused his side some confusion in the matter of their not knowing the form, it really did not bother us. With that spirit of real democracy abroad, even his parents caught some of it in the end and grudgingly welcomed me into the family. I remember Francis's mother saying, 'Why only six months?', and looking at me suspiciously. 'Because I can't wait any longer,' he said. She looked a little shocked at such a wanton display of emotion and pointed out that there was barely time to get our list out to Peter Jones and the Army & Navy . . . I now understood this particular emporium perfectly.

I was astonished at the wedding presents – really astonished. We were given a whole canteen of exquisite silver cutlery, *linen* bedlinen, silver wine coolers, crystal glasses, so that my mother's towels from the Co-op and my various aunts' and uncles' gifts – Cora's teak salad bowl, even the upwardly mobile Arthur and Eliza's cut-glass vase – looked cheap and tawdry by their side.

Francis was being accurate when he said he couldn't wait. He was nearly beside himself with the waiting – and I wasn't far behind. For some crazy reason he had suggested – and I agreed to – our not having sex until our wedding night. If there was something very pure about the concept, there was nothing pure at all about its heightened consequences. In restaurants I teased him with asparagus, in the street I wore mini-skirts bordering on the prosecutable, and when we parted I gave him a long, lingering, dangerous kiss. During those months we very nearly eloped several times and I was driven so nearly demented with frustration that I never could think beyond it to the more delicate matter of Love.

At the wedding my mother behaved with great dignity and wore what she called a 'nice two-piece costume in navy' and a small, elegant piece of millinery which I helped her choose. She showed a flair for good dress sense that I never knew she possessed. It was Francis's older sister, Julia, who suggested a small hat. Quite rightly, she said that people who were not used to hats got into terrible muddles with them. The only sign of how strained my mother felt among my new family was that she stuck out her little finger when sipping her wine and nearly jumped out of her skin when the master of cere-monies banged his gavel on the table. Apart from that she seemed quite serene. And she was so happy for me. And for herself. If her daughter had married well then she would be looked after in her old age. And she would have been, too, if she had lived. No matter how unsure of herself she felt inside, ultimately she knew she was the bride's mother and therefore carried the dignity of the day.

But Virginia, my sister, was another matter. Something had got right up her nose and there was nothing to be done with Virginia. She was eaten up with envy for my job, and now for my good fortune (both spiritual and fiscal) in my husband. Some time before, she had married a lovely man called Bruce who worked in his father's three-hander building firm, and they had the usual local church and local church-hall wed-ding at which I was, very grudgingly, allowed to be the chief bridesmaid. My Grandmother Smart said to Virginia that there was no way out of it – a family wedding was a family wedding and a sister was a sister. The implication being that I was still that irritating little insect. To Virginia my high-class wedding seemed a snook-cocking exercise. Bigger, grander, richer than hers, one she and the family could not interfere with because they weren't paying for it. The cost of it was beyond them. It was also announced in *The Times*. When Virginia heard, she rang me up about that, calling it a very silly bit of showing off. She was a little flummoxed when I said I agreed with her, but that Francis's parents had insisted.

The other thing that got up Virginia's nose was that she could take no ceremonial part in the big day, because she was about eight-and-a-half-months pregnant. Even my mother intervened – not something she usually did – to say to Virginia that she wasn't going to boil the water if all the standing around and whatnot brought it on. I think even Virginia realized that she had gone too far when she said that we'd just have to change the date. My husband-to-be stared at her wondering if it was a joke. Just to make sure, he put his arm around me and said, 'We have to remember that this is Dilys's day, Ginny.' And though she didn't look at all convinced, so it was.

But if she couldn't walk down the aisle with me, she was damn well going to show the world that she was as good as *anybody*. When I said that nobody doubted it in the first place, she wheeled around and yelled that 'there I went, patronizing her again' – it was a favourite accusation of hers. 'You might have persuaded Mum to toe the line with her hat,' she yelled, 'but you're not dictating to me. Not *you* . . .'

Thus, in the matter of wedding headgear, there was no telling Virginia. She wore a huge cartwheel hat, the brim so stuffed full of flowers that she looked like a woman whose preferred form of shopping trolley was on her head. One who had not – quite – got the hang of it. The brim kept catching in people's nostrils, and at one point her husband, the mild-tempered Bruce, thought someone had punched him in the jaw and even raised his fist slightly before he saw her peering up at him like a pregnant mushroom. At table she sat rigid-backed, which pushed the bump out aggressively. And she tried not to be impressed with anything. The bishop seated next to her helped her to more wine – drink not having been banned by the pre-natal lobby at that point – and on her other side Francis's seventeen-year-old cousin engaged her in a conversation – well-meaningly enough – about the pleasures of the Hunt. Virginia never forgave me. It wasn't the foxes she minded, it was how inadequate and hunted it made her feel. In our family Virginia was not used to feeling either. I muttered something about the unspeakable in pursuit of the uneatable and that the lack of dignity was all his – and that he was only seventeen, after all – and she turned on her heel, called me patronizing, and refused to speak to me in anything but the coolest of ways for several years, until our mother developed the first of her cancers. The usual pattern of our vast family's weddings. Generally someone ended up in a huff.

We honeymooned in a quiet part of Corfu. In a villa owned by one of Francis's friends. All the way there Francis exuded repressed lust and I was as much amused as excited as gripped by the power I held as by the need for sex myself. I had no idea, then, that this would be the basis of our love life. What all this suppressed desire did, of course, was cover up the quiet way I felt about Francis. The pragmatic sense of relief at having finally tied the knot. 'Well, now that's done and I'm glad it's over,' as T. S. Eliot's typist would have it. This settled state was hidden in amongst all the buzz of the excitement of our four months' denial. By the time we staggered off the plane and our driver dropped us at the villa, we were both crawling for each other. And although we both vowed we'd never wish it on ourselves again, it was not quite so odd then as it would be considered now.

Once in the legally wedded Kingsize, with the sound of the sea and the crickets, he proved himself to be an enthusiastic lover, very English public school – bags of energy but no style. Not that I was sure of anything. Neither of us was a virgin – but that we were to each other made it feel that way – and on our first night Francis was so completely overwhelmed with fear and desire and, I imagine, the eternal guilt that befalls the British and the pleasuring of themselves that we ended up at three in the morning sitting on our terrace playing Scrabble. It was all right eventually – by the time we returned to London we had competently rogered the hide off each other, and Francis was relaxed about our love life from that day forth. Indeed, I swear he preened himself as we came back down the aircraft steps at Gatwick. I was always happy and satisfied with the way we were together but never electrified like Francis. He liked it and made no bones about it and in all our years together he was never uninterested. Of course, over time it died away a bit, but it never went away completely. Well, not for him.

I had no other grand passion to compare. My previous experience of any significance, with an out-of-work performance (called 'Happenings' then) artist and poet of nineteen, had not been any wilder. He smoked so much marijuana that it was always touch and go whether he would quite make it or not – and I certainly never did. But he *did* – bless his heart – teach me how to go solo. For which I was ever after grateful. Even if he did teach me so that he could fall back into a brain-dead Nirvana with a clear conscience because I knew how to get on with it. Nevertheless, after Corfu I had a sense that there was something wild and wonderful out there that I had never experienced, and now never would. I didn't pine for this Great Unknown. I just knew that there was something so all-engulfing that people were even prepared to die for it. Unless Balzac and Shakespeare and Puccini were liars.

But I *was* blessed. Francis could not have been more different from what I knew, very hazily, about my father. I knew he would never demean me in any way, and I thought that if I kept that other little bit of myself, the bit that he didn't reach, the streak of passion, if you like, as my secret place, then we would be fine. And there it was. In that Royal Chamber. Dormant but not dead.

We were happy. I went on working at the art gallery for a few more years, until our first child, James, was born, whereupon we moved from Francis's flat in Holborn to a smart little house in Fulham and had our next child, John. After which we moved to a considerably grander house in Fulham where we stayed. Virginia watched all this enviously.

I did the motherhood bit, working from home with a regular round-up spot in *The Art Buyer* and reviews for other magazines. For me, working was a kind of sanity. In the soothing silence of the Tate's archives, going through old Richard Hamilton catalogues or choosing a slide or two, I often forgot that I hadn't had a complete night's sleep for two years.

Virginia considered it all self-indulgent. It was hardly real work. She was struggling with her two and doing all the business side of things for Bruce, who was now working solo. He loved plumbing and that was what he did. As our children got older, while I pottered around the fringes of the art world and began curating the odd exhibition here and there and writing the occasional bit of catalogue copy, my sister burned the midnight oil over account books and invoices and the cost of copper piping. And she was not at all pleased when my picture appeared in the press – as it very occasionally did – at the launch of a show. I always thought there was an edge of hope in her voice if ever she rang up and asked, 'And how's Francis? Everything all right between you two?' Our lives diverged, especially after our mother died, and that was a much easier way to be.

When James and John were both at senior school I had a miscarriage, with complications. The daughter we both wanted. It was suggested by Dr Rowe that we left it at that. I did not recover very quickly. I was angry, miserable, unkind for a couple of years afterwards. And Francis had a brief affair with one of the pretty girls with shoulder pads who worked at his chambers. It's possible that she thought she was on to something, but he was too good and honourable at heart.

The affair lasted about four months. 'I don't know how it happened,' he said to me. 'One minute we were sitting talking at the office. The next I was in her bed.' He blinked with puzzlement. He had no idea what a trophy he was. He ended it and told me about it and asked me to forgive him. Which I did, because I really could not blame him, and because it brought me to my senses. If I carried on behaving the way I was, I would lose everything. It never occurred to me to wonder if everything was what I wanted to keep . . . For a long time afterwards he flayed himself, metaphorically, for this fall from marital grace.

After that we settled down quite peacefully. He arranged a long holiday to coincide with my fortieth birthday and we took the boys all round America. I'm not sure if love was reborn between us. Had it ever gone away? But we got back into the routine of intimacy, and James and John loved the trip. For them it was the journey of a lifetime – they now talk to their own children about it and still remember a surprising amount. I remember less of the travelling and the places, more how Francis and I were with each other. When we began sharing a bed together again we were so careful, so newborn, so considerate and gentle, that it was like another honeymoon. Looking back, I realize that was what he had in mind, though he never said. It still wasn't Krakatoa, but it was like coming home again. Warm, reassuring, peace again. Of the two of us, I think Francis was the more bruised by his straying. He had hurt me, so he thought, at a time when I was weak, and it was unforgivable. I, on the other hand, took it in my stride. These things happen, I told myself, and closed the door on it. Francis thought I was being wonderful, but I wasn't. The fact was, it hardly touched me at all. That was the bigger shock and the one I kept to myself. I did not, really, mind that my husband had been making love to another woman. Like the vignette of the scullers, this was, perhaps, something of which I should have taken more notice. In a way I thought it was funny. The whole thing sat so awkwardly in the nature of Francis. I also had to keep a straight face during some of the confessional. Apparently the power-

19

suit took him to the Ministry of Sound for his one and only experience of clubbing and he was convinced he would have a heart attack. She also told him that he should drink his beer straight from the bottle and introduced him, for wacky fun, to the delights of the Late Nite Drive-Thru McDonald's – both of which he made a mess of. 'The only thing I could taste', he said, with some perplexity, of the burger, 'was the gherkin.' Memo to young women seeking older men: dignity is all.

As a final full-stop to the whole thing, Francis bought me a Ceylon sapphire, the lightest, clearest blue – a symbol of fidelity, he said – and vowed he would never betray me again. I think he had frightened himself at how close he came to busting his world apart. Virginia looked at the winking bright blueness of the ring with a mixture of admiration, envy and contempt, and said very crisply that he should have waited, since sapphires represented your forty-fifth wedding anniversary. I laughed at something that seemed impossible and so far away, and Francis – who knew human nature rather well and understood my sister's hidden scars – said bravely, 'Well, I'll buy her another one then.' Not the kind of thing to say to Virginia. But there was no time for her to take offence again. She and I needed each other in the following year, because our mother finally died.

The battle against cancer had been long and arduous. Twice she went into remission, and eventually it went to her bones. I was angry. She had neglected to think the aches and pains it began with were anything more than the sufferings an ageing woman could expect. A long, hard working life in a factory – its structure lined with asbestos – and the accompanying lifestyle of stress and smoking was more than likely to end that way. She was also lonely and bitter, and the past, like the cancer itself, gnawed away at her. The family was all. She had no friends. Shame made her wary of people. As she said, 'Once you have been kicked in a gutter by your husband, in full view of the street, you don't want to meet anybody's eye . . .' My growing up had been rich with graphic morsels such as this, the whole story of which I could only imagine.

Francis and I made her life more comfortable, but it was always difficult with Virginia. She watched our relationship and our gifts to my mother like an angry hawk. I was obliged to consult her on everything. My mother knew this – and sometimes she would whisper to me, looking very nervous, that she'd better not do, or accept, something because 'You know what Ginny's like . . .' The cancers were relentless. She battled for too many years to count. If there was a God, I vowed, then it was not the kind of God I could worship.

There was no room for envy or recriminations between Virginia and me during all that final suffering and they were set aside, I hoped forgotten, in the greater task of getting through the pain of it all. After the funeral, when it came to sorting through my mother's possessions, I found a large brown cardboard box containing her hat from our wedding, never worn again, and the corsage presented to her that day by Francis's father. These were both swathed in tissue paper and surrounded by stalks of long dried lavender from the garden. She had also saved the order of service, the wedding breakfast menu and one of the champagne corks. I knew my mother had loved that day. Had loved the dressing up, the perfect little hat, the matching shoes and handbag, gloves – being at the centre of it all and coming out of herself for a while. It was a precious find that I kept from my sister. There was not a trace of her wedding, apart from a photograph on the mantelpiece of the smiling bride and groom, with me standing somewhat edgily behind.

Even then I could not win. I made the mistake of suggesting to my sister that she take everything of our mother's that there was, which was not very much since the house was rented, including the small savings our mother possessed (the pitiful amount she put away for her funeral), for her children. James and John were content with some of the family photographs and a cup and saucer each, and I just took the green glass dressing-table set – always the essence of mother. But Virginia saw this as just another flaunting.

'We will share it,' she said of the money.

I suggested that we gave it to a cancer charity. Mistake.

'*You* may be able to afford that sort of thing,' she said. 'We can't.'

All the good that had built up between us during our mother's illness just melted away. It was *en guard* again. And very wearying.

Virginia was just too late for the sixties revolution. She had worked at a bank – which was considered an excellent job until the sixties burst all that wide open – instead of at an art gallery, and she had married a plumber instead of a lawyer. Blue collar, not white. After leaving his father's business, Bruce was a one-man band, and he remained a one-man band, and he made plumbing an art. After he put in our central heating, we used to show our friends the piping. It was beautiful. Exquisite. A symphony in copper. A Morris Louis of lines. He never had to advertise. When I saw the work in progress on the refurbishment of the London Underground, which had exposed the hidden perfections of the Victorian builders, I told Bruce that it reminded me of his work. Pure artistry for artistry' s sake. He went to see it. Virginia thought I was both showing off and comparing him with the navvies. 'How *bloody* patronizing,' she said. Even Bruce dared to tell her to shut up over that one. But it was never going to be resolved, this resentment, and I walked on eggshells with her in case admiring their new patio, or some new purchase, caused even more of an outburst. Conversation between us became stilted and false. She was still locked into the old way. I had gone up in the world, and that was turning yourself into someone who was no better than they ought to be . . . Well, certainly not that irritating little sister. Fortunately I had Carole cheerfully buzzing about in my life. Virginia resented that too. It was as if I should never have existed.

I never really understood the game. It seemed to me that

success or good fortune was something you celebrated – not resented – and besides, Virginia and Bruce were comfortably off with a between-the-wars villa in Kingston and a half share in a small villa in Spain. Their son, Alec, is a bank manager in Leeds, and their daughter Colette teaches games and sport to under-elevens and runs the marathon when she can. So, as Bruce would say, A Result. But not quite for my sister. Virginia was both proud of my marriage to a high-earning, high-achieving lawyer – and eaten up about it. And the only time I really let rip at her was after Colette's wedding, when she said, 'Of course they won't be going to Barbados for their honeymoon . . .' (we had paid for our son John's honeymoon there) and 'Sorry it's only hock and not champagne . . .' once too often.

'Hock', I said, driven beyond endurance, 'really betrays your origins. A nice white burgundy would have been so much more stylish . . .'

That was another six months of sisterly union down the drain. Fortunately I stopped myself just in time from also telling her that I had earned my sapphire on account of my husband shagging one of his secretaries. That would have stopped her in her tracks. In her eyes Francis was the perfect provider and she often told me so. With many a sigh. If she'd known the truth she would probably have told me to keep quiet, let him get on with it, don't rock the boat, think of the mortgage . . . Actually, we didn't have one, but I would never have dared to tell her that either.

There are three holes in people's lives. One is the hole that remains open because you do not get enough love to fill it. The second is the hole that remains because you do not find a fulfilling direction to live by. And the third is the hole that remains because you do not have enough money to make up for one or both of the other holes. I had, it seemed, plugged each one. Virginia was not even sure she had plugged any of them. Love for her was a controlling thing. If you love me, you will do this, be this, not do that . . . Her family learned to love her around it. And if she was unsure about love, well, she *certainly* did not feel she had fulfilment, nor enough money. And her little squirt of a sister apparently had it all. How maddening it must have been when I said, from my lofty heights, that of the three of them I would give up the money most easily. How smug I felt. It was *so* good to know that. I never seriously thought it would be tested.

So, there I was, with a little bit of blue fire on my finger symbolizing forgiveness of sin, and bugger my sister's Look Through Green Glass. Francis loved me and I loved him and the boys were coming along nicely. Total happiness. Interview us about our marriage for the posh Sundays and there would be no angle. Mr and Mrs Couldn't-Be-Better. And if part of all that was having nice things – well, why shouldn't I? On we went. Francis and me. Me and Francis. There is something very seductive, very soothing, in being cared about, while being cared for. No wonder women took so long to gain the vote.

Francis was – no – *is* a good man, a good husband, a good father, a good lawyer – though I had very little to do with that side of things. I went to the necessary dinners and anything else to which he invited me and we discussed a few of his cases. But work and home were generally kept apart. His only two stumbles on the path of honour were his affair with the shoulder pads, and being stopped late at night, breathalysed and found to be a little over the limit. His donation to the Policeman's Ball dealt with that. 'Look,' he said, when I teased him for corruption, 'I made a very small mistake for which the penalty and opprobrium would be out of all proportion because of who I am . . . I don't want to lose this case, and if a couple of bob to the local nick does the job, so be it.' It was the truth, too. He was working on a child snatch at the time. A Muslim father had exerted his rights over his estranged British wife and taken their sons back to Lahore. She had snatched them back again. The case was so sensitive that it seemed everybody from the Attorney General downwards

24

was on tippy-toes. Francis was right – a glass of wine over the limit, or his client's and his client's children's future happiness? Francis saw it as no contest. He won the case. And that was it. A couple of misdemeanours, of no great import, during a marriage of over thirty years. An existent, if not volcanic, sex life. The occasional display of temper, the occasional streak of selfishness, the once-in-a-blue-moon bouts of depression – and there you have it. A good marriage compared with many people – but for the nagging little gnawing something or other, That Royal Chamber, sealed, safe, never quite going away.

Back to flirting. The thing I cannot do. The thing I now know you do not have to do in order to attract. For in my case, I wasn't flirting at all. I was waiting for my train alone because Francis had flu, and I was rapidly discovering that Bristol Temple Meads station in March was not the most conducive of places for any activity – and certainly not that one. A chill breeze whipped around the benches, my black wool coat was pulled up tight around my neck, a black and white scarf hung down as limp as I felt, my hands were chilled even in black leather gloves and my exposed ankles were covered in goosebumps despite the thick black tights. I slumped on to a bench in the rawish, dampish air like a defeated magpie and the misery of the loss of my friend Carole overwhelmed me again. With shades of my own mortality thrown in. The cold had penetrated through to my bones; I, too, could be lying in clay. I began to weep. She was a year younger than me and part of my own history died with her. She alone, for example, knew about the Henley moment, and she alone knew that when John was seventeen and his school did Plautus's *Pot of Gold*, I went all peculiar looking at one of his friends who was up on stage with not a lot on. She was my friend. When comes such another?

She was the first of my friends to die. Parents go – and that is not easy – but it is expected, it fits the pattern, even if they go too early. But a friend, a contemporary, one of those whom you took to your bosom out of choice and, more to the point perhaps, one who also chose *you* . . . Now that is hard and cruel. Besides which, Carole was wonderful, exceptional, gifted; the best teacher of remedial children that money could not buy. The dizzy, Biba-booted girl of the sixties and early seventies turned into a woman of honour, commitment and dedication – which gives hope to even the most faint-hearted parent. Her life was worth something, and now she was dead. Horribly dead, too, with no hair left, no flesh left, her sense of humour all gone. Dead and praying to die. We used to joke in the old days and say that they could send a man to the moon but they couldn't cure the common cold. Now it was no joke. They could build a little kingdom of men in the moon nowadays but they still couldn't cure either the common cold – or the common cancer. Fishy, in my opinion. For what would all those big profitable drug companies do with their expensive treatments for either colds or cancer if a cure were suddenly found? Carole couldn't hang around to see. So what the fuck if I cried in public? They were lucky, in that station, that I did not run down the length of it and beat my breast and rend my clothes and push lumps of dirt into my mouth. But I only wept, and not very loudly at that.

I was remembering the Humanist burial service, chosen by her, with me much consulted, and staring at the railway lines, and hearing her voice, and hearing the voices of the people who stood up and delivered their messages of how wonderful she was – and the tears started. I was also thinking that I had lost my one true sister. Hand-chosen, unlike my biological one, and capable of all those pleasures that sisters in books experience. Katy and Clover, Marianne and Elinor, Gudrun and Ursula. A mighty great hole had opened up inside of me and I couldn't think that it would ever be healed.

That was when the tears turned to little sobs, and then bigger ones, and then – as if in the nick of time – someone sat next to me on the bench and handed me a large, clean, white handkerchief. I looked up, gratefully, into the concerned eyes of a man wearing a leather jacket, jeans and a thick woolly hat pulled right down over his head. Muggers don't carry clean white hankies, was my first thought – such is urban life. He didn't look dangerous on any level – criminal or otherwise – though the hat did give him a vaguely sinister air. If he had walked away from me at that moment and I had later been asked to describe him, the first word that would have come to mind would not have been attractive. But his eyes, I remember noticing, were brilliant blue – the colour of my sapphire – their sharpness probably due to the extreme cold, because his nose was nearly the same colour too in that unkind air. Grief is a sturdy shield from cold, but he, apparently free of it, was obviously suffering.

He smiled a little tentatively and said, 'Don't let me disturb you, but I thought you might need this.' I took the handkerchief, sobbed into it, and then had the embarrassment of seeing mascara streaked all over its whiteness – closely followed by the thought that if it looks like that on his handkerchief, what must it look like on my face? Which made me sob a bit more thinking that there was no longer a Carole to share the joke with . . .

'Why do we go on?' I asked. Not really of him, more of the world in general. I was still staring at the railway lines.

'To see what's round the corner?' he asked.

'Hrmph.' I said. Sorrow allows you to be impolite.

'To see if there's anything *better* round the corner, perhaps?'

That seemed adequate, so I nodded.

Then there was an announcement saying the London train was delayed.

'*Plus ça change,*' he said with irritation, and stood up. 'Are you going to London?'

I nodded again.

He reached down and touched my elbow. Just that. Unthreatening contact and about as much as I could take. And then he added, 'Come on. Let's have a coffee in the buffet. In the warm.'

I stood up and I thought, This will probably be the very last time I ever come down to this town. I took a last look around the platform, the station, and beyond it to the familiar rise of buildings. He cocked his head in gentle inquiry: should he go and leave me there, or was I coming?

'Just taking my leave of someone special,' I said. 'A sister.'

Perhaps a warm drink with a stranger would help that cold, hollow place inside. He opened the door of the buffet and held it for me. 'Not a real sister,' I added, as if strict truth were paramount. 'Better than that.'

He nodded and I felt that he understood.

I was suddenly immensely pleased to be back in the warmth again. There was a table for two straight ahead of us, as perfectly placed as if it were part of a film set. And as I walked towards it I suddenly thought, Oh my God – it's *Brief Encounter*. Without the grit but with the handkerchief . . .

And that made me laugh for a moment because I distinctly heard Carole's voice saying, 'Shame on you. Picking up a man on the day of my funeral . . .', followed by her laugh.

'You're not a doctor, are you?' I asked.

He shook his head.

2

Brandy Nights

When I arrived home that evening, Francis was sweltering in his flu bed. Our daughter-in-law Petra had called in to see him and given him a cup of something that smelled very like liquorice water and some charcoal tablets.

'To detoxify me . . .' he groaned. 'I told her I'd rather be poisoned.'

He was not in the best of spirits and he did not smell very nice either. This is no way to present yourself when your wife has just had a touch of the *Brief Encounter*s and sobbed her heart out for an hour to a stranger of the opposite sex, with sapphire blue eyes, in a station buffet followed by two hours in a train. Peevishness is one of the least charming aspects of the human condition. I wanted love, I wanted sympathy, and I didn't want to give any at all.

As I slumped on the pillow next to Francis and the sour smell of a body in the advanced stages of needing a bath wafted around me, I thought, I don't want to be here – which I took to be a symptom of the continuing sense of loss. I made my poor husband get out of bed and get into a bath, while I changed the bed linen and cleared up the crumpled tissues and wiped down the bedside table, which was sticky with all manner of dripped medicaments. I was hardly doing it in the style of Florrie Nightingale, more like a very put out Mrs Gamp. Every used tissue, every crease in a pillowcase, every sticky tumbler was a personal affront, and I made a lot of noise and confusion. I stubbed my toe on the bed and banged my shin and then, in high dudgeon, I got Francis out of the bath and into fresh pyjamas, above the pale blue collar of which he looked like a well cooked lobster. I glared at him as I tucked him back under the covers, but fortunately he was entirely indifferent, it being a particularly virulent influenza doing the rounds that year. I went off and had my bath and another line from Eliot repeated itself as I cleaned my teeth – 'I have measured out my life with coffee spoons' – over and over again. I wanted to cry and I wanted to sing; I suppose I was manic. I put my ring on the side of the basin, as usual, and immediately thought of the colour of that man's eyes. And the little secret place in me, the place that had been kept secret for so long, creaked open just a crack and became charged with a ticklish energy. No amount of toothscrubbing seemed to subdue it.

Coming back into the bedroom, another verse of Eliot's suddenly made me laugh: 'But Doris, towelled from the bath/Enters padding on broad feet/Bringing sal volatile./And a glass of brandy neat.' I asked Francis if he wanted a glass of brandy and took it very ill when he said, very forcefully, that he did not.

'Good grief, Dilys,' he said miserably. 'Are you trying to kill me?'

'Oh, don't be so silly,' I said, completely without sympathy.

'You've just pumped me full of pills,' he said complainingly, breaking out into a sweat again. 'Lots of pills. Probably too many anyway – without finishing me off with booze.'

It was true. I had also shovelled a hefty dose of paracetamol down him. A glass of brandy was hardly a kind suggestion. But I was in no mood to apologize. 'I was quoting Eliot,' I said stiffly. 'Loosen up.'

Telling an influenza patient to loosen up is tantamount to suggesting he should pick up his bed and walk . . .

'I'm not in the mood for poetry,' he said irritably. 'But a little fizzy water would be nice.'

'Oh, Francis. A brandy wouldn't kill you.'

'I'm not so sure about that. I don't feel very far off dying anyway.'

'Maybe I'll have one.'

'Do.'

So I did.

We both looked surprised as I sat there on the side of the bed sipping it. We both looked surprised because it is well known that I hate the stuff. When the dog was run over, one of my neighbours handed me a brandy and I downed it without thinking and immediately threw up. So I was *renowned* for it. Except that evening, on the train, the white knight bought me one – and I drank it like an obedient child. The face I pulled made him laugh. And that laugh made me feel very young. Like I was kicking death in the teeth. I had been with death that day, and I had escaped. See? I was saying, I'm not ready for you yet.

Francis, now looking both wan and puzzled, said, rather forlornly, 'But you don't like the taste.'

And I said, 'It's the *smell* I can't stand . . .'

'Smell is taste,' he said miserably.

Of course, this was true. And even the smell, until now, had been so repugnant that I put rum in the Christmas puddings. But as I sat there on the bed, sipping it, I felt a warm inner glow which was not entirely due to the drink. I took it slowly.

'Hurry up,' said Francis, with the peevishness of illness, 'I want to turn the light out.'

'Oh, well – I'll just go downstairs and drink it then.' I got up. 'Shall I?'

'Oh, by the way,' he said wearily, 'Ginny rang. To see if you were all right.'

'To gloat more like,' I said, with unaccustomed venom.

Then he just looked exasperated and I thought he might be going to shout at me or burst into tears – flu being a notably depressing illness – but then he suddenly smiled very tenderly and said he was sorry. He was being selfish. Please, sit down again. And he asked me how the ceremony for Carole had gone. And then, full of remorse myself and relieved to have safe ground, I said that it had gone well.

'And our flowers?'

'Were lovely.'

Tears spilled. He squeezed my hand. But his felt too warm and clammy so I pulled mine away and wiped my eyes.

'I'm sorry I wasn't there.' His voice had gone wobbly, too. When we signed the card for the flowers he surprised me by writing 'Frankie'. 'I really liked her,' he said.

'She liked you, too.'

But I still didn't put my hand back. It was as if that little refusal had a private power all of its own. Francis didn't notice, of course.

'It was perfect,' I said. 'Just what she wanted.'

'I wish I'd been there.'

'I wish you had, too.'

Did I?

Yes and no.

If he had come, I knew, everything would have stayed the same. And that was easy.

Because he had not come, I was aware that something had changed. And that was going to be hard.

I looked at him. He was like a trusting child lying there. And I was like the nurse who says, 'This won't hurt a bit.' And it does.

'And how were you afterwards?' He put a hot hand on my cheek and looked as kind and loving as anyone can with a temperature of one hundred degrees and a rampant daughter-in-law with a health-food fetish and a shop to feed it. I was about to launch in – about to tell him the minutiae of the pain of it all – but the only words that came out were, 'Oh – not so bad.' And that was that. I realized that I had given it all to a stranger and did not need anyone else's concern.

Francis, dozy from the bath and the Night Nurse and the pills, said, 'Finish your brandy and come to bed.' And fell asleep. I lay awake. A third double brandy for a woman who had never had one successfully in her life before and it did not send her off dreaming into an alcoholic stupor? I put it down to the sorrows of the day. Very firmly put it down to the sorrows of the day – and I was still wide awake. Wide, wide awake.

Eventually I slid out of bed and padded downstairs on my broad Doris feet and went to the telephone directory. Is there any surer sign of the hook of attraction than looking up the object of the attraction in a telephone directory? I hadn't done anything like it since, in my one stab at eleven-year-old groupiedom, I tried to trace Tommy Steele's number in Bermondsey.

His name was Matthew Todd and he lived near Paddington Station, that much I knew. He told me he had worked in a hostel for the homeless until it was closed down and his reason for the trip to Bristol was to see about working in something similar down there. In other words, he was unemployed. He said this – rather than me thinking it – and as he said it and I sipped my First Great Western brandy, he smiled, as if to say, 'So what?'

I thought, How wonderful. To be honourably unemployed and not be ashamed. I said, 'So am I. Temporarily.' And I told him about the Fogal Institute and the funded exhibition space at Stepney I had helped to set up. 'I'd done all I wanted to do. It was time to go.'

'Sometimes', he said, 'you just know when it's time to get out.'

My innards flinched at the sentence. Which was odd.

'I'm on benefit for the first time in my life,' he said. 'Now I know what it's like from the other side.'

'And what is it like?'

I expected him to say that it was not very good. But he smiled. 'It's not bad at all,' he said. 'Gives you time to look around. Time to think. Difference is, of course, that I know it's not for ever. And I've got a roof over my head.'

'Where?' I asked, perhaps a shade too quickly. Which was how I knew where he lived. 'And if the Bristol thing doesn't come off?' I said, trying to sound neutral. I did not want to sound prissy and on your bike-ish. Besides, as anyone who

33

has worked in the business knows, the greatest modern patron of art and artists in this country, the Medici of our times, is the dole. We wouldn't have half the artistic output we are blessed with if the government didn't sponsor it as unemployment benefit.

He was engagingly relaxed. 'Oh, I might do a bit of travelling. I might write an alternative self-help guide – I've been asked to do that,' he leaned back in the seat. And he shrugged. 'Or I might not. I've spent nearly twenty years trying to change the world. I'm not inclined to be bothered by the work ethic just now – I might just slob about for a while . . .'

Carole would have loved him. I heard her saying, Good for you . . . Give yourself some space. It was a phrase she used often enough. It always drove Francis nuts. He, of course, was continually picking up the pieces of people who had given themselves too much space and time. I could hear him pointing out to Matthew that it was a bad role model to offer to our youth, and *in particular* it was a bad role model to offer our black youth, since the black community was desperately trying to get them to consider education as the new fashion statement, rather than mobile phones, music and cars. Even when Carole was quite ill she and Francis had a firm and frank exchange of views over all that. She was a great one for freedom of the individual – I suppose it came from having to deal with so many square pegs and round holes. I always tended to side with Francis, but now, sitting opposite this smiling man who looked so relaxed about it all, I just made sure that my mouth was not remotely reflecting sour disapproval and smiled back at him.

'That's the way,' I said, very seriously. 'Give yourself some space.'

'I'm researching the demise of the individual and its direct correlation to daytime TV,' he said.

Fortunately he smiled to show it was a joke, or I would have taken that very seriously, too.

And then I had another thought, there in that stifling carriage – much more intimate and shocking, and quite unbidden – and it was that this man with the useful hankie, when he was blowtorched back to normal body temperature, was probably quite attractive. At any rate, not unattractive. Young looking, in fact. Young dressing, too. And way, way off my usual beam. And then I realized that he was neither particularly young looking for his age, nor young dressing. It was just that I had been used to someone older. Francis, being eight years my senior, made quite a difference to my self-perception. I tended to think that I was nearly sixty too. And I wasn't. And what's more, sitting there with that man, I didn't want to be.

It's amazing how good you can be with sums when there is a practical point. Miss Brettle's hopeful lessons in the filling up of baths for understanding cubic capacity, or the cycling up an incline for understanding gradients never worked. But for matters of the most personal – well, my innumerate brain, the one which cannot work out litres and grammes and how many beans make five, easily reckoned that if he graduated at the age of twenty-one – or twenty-two at most – and had worked in the social sector for nearly twenty years, well, he must be very close to the life-begins-at . . . And for some reason the thought made me incredibly happy. I was at least ten years older than him, and yet I felt ten years younger. Despite the miserable occasion. Carole, my golden girl, had come to dust, but I was still here, still dancing – if I wanted to. That was when I said yes to the second brandy, and sat back against the seat watching for his return in the reflection of the window.

Now I was like a thief in the night creeping around downstairs. My heart was bumping extraordinarily loudly as I turned the pages of the telephone directory and ran my finger down the list of names. Guilt, of course. Confusion, naturally. But also, undoubtedly, excitement. Just to see his name in print and confirm his existence. And there it was – Matthew Todd, 12a Beeston Gardens, London W2. Well, Matthew

Todd of Beeston Gardens, I thought. Like the ladies of yore, I have your favour. When I am ready, you can have your handkerchief back and it will be delivered personally. That is exactly what I thought, without any preparation whatsoever, and I took my own breath away. There was no morality in this hinterland, only strategy.

I didn't even bother to argue with myself. It was too late for that. And if I had hoped it was merely the effect of the brandy, it wasn't.

I knew what to do, of course. I knew because deceit is written into our psyches along with the blueprint of our birth. We all know how to deceive and manipulate and manoeuvre. Those who say they don't have never had cause to try. Until that moment, neither had I. But it was there as if the bolt had been oiled every day in readiness. I just had to draw it back. My hand would not stop shaking as I jotted down the phone number and the address. Then, heart still bumping, I crept upstairs to bed. Francis, smelling of soap and eucalyptus, had not stirred. I snuggled up to him, that warm, comforting, irritating presence in the bed, and I thought it was perfectly understandable to be doing such peculiar things on the day we interred my best friend. The gnawing, niggling something had given way to a more urgent sensation. The scullers' revenge. And I could do nothing about it because I did not want to.

I lay there feeling my husband's steady heartbeat and willing my own to calm down, and thinking that it would all look different in the morning. It was all to do with Carole and the shock, and how, despite knowing it was going to happen, I was totally emotionally unprepared for her death. That sudden knowledge that, as the last breath expires, there are no more answers, no more shared jokes, no more turning and saying, 'What did you mean when . . .?' Nothing prepares you for that. Nor, God help me (and He wouldn't), does it prepare you for the wild sense of *carpe diem* such a death leaves behind. I turned from the hot body next to me. Brandy and the stillness of the night combined to make me think indulgently that when one door closes, another always opens. I deliberately switched my thoughts away from old pain to new brightness. Even if thinking about Matthew Todd was a comfort for this one night, it was something. Carole would forgive me. In any case, we did our mourning together over the last year, knowing it was inevitable that it would come to this. I was on the stage alone now. Anything I did was all right, and – as the poet said – the grave's a fine and silent place but none I think do there embrace . . . Losing Carole made me think about my own failings. The gaps. And no matter how I lay there persuading myself that I would be mad to embrace whatever life threw my way while I was in such a mixed-up state, I wasn't convinced.

My only hope was that the object of my fantasy was even now lying in bed as I was lying in bed. That he was sleeping locked in the arms of his beloved. That, unlike me, he had no emptiness to fill and that I had faded from his mind as the lights of my taxi disappeared down the Marylebone Road. But somehow I doubted it. He had not talked like a man with a beloved, nor did he have the air of one concerned over much with the feelings of anybody close to him. None of those ordinary phrases such as 'Well, my wife always says –' or 'We quite fancy moving out of London –' Or was that wishful thinking? In my startling new-found interest, I understood, suddenly, why Carole had been so angry in her last few days, so uncharacteristically humourless. The losing of your life is the losing of such possibilities . . . The adventure of it all. Life – ever interesting, ever changing, always unknown and full of potential. This is what my friend bitterly resented losing. The unknown promise even in the darkest hour. Death removes the unknown. It is, as they say, the only certainty we've got. And what had happened to me at Bristol Temple Meads Station that day – the unpredictable – was pre-cisely what death had taken from her.

I understood, quite suddenly, how lucky I was to be alive.

Which was immediately followed by the cold-water panic of remembering that I had not rung my sister back. But instead of lying there feeling twitchy about it, I just turned on my side and switched off the lamp. Sod her. This was my moment of secret pleasure and I was not going to put it on hold for the sake of unsisterly equilibrium.

Better get on with life then. My pleasure was not this, not the Now. Not the lying in this comfortable bed with the solid sound of my husband breathing next to me and being loved by him. My pleasure was waiting and wondering about the Next to come. Matthew and Francis, I thought, as sleep and the brandy finally crept over me. Matthew and Francis and Me. Now that was a new dimension. I had stepped out of the door this morning as Francis and Me. And tonight . . . No doubt about it – we were three. Whereupon I slept.

3

Cocktails with My Aunt

Unemployment has much to answer for. Including the fur-
therance of illicit affairs. If Matthew had been required to get
up at seven-thirty in the morning and get a bus, things might
have been different. And if I had been required to get up and
drive to Stepney four days a week – things might also have
been different. As it was we had all the time in the world. He
was funded by the Department of Social Security, and I was
funded by my husband. Two little paragons of virtue suddenly turned into monsters of deceit and neither of us
thought twice about it. We were like a pair of teenagers bunking off school. Only considerably more erotically inventive, I
like to think. I was having a misspent youth – thirty years
later than usual. And I was savouring every wicked minute.
And Matthew, of course, whose youth had most certainly
been misspent, was just having me.

It began inauspiciously. Having laundered the handkerchief, two weeks later I sent him an invitation to the private
view of an exhibition of Indian prints and carvings at the
Wiesmann Centre, not far from his flat. One of the things he
told me across our *Brief Encounter* brandy, amid the mopping
of my tears, was that he had spent a month in India earlier in
the year and wanted to go back again. He'd got a cheap flight,
a visa, a backpack, and set off, starting in Mumbai and going
south. Now he wanted to do the north. He offered it as a possible comforter.

'I don't know,' he said. 'India just feeds the spirit. They have
a way of being balanced – the whole structure is one of balance
– hot and cold become warm and cool – that kind of thing . . .
You can take your grief to Gandhi's memorial and the place
blesses you somehow. Different values. Life changing, really.'

His face was transformed with enthusiasm. 'Have you been? I've never wanted to go back anywhere as much.' I noticed that he used the subjective first person, which delighted me.

Well, of course I had been. But only once. Like me, Francis was Europe-orientated. We favoured hot Tuscan vineyards with Florence nearby, or the Paradors of Seville and Madrid, or cold, quaint Bruges and Amsterdam where only the art heats the blood. India had not featured again in my travel thoughts. We loved it while we were there, staying at the palaces in Rajasthan and Gujarat, taking a boat and a uniformed guide around the lakes, and hiring cars and drivers – doing it in luxurious, sometimes quirky, but always extremely comfortable, style. We were there for just over a fortnight. It was, we agreed, quite an experience. Soul touching. But the next year we chose to go to Ravello.

'I'd love to go back one day,' I said to Matthew. 'I've always wanted to.' And then I couldn't resist it and I had to add, 'I'm not sure my husband felt the same . . .'

I watched to see if the lemon juice would touch the oyster – and there was just the faintest flicker of something. I smiled, quite involuntarily, into his eyes. The kind of thing I never do. And I was pleased to see that he looked away, a little bashfully I thought. And then the subject was changed in the way of these things and suddenly we were talking about the pleasures of the nights getting lighter and how long winter had been.

So this private-view invitation had a point. I hoped he would read the relevance of my choice and understand that there was a message for him. And I prayed that he would not be as obtuse as most of the men in my family – Francis for example, shrewd as a polecat in court, and guileless out of it. It was never any good hinting at things with him – especially in those most delicate of areas. On holiday once I tried to suggest that he and I slip away to bed in the afternoon – at which he announced to our lunch companions that 'Dilys is just going up for forty winks.' With Francis, if you wanted

40

something you had to say it outright. After all, there was no reason to elide. The subtext of this particular invitation was that I was interested enough in Matthew to remember everything he said. And to want to see him again. I wrote on the card, 'Thought you would be particularly interested in this. I shall have your handkerchief clean and ironed and return it to you then. Many thanks. Dilys.' Not Dilly. Hmm? Was that significant?

I wrote my mobile number in the corner of the card and banged my head three times against the wall to remind myself to switch it on. I then spent a week in complete day and night agony. Nothing. Not a peep. Francis thought I'd got ants in my pants, as he so winningly said. I even asked my daughter-in-law to ring me, just to check the thing was working. It was. Despair. Thus, in a lather of self-mortification, I had all but given up. If we'd had a cat I would have kicked it. Fool, I told myself six times a day. Stupid bloody fool. And then, of course, he rang, the evening before the private view, when I was sitting in front of the box with Francis watching *Great Expectations*. Rather appropriately, I suppose.

Fate. Fuck her. I could have been anywhere. I could have been out at the shops, I could have been in the bathroom, I could have been driving the car. But no. Fate designed that he should ring at what was the absolutely worst time. One minute I was calmly sitting beside my husband, the next I was leaping around the room like a scalded budgerigar. And I was spontaneously hearty.

'Splendid. Wonderful. Yes, I did. Thank you. You can? So glad. Yes – no – six-thirty. Splendid. Terrific. Tomorrow. Jolly good! Oh, no – thank *you*. Bye.'

He must have thought I was a closet Sergeant Major.

'Who was that?' asked Francis.

Well – yes – who was that? Fair question and God rot him for it.

There was one frozen moment, and then, 'My Aunt Eliza. Auntie Liza.'

Where *does* the ability to deceive come from?

Francis looked suitably incredulous.

Why, oh why, did I say that?

'*Eliza*?' he said, understandably fazed. 'You were a bit abrupt with her. She must be nearly ninety.'

I nodded towards the television. 'I didn't want to miss the fire scene.' Even as I said this it struck me as wholly inappropriate to be keen to watch another old lady, albeit fictitious, going up in flames.

'Nearly ninety,' he repeated, watching Miss Havisham burn.

'Who?'

'Liza.'

'Something like that.'

My heart was giving a fairly good imitation of the Porter at the Gate's little problem: Waking the Dead.

'She was knocking sixty at our wedding.'

'I suppose she was. No – a bit younger I think. She's nearer eighty-five. Three maybe.'

'This is sudden.'

'I just thought I'd get in touch with her.'

'I thought you couldn't find her when your mother died? Or you didn't want to, or something.'

Guilt is a very dreadful thing. Francis was asking me very reasonable questions, in a very reasonable voice. I was listening to those very reasonable questions in their very reasonable voice as if he was a combination of the Stasi and Gestapo.

'What is this?' I said sharply. 'The third degree?' Then I tried to laugh. 'Tee hee' came out sounding as if I had *strangled* the bloody budgie.

'Well – it's rather nice. That's all. You haven't got much of your older family left.'

'She's not really family. She's an aunt by marriage.'

'All the same . . . Now there's only Cora and we don't see much of her. We ought to go up there again . . .'

Francis was keen on family. Love them or hate them, they were blood and to be nurtured.

'Hmmm,' I said.

We watched a bit more of the film and then he said, 'Where are you going?'

My heart nearly stopped. I had forgotten my aunt.

'When?'

'Tomorrow.'

I stared at him.

'Six-thirty? With Eliza?'

Relief.

Except where on earth could I be going at six-thirty on a Wednesday evening in March with an old woman approaching ninety?

'Oh, for a cocktail. It's her birthday. She loves – oh, you know – that one with the Cointreau and the lemon juice and the –'

'White Lady?'

'Yup. She loves them. Downs them like lemonade.'

Taking a nearly ninety-year-old aunt out for a *cocktail*? Still, he looked as if he believed it. Sort of.

'Where?'

'Oh – there's a place near her.'

'Where does she live now?'

I hadn't a clue. Francis was right, I had not been able to track her down for my mother's funeral and since that – when half the family weren't talking to the other half anyhow – I had more or less lost touch. I did Christmas cards with a couple of cousins and very occasionally saw Aunt Cora, who lived in Norfolk. The other aunts and uncles, on my maternal side, were all dead. Eliza married my Uncle Arthur, the youngest of the men, but when he died, she just slipped out of sight. None of the Smart family had much to say that was kind about her and I had no idea where she was. Or even if she was still alive. She had always been something of a game bird, so she probably was. Traditionally Auntie Liza was known to like *men*. A quite shameful attitude in a woman, certainly according to Grandmother Smart. In her time she

43

was considered flighty. Whatever that meant. In our road, when I was growing up, it was considered flighty to give the milkman a cup of tea and flighty to go to bed with John Profumo. So it could be a flightiness of any degree bar, at a guess, actually working in a brothel. I was never very close to my cousin, Alison. She was a couple of years younger than me, Eliza and Arthur's only child, and a great one for flaunting the fact that she had a father and I did not. So I wouldn't really know where to begin looking for her, either. But the lie had been said and I could hardly undo it. So then – where did my aunt live now?

The first law of lying being to stick as close to the truth as possible, I did so. It wasn't until it was halfway out that I realized it sounded very odd.

'Paddington,' I said to Francis.

'Paddington?'

That made him take his eyes off Magwitch. The last Francis knew of them they were living in Finchley, very proper Thatcher territory, whereas Paddington had quite a reputation for its transient, mixed population – and was known to have quite a drug culture.

'But she's about to move.'

'Where to?'

'Don't know,' I said, smiling at my sudden brainwave. 'I'll find out tomorrow.'

He laughed. 'Well, go easy on the Cointreau – you don't want to kill her off. Shall I come?'

'No –' I said, far too quickly. 'Don't worry.'

'I could pick you up after. Just say hello and take her back, and then we could go on for a meal.'

'She's shy with men,' I said. 'Bit afraid of them. Don't know why.'

I prayed he would not remember that she was the one at the wedding who danced with him very closely while staring into his eyes, who rolled her own suggestively while saying that if she'd been twenty years younger . . . , who showed

44

absolutely no fear whatsoever. And who also told him, in the clipped posh vowels of a thirties news announcer, that her father would have been a lawyer himself if he had not been a clever businessman.

She was always one for grandeur, my Auntie Liza. And only just tolerated by the family – much as any outsider was tolerated – but never forgiven for giving herself airs. Scraps of the overheard conversations of childhood came back to me.

'She was always a cut above herself,' my mother said. 'Businessman my foot. Her father had a couple of butcher's shops.'

'You used to be thick with her, Nell,' said my grandmother, in a sharp voice.

My mother looked uncomfortable. 'Yes, well, that was before she got so above herself. Tuppence to talk to her now.'

But my grandmother was much more blunt. 'She's a bloody snob,' she said. 'And she likes the men. No wonder Arthur took so long . . .'

And the two women nodded together, silently, disapprovingly.

'Uncle Arthur took so long at what?' I asked.

But that was as far as they went.

My family was poles apart from Francis's funny old ex-military lot. Both his father and his uncle were still alive, in the same home for retired army folk, Richmond Lodge, where they played bridge and drank pink gin. His father was eighty-six and, apart from a little deafness and a gammy knee, was in good nick. Uncle Samuel was two years older and a little more decrepit, which is why Francis's father joined him in the home. It was the perfect example of what a difference money makes at any age you like. Richmond Lodge was run as a cross between an officers' mess and a good quality hotel. It was subsidised by an army charity and it was still expensive, whereas my Aunt Cora, in Norfolk, lived in a local authority home which, if pleasant, was not designed to work for the individual. I would have offered some long-term financial help – maybe to get her into somewhere private and better – but my cousins would not hear of it. She was their mother and they would deal with it all.

My family were what Shaw referred to as 'the deserving poor'. Ten aunts and uncles. Ten children in a four-bedroomed house in Islington, next to the wet-fish shop, and taking in washing. With lodger. My grandmother brought all ten of them up alone after my grandfather pottered off round the corner to live with someone new. Perhaps the new one was prepared to say that she loved him occasionally. As far as I remember, the only time my Grandmother Smart referred to Grandfather Smart was when she told the story of him coming home once a little the worse for the threepenny ale and her hitting him over the head with the bloater pan. I supposed you would consider moving on after that.

My mother was number nine and all set to be the adored final baby of the family, until number ten, Auntie Daff, arrived. My poor mother – nothing ever quite went right for her. It seemed that throughout her life she was to be handed the cup of happiness over and over again, only to have it dashed from her lips.

All the aunts did well for themselves except my mother and my Auntie Daff, the two youngest. Those two did badly for themselves, very badly indeed. In both cases men were their ruin, as I remember hearing. My mother because she met and married a bastard, my Auntie Daff because she bore an illegitimate child by one. A man who was married at the time and not intending to get unmarried. Some years later he came to court my mother – fair-haired, thin-faced, smoked incessantly. By the time he got to her he was a widower and a bus inspector – *very* acceptable. I remember overhearing one of my aunts urging her to accept, saying that marriage would ease her burdens (which put an image in my head of my mother struggling through the jungle like the natives in books). But my mother shook her head. 'Not necessarily,' she

46

said. 'And anyway, how can I marry the man who gave Daff a baby?'

It was all confusion to me. Auntie Daff ended up living in a council house. While we lived in private rented. It might not have been grand but nevertheless – it was not *council* . . . Another puzzle in my childhood. What was so bad about *council*? The Deserving Poor could tell you: it smacked of the workhouse and charity and – oh, guardian angels, stop her – being *common*.

As children, Virginia and I went to stay with various aunts and uncles to give our struggling mother a break, each of whom dealt with us in their own way, which was generally kindly. At my Uncle Arthur and Auntie Liza's house it was more difficult. We went fairly often until Virginia was old enough to say no, and then I went on my own. I was about nine or ten – and after that visit I never went back again. This, apparently and according to my grandmother, was due to Liza's 'big mouth'. She had said something that rendered her a pariah. The family, no less than any Mafiosi, had its honour. Eliza had told the local bus conductor, when she took me and Darling Ally, her daughter, to the shops, that I was her 'poor relation'. A description which sounded very romantic to me and was therefore passed on to my mother when I came home. It caused the family equivalent of the Third World War. The more so because it happened to be true. 'After all I've done for her –' my mother kept saying over and over again. 'I've a good mind to . . .' I hung on her every word, wondering what she had a good mind about, but she caught my look and went quiet, just shaking her head.

'No butcher's daughter from Marylebone is going to call *my* family her poor relations,' said Grandmother Smart. And then she looked at me and narrowed her eyes. 'I might have known', she said, 'that you'd be the troublemaker.'

Virginia took up the theme. 'You can't keep your big trap shut,' she said, in a perfect copy of our grandmother's tone. 'Double trouble.' They were great allies.

Auntie Liza was barred from the familial inner sanctum from then on. Oh, she came to weddings and funerals and all the other stuff, but she was very much out in the cold and no doubt she, too, knew it was my fault. Which made the choice of Auntie Eliza as a cover for my illicit date quite an odd one.

I must have smiled at the recollection of all this, because Francis looked at me and smiled back. 'You are so kind,' he said, almost thoughtlessly – a throwaway remark offered as we watched the television credits rolling. In the space of a few days my marital antennae had grown extra sensors. The mixture of elation and terror his words caused had me turning into water inside as I read what was to become a very terrible thing in his eyes. It was love. And the shocking thing was that I just felt . . . irritated to see it. There was also The Question: Here we were, ten o'clock, all snuggled up on our own – perhaps we should just go to bed a little early . . .? And that I could not do. 'I'm really sleepy tonight,' I said. He squeezed my knee, understanding, not the slightest bit alarmed. We turned the television off. And I yawned a very positive yawn.

Deception. I was getting good at this. Just as we turned out the light that night I said, yawning convincingly again, that I thought I'd pop into an Indian art exhibition tomorrow evening, while I was in that neck of the woods and before I met up with my aunt. I did not specify the Weismann. Francis just grunted. But at least if someone saw me and said something to him – not very likely but still – at least there would be nothing suspicious about it.

And the next afternoon, off I went. In a black cab because I wanted to arrive in pristine condition. I had the clean white handkerchief in my handbag, hair newly done, the roots covered by the best black dye that a hairdresser and money could buy, bright eyed and bushy tailed and in a brand new white cashmere dress. Which, I reminded myself excitedly, reflects on to the skin and makes you look younger. On the other hand, when I reflected on the cost of the dress, I felt considerably older . . . But – heck – I could afford it.

The taxi got me there early. I positively bounced into the Weismann, all teenaged anticipation, collected a glass of wine, and wandered around looking as if I cared what was on the walls. Really, at that point, I couldn't see a thing. Except that he was not there yet. I relaxed. By the time he arrived the thumping heart and the apparent loss of control over my entire urinary tract would be sorted out. And then –

'Hello?'

I turned.

There he was. Those blue, blue eyes, the thinning fair hair cropped very close to the head, that smile with his too-wide mouth, and some kind of loose black suit, with a denim shirt under it. The very opposite image of Francis. Francis somehow managed to look slightly manicured, even in jeans. It took the entire combined forces of the family to unite against him and his desire to have a crease in his Levis. Matthew looked like an advertisement for cool relaxation to the point of falling asleep. It was not high style. It was not creamy white cashmere, but it was Very Now, that was for sure. But he could have been wearing a tutu and I wouldn't have cared – I was just so happy to see him. He looked happy to see me, too, smiling from ear to ear and looking, I decided wishfully, appreciative. Though whether that was the art or me I could not say . . . He was not at all handsome, with no regular features, not even tall and distinguished looking like Francis. Just a common or garden face, on an average build – with those sharp blue eyes. He also looked much younger than I remembered, polished up, as if he had shed a few years. Which is what my hairdresser had said of me. 'Something's perked you up,' he had remarked as he whacked on the ebony dye.

Matthew looked, I thought, a bit shy. None of which mattered because here he was, in front of me, smiling away.

Then came the inauspicious bit.

'And this', he said, 'is Jacqueline.'

I can barely remember what I said. But I hope it wasn't

what I thought, which was: What a very horrible thing to do to me and I think I'm going to cry. It was like opening up your birthday parcel and finding it contained a dead rat. It was a cruel thing that he had done – and he didn't even know it.

'Have you had a drink yet?' I do remember saying that.

Jacqueline, who was approximately the same age as Petra and had the same pale, unhealthy, unmade-up look of one who is saving the planet and not eating meat, took water. I saw Matthew's hand waver – over the orange juice, over the water, over the wine – and I thought, I'm not having this, so I shoved a glass of white wine into his hand. He looked surprised to find it there but carried on.

'Matthew was very kind to me the other day . . .' I began, and launched into a whole self-deprecating tale of our meeting. Inside I was like bruised jelly. How could he have brought her? How *could* he?

'Is your husband here?' he asked, looking beyond me and round about.

'No – India is not his thing,' I said. And then, turning to Jacqueline, I said, 'Have you been?'

She shook her head. 'Mattie went alone. I'll go next time.'

Mattie?

Gift of God, evangelist, tax collector turned saint, successor to the evil Judas Iscariot and she calls him *Mattie* . . . What the hell right had she to call him after a diminutive rug? My blood was up.

'It's wonderful,' I said. I looked him full in the eye and added, 'And I have every intention of going again. You have rekindled my appetite, Matthew . . .' I gave it all I'd got and then paused for a moment before finishing with a bright and careless 'Maybe we'll all meet up there . . .?' Tinkling laugh. Curtain. I, Dilys Holmes, had flirted.

Sometimes the gods are kind and sometimes they are not. And at that point they decided to bestow a little favour. For hanging on the wall directly behind *Mattie* was something quite extraordinary. And very probably not the sort of thing a vegetarian named Jacqueline could handle. I wasn't entirely convinced I could either. The carvers of Vrindavan have much to answer for in their celebratory rendering of earthly passions and cowgirls losing their clothes. Especially when you are a bit in the mood yourself.

I said, 'Oh, ah, um. I wouldn't turn round if I were you.'

Of course they both did, and I had the benefit of seeing her go very rosy indeed, and his neck and the tips of his ears turn a fetching shade of peony. OK, Littlerug, I thought. Where's your sense of balance now? Warm and cool indeed. That's hot and hotter if I'm not mistaken. Out loud I said, 'Hmm, yes – I can see what you mean about the sense of balance being different in India, Matthew. I'm sure if I did that I'd just fall over.'

'Not if you were held correctly,' he said smoothly, gliding towards the carving like a man on buttered wheels.

Jacqueline laughed. It was a laugh that said she knew *just* what he was talking about.

I laughed, trying not to sound like someone who wished she did.

Later, as we shuffled around the show, the three of us, he asked me how I was feeling about Carole, and when I said not good, he touched my arm and said the usual thing about it taking time, a lot of time. To be gentle and not try to get over it too soon, to talk about it . . . Oh, lots of correct things – and they all sounded completely meaningless because Jacqueline had on her sorry-for-you expression, and I thought, If only you knew how sorry for me you ought to be, you pale little vegan-thing. I then apologized and said I had to leave to see my aunt, and they left with me. On the steps, while Jacqueline wrapped her very large, very hairy scarf around her very small neck – which took some time – he said quietly, 'It's been nice seeing you again.'

'Yes,' I said, brightly.

And that was that.

They went off to catch a bus – Jacqueline hooking her little

51

paw under his arm – and I wandered off blindly, looking for a taxi. It was only once I was in the cab and in need of something to mop the tears – mostly of rage at myself – that I realized I had not given him back his handkerchief after all. So I blew my nose into it, very hard, and decided that she, his ladyfriend, could wash it this time. With those ecologically sound soap powders, the process of getting it clean could take her quite a while. There was mascara all over it again. Perhaps this was to be my life from now on? Weeping and wailing and gnashing my teeth in a terrible vortex of unrequited something? It didn't bear thinking about. It was Carole's fault for going and dying. It was Francis's fault for getting the flu. And it would pass.

I got the cab to drop me about half an hour's slow walk from home, so that I wouldn't be in too early. It was still only just after eight. I felt wretched, humiliated, and a stupid fool. Suddenly I was nearly sixty after all. How could I *possibly* have mistaken friendliness for fancy? At the same time I couldn't forget how he said, 'Not if you were held correctly . . .' Walking helped. Stomping might be more accurate. It is just as well that no one decided to mug me that night. They'd have been dead meat.

When I reached home Francis was out. I rang his chambers and he was there, working.

'How were the cocktails?' he said, with his mind on other things.

'Very strong. She had two and smacked her chops for more. Will you be late?'

'Not much before twelve I shouldn't think. You go to bed. Oh, and Dilys?'

My heart lurched a bit at his tone. 'Yes?'

'Don't forget to drink a lot of water.' He laughed in his Oh, You Girls way and rang off.

I put down the phone and paced about a bit. Ran a bath. Tried not to think. Ate an apple. Turned on the television. Turned off the television. Re-ran the bath which had gone cool. Told myself it was all fine, everything was fine. Face and marriage, both had been saved. I was just being absurd. Then I undressed and was just stepping into the water when my mobile rang. I went all quivery. Probably a wrong number. I really only have the thing for emergencies. Fat lot of good that is when I forget to switch it on, as my sons are so fond of pointing out to me. But it was on now, and ringing. My heart started thumping again. No. It couldn't be. But I answered it and there he was – Matthew Todd.

He said, 'It's Matthew.' And I didn't know quite what to do. 'I just wanted to thank you.' Articulation was suddenly missing. What wasn't missing was a cattle-prod bullseye right in the solar plexus. All I managed to his further, perfectly resonated 'Hello?' was 'Eeek.' He enquired again. 'Dilys?'

And I managed. 'Hello.' And then I sat down on the cold side of the bath, naked as an ageing Botticelli, and listened. It was all I could do.

He repeated that he was ringing to thank me again – and even I thought this was a bit thin given that the clock was now striking ten. I said that I was glad they had *both* enjoyed it.

'We did,' he said, more stiffly.

'Good,' I said.

He floundered a bit, saying that it was kind of me to remember the Indian connection, that it brought back good memories. Then he paused before adding that it was – also – good to see me again.

'Yes,' I said. Be damned if I was going to give anything away.

There was another short pause. Don't say a word, I told myself. Do not fill that gap.

'Well, then –' he said. It was valedictory.

'Oh,' I said quickly, 'I forgot to give you what you came for.'

There was just the merest hesitation at this, as indeed there might be.

'What was that?'

'Your handkerchief.'

There was a proper pause this time. Then he said, 'What are you doing now?'

Well, honestly, how often does fate offer you that most perfect of moments?

I said, 'Funnily enough, I'm just stepping into the bath. Literally – just about to put a toe in the water.'

There was another pause and he said, very faintly, 'Oh.'

Then I heard what sounded like a bus going by at his end. 'Where are you?' I asked.

'At the corner of Pittsburgh Street and . . . er . . . Prebend Place.'

It was my turn to say 'Oh,' as the heart started cranking up again. 'That's just round the corner.'

'I know.'

There was no going back. That was the moment for me to retreat. Which, of course, I did not. 'Are you alone?' I said.

'Yes. Are you?'

'I'll come out. Give me ten minutes. I'll have to put some clothes on first.'

And then I heard it. Very faint. But very definite. Like the first longed for cuckoo in spring. Definitely, definitely, I heard what I was listening for.

'Must you?' he said.

'Jacqueline –?'

'My ex – or almost my ex –'

'She doesn't see it that way –?'

'No –'

'You live together?'

'At the moment –'

'Difficult.'

'And you – your husband?'

'Shall we agree not to talk about . . . either?'

'OK.'

'Shall we go for a drink?'

'No – let's go towards Hammersmith. Walk by the river. Talk. Where is your . . .?'

'I've got about an hour.'

'I suppose it's like this –'

'I suppose it is.'

'Do you –?

'Never. And you?'

'Nope.'

'Always a first time.'

'Yup.'

I don't think Francis had ever said either 'Nope' or 'Yup' in his life. Even that – God help me – was different . . . *exciting*.

Dangerous, stupid . . . were other words that came to mind.

It is a very terrible happiness that particular happiness. Forbidden happiness that you cannot stop happening, no matter how you try. You laugh, you walk in silence, you touch, you retreat, you touch, you explode in your head and your body and you think you would throw everything you own away for that one bit of time to go on for ever. It is the last vestige of your innocence, what Sartre called the formation in the womb, when you are almost too tender to touch each other. You go over the minutiae of your attraction – when did you first know, why did you? You find the places which are not ready to be found and you pry them open. You make pretences. He doesn't ask about your children, you don't ask about his girlfriend. You live in immediate time. No past, no tomorrow. Just now. You show the best of yourself and he shows the best of himself. It is like a very subtle advertising pitch or the first days of a new, golden recruit. Every joke is funny, every pronouncement important, nobody else exists. And then there is the stumbling moment when you both pause to look at the river, you pretend, and you look from the river into each other's eyes, and you kiss. There it is. Out in the open. Too late to ever go back. You both make excuses. You say you have never gone out looking for such a

55

thing. You don't, really, know what has come over you – and then you kiss again and walk tightly bundled up together, just about daring to say how happy you feel, knowing it is already cursed.

Then comes the goodbye, hidden, round the corner, away from the streetlamp, exciting until it suddenly dawns on you that this hiding is no children's game, but something very grown up indeed – so grown up that it is even known as *adultery*. You push all that to the back of your mind and you make the promise to meet again soon – the codes arranged, the farewell touching, the understanding of where this will lead – which is frighteningly erotic and also just plain frightening. The relief almost of being alone to savour it, to think about it, to wonder over it. And then the heightened world as you totter up your steps and open your familiar front door and go into the warm, light space that is no longer clean and honest but as shadowy and malevolent as a cell – because you have changed it for ever. No going back. This pale grey Wilton carpet, those pictures, these flowers, that mirror in the hall that you chose with your husband – all are meaningless now. You go up the stairs, knowing all this, yet you are humming – you are happy. It's mad but it's as inevitable as a sneeze after pepper – and just as uncontrollable. Your happy home. And you have just sent a bomb rolling right slap bang down the middle of it.

4

Paddington Bare

Having sex with two different men on separate occasions is a dangerous business. If you are in bed with both of them, and they are aware of this, then you might be excused a little leeway in the names department, but if you have them one at a time and in different places, beware. Apart from the possibility of whispering the wrong name at the prime moment – and finding a pair of startled eyes staring into yours and saying something along the lines of 'Excuse me, I'm George' – there is the likelihood that one of them will notice, sooner or later, that your heart isn't in it. There is also the third likelihood – that you will drive yourself semi-mad with the horror of what you are doing to someone who trusts you. I don't recommend it, but I couldn't give it up.

Somewhere inside me burned the inevitable little flame of resentment that my lover had it so easy, while I had it so tough. I had to face Francis every day of my life, except when he was away from home – and even then he telephoned unless I made up some convincing lie about going out. My newly discovered Auntie Liza was a feature. I was throwing everything down her eighty-odd-year-old throat, as well as those lethal cocktails: afternoon tea, dinner, a bottle of champagne from our cellar that Francis caught me putting into the car, a tray of gingerbread men complete with genitals (aroused) that he smelled the baking of but fortunately never saw . . . And he took it all at face value. A situation that, in those heady first days, I managed to blank. But even in the most trusting of men, there must come a time when he thinks his wife's desire for the company of an octogenarian-relation-by-marriage is strange. I dreaded that moment more than anything. The moment when I would have to find other deceptions, a deeper tangle, a stickier web.

There is, of course, no sympathy vote for this. You don't like deceiving your husband? Then *don't*. Thank you, St Agnes of Bow. I hated every minute of deceiving Francis. But I loved every minute of being with my lover. And while I sweated and thraped to keep the whole thing going, Matthew was suddenly free. Which both helped – and didn't. If he had not become free so soon, he might have understood a little more about my tormented marital jugglings. But he became free, single and twenty-four-hours-a-day available – which was such a relief and such a joy to us both I forgot to remind him that I, most definitely, was not.

Before he became free, it seemed the only way for him to separate from Jacqueline was by moving out of his flat and finding one somewhere else, at least for the time being.

'I'd be sorry to go,' he said. 'I've rented this place for nearly eight years.'

This had a touch of excitement about it – a touch of the poor Bohemian – after the absolute security of my domestic arrangements. 'Didn't you ever think of buying?'

He laughed. 'I was always moving on.'

'We'll find something,' I said. 'I can help with the rent.'

Cheap any flat had to be, but I drew the line at Matthew's thoughtful suggestion that he might invest in an old Dormobile. A love wagon, he called it. At times like that you feel your age. Dormobile by any other name, I said – and wouldn't. Even so, some of the places we went to see together, so-called 'studio' flats in the seamier parts of south and west London, were not much better than being parked at the roadside. In Acton, when we found one with an actual separate bedroom, the landlord stared us out in the matter of furniture.

'There's no bed.'

'You'll want to bring your own then.'

'There's no table, or chairs, or fridge –'

'There are curtains. Which planet are you from?'

Nevertheless, we nearly took it until – after our initial agreement – the owner said that there was also the matter of the deposit. £2,000.

'I could,' I said reluctantly.

'No chance,' said Matthew. 'I wouldn't give him the pickings from my nose.' He stormed out, leaving the astonished landlord to stand there delivering some choice abuse. 'Now you know why so many people live in doorways,' he said to me. 'Because of filth like that.'

'Listen,' I said to Matthew afterwards. 'For next time, I can get the money – quite easily. I just need a bit of notice.'

I did not add that the real problem was because everything was in joint names. Or that Francis had already shown uncustomary surprise at how much I'd run up on our credit card and plundered from the current account. I paid for most things to do with the affair in cash – but it was quite hard to justify. I used my Auntie Liza as an excuse for some of it – but even sweet, trusting Francis was unlikely to believe that I'd bought her a leather jacket from Harrods. (Like a child, I wanted to wear the same clothes as Matthew.)

'An odd purchase,' said Francis thoughtfully. It was, since the spring sun shone warmly, as I said, every day.

It was all like visiting a far-off land, the economics of everything. Juggling figures and wondering if you could have this, but not that; if you got rid of this and kept that, could you do this? These were not things I had considered since I left my mother's house. Now here we were trying to work out a budget for our wicked ways. And all we wanted – as you do in those golden, early days – the innocent days if you like – was somewhere to take off all our clothes and be naked together. Often. And there was nowhere to be found. I felt paranoia creeping up – all landlords and agents knew we were a couple of adulterers and acted accordingly. I was convinced of it.

Matthew said, somewhat despairingly, and only half jokingly, that we could join a Naturist group, but I thought they might notice that we weren't joining in the activities – volleyball not being something I had a penchant for at the most dressed of times. But it wasn't funny. It was desperate. And we got past the stage of finding Travelodges excitingly sleazy. I wanted somewhere to bring flowers, to leave a bottle of scent, to hang a robe, leave some underwear, make my permanent mark. But in those first few weeks Jacqueline was too unpredictable to risk us even just using the flat. We'd tried once and missed her return by a whisker – only because we nipped round to the off-licence to buy a bottle of wine. After that we borrowed one of his friend's flats, only to be disturbed *in flagrante* by someone else who had a key. You have to be at the very peak of your powers as a new lover not to run off screaming into the day when something like that happens. I remembered the scene in *Brief Encounter* where the same thing (though not quite *in flagrante*) happened. Art and life fuse. I now realize that there is no point in calling out to the screen, 'Don't go, don't run away,' to Celia Johnson, because that's all you can do. It makes you feel like something stuck on someone's shoe. A social alien. What to you is beautiful, to the outside world is merely a shag. Sleazy, transient space was all we could use. Those Travelodges were like sucking on bones. I often wonder, if it had continued like that, would we have survived past the first few weeks?

Matthew asked about my house. When we couldn't find somewhere for him to rent, and we were yet again returning from the post-modernist hell of an A1 stop-off, complete with kiddies' castle, he said – quite pragmatically – 'Maybe needs must.' But that consideration had been torture. On the one hand, Francis did stay away when he couldn't possibly get back for a night; on the other, I could not bring myself to do it and Matthew – I could tell – just did not understand. After all, if you cheated on your husband in one place, what was the squeamishness of the marital home all about? 'Or,' he said, stopping suddenly to turn to me, 'you could just tell him.' Another warning vignette – and one which should have been placed along with the scullers and the easy way I accepted

Little Miss Power Suit where Francis was concerned. Matthew had no concept of how torn I was about Francis, how I had to keep two relationships afloat. One in calm seas, and one in the proverbial boiling cauldron. A dangerous omission, not registering his suggestion as serious. But I didn't see it. And then, at last – at just about crisis point – I didn't have to. Because the issue resolved itself. Magically, Jacqueline suddenly announced that she was moving out.

This was about a month after our affair began and Matthew was only *just* starting to find the deception a strain. I found being with him the only calm experience in my life – the rest of it was now fully shot to hell. To be at his flat without fear of discovery and to not have to hide every trace of myself was like having a stone lifted. When he rang to tell me she had gone, he was as excited as a child. And I rushed up to the airing cupboard (the things you do) and took out fresh sheets, fresh pillow cases, fresh towels to take over there. Oh, the relief of it. I wanted to tell *someone* – share the moments like these – but there was no one. I could trust no one. Without Carole I was on my own. I certainly could not tell my sister and I had no friends who were solely for me. I couldn't tell any of our local coterie because they were couples and sooner or later the word would get out; I couldn't tell anyone in the Stepney team because I didn't work there any more; and, of course, I couldn't tell the one person to whom I had confided everything else in my life – Francis. So Jacqueline's sudden departure saved me from any further heartsearching about whether I could ever bring Matthew into my home. At least, hand on heart, I never did that to my husband.

When, in our own bed together at last (and with my best sheets and pillowcases to protect us from the influence of its previous incumbent), I asked him why she had suddenly taken herself off like that, he said that he'd stopped having sex with her when we met. Given that they were on the skids already it was fairly negligible anyway, so ceasing to sleep with her was a reasonably unsuspicious development.

'Negligible?' I asked. 'What's negligible?' I was thinking of me and Francis. We were sporadic but not really negligible.

'Three or four times a night,' he said. 'Every night.'

'Lucky you,' I said.

'On the contrary,' he said, shifting towards me. 'Lucky you.'

'But seriously –'

'Let's just be grateful,' he said.

End of conversation.

Jacqueline was gone and I would be happy with that. It was enough. Space and time. This is enough, I thought. Oh, but . . . Is anything ever enough? Is it in the nature of human endeavour to be given what you think you want and then to find you want more? Even when you know that getting it can destroy lives? It must be. Because, almost immediately, we did. We not only wanted a whole night together – which we managed – but we wanted a whole weekend together, which we did not. And then we wanted a longer time like a holiday, and Matthew said, 'Come to India.' Just about the cruellest thing you can do to a respectably married woman who couldn't even manage a weekend in Bognor and who appears to be falling deeper and deeper down the well with you. But he was falling deeper and deeper down the well with me, too. Neither of us was in control. The whole thing was like an inflatable – we had pulled out the valve on what we thought was a small and containable dinghy, and it was rapidly turning into an air-filled replica of the Belgrano. I couldn't even go past a shop without wanting to buy him something . . . And he couldn't let a day go by without some kind of meeting or phone call. The job in Bristol was offered. And he refused it. The outgoing manager rang him and urged him to think about it. But he said no and they appointed someone else. I tried not to think of the enormity of that. On Bristol Temple Meads Station he had told me how much, how very much, he wanted it . . .

The flat became ours alone in May, and May is the most

beautiful month in which to be newly in love. I suppose I would say that of November, if it were November. But May is benign. It's warm, it's brimming with the fulfilment of promises, and you can believe that the summer, like your happiness, will never end. It is also, to return the feet to earth, the month of Francis's and my birthdays. Two days apart. Him on the twelfth and me on the fourteenth. Just think, we used to laugh, his parents and mine must both have had a preference for September sex. Now it was no laughing matter.

One of the most painful aspects of what I was doing to Francis was that he always tried to make me happy. When we became engaged that was one of the first things he said. 'I will make you happy. I will make it up to you.' His own childhood had been unremarkable and happy – apart from school fears – and the idea of me growing up amid all that depression and lack of worldly comfort he could barely understand, let alone forgive. He knew about criminals – but he had absolutely no idea of the way women just had to get on with it then. That you might be beaten black and blue but you thought long and hard before taking your children and leaving home for the great and alien unknown. Nor – despite his profession – did he have any real concept of how the law turned its back once upon a time. Indeed, until very recently. I was told, or heard it said, that my mother's neighbours became vigilantes and protected her during my father's worst excesses. The police did nothing.

'I'd have thought their simple humanity would have made them do something,' he said.

'Some of them drank with my father,' I replied. 'It was a domestic. In those days you didn't interfere with a domestic. You know that.'

'How did you grow up so sane?' he sighed.

I tried to explain that it really had not felt that bad – that it probably sounded worse than it was. That I remembered very little. But he wouldn't have it. To him it was an unacceptably unhappy experience and he was determined to make it all better. And he did. So to be deceiving him was like spitting in the eye of all that is best in the world. I knew that without him the love and protection would be gone. Some people love generously, benignly; others love rapaciously, cruelly. I was aware of that. And I was aware that my husband was a very special man. That what we had together was very special. But I had discovered the love of Balzac and Shakespeare and Puccini and the balladeers and the poets. There is this thing called love and its power is so strong we cannot help but risk our very lives for it. Truth was, I wrestled with temptation, but not very hard, and temptation won. Truth was, I did not want to be with my husband, my paragon, I wanted to be with my lover. Truth was, despite the loving kindness and the years of feeling safe and secure, the very thing that Francis had promised me, it now seemed he could not provide. I was only happy when I was with someone else. Not only that. For the first time I knew what it meant to be really happy. To feel truly alive.

So, our birthdays. We always go away for one or two or even the full three days and nights. A tradition in the Holmes' marriage. And this year the whole bloody lot fell over a weekend and we were meeting up with Tim and Charlotte Jennings in Bath. I liked Tim, a doctor and old college friend of Francis's, and I liked Charlotte, who dabbled in antiques, and I loved Bath. But it was booked Before Matthew. Now I didn't want to go and there was nothing I could do about it. Not only that, but Francis – innocent, unsuspecting Francis – who one way and another had not been getting much in the way of his conjugals just recently, and who, I think, put it down to Carole's death – would be expecting something a little more sexy in the affection department than a wife who yawned in his face. I was less and less inclined to suffer this one last great betrayal: to make love to my husband while wishing he was another man.

Matthew and I sat down to discuss it all a couple of weeks

before. Just to clear the air. Man to woman, sitting across from each other at the table in his flat. Only we were naked. And he kept reaching across and stroking my nipple, which had a powerful effect on my capacity for logic and reason.

'I'd better dress,' I said, trying to move the discussion forward. But there was something very focused in the way Matthew said 'No' that stopped me. Almost as if he was testing me in some way. So I didn't.

'Look,' I said firmly. 'We do this birthday thing every year. It's traditional.'

'You won't enjoy it.'

'I know,' I half groaned. What with what he was doing to me and what Francis was undoubtedly thinking about doing to me, and the thought of being away from Matthew for three days, groaning seemed the only option.

'Just don't go,' he said. 'Please.'

'I have to go. Unless I'm ill.'

'Be ill then. I mean, pretend you are.'

'Don't touch me like that. I can't think.'

'Like this, then?'

'I can't get out of it.'

'You can't go.'

'I must.'

He took his hand away. 'Just say you're not up to it.'

'Matthew – look at me. Can't you see what everyone else can see, including Francis?'

'What – Mrs Holmes without her clothes on?'

'I'm serious. Take a look. I'm blooming. I run up the stairs at home. I sing. I look and feel on top of the world. My hairdresser says so, my neighbours say so, even my son says so – my *son*, Matthew. And no doubt if my other son were in the country he would say so too. Much more to the point, Francis says so. In fact, for a lawyer he's being remarkably obtuse given that on the one hand I look radiantly well and full of life, and on the other, come ten o'clock at night, I'm suddenly too tired to besport myself upon the bedsprings.'

Matthew winced. I took no notice. Just went running on. No warning bells rang even faintly. I stopped to consider. 'Well – he has made the odd murmur in the direction of "You don't look very run down" when I say that's what it must be. And he's quite convinced that a few days in Bath is going to perk me up something amazing. Indeed, he's been going on about how our trip to Bath will produce such a miracle of energy and health in me that it's like taking part in a Jane Austen bloody *novel* . . .'

'Temper.'

'I don't know what to do. I don't want to make love to him because I shall want it to be you. I always do. On the rare occasions it's happened with him since we met you just swim in and swim out . . .' I laughed. 'Almost literally . . .'

But he was not laughing.

Very far from it was He Not Laughing.

He stood up. His hand was still resting on my neck but the whole of him went rigid. I expected to hear something snap or ricochet as he moved away.

'Matthew? What on earth's the matter?' He took his hand from my neck and pushed me away. Then he left the table.

I felt cold all over, which was nothing to do with my nakedness, and just about managed to croak out, 'Where are you going?'

I walked into the bedroom. His face was chalky. His lips pulled into almost nothing, that wide and generous mouth all gone – no smile now. He dressed. I heard the soft sound of cotton and then the harshness of a zip. Breathing. Space and time were held between us – the weight of something malevolent hung in the air. Then he came out of the bedroom again. I wondered if he had been crying. He leaned his hands on the table and stared at me. The blue of his eyes was very, very hard.

He said, 'When did you last fuck him?'

5

Crammed Hotel

You see what I mean about innocence? It had never occurred to Matthew, because he almost immediately stopped doing It with his partner, that I had a physical marriage to continue. He was absolutely beside himself with pain and rage and jealousy at the thought of me making love with Francis. I remembered how agonized I felt when he just turned up with Jacqueline at that private view. Multiply that a few times and I suppose I would have been chalk white and beside myself too. It didn't matter how much I said (hating to do so on my husband's behalf) that I did not enjoy it, that I found it a terrible strain, that I only ever thought of him. It just cut him to shreds. I've always thought men were by far the more romantic of the sexes. Women are the pragmatists really. They have had to attract to survive for a lot longer than men.

'Do you still come?' he wanted to know. I wanted to say that this was forbidden territory. But his pallor told me to tell a lie.

'No. Never,' I said. Though the truth was that I did – if I put my mind somewhere else entirely or imagined it was him and not Francis. Despite the total shock my machine-gunned brain was suffering, I knew better than to say that out loud. He looked so altered that I felt frightened. Not for myself but for him, because he, too, was tasting the reality of the well we had tumbled down together. He said quietly, 'Just don't go.'

'Matthew, I have to,' I said. 'If I stop, Francis will either start dosing me up with St John's Wort and talking in a low, kindly voice, or he will begin to suspect. He's a lawyer. I can't risk it.'

'Risk what?'

I was about to say, 'My marriage, of course,' but then I looked at his expression. 'It,' I said lamely.

Somehow he calmed down. And apologized. There was nothing to forgive and no way out of it. The weekend would happen. At least he had things to do and he wouldn't be sitting around fretting. There were friends to catch up with, several job negotiations with various organizations going on and he had also been asked to write the Mission Statement (terminology that made me laugh and him wince) for a new approach to Young Offenders Institutions. Given the latter, I was even more aware of how much he and my husband would like each other, an awareness that played around bizarrely in my head and bred its own wild imagery: a Seurat of Francis and me strolling along by the river and me passing Matthew by with merely a nod, only to find the two of them falling into each other's arms with sincere, respectful recognition; or, worse, the two of them sitting on grass, fully clothed and in deep debate, with me naked and unnoticed sitting between them, a monstrous version of *Dejeuner sur l'herbe*. I didn't think that this was a particularly good time to share either of those thoughts with Matthew, so I told him that I loved him and took my leave. And then . . . the weekend arrived.

Francis and I set off on Friday afternoon. I had not managed to see Matthew the day before because I had to be at home in the morning to get James's call from Cape Town and then have a late lunch with John and Petra, at the end of which we were joined by Francis and his sister Julia (very clever – they came to the health-food restaurant in time for the puddings. Have you noticed how health-conscious eaters go bananas when it comes to dessert?), after which we took Julia back home with us because, as usual, she was going to house-sit. Another little tradition which, until now, I had blessed. Whenever possible, when we went away Julia upped sticks from Hove and had a few days in town. Which she enjoyed and which gave us peace of mind. Once burgled, never forgotten. By the time Julia has been in London for a few days, she's longing to get back to the south coast, so it is the perfect solution all round. We get on very well in these short bursts, and in the past I always welcomed her occasional visits. Now I resented it dreadfully and was not a very nice sister-in-law to her. Very short, I was, when she rang to confirm it all.

'Do you really want to come up again?'

She did.

So no chance to slip away for an hour or two on Thursday evening, either, then. It made me twitchy and ill-tempered and I found myself glaring at her that evening as if she were the sole harbinger of some great misfortune. When she suggested that we might all take our after-dinner coffees into the garden because it was so mild, I said I felt *quite* a chill, and that I was going to bed. The fact that it was only ten to nine obviously did not go unnoticed and nor was it meant to. Uncheckable childishness had descended. I saw Francis raise an eyebrow but beyond that he didn't say anything. And then Julia came upstairs and put her head round the door and asked if she had offended me, so that I had to shove the mobile back under the duvet and stamp a bright and welcoming smile on my face. I must have looked as glitteringly guilty as Titus serving Tamora's pie. So there was no hiding place. When I did finally manage to be alone, it was late and his phone was switched off.

In the morning, Friday, Francis's birthday, Julia was there and, given my thorough upsetting of her the night before, I could hardly dash off and leave her. We sat mute over morning coffee and then I took her to Peter Jones as she asked. I have never hated Peter Jones more. Wretched shop. I categorically refused to have my usual piece of their carrot cake, and Julia was moved to say, 'I think Francis is right. You do need a break . . .' Which brought me up short and made me at least be civil. And I thought, as we chatted about the shopping and the traffic and the other customers, that this was what my life had become: Peter Jones, Private Views, Mini-Breaks in Bath, slightly blue-rinsed ageing relations, sons and grandchildren, halfway freedom, the smug and slippery slope of the not very chattering classes . . . I'd been so happy with it all, a part of me never ceasing to congratulate myself on having shaken the dust of the past so cleanly from my shoes. And now?

Julia was saying something about cotton as opposed to Percale.

'I think those pillowcases were a very good buy.'

'Yes,' I said, thinking pillow, pillow, pillow – I want to be on his pillow right now – NOW!

The messages left on my mobile were unrepeatable. I found the first when I went to the Ladies before we left Peter Jones. They made me hug myself and they made me randy as hell. Matthew had excelled in making his presence felt. Pillowcases and carrot cake melted to nothing in the heat of a little, gentle bondage . . . There were others, just as hot, waiting when I got home.

'You look flushed, dear,' said Julia when I re-emerged from my bedroom. 'Everything all right?'

'Perfect,' I said. I could feel the phone in my pocket, still warm from my hand and my ear and it was almost as if it was him pressing against my belly. 'Call me,' were his last words. I tried – but again it was impossible. On the one occasion I managed to get far enough away from Julia to have a go, Matthew's line was engaged. Irrational pain, deadly fear hit me as I imagined that he was talking to Jacqueline and asking her back. After all, I was going away with my husband . . . I could hear him saying it to me with cold, acidic logic.

Then, mid-afternoon, Francis came home and we prepared to set off. I did not dare check my mobile for more messages because Francis stayed wittering around me the whole time. I could hardly get irritated with him on his birthday, though he remarked that I seemed a little twitchy. 'Eager to be off,' I said. Which in a way was true. I'd had quite enough of trying to avoid Julia's friendly presence and his cheerful impatience to try to make another call. Various attempts had singularly failed and were entirely unconvincing anyway. Desperation drove me to say that I would just go up the garden to check on the lilies. That they might be too dry given this heat. Both Francis and Julia stared at me rather oddly. I got up there all right, and I was just bringing out the phone and tapping in the number, heart beating as it had done right at the start of the affair, when Polly Savage from next door popped her head over the fence and said, 'I thought you'd be off by now . . .' So that I jumped sky high, much to her consternation, and just about stopped myself falling backwards into those perfectly damp and happy *Bellisariaii*. No wonder Francis and Julia had looked at me so oddly. It had rained first thing that morning.

Believe me, you have no idea how closed-in your life is until you don't want it to be. I went into the downstairs cloak-room – last resort – just as we were about to leave, but then Francis dashed back from the car to get the camera and I knew that if Francis heard me talking to myself in there, fol-lowing my check-up on the lilies, I'd be hospitalized. Then he went back out to the car and I excused myself and tried the downstairs loo again but couldn't get a signal. So we drove off, Julia waving at us from the gate and telling him to take good care of me, and me with a smile clamped on my betrayer's mouth. Believe me, you have no idea how closed-in your life is until . . .

'I'm looking forward to this,' he said, as we negotiated the motorway.

'So am I,' I said weakly. I sounded as enthusiastic as Marie Antoinette in the tumbril.

'We can turn off the motorway and take it slowly if you like,' he said.

'No, no – let's just get there.'

Somehow the idea in my head was that the sooner we arrived, the sooner it would all be over. I probably even *looked* like Marie Antoinette in the tumbril. Francis asked me if I was OK, and I said through gritted teeth that I was just about in Heaven, while staring stonily ahead. Childish. He pursed his mouth and drove in silence. A bad sign. I had to speak to Matthew, or leave a message, or *something* – I needed the contact like a fix, I suppose.

Eventually I asked if we could stop on the motorway, and when we did I dashed off to the lavatory, but I couldn't get a signal. There were no further messages. Short of wandering around the forecourt of Membury Services in full view of my even-nearer-to-sixty-year-old husband with a telephone glued to my ear, I could only fail again, and – as Beckett would have it – fail better. I crept back into the car and imagined what was taking place in 12a Beeston Gardens. Agony, mayhem . . . Hell on earth . . . Jacqueline? I was terrified I would lose him.

'Insides all right?' asked Francis.

'Oh, fine.'

'It's just that you seem to be going rather a lot.'

'Time of the month.'

'You only finished one last week . . . Sure you're OK?'

It was so genuine, so caring, so really and truly concerned.

I'd forgotten. I'd used it as an excuse to avoid sex after the debacle with Matthew. Oh, God. Oh, how I hated all this.

'Maybe you should see Dr Rowe?'

'I'm fine. It's probably all those lentils yesterday. It's OK now.'

'Well, you could always ask Tim.'

'I'm fine . . .' Those gritted teeth again. 'Fine.'

He threw something on to my lap.

'Good,' he said, 'because I got these. Happy birthday.'

I opened the packet. Tickets for *The Magic Flute* on the following night. Three months ago I would have been ecstatic. Now, After Matthew, I just felt numb. What was seeing Mozart when I could be sitting naked with my lover in a tatty little flat in Paddington?

'Lovely,' I said.

'Hmm. I think you ought to see Dr Rowe.' And then he lowered his voice as if the car was full of spies. 'Do you think it might be *the change* . . .'

72

Something else occurred to me. I had invented so many periods that, apart from a serious need for a blood transfusion if t'were true, I had no idea when a real one was coming. They were a bit erratic nowadays anyway – due to the forthcoming delights of *the change* probably. And of course, I had never had to give them a moment's thought – except to be prepared. But now it occurred to me – mad, wild, stupid, impossible thought – that I might actually be pregnant. The last genuine one seemed such a long time ago. Oh my God. I stared around the forecourt. All the cars seemed suddenly to have baby seats in them. It couldn't be, it just couldn't . . . Oh, but it *could*. That amount of sex, and a lot of it caution to the wind stuff – it could very well be.

Up until Matthew, I was a sensible woman. When Dr Rowe said I should come off the pill and revert to the cap – progesterone being such a naughty little hormone – I did so. After all, the one and a half per cent failure rate was scarcely a worry. I was having legitimate sex on an acceptably occasional basis with only my husband. If anything happened – well, we could cross that bridge . . . It was highly, *highly* unlikely. Then. But now I had only been taking the pill regularly for five weeks. In that time, I'd had more *coitus non interruptus* than a bevy of girls in a wayside bordello. And let's face it – when you are in the first throes of an almighty love affair, contraceptive procedures tend to slip a little. Oh. Oh. Oh. I stared at the mumsy hatchbacks surrounding us, prayed, became convinced that I was now a mother-to-be and really did need the lavatory following the thought.

'Just once more,' I said to Francis. 'Just to be sure.'

'Hurry up then,' he said, unable – understandably – to keep the peevishness at bay.

Once in there I took deep breaths and thought hard. Pregnant? I probably was. I touched my breasts. They did feel tender. And I was – well, glowing, just as I was with all three of my pregnancies. I nearly wept. Whatever metamechanic ruled the Universe, it assuredly had ways of punishing the

73

adulterer, and I found myself wondering, in a mad and idle moment, whether we'd still kept the cot. I was grateful to be still sitting on a loo at that thought. Here I was, probably pregnant, and not having had sex with my husband for weeks. Even Francis, who would trust me to Infinity, might have a problem with that. And then I had a revelation.

I rushed back to the car, virtually leapt into the passenger seat, gave Francis a very bright smile – as seductive as I could manage – and said, 'I can't wait to get into bed tonight.'

He looked disappointed. 'Tired again?' he said.

'Not at all. I feel really randy. *Really* randy.'

'Well,' said Francis, looking pleased and excited, 'Tim and Charlotte aren't getting down till gone seven. It's only just after five now. We'll be there by six easily. So – the lady can be accommodated.'

'Good,' I said. 'Oh, good.'

If I was pregnant, went the logic, I could pass the baby off as my husband's. See what I mean about deception? It is in our bones. The enthusiasm of my tone, however, still had the undertow of one who has just been told that her scaffold is nigh. Nevertheless, Francis was beaming. He put a Bryan Ferry cassette on. *Let's Stick Together*. And beat time on the steering wheel. It was an album the boys gave him years ago – to liven him up. He had listened to it dutifully and eventually got to like it. He was humming along to it very happily, which made me feel even bleaker. Somehow, by the time we'd pulled off the forecourt and back into the traffic, I was feeling sick and even more convinced I was pregnant. Well, sick or not, Matthew or not, I would have sex with my husband as soon as possible – which would cover all possibilities. No wonder Henry VIII got rid of five of us. He'd probably have dumped the sixth if the pox hadn't taken him.

The hotel, the Royal Edward, is lovely. It is big and sumptuous – the kind Americans adore and which, thanks to our transatlantic cousins, nowadays offers proper plumbing and a desire to serve. When you press shower, you get shower. When you require room service, it arrives with a smile. We'd stayed there before and this time Francis had booked a suite. It was right at the top, away from traffic noise and with a wonderful view of the Abbey. I went straight into the bathroom – on the pretext of getting ready for our love-making – and checked my messages. There was one. 'I love you. I miss you.' And I was so relieved. No 'Where the fuck are you? Why haven't you called? We're through.' Thank God he was being reasonable. Even while I was doing this, I heard the pop of a champagne cork. Francis was getting into his stride.

We undressed and put on robes and sat at the window sipping champagne and looking out. The Abbey looked golden in the sunlight. I wanted Matthew to see it.

'Nice,' said Francis, stroking my knee.

I gritted then clenched my teeth yet again – God knows what I didn't do to them – and had a hysterical moment when I thought, Lie back and think of Maternity . . .

We began to make love. And, truth to tell, Francis looked so familiar and happy and – well – just uncomplicated – that I was not entirely disliking it. Then the telephone rang. Making love within a marriage means that if the telephone goes you sometimes answer it. I took it as I was nearest. A slightly foreign voice said that some flowers had arrived for me and should they bring them up. 'No,' I said. 'Not yet.'

'What not yet?' asked Francis, lying there next to me as if the world which we inhabited as husband and wife was the same unchanging, kindly place it always had been.

'Something about ordering dinner. *Really* . . .'

If the flowers were his idea, their lateness would not matter. But if they were not . . .

And on we went. Champagne, dim lights, crisp white sheets and a silken coverlet to slither around us. Just the wrong man.

Then – a knock at the door.

'Don't go,' I said, trying not to sound alarmed. It would be the flowers and I would be sunk.

The knock came louder.

And louder.

Francis left the bed, pulled on his robe, went out into our little sitting room, and opened the door. I heard the same foreign voice announcing flowers for Mrs Holmes. I heard Francis react – and be brushed aside as the flowers were brought through the sitting room and into the bedroom, where I sat up on the bed, wrapped in the coverlet, naked of body and naked of speech. For the person delivering the flowers was Matthew.

Matthew . . .

God knew where he got that suit, but he looked perfect for the part of Discreet Flunky. Navy spotted tie and all.

'Madam,' he said, and bowed, and put the basket – a vulgar outrage – down beside me on the bed. His face was absolutely stony. His eyes like blue steel. I tried to look as if I was just having a nap. I could not say anything because Francis came up behind him looking astonished. I stared at Matthew, who stared back. I had never seen eyes glitter like that before. It can be very menacing and I fully expected him to punch Francis on the nose or do something really bad. But all he did was give a little bow.

'I am so sorry, Madam,' he said, in his quaint foreign accent. 'Should you require any further assistance,' and he handed me a card.

It was very well done. It looked perfectly natural. Except no hotel employee would march into a bedroom without invitation, never mind flowers. But I suppose it was the old maxim about doing anything with enough confidence and you can get away with it. Francis looked distinctly chilly, but before he could say anything other than, 'If that's all –' Matthew turned away. And just as naturally as he had walked into the place, he left it. I slipped the card under the pillow.

Francis followed him out of the bedroom and watched him leave.

'Bloody cheek,' he said crossly, as the sitting-room door

closed loudly. But if Francis thought it was anything more than very odd, he did not choose to dwell on it. Instead he came back to the bed. 'Well,' he said, touching one of the orange carnations which nestled next to the green ones, 'someone's gone to town. I've never seen such a dog's break-fast . . . Who's it from?'

He picked up the little envelope and pulled out a card with flowers drawn in one corner and the words 'In Loving Sympathy' printed over the top of them. 'From all at number 12a,' he read.

He looked at me and shrugged.

'My Auntie Liza,' I said. 'Bless her.'

'Who's the All?' he said.

'The cats.'

I could have taken on MI5.

Francis forgave the vulgarity of the harlequin display. 'Shame she won't meet me,' he said. 'She seems like a nice old bird. I suppose she feels her days are coming to an end – hence all this attachment to you . . .' He flicked at a tight, shocking pink rose bud. He looked at the card again and smiled. 'Got this a bit wrong, though.' And he tapped the words 'In Loving Sympathy'.

The thing was that, beneath the anger and the fear of dis-covery, I loved Matthew *more* for pulling a trick like that. It made me feel young and daring – like a child who knows something is dangerous but still just *has* to go and do it.

'Where were we?' said my husband.

He laughed. I attempted it. But now it was as if old Marie was having a chuckle while the executioner checked the blade. Matthew was not only in the hotel – he could make another dramatic entrance at any time. My marriage could be over quicker than the snap of his fingers. Part of me, the angry part, gave way to a softer sense of loving him all over again. Such planning, such forethought – it put *The Magic Flute* into the shade. Then the angry part overtook the soft love and I was ready to march after him and find him and ask

77

him what the bloody hell he thought he was doing to my marriage. To which he, of course, would have the obvious answer: 'What marriage?'

I did the only thing possible: had another glass of champagne and finished making love. Undisturbed. Perhaps because I had the presence of mind to just *tip* the telephone off its receiver. If anyone was trying to get through during the next half an hour or so, he couldn't.

Our suite number was 505. The room number on Matthew's card was 215. At least he wasn't next door. Or even down the corridor. Oh God, why did Carole have to go and die? This was all her fault. And now that it had happened she wasn't even here to confide in. I needed her. Having to keep everything entirely to myself was almost beyond endurance. Not only did I want to tell someone about this crazy, absurd, wonderful bit of theatre put on for me by my lover in this very hotel and under my husband's nose, but in general, and often, I wanted to tell someone how it felt to be in love like this. I wanted to share the jokes, the telling little moments, all that stuff that women confess to each other about such things. Not the size of a man's equipment, nor how many times a night, but the apparently enchanting peripherals. No one has been tried as a true friend until they have sat through at least a month of ecstatic conversations regarding the new man's *bon mots*, and if he said that but did this what did that mean in relation to this, and he's got a dimple when he's thinking hard, and he's the only man I've ever met who can get away with wearing yellow, and have I told you what he said last night when we . . . On and on and on. I had no one I could trust – certainly not my sister, I thought sourly, the one whom I *should* have been able to trust. No one. And that isolation bred its own kind of demons. Absolutely no one was out there showing the good sense of detachment. The madnesses were all my own and stayed so – I was worn ragged with it all, but there were no solutions. At least, no solutions I was prepared to consider.

As soon as Francis was holding me and we were thanking each other and touching each other in that sweet and civil way, I got the shakes. Matthew Todd was *staying* at the same hotel as me and my husband and our two good friends. He had come right into this bedroom, walked past my husband, and seen me on the bed in a condition that could only lead him to conclude one thing. That I was so keen to get into Francis's underpants that as soon as the door closed on the luggage we were unrestrainedly At It. I shook some more. It took so long to calm Matthew down after he discovered that a wife having an affair has to go on sleeping with her husband – and now he had seen it in action. I just wanted to die. I wanted to lie back on that bed and say, 'OK, fate – I give up. Have me. Take me. I don't know what to do any more.' He was out there, he was dangerous and he could do anything . . . And part of me wished that he would.

Francis stroked my forehead.

'You look a bit stressed,' he said. 'Take it easy. We're here to relax. Just lie there for a little while – I'll run you a bath.'

Well, of course, I burst into tears.

And he comforted me. Or he thought he did. While he held me I slipped the receiver back on to the machine. It rang. 'Take me, Fate,' I said silently. But it was only Tim to announce they had arrived. Francis said he would shower and go down and meet him while I got on with the bath. Space at last.

6

The Man with the Iron Mask

If I once thought that I measured out my life in coffee spoons, that had all changed. I now measured out my life by sitting on various lavatories manically punching numbers into a telephone. I'd tried his room – no reply. Now there was no reply to his mobile. I really was panicking. Back in the bedroom I tried his room again – nothing. I rang reception and asked if the guest in number 215 was in the hotel. As far as they knew, he was. His key was absent. I tried his room number again. And his mobile. Nothing. Then I plunged into a tepid bath and gave myself a stern talking to. No good would come of my dying in these circumstances. Also – and I suppose this was innate, atavistic pragmatism – I should let him get on with whatever it was he wanted to get on with down here. He could lead, and I would follow – and just hope that Francis never found out. The sternness lifted. I was back to being amused and excited. I smiled into my soap bubbles. I might manage some time with him. Complete stark staring madness, of course. But much greater than the fear of being caught was the thrill of that possibility. Like all Guineveres, I was tickled by his derring-do – and foolishly pleased that he had done something so rash for me.

I dressed and went down to the bar. On the way I called at room 215, but there was no response. Plan B. I had written a note. Plan B useless. Note would not slip under door. Fine. I would take it downstairs and leave it for him at Reception.

By the time the lift deposited me on the ground floor, I felt calmer, fatalistic. I had two goals. One was to see him alone as soon as possible. Two was not to hurt Francis. The first I might or might not achieve. The second I was determined to ensure. Pathetic, really, given what I was doing behind his back. Francis was not silly or daft or arrogant and therefore worthy of being duped – he was just a man who trusted his wife.

Charlotte was just crossing the foyer as the doors of the lift opened. No Plan C then. I tucked the note back into my bag and we embraced. Then she stepped back and looked me up and down.

'You look bloody marvellous,' she said. And then added sceptically, 'Francis said you hadn't been completely well.'

I had a terrible urge to tell her everything. Happily, the moment of madness passed. Act normal, I told myself, and hooked my arm through hers. 'It's so lovely to see you again,' I said.

We made our way through the foyer towards the bar. Charlotte looked just the same. One of those beanpole women with neat grey hair, good bone structure and long elegant limbs. She wore pastel floaty skirts with pastel floaty jackets to match and pale stockings, which together somehow looked all right on her.

'You look just wonderful too. Even more elegant . . .'

She interrupted. 'No,' she said. 'I mean it. You look *really* wonderful. What's the secret?'

I looked up.

I smiled.

Then I focused on something as I smiled, and I gasped.

I was speechless, gaping and completely rigid. And she was completely stumped.

We both remained speechless and stumped for a moment longer until she eventually said, slightly hesitantly, 'The secret?' In a way that suggested she was really saying, 'Hello – I'm over here.'

For my eyes were transfixed on a place behind her. *Secret? What was my secret?* Well – not to put too fine a point on it – there it was sitting in an armchair reading a newspaper, or rather, looking over the top of it and raising his eyebrows. He was not smiling.

Neither was I.

'No secret,' I said to her, forcing myself to breathe again. 'They're in the bar, aren't they?' And with my arm tucked into hers and me nearly fainting, we headed off.

Matthew stood up and followed us. It looked perfectly normal. Well, *it* might have looked perfectly normal, but he didn't. Where had he got the clothes? Now he was wearing a blazer and flannels – with white shirt and tie and even a *tie-pin*. He looked as far removed from my casual Matthew as Fred Astaire from a break-dancer. He had transformed himself into a refugee from the Hastings Bowls Club. I would have laughed out loud (or possibly cried) if he had not been looking so wild. As it was I stared straight ahead, as did he, and almost abreast, with me still holding on to Charlotte, into the bar we three went.

Francis and Tim were sitting by the window. There were no free tables near us and Matthew made for a stool at the counter. When Francis kissed my cheek and said I looked wonderful, I nearly shouted at him, *'Don't.'* Electricity was pouring into the space between the bar and me. I glanced round but Matthew had his back turned. Then I saw. Two pinpoints of blue light reflected from the far side of the bar. He was watching us in the mirror.

Tim said something about me looking ten years younger. Francis said something about champagne or gin and tonic, to which I said, 'Yes,' and he said, 'What, *both*?' And while he and the waiter were amusedly sorting that out, I put my hand behind me, in the small of my back, and gave a little wave. Matthew did the same. He still did not smile. And then somehow I was seated at our table with my back to my lover and I didn't know whether that was better or worse.

I should have known. I should have known from all his questioning about the name of the hotel: when exactly were we arriving, did we eat in the restaurant there or somewhere else, what kind of things did we do on these weekends . . .? I thought it was all down to jealousy, but it was all down to planning. I had given Matthew the information – and by God he was making full use of it. For, as if sitting in the bar chatting to friends, being hand-squeezed by my husband, trying to sip a gin and tonic – which I badly wanted to down in one so that I could sink to the floor in oblivion – and generally trying to comport myself were not enough with his unforgiving eyes upon me, when we left the bar and made for the restaurant, he came along right behind. He was placed at a table across the room, by the door, but I could see him perfectly well. And he could see me. He stared. No emotion. Just his face, staring unflinchingly across the heads of the other diners. I smiled. He did not. He just raised his empty glass and set it down again and folded his hands on the table and went on staring. If he hadn't possessed such a basically innocent, cheery face, which even his glare couldn't entirely render evil, the hotel staff would have arrested him. Not a hint of emotion anywhere in either face or body. He could have been wearing a mask.

Once our order was taken and the wine on the table, I excused myself. I had the perfect reason for this. I had forgotten Francis's birthday present. It was sitting on the dressing table upstairs. I stood up, said, 'Won't be a moment,' and fled. I felt Matthew follow. At least my lot were still chattering away heedlessly. Matthew's waiter, as I turned out of the restaurant door, was still standing, bottle in hand, dumbfounded at the sudden emptying of his customer's chair. I heard him say, 'Sir?' And I heard Matthew say, 'I'll be back,' and then I was out in the foyer running. He caught up with me. 'I love you,' he said. I ran. God knows what the sober people sitting and milling around thought of us. This was not a hotel in which people usually sprinted.

'You're angry?' he said.

I said nothing.

We ran up the stairs to the next landing and then he took my hand and we ran up the next flight to his floor. We reached his room. Number 215 was in the less salubrious part of the hotel and we went down corridor after corridor as if we were Alice and the White Rabbit. The room was small, narrow, with a single bed and a poky en-suite shower. One of the rooms once used for accompanying servants perhaps – or set aside for the occasional impoverished single guest. Who knows. After 505 it made me feel ashamed.

'This is dreadful,' I said. 'Really nasty.'

We put our arms round each other and stood on the narrow bit of carpet. 'It's all I could get and it's a lot better now,' he said.

'How could you do this?' I asked. 'It's completely crazy.'

'I couldn't think of anything else to do.' He was feeling for my zip but the dress didn't have one. He didn't seem to notice. 'It helped,' he said in a mixture of reproval and misery. 'The planning, the secret, the coming down here. Took my mind off you and him.'

Something was not quite right in all this. Surely those words should be uttered by the wronged husband, not the new lover.

'The flowers – that was funny.'

He ignored my laugh. '*Funny?*' He gave up on the zip and put his hand between my legs. 'Did you –' he said – 'this evening . . .?'

'There's no point. I did what I had to do. He's my husband, Matthew. My husband.' I was shouting suddenly, fear and anger rose above the childishness of it all. 'I bloody well had to,' I said.

'There are ways,' he said.

'There are not.'

He moved away from me and stared at my face as if I'd stuck a knife into him.

'I've tried them all. I just had to. Now forget it, please.' I advanced.

He retreated, his face cold as a mask again. 'Was it –'

'I don't think any good is going to come out of this conversation . . . I love you and I want to be with you –' I tried to kiss him but he jerked his head away. I took his hand and held it

84

and hated Francis at that moment. This was what I wanted. Now.

'Stay,' he said.

'I can't.'

'You can,' said Matthew. 'Please.'

We were like a couple of demented beings.

'I've got to go back. They're all down there. If I don't get back, they'll come looking for me. They already think I'm unhinged – or unwell, as they put it – and Francis thinks I'm both unhinged, unwell *and* incontinent.

'*What?*'

'Because I've tried to ring you from every public lavatory between here and the Hammersmith flyover.'

There was a pause. Then – from relief? from nerves? – something made us see how funny it was and for a while we couldn't stop laughing. At least the mask had slipped.

When we eventually managed to stop, he began stroking my neck. 'You could', he said, 'just walk away from it all. You'll have to one day.'

That was the place I dared not touch. The place that the fear and anger protected. There was nothing to say except, 'I've got to go. I really have got to go. If I don't go he might find out. And then –'

He looked at me with the blue of his eyes all hard again. 'Then?' he said. 'What then?'

'Er . . . no.' I backed off. 'Er . . . no. I'm just not ready to have that conversation.'

I kissed him. He was back to being wooden again, face a mask . . .

'Don't do this. Please, Matthew . . .'

I was supposed to be letting go of him but instead I was holding on. I think if he had asked me to stay one more time, I would have. But he just kissed my hair and pushed me towards the door. Out of the room we went. Silent.

'You go down,' I said eventually. 'I've still got to collect Francis's present.' I was near to tears. At any moment I expected him to say the age-old words 'If You Loved Me You Would', and I had a sudden crazy sense of us being as young as Romeo and Juliet and just as trapped. Everybody dies, I thought, irrationally. Those two, Madame Bovary, Thérèse Raquin, Madame Butterfly . . .

When we got to the end of the corridor he went one way and I took the lift up to the fifth floor. By this time I was really crying. It was just too much and I didn't know what to do – I was torn in two by it all. Perhaps I *would* end up mentally deranged and incontinent.

As I hared out of the lift and ran along the corridor towards our suite, I saw Charlotte walking in front of me, checking the door numbers.

I called to her, and she turned and smiled.

'Francis was worried,' she said, 'so I came. Are you all right? You look a bit –'

'I thought I looked wonderfully well an hour ago,' I said, far too snappishly.

She blinked. Nice, kind, proper Charlotte. I very nearly said, 'No, I'm not all right. I'm shagging two men and I don't know what to do . . . Because I love them both. Or I think I love them both . . . At any rate, I love one of them, and though I love the other one, I also hate the sight of him . . .'

Fortunately she intervened. 'Well, you *have* been crying,' she said to exonerate herself.

'Yes. Oh – sorry. This is it.'

I let her into 505 and sat in one of the chairs. She perched on the other, looking concerned. Not least at the extraordinary basket of flowers.

'*Is* it the menopause?'

I shrugged, remembering to stick to the truth where possible. 'One minute I'm happy and the next minute I'm like this . . .'

She relaxed. 'Oh, I know. I'm the same. I can be perfectly all right and then – pouf! I was weeding the front garden last week and I suddenly felt all weak and wobbly . . .'

Dear Charlotte. Weeding the garden!

I stood up. 'There now. All better. I'll just get the present and then we can go down.'

'You can always talk to me, you know. I promise I wouldn't tell Tim.'

I stared at her. Did she suspect?

'Besides,' she added, 'you've got your own doctor.'

I collected the gift – a wallet – impersonal – I just couldn't bring myself to buy him anything that was for ever, like a ring or a watch – and down we went. Serene, confident, two ladies of a certain age attending a jolly weekend with their husbands in lovely historic Bath and dining in. Except that one of them happens to have her lover sitting at another table, who glowers as the two serene, confident ladies saunter past. Just for a moment I thought I might sit down with him – 'Can I join you darlin'?' – and then it really would all be over.

But I carried on and walked straight by and sat down with my party. I knew Tim and Francis had been discussing me. Though whether it was the state of my hormones or the apparent blossoming that had taken place, who could say. Tim just smiled genially, Francis took and opened his present, expressed deep satisfaction and showed it by kissing my cheek, which must have given Matthew a nice moment. The starters, which had been held back, then arrived. I took a quick look across the room. Matthew and I had chosen oysters. I thought it was some kind of sign. Twin hearts . . . Crazy stuff.

And then Tim, glancing at my plate, said to Francis. 'Ah-ha – this might be your lucky night.'

Francis's plate arrived. He, too, had ordered oysters. He winked at me as they were placed in front of him. 'Sexy old oysters,' he said. The others tittered.

'Rules,' he said to include Tim and Charlotte in the joke. 'She wooed me there with oysters on our first date.'

A sudden sadness opened up inside me for the happy, uncomplicated person I was all those years ago.

After the main course, Matthew left. I turned to look at him, and his table was empty and being cleared. My immediate, banal thought was, Oh, well, he doesn't like puddings very much. And then I had to stop myself smiling for the sheer ordinariness of thinking such a thing and for understanding that beneath the passion and the fervour true affection grew.

'Dilys?'

Francis had said something.

'Yes?'

'Tim was just saying that we're all very lucky to have made it this far. Still in one piece.'

'I thought everyone was living longer and healthier?'

'Not staying alive,' said Tim.

Charlotte laughed.

'Staying *married*. It's the best thing for you.'

'Really?' I said. Paranoia made me wonder if this was some kind of test. 'I thought marriage kept men alive but that women on their own lived longer. Isn't that what the statistics say?'

'Oh, statistics,' said Tim.

'A much bigger proportion of marriages fall apart now,' said Charlotte. 'Half of our friends' marriages are crumbling around us. And their children's.'

Francis said, 'I think that nowadays they confuse the wedding with the marriage. One's easy, the other's hard.' He laughed and tapped my hand. '*Bloody* hard.'

It is a very good job that alcohol goes down without need for chewing and almost no swallowing. Any activity demanding muscular control was almost beyond me. Why were we having this conversation? Did they all know I was an adulterer? Were they baiting me? Had they secretly got together and decided to give me a terrible time before revealing the truth?

Tim went on, clearly oblivious to any darker meaning. 'Anyway, can you imagine doing a Jeffrey Archer or an Alan

Clark? Adultery. With all the risks. The very thought of it gives me the willies.'

'That's their problem, I think,' Charlotte said, laughing. 'Willies.'

Tim raised his glass to her. 'We've done almost thirty-five –' he said. 'And you must have clocked up thirty.'

'Yes,' I said. I was back in the tumbril again. I felt Charlotte give me a long look, so I reached over and squeezed Francis's hand – and felt sick as I did so. Judas and Marie unhappily side by side rattling over the cobbles.

'We're going for forty-five,' said Francis. He touched the ring on my hand. 'I just bought the sapphire a few years early.'

'What happens after forty-five?' I asked.

'I chuck you out into the snow,' he said.

Everybody laughed.

All I could think was, *Forty-five years*.

'I think I'll have a brandy,' I said cheerfully.

I saw Francis and Tim exchange the faintest of looks. Francis had obviously remembered the brandy and Carole's funeral and how nothing had been the same since. 'I've grown to like it.' Bugger them. 'Why don't we have our coffee in the bar?'

I was suddenly desperate to find Matthew again. Just to be in the same room as him. I thought he had probably gone to drown his sorrows. I know I was ready to drown mine.

We all trooped off and settled ourselves. The room was nearly empty. He was not there. I sipped my horrible brandy miserably.

'Mozart tomorrow night,' said Charlotte. 'What a treat.'

It crossed my mind, not without a sense of humour, that Matthew had probably managed to get himself a part in the production. I wouldn't put anything past him. But he hadn't. He had left a message for me on my mobile. It just said:

'Couldn't stand it. Have gone home.'

I felt completely bereft.

7

To Have or Have Not?

'What are these?' said Francis, as we were packing to go home.

'Hormone pills,' I said. 'And don't go down my bag. Ask.'

'I'm not –' he sounded injured. 'I'm just looking for a pen.'

I was furious. 'Well, use your own.'

I knew I should have just taken two of the pills out of the packet and left the rest at home. Laziness and adultery do not, I was discovering, go hand in hand. 'My bag is personal. Very personal.'

'I'm sorry,' he said.

I went thin-lipped, hardly Dunmow Flitch behaviour when your husband has arranged a lovely weekend.

'I'd forgotten it's the Chatelaine's seat of power.'

'What is?' I snapped.

'Her handbag.' He smiled a little cautiously. 'I promise to ask next time.'

He waited.

I continued to sulk.

He said, 'You may now stamp your foot.'

And, of course, I was instantly ashamed, instantly sorry.

'The Mozart was wonderful. Thank you.'

'I saw the tears,' he said, pleased. 'It was a good production.' And he began to hum 'O zittre nicht, mein lieber Sohn . . .'

Be not afraid, oh noble youth, seemed exquisitely appropriate.

'Don't,' I groaned involuntarily.

He laughed as he packed. 'A little excruciating now and then . . . Pamina was a very large Pamina wasn't she?'

'She certainly was.'

He closed the case. 'If you had to choose between Wisdom,

90

Reason and Nature, which temple would *you* enter?'

'Wisdom, of course,' I lied. 'And you?'

'I'd have said the same, but –' He looked up from his packing. 'I think I might choose Nature now . . . Take a walk on the wild side.'

In the olden days I might have stepped across to him, touched him affectionately, kissed his cheek – more, perhaps. Now I practically shot across the room and into the bathroom. Even he looked surprised as I catapulted past. I began cleaning my teeth again.

He called, 'Anyway, I'm looking forward to retirement.'

'Um,' I said, through the foam.

'Tim's finishing at the end of next year. They want to go round the world. They were making noises about us all joining up.'

'Lovely,' I said, re-emerging from the bathroom on the assumption that any danger of intimacy was over. He touched my ear. In which nestled a sapphire earring. One of the pair he had presented me with just before we went off to the opera.

'Not lovely,' he said. 'We want to be on our own, don't we?'

I couldn't bear it and I moved my head.

He gave the lightest of sighs.

'I thought we might stop for lunch. Take it slow getting back. Would you like that? I rather fancy Henley.'

If there was pathos attached to the suggestion, it was not very evident. But it stung me to the quick. 'I'd just like to get home. That was a huge breakfast. Anyway, it'll be nice to have a bit of time with Julia.'

He nodded. Disappointed. As he had been disappointed that morning in bed when he began to touch me and I moved away. I put my arm round his waist and gave him a dismissive hug, which made me feel even more cruel.

'Tell me about the Hogan case,' I said.

While he talked, my mind was working out a way to see

Matthew this evening. I had to. Every single bit of me was hot-wired to him. Whoever compared love to a drug – Mozart to Bryan Ferry – was just about right. You just don't think about the danger, the cost, when you need a fix . . .

All the way home I was racking my brains. How could I get out of the house legitimately, and alone, tonight? *How?*

Dare I do it once more?

Sweet old Auntie Liza.

The drive from Fulham to Paddington on a warm summer's afternoon takes about thirty-five minutes. This time, while negotiating it, instead of letting my mind behave like a parched pea in a frying pan, I tried to concentrate on Useful Thoughts. I had not had one of these since the day of Carole's funeral, and I was not sure I was capable of having one now, but I meant to try. If there is one thing passion does to you, it is to reduce your brain to childlike proportions. Anything grown-up that comes along just cannot find space among all the spangly candyfloss. So I concentrated. At least I might get some idea of where this Wrong Thing was going. In the name of sanity, if nothing else, between Fulham and Paddington I focused.

As I pulled into the first bit of serious traffic at Hammersmith, I considered these two men. Francis and Matthew. Husband and lover. Respectable lawyer and unemployed of Paddington. Write down a list of their good qualities and there would be scarcely a leaf between them. At least I wasn't cuckolding Francis with someone of whom he would disapprove. Which brought no comfort at all. As it would not, if he ever found out, bring any to him. And on the odd occasion when I tried to talk to Matthew about Francis, he either put his finger to his lips, or to mine, and changed the subject.

Both believed in the ultimate good. Both held liberal views. Both dealt in the stark realities of life as opposed to the kingdom of untried ideals that most of us inhabit at one end of the political divide or the other. The beautiful, clean, untried ideals of 'Give people a nice house to live in and food on their table and they will become socialized and not beat up old ladies in the street.'

Francis was continually dealing with people who had a nice house, nice food, clean duvet covers every Monday and who still went out and beat up anyone they could find. He had a football thug on remand who got his last Spurs ruck off the ground by sticking a knife in a cheering pensioner's ear. When his house was searched, and his wife held the baby and looked on in disbelief, the police found themselves rifling through drawers and cupboards of neatly ironed and folded bed linen, personal linen and baby clothes, and throwing the contents of drawers out on to immaculately hoovered fawn Wilton. And she said she had no idea. I wasn't convinced then – I believed it now. You could cheat anyone if they loved you.

At the other end of Francis's professional spectrum were the vulnerable misfits, the damaged goods of society. The hapless and hopeless who needed protection from the 'If you can't hang 'em, at least flog 'em' school of correction. He was their champion, 'There but for the Grace of God', and all that. Francis dealt all the time with clients who had mysteriously found their heads beating hell out of several policemen's boots, or who had tragically slipped down the stairs at the police station. He had been called, in the night, to remand centres where, when his young clients' bodies were cut down, they displayed more than just bruising on the neck. He took a direct line back from the bourgeois thug with his fawn Wilton, through the swastika-bearing mugger and drugger and the despairing young disenfranchised, to Margaret Thatcher and her 'Are you one of us?'

Francis, coming from a world in which privilege meant that nothing need be denied you, believed in social rights for all. He pointed the finger whenever he could. Thatcher and her No Society claptrap had shored up the brutal arrogance that pervaded our institutions. To him it was incomprehensible that lack of money or job or home still rendered you vulnerable to institutional abuse, never mind social exclusion. He was in tears of grief and rage when the news broke about Hillsborough. There it was, on our screens – second-class citizens, treated like scum, locked into a living graveyard, fathers kneeling over sons, brothers holding brothers, police losing their minds and – later – getting them back enough to realize they should lose the video that damned them instead. It was, he said, Dickensian. And that was what he blamed Thatcher and her ideology for – that she dressed up the brutal cynicism of Every Man for Himself as Self-Help. True Victorian Values. He loathed her with a passion.

It was odd, then, to lie in bed on our first full night together and watch the dawn, listening to Matthew going on about the same things, in the same way. I could have filled in the pauses with exactly the right words – I knew them off by heart. It was all I could do not to tell him. In his already heightened state, he would have just *loved* to hear how much he reminded me of my husband . . . Thatcher was the only human being that Francis could cheerfully have strangled with his own bare hands; Matthew's chosen form of execution was to stove in her head with one of her iron handbags.

Neither was there much to choose between them over the Falklands War. For Francis it was one of those experiences that deepened his political commitment just at a time in his life when he might have begun to Go Gentle . . . On the night of the Great Victory Parade, that painfully ludicrous occasion when the injured and mutilated veterans were banished, we were in a local restaurant. One of the other diners made the mistake of raising their glass to us for the Glorious Victory. Whereupon Francis strode across to their table, told him where he could stick his Victory salute, and brought his fist down with such force under his nose that the glasses jumped. Fortunately the manager knew us . . .

To remember that night was suddenly painful. The combination of being known at a restaurant – such a commonplace once – and the memory of Francis's fearless morality, I suppose. Whatever I was doing to my husband now, my admiration for him never wavered. It only added to my shame that I should be hurting someone so good. How much easier all this would have been if I could just say that Francis was a bad husband, bad person, bad, bad, bad. I knew that Matthew needed to hear such things (as I also would, obviously, if he had a wife), but the truth was that Francis was good, good, good. And I was proud of him. Proud of him and also betraying him. Bastard Love. I wanted, so often, to tell Matthew the good things about him – about the restaurant and the Falklands Parade, for instance. But I kept quiet as I lay in his arms, and I listened as if innocent and learned that on the same Glorious Parade night the student Matthew spent the time with two homeless veterans, getting legless. They, apparently, already were.

Francis was comfortable with the Blairite Revolution, even though I think it brought him up short to find himself a dozen years older than the new Prime Minister. Matthew had gone off the idea completely. His expectations of a new investment in the underclass had died, whereas Francis took the long view that only when the middle classes were truly on-side could reforms begin. It was the way of history. I floated that idea to Matthew. 'Fuck that,' he said. 'The so-called Blairite Revolution is a betrayal of the whole Labour movement. When you get into government and your first piece of serious legislation is to charge fees for further education and you count among your aims a zero tolerance on the homeless, then, baby, you've lost me –'

'Who will you now vote for then?'

'Let us not bring politics into the bedchamber . . .'

'Does that mean you don't know?'

'Yup.'

'Then why not give Blair and Co. a chance?'

'Because, my sweet little running dog of Capitalism, it's giving them a chance that I'm afraid of . . .'

But Francis and I had waited so long for this change of direction. It held the seeds of the guilt and despair I felt now. For when it came – such a long time in the waiting – he was finally ready to leave the field. That was when he began to talk seriously about retirement. Youth, after all, was what counted. We – he and I – were free of responsibility at last. It never occurred to me to think that I was still in my forties then, still comparatively young. We were the Grandee and His Lady, going off into the sunset, a job well done. We had kept the faith and Labour had finally made it. Matthew's view was rather different. 'They have ditched principle for power. It's government by board meeting. I used to be invited to address board meetings sometimes – when I was pitching for funds – and it was all corporate speak. Unreal, what you'd like it to be, not what it actually is. This government is no different. When did you last hear someone say "Yes, sorry, I fucked up?"'

'Stephen Lawrence?' I said.

I thought Matthew would die on the spot. 'Whitewash,' he said eventually. 'Oh, come on, Dilly – you surely see that? How many black or Asian high-fliers are there in the police? How many black or Asian high-fliers are in Francis's chambers, come to that? Even more relevant – how many friends have you and he got who aren't white?'

This was all an uncomfortable puncturing of the cocoon. How could I tell him that the only person I knew well from any ethnic minority was – my cleaner? Until that moment, everything felt in harmony with *Desideratum* – that the world is unfolding as it should.

At last, Francis was convinced that real change had begun. Coming home from the dramatization of the Stephen Lawrence enquiry, he was even more convinced. The police's bungling and prejudice were finally spotlit for a public who could no longer look away. The white sepulchre was open at last. It was the battle he had been waging for years, and now he could hand it on.

'I'm glad,' he said. 'And I'm tired. Time to do something purely selfish.'

We deserved it, we thought, as we snuggled into our nice black Saab and drove to our favourite local eatery, where we would spend the equivalent of a pensioner's weekly income on our meal. I wish I could forget those moments. I was so genuinely happy. It was the hardest thing to remember, that sense of clear-conscienced happiness. You don't think of the word 'happiness' until something removes it. Since meeting Matthew, I knew this happy state – the peace of mind that he laughed at and called my smugness – would never return.

And I was happy then. Half my women friends had husbands who, as time moved them into their fifties and sixties, showed no obvious signs of giving up the rat race. Indeed, Jessica Pine next door on the other side from Polly, whose husband, Edgar, was something pivotal in a large drugs company and who was only a little while off retirement, came to me in floods of tears one morning because Edgar had gone off to work the previous day with only eleven months left on his contract and had come home with another three years added on.

'And we were supposed to be buying a place in Sicily next year,' she said miserably. 'He promised. I've been waiting thirty years to watch the sun go down over Agrigento from my own doorstep. And now I know it will never happen.'

She was right. He's still getting the tube into town each morning, and she's still doing good works and rapidly disappearing down the wrong end of a bottle.

She wasn't the only one. I knew other women who were desperately filling up their time with book clubs and badminton and working out at the gym while their husbands said, 'One More Year', and then 'One More Year' after that . . . Women who had fulfilled their own lives – with family, career, home, friends – and who were now a few years off retirement and quite ready to wind down. One More Year did for the Bensons round the corner. While he was having his

One More Year, Sylvia Benson had a stroke, the cruelty of which being that it did not kill her. Just made her bed-ridden and dribbling and most often in tears, sad beyond measure that her bright brain was locked away for ever in her damaged body, knowing that she never would, now, visit Australia and her grandchildren, or follow Eric Newby through the Hindu Kush. You have to wonder what life is for when you see something like that. I made Francis promise that if it happened to me he would shoot me. He promised that he would. It occurred to me that now he just might. Only for a completely different reason.

Given all that, what was I doing? The woman who now had so much and who knew what it was to have so little, risking it all for the sake of a bit of fresh trouser? When I was thirteen, at the threshold so to speak, and watching all my friends take their first tentative steps in the fascinating world of brassieres and lace slips and girly underwear, I was so poor that I had two pairs of knickers – one pair on and one in the wash – and a vest, all of them so grey and frayed that I never dared show them to anyone. So I could never undress in their company. I was branded a prude. Prudes were excluded from girlitude. I think if there was anything I ever coveted, it was belonging. Now I could boast half a Marks & Spencer's underwear department and belonged in the heart of a family – loving husband, our sons, their wives and our grandchildren – and just at that perfect, most perfect, point I decide to Vulcanize?

So much easier for a man, I decided. A man would just say to his mistress, 'Well, Cynthia, that's it, take it or leave it.' And Cynthia probably would. The wife would then continue in blissful ignorance, having the holidays and the Black Forest gateau at the firm's dinner dance, and Mistress Cynthia would sink into wrinkled bitterness as the years took their toll. Whereas if I said to Matthew, 'Take it or leave it, sunshine,' he would go. Because he was no Rover and this little drama we were starring in was Congreve rather than

Behn. Sticky endings were everywhere. High moral ground coming out of its ears. Two honourable men in one woman's lifetime might be more than this particular woman could handle. Matthew would go, I knew, if I gave him the Cynthia ultimatum. And I just couldn't bear the loss. But yet, oh yet. What loss would be mine if I continued?

But even as I drove nearer to where he waited, my heart was beating faster, the world becoming more beautiful as each street was travelled.

Stop it?

I didn't want to.

Simple as that.

Quite suddenly, the thought of Francis being around permanently was the last thing I wanted. The nice man that I married was now surplus. In that one night after the Indian exhibition I had changed my life. Not even in that one night. I had changed it at Temple Meads Station and I had let it happen. Gone from being a contented woman with the future all wrapped up in golden paper, with neighbours who dined and talked sense, with – pinch me, I'm dreaming – the easy life, the old rags-to-riches story – gone from all that to this urgent quean. How could I set out to destroy all that? If it was for love, then I was loved. By my husband and my children and my grandchildren and even – remarkable fact – by my daughters-in-law. And now Matthew had come along and blown the whole thing out of the water. My loving, successful, loyal husband had just become a nuisance. The world had, apparently, turned on a sixpence. I was nineteen again, looking back at those scullers' thighs through the hanging willows at Henley and wishing, with all my heart, that I had dared to Just Say No.

A few months previously Francis had emerged from one of the Sunday paper property pages and said, 'We can sell this house if you like and buy one of those warehouse conversions. Or just rent somewhere. Kick up our heels a bit. Relive our not-so-misspent youth. Or at least *my* not misspent youth.' Even thirty years on, Francis was convinced that I had led a life much more dissolute than his by the time we met. Something to do with that poet and smoking dope. I denied it as usual. But he was looking to me, now, to lead him to the lively.

He put down the paper and said, 'Perhaps I'll have a tattoo. And an earring? What do you think?'

I said, 'Not half,' and meant it. I was as enthusiastic as he was to do something wild. Obviously. As it turned out.

That is what made all this so much more painful. I was cheating on a man who had paid his dues, waited to be irresponsible, and now –? It was like Sylvia's stroke. I was cutting him down in his prime. We might not have got on the Magic Bus all those years ago, but I couldn't blame him for that. I had hardly wanted to climb aboard myself. If a girl can't flirt, she probably can't survive the North African desert without her Tampax. And as I had only just got enough of the stuff, I was untempted to go where there might not be a clean set of underwear either. Neither of us was hippy material, but somewhere under all that propriety Francis, too, had a wild side. A side I could not, quite, fathom. The little bit of mystery, the inexplicable, that occasionally gave him an edge. I'd seen it in the way he liked some of his villains.

In his job he met a lot of what he called Real Old-Fashioned Villains. Men and women who took the breaking of the law and the conning and the fiddling and the laundering and the finger-in-pie-ing to an art. He didn't approve of them, but he liked quite a lot of them, which I never reconciled. Matthew, of course, would. And though Francis drew the line at the Krays, whom he designated psychopaths, he was curiously sympathetic with a diverse bunch of felons. He always said that a straight villain was worth more than a bent copper, which I suppose was fairly standard among his peers. A client of his, the head of a gang who stole cars to order – and we are not talking ten-year-old Peugeots – was like a farmer's son. The 'profession' had been passed on to his father, and his father had passed it on to him, like farmers pass on their land. It was less about sentiment, more about codes of practice. I said this was just boy-talk – that a villain, was a villain, was a villain . . . He agreed that violence was part of the code, but that nevertheless it *was* a code. You knew where you were with them. What he and his legal colleagues found frightening, post-Thatcher, was that these codes, just as everywhere else, had almost gone. The Self-Regulatory, Non-Bonded, Non-Existent Society had spread out to those who lived beyond its lawful boundaries. If the beatifying of market forces as the only morality prevailed enthusiastically in the market place, so it did in the jungle of crime. The criminal fraternity cut the fraternizing and began to operate without conscience or code, wholeheartedly, feet first and with brass knobs on. Like his football thug who just liked to get blood on his hands.

The new kids on the block had the amorality of children. Nothing in Francis's professional world had ever been savoury, but now everyone was turning into a little fascist mafioso who'd slit your nostrils as soon as look at you. Which, metaphorically speaking, Francis argued, was exactly what the Tories under Thatcher became. Just as there was no longer much Honour Among Thieves, the Thatcher years had finally wiped out any Honour among the Tory Old Guard. At least the patrician classes would give a tramp a biscuit in the old days. So – according to Francis – in much the same way, old-fashioned, true villains – just like the Tory Old Guard – began to look like persons of honour. They might whip six Range Rovers from under the noses of their well-heeled owners, they might poison a dog here and there to get hold of a bank manager and his keys, and – yes – they were not averse to hurting people or carrying a gun in pursuit of success, but they would never bash a child over the head with an iron bar for the sake of the thrill of a gout of blood. In clean, out clean, was the old-fashioned villains' motto. Having seen some of the cases that passed through his hands more recently, I could see his point. He didn't need to watch Greenaway or Tarantino – that stuff he was dealing with every day.

When I suggested that this was a dual standard, Francis just said, 'There are degrees . . .' All the same, he used to get a bit pink about the ears when we were sent hampers from Harrods and boxes of Scotch from distilleries at Christmas, with little cards saying cryptic things like 'From Tinkerbell and the Shadows' or 'Free Pig'. We worked out what the latter meant, if not to whom it referred – it was 'Free Pig' because Francis had saved his bacon. Or hers, I suppose. It was a far cry from the successful young City lawyer I married.

I remember exactly when he changed, this husband of mine. He was thirty-three and he was doing as fabulously well out of the City as everyone else was then – nothing to get your hands dirty with – and he looked the part, too. Long black overcoat, plain scarf tucked in just so, black leather gloves, discreet trouser bottoms, polished black broguish shoes and hair just a trifle long over the striped shirt collar. On any weekday morning, if you stood near the exit of Moorgate or Temple or Bank, you would see hundreds of them coming out and strolling to their places of work. Which is just what Francis said that evening. We'd been to his club, and he suggested we walked down Piccadilly instead of taking a cab. And while we walked he said he'd decided to change professional direction. He was going to join a different kind of practice and give up the dream of one day owning a Morgan and a small yacht and an apartment in Antibes. It was time, he said, to give something back.

I didn't know what to think. I imagined us plunged into poverty. Quite irrationally. Because, of course, what I did not realize, coming from my background, was that the cut in our income would only be relative. That fees would still be generous, that we would still live well and that what Francis earned per annum would have kept several members of my family very happily. Being unaware of all this, I was aghast and enraged and I lost my temper. First time ever, there in Piccadilly. Which shocked us both. I went from sweet and dutiful wife to cornered tiger-mother.

I spat out, 'You might have asked me about it. After all, we'll both be suffering . . . Or doesn't my opinion count?'

And he stopped, right by the Arts Council's building, which was at the Hyde Park end of Piccadilly in those days, and he looked up at it and then at me and said, 'We won't be suffering – unless you think not having a Morgan is suffering. And if we were, then of course it would be different. But in matters of what we want to do with our chosen careers – well – I'd never *dream* of hindering you if you wanted to change what you were doing.'

He was missing my point. 'What about the money?' I shouted.

He looked at me as if I were talking double Dutch.

He looked puzzled. 'We'll manage.'

'Manage? *Manage?*' I was terrified. 'I don't bloody want to manage. I've done managing – I've lived with managing until I almost didn't exist. Oh, no. I want – I want –' And then I saw his face – concerned, frightened – and I stopped

We really were from different planets. When he used the word 'manage' he meant it as a positive, something unquestionably achievable. In my growing up the word 'manage' was different. It meant hand to mouth, coping against the odds, going without, sacrifice.

'I'd never do anything to make life difficult . . .' He was horrified.

I controlled the shaking somehow and pulled myself together enough to speak coherently. 'Doing anything in the arts is poorly paid,' I said, still angry but trying to be emollient. 'Rewarding in other ways, though,' he said mildly.

'We'd never be able to rely on what I earned.'

'I don't think it'll ever come to that,' he said. 'But it feeds the spirit.'

And then we were friends again and continued to walk,

and I understood that I really had moved into a different league. I knew, finally, that I was safe.

'I think', he said, 'that something rewarding, something good for the soul, is the same thing I'm looking for, I suppose. Giving something back. Only mine pays considerably better than yours – unless you get a bestseller.'

'Not likely in art history,' I said.

'Oh, I don't know,' he laughed. 'Think of Gombrich. Think of Berenson!'

Gombrich? Berenson? Any immediate thoughts on what I did for a living was irrelevant at the time since I was up to my neck in potty training and Babygros. I managed to slip off to the major shows, but I was barely touching base with the world of art; any stolen moments curled up with a serious book – let alone an art history – were rare and sweet. As for writing one of my own, that seemed – from the depths of my happy, soggy motherhood – pie in the cerulean sky.

But things move on, and a few years later I began work on a book about Davina Bentham – a painter cousin of Jeremy's and one whom he referred to in one of his letters to Rickman as 'a bit of a dabbler in oils but shocking unseemly for a female'. Francis was all for it. He bought me an Amstrad computer, state of the art in those days, and never – throughout all our trials with various nannies, home helps, au pair girls – did he show any regret. He even found a summer camp for the boys – I think a colleague told him about it – and they went there for three weeks while I went to Hell and Back trying to finish the first draft, which I did. Francis had a naïve love of art and he liked my knowledge of it, so I could hardly fail, given all that material and psychological support. It occurred to me that it was the very opposite of poor Davina Bentham's experience, where every professional step she took was larded with disapproval and weighed down with considerations of feminine propriety – as well as the more pressing constraint of having to earn her own living. Her grandfather lost most of the family's money in the South Sea

Bubble, so she was brought up in genteel poverty and required to find her own way in the world. The family were somewhat horrified to discover her commitment to do so by means of her brush and palette. It also occurred to me, because I never got past the first draft, that while she fought against all the odds to succeed – and did so – I, who had nothing to worry about, lost the struggle. A little lesson there, no doubt.

If I had been hungrier, I might have pushed myself harder. My book was more to do with the character and nature of a woman and an artist making it in the Age of Reason. I admired the way she remained focused and I found her remarkably sassy and appealing, as well as prodigiously talented. She still hovered in the back of my mind. Unformed, unfinished. I became very close to her during all the research, but somehow there was a dimension to her that I could not quite reach. A bit of the jigsaw I had not found. If I was ever to succeed with her, I would need to discover and understand the part of her I had not found. But I just couldn't quite put my finger on what was missing.

She was already modern in an age when women had lip service paid to their qualities and little else. She was, for example, bossy and acerbic with her sitters, which was acceptable for Gainsborough and Reynolds, but no good at all for a doe-eyed young lady. She also painted a study of Hercules, which she refused to clothe and which, on presentation for exhibition, the Academy destroyed on the grounds of corruption. When a priest was sent to her she hurled herself to her knees and appeared to sob all over his feet. Later it was seen that she was laughing. The story did her reputation no good, and the commissions for children's portraits, at which she was considered very talented, all but vanished overnight.

She then had three choices: she could go on making very little money at her art, or she could marry a wealthy man, or she could become the mistress of an even wealthier one – in her case Lord Sidon, who fell for her when his two children sat for her. Lord Sidon made his considerable wealth out of an advantageous marriage to a plain woman of great fortune, some years older than himself and pleased to be asked. Lord Sidon had never implied, as he wrote to Davina, that he would stay faithful to his wife, but he did assure her that he would never leave her bereft in society. It was, after all, no different from the Prince of Wales's conduct. Therefore, if Davina was willing to accommodate him on those terms, she would find he could be very generous. 'I love you more than Aphrodite is known to be beautiful, more than Philomena's singing is known to captivate,' he ended his letter with a flourish. In the margin of that letter Davina scrawled, 'Then it shall cost ye!'

She wrote to her sister Rowena, quoting this, and saying that he had a small nose, somewhat like a button, which betokened small everything. Her sister wrote back tartly saying she should be very glad of it, as many women would be. Though whether she referred to the smallness of a male member or, more innocently, to the potential of being someone's mistress was unclear. For her part, it is certain that Davina referred to Lord Sidon's genitals, the mysteries of which held no fears for her, which was quite clear from her studies for the doomed painting of Hercules. It is not known, and I could not find out, who the model for that painting was, but certainly in some of the studies the youth has a look about him that is not, altogether, unawakened . . .

But Lord Sidon wanted too much of her freedom. She would certainly not give up her art. In the end Davina Bentham chose the road alone, believing that her talent would win through. It did not. She continued to make very little money, though the few portraits that exist show an expertise that would not have shamed any Academician. She had a remarkable flair for colour, and though she subdued it for her commissions a little, in her private work – landscapes, still lifes and studies of friends – she never held back. She was

also fond of the domestic interior and painted it atmospheri-
cally many years in advance of Turner and his Petworths.
Indeed, Turner himself owned one of her dusky, ill-lit rooms,
and it was framed expensively enough to show he valued it.

She was interesting, both as a painter and as a woman.
When Rickman was working on the first census in the late
eighteenth century, she travelled with him occasionally and
painted some of the country people and the poor in a few of
the big industrial towns. Rickman observes in a letter to
Bentham that she 'gets a fearsome look in her eye and
splashes as much paint on the carpet as she do on the paper –
but she does work very quick . . .' She felt she had a right to be
as free as – say – her cousin Jeremy and his radical, intelligent
(and bumper drinking and whoring) academic friends.
Bentham did what he could for his cousin, but her only surviving close relative, her brother Edward, did not. He disap-
proved of her manner and methods – he harangued her
heartily in several letters while she was travelling with
Rickman – but she paid no attention, merely doodling in the
minuscule edges of the paper. She wrote to her cousin
Bentham that 'Edward do consider me too wild to be even on
separate horses here with Mr Rickman so, compliments to my
brother and would you please convey to him the enclosed
portrait so that he may see for himself how Mr Rickman is
wholly without attractions.' The picture is lost, but there is no
doubt from Bentham's diary that it was of Rickman naked.

In the end she quarrelled with Bentham and his wife, and
they abandoned her – or she them. Like Mary Wollstonecraft,
she was at the mercy of her temperament and her high intel-
ligence, in an age when both were considered unnecessary in
a woman, but unlike Wollstonecraft, as far as I could tell, she
never fell in love to her detriment. She loved her art. 'Take
that from me and I die,' she ended a letter to one of her
cousins, when they tried to persuade her to settle down.
Which made me smile for being so over the top. It was generally thought that the illness she died from, when she was only

forty-six, was syphilis, though some Wollstonecraft mix-and-matchers have suggested that she, too, died from childbirth. There is a good argument for it being, quite simply, poverty. But how could she let that happen in a world that wanted to care for her?

Given the drama of her story and the few remaining paintings that were known to exist and the others that must still be hidden away in private collections, and her peculiar placing in the modern history of women, it was silly of me to give up on the idea. But – well – comfort breeds sloth, I suppose.

Francis's mother viewed my 'work' much as the charity work of genteel women was viewed: something to occupy them; something that Dilys can *do* to keep her fingers from being idle. She never did understand his marriage to me, nor why he gave up the City, nor why we had a Labour Party poster in our windows ('Darling, couldn't you just vote *Liberal* if you must . . .?') during elections. Julia, who was then married to a stockbroker, just smiled at him indulgently, as if he were still eight years old, and shook her head and said, 'Oh, Francis, *Francis* – always wanting to do something different . . .' But my relationship with them was uneasy for a while. It took his mother and his sister about ten years and our two children before they could accept me. The various liberations of the sixties and the seventies cut no ice with them. Coming from the great unwashed, I must be a social climber after Francis's money and out to scupper the good family name. He should have married a girl like Tim's Charlotte. Indeed, when we hooked up for a foursome down at the family home, I quite often caught Francis's mother gazing wistfully at Charlotte and then bleakly at me. It was only later, when I led the vanguard against Francis and stopped John being sent to the nearest state senior school – making sure he went to a grant-assisted a few miles away instead – that his mother and his sister finally accepted me. Of course, they came at it from the opposite end of the educational axis. One simply did *not* attend state schools. I came at it from the maternal point of view. It was not the right place for our son. Francis and I sparred endlessly over the question and it was our first real parental falling out. The only serious one ever. We did not speak except to pass the marmalade for weeks. But I knew John would get bullied. Only when you have been on the other side of the educational tracks can you really know what you are talking about, and I wasn't going to have my son suffering as a guinea pig to principle.

After winning that one, my mother-in-law and my sister-in-law were best-grade putty in my hands. I had come of age in the upper reaches of the middle classes. Julia was entirely on-side, my mother-in-law grudging but willing to trust. The latter, thank the gods, was now long gone, but the very thought of dear, trusting, kind Julia finding out about the affair left me feeling very, very ill.

I had shed my socially inadequate past, buried it as far as I knew, and was now on the side of the angels. You only had to see how Virginia behaved towards me to see that, in the eyes of the world, I had crossed over. I was protected from her, too. I was protected from everything and everyone while I was with Francis. Protected, loved, respected. Everything in the world a woman could wish for.

Until Matthew.

Now that shining white wife, the one who wrapped bacon round myriad dates and made platefuls of mini-pizzas for our party to celebrate the Sleaze Bust of Treddick and Co. – with which I so heartily concurred that my hangover lasted into the middle of the following week – was shaming. I had now created a personal cesspit of my own. So what if a handful of Tory MPs were made to walk the plank? If Mrs Perfect Mini-Pizza found that so shameful, what about that same woman now? Slinking off to fuck her lover in a shoddy flat in Paddington, while paying lip service to her husband's fond and future plans? I was no better than any politician who told the world to behave in one way, while behaving quite improperly themselves. How could I face my mirror each morning? How could I have sneered at those brown envelopes when I was now slipping greasy bits of cash into motel tills? How could I join in the cackling over Jeffrey Archer's wandering willy, when my little honey pot didn't try to stay at home either? How could I do it? Yet I had, and I would, and I did.

What demon drove me in this Congreve that was all blood and bone instead of bawdy red lips and thoughtless warm thighs? None. I drove myself. All the characters in this play must come to a sticky end if I pursued what I desired. Yet I could see no way out of it because I did not seem capable of making that choice. No use putting my head in my hands and saying I was driven to it. I was hurtling towards a disaster at my own volition, almost triumphantly. Almost as if I was saying, 'Look, look – I am really a sham.' Bad blood will out. Dear Francis. Dear, good Francis. Equable, cultivated, highly developed social conscience, good son, good brother, good husband, good father. What was I doing? For what? And with whom . . .?

It would serve me right, I thought as I crawled in the traffic down Bayswater Road, if I really was pregnant.

8

Down and Outs in the Palace of London

And Matthew? What was he like, this man whose company I thought Francis would enjoy if they ever met over a warm beer at the Rat and Parrot? Matthew Patrick Todd. What made *this* honourable man tick? *This* honourable man who, like Francis, had found a new direction with the discovering of his conscience? He, too, had changed direction and combined work and the ethos of worthy citizenship in a single move. Sometimes, if I thought about it at all, I wondered if it wouldn't have just been much easier to revert to my maternal blueprint and gone out and found myself a big, butch bastard.

Matthew. Lying in bed in a Travelodge somewhere a week or two after we met, I began to learn about his past. After graduating brilliantly – his word – from Leeds University and teaching English in Namibia for a year – where he met and fell in love with Alma, a graduate from Edinburgh doing the same – he came back to London and slid into exactly the kind of job he thought he wanted. Certainly the kind of job that Alma and his parents – both teachers – wanted for him: in the education department of a radical London borough. Articulate, attractive (for which, alas, I could vouch), passionate (ditto), ambitious and highly motivated, he was groomed for, and looking forward to, a career in politics. Given the devastation being wrought on the poorly paid and those at the hopeless bottom of the pile, he learned quickly how to influence, lobby, manipulate. His borough housed a high proportion of immigrants with the usual high proportion of women outworkers – thus his crusade was made. The beautiful young man with fearsome blue eyes and hair like a blonde Byron's, preaching unfashionable socialism.

'I was not beautiful,' he said defensively. 'And I was already going bald.'

But I stuck to the fantasy.

'And anyway,' he said, 'Byron loathed women . . .'

'But they adored him.'

'That's what he both adored and loathed about them. I like women.'

'I'd noticed.'

'All except one.'

There was no getting away from it. That grocer's daughter from Grantham had a way of getting a response out of even the most liberal of men, even if it was demonic. At least, I thought privately, Thatcher was convinced she had right on her side . . . Much, no doubt, as Vlad the Impaler believed, but at least she believed *something* . . . All my beliefs seemed to have melted away.

'What I love about being with you,' Matthew continued, 'is that we think alike.'

'Yes,' I said, thinking, All three of us, actually. Pillow talk among socialists, even in a Travelodge off the A1, is heady stuff. Francis and I used to do the same thing when we were first together – lie in each other's arms and discuss 'Grocer' Heath, stuffed and fried. Francis did a fair imitation of those shaking shoulders and the very silly laugh, and we both found his current gravitas as the thinking person's sage too silly by half. But at least he gave the Grantham Girl a kick up the eighties. Now it was a kind of déjà vu.

'So, Matthew Todd – you were set for the stars at Westminster and then what?'

He laughed. 'And then one of the tabloids tried to out me as a "loony leftwing pinko homosexual" and I won an out-of-court settlement.'

'How did you disprove it?'

If I hoped for a demonstration it was not forthcoming.

'They'd bribed someone and he came clean about it. Anyway, after that I knew that I'd arrived politically. Interest in whom I had sex with and how I did it meant I'd got a profile . . . So I thought, What next?' He laughed again. 'What cause can I take up that is so unfashionable it needs my Loony Leftwing Pinko publicity? And you know what I found?'

I shook my head, lulled.

'Bangladeshi women.' He waited. 'Ring any bells?'

'Well –' I began – 'I knew all about it because . . .'

He was smiling very broadly.

'Because?'

'Well, Francis was working on a number of cases of exploitation and – oh my God . . .'

'Exactly. He – um – put them in touch with me.'

This was the first time Francis's name had been spoken willingly by Matthew. I waited. It could not have been odder, really, but then – what was not odd nowadays?

'He was very clever, your husband, because he realized that before we could get anywhere in the courts what we needed was the approval of the Bangladeshi community, particularly their menfolk.' He put his hands behind his head and smiled up at the ceiling. 'So I have much to thank your husband for. After that success, television and radio started to wheel me on as a young, dynamic talking head. I was twenty-four.' He gave me a strange look. 'And all thanks to your husband.'

'Why are you telling me about this?'

He shrugged. 'To tell you that I know he's a good man, maybe. To show you what I am . . . And to tell you that I feel a shit but I can't help it. Who was it said that love is a tyrant?'

'Don't know. Then what?'

'Corneille maybe?'

'Then?'

'Then everything changed. Just as I was about to buy a house with Alma – and settle down – I walked away from it all . . .'

'Were you engaged?' The question shot out of me so fast I was surprised it didn't put a hole through him.

He paused, looking a little thrown, and then said, 'We were – but only because her parents were rabid Scots Presbyterians . . . Anyway, I discovered my vocation, which was not to be a dashing political figure on a dream ticket but an activist, apparently, with a life devoted to society's trash. If it surprised Alma, it sure as hell surprised me. One day I was sitting at a meeting of councillors who were discussing the Problem of the Homeless, the next I had walked out of the building to set up a hostel in the area. Because I knew how things worked I knew how to manage it. My Damascus . . . It was semantics. The word "problem" at the meeting. The Council's view was that its job was to charge the ratepayers as little as possible to eradicate *the problem*. The nice, clean Meals on Wheels, the brownie points of Adoption, a caring Old Folks' Home or two were fine . . . But not dregs. They didn't want dregs. It was cousin to fascism and eugenics. Ratepayers, of course, voted the council in or out, ratepayers paid the council workers' wages . . . They didn't want to *do* anything about it. They just wanted the *problem* to disappear . . . They were even adding to it – tipping out the asylums and waving goodbye to all those kids in care when they hit eighteen. So enter the shining white knight . . .'

I was just thinking that even new lovers, engirdled by their socialist dream, can overdo the political pillow talk, when he said, 'That's it. I just wanted to make a difference. And I did. I left Alma for the Common Weal,' he added, poking fun at himself. 'Bit by bit we got there. The high spot was persuading the council to give us Sheldon Point as a hostel for the homeless. We called it "The Palace of London".'

'And Alma?'

He put his arms round me very tightly. 'You should know that if I had to make that choice now I am not sure I would risk losing you . . . From now on,' he said, half laughing, half serious, 'you will be my Palace of London.'

I heard the ticking of my little travelling alarm clock but apart from that it was as if the entire motel, the entire world, held its breath. And then he added, 'Your husband sent me a letter of support and said that, if ever I needed his help, I had only to ask . . . Fortunately I never did.'

Make that *two* pints at the Rat and Parrot.

When breathing was restored I had only one real, burning question. Not what happened to the Bangladeshi women. Not what happened to the housing dream. Not even what did you do next to Save the World, Matthew? . . . Of course, in my present state, the only thing I wanted to know was '. . . And what about your fiancée?'

'My . . .? Oh – Alma . . .'

I held my breath for signs of an unmended heart.

'I asked her to wait, and she said she would, and then she didn't.'

'Poor you,' I said, guiltily delighted.

'Nope. When I asked her to wait I think I was hoping she'd give up. I didn't want to be tied to anything any more. Didn't want a steady job, mortgage, kids, car. I'd done everything by the book – trodden the planned path and found that it was just a little too golden, a little too easy . . . I wanted another *crusade.*'

And now look at you, I thought, running my fingers over his skin.

Pride crept into his voice.

I was jealous even of *that*.

'And we turned it into the biggest place of its kind in the country. A result or what?'

I remembered the Grand Opening. Francis and I went along to the ceremony – the fantastical party in celebration. Francis was unqualified in his praise of the scheme. To say recalling all this made my blood run cold would be an exaggeration. But to think of those two, in the same room, drinking to the same success? They were born to be buddies . . .

'I remember,' I said. 'Francis went to the opening.'

'I know,' he said. 'I spent some time talking to him. He'd just begun working with Lawyers of Conscience.'

I waited for him to say that he remembered me, too. He did not. And whilst I did not remember *him*, I did remember that I was wearing a particularly striking little black number that even Francis still remembered with affection. Ah well. For a moment I thought about throwing him a left hook. After all, we were lying in bed together, we had just made love, I was living flesh and he ought to have remembered. Or pretended. Needy, that was me. But Matthew's eyes were shining with the light of real evangelism. 'It was fantastic,' he said, obviously transported back to his greatest triumph. 'You should have been there . . .'

'I was.'

'Good grief.'

Quite.

Two men in my life of any importance and they *both* had to be a combination of Lancelot, Charles Dickens, Keir Hardie and Bronowsky.

'So the change of direction was right?'

'Completely right.'

'On every level?'

He looked puzzled.

'The whole man?'

He shrugged, still unclear. 'I think so –'

'Every single level?' I emphasized.

'To the very nerve endings,' he said, pretending to humour me and obviously not having any idea what I was getting at.

I took a deep breath. I wondered, fleetingly, where the woman called Dilys, who was known to be a little too serious on occasion, had fled. Perhaps I flatter myself but it was a little like Buñuel suddenly deciding to make his next movie along the lines of *Carry On Up the Berlin Wall*. Love had made me a fluffhead.

'What?' He was still waiting.

Another deep breath. 'And also – in your love life?'

The light now dawned. 'Oh, that,' he said dismissively. 'You mean without Alma?'

116

I nodded.

'Well, I missed out on that old sixties thing Free Love,' he said, 'so I reinvented it for myself later on . . .' He gave a little smile, with just a touch too much of the gloat about it. And he nodded with satisfaction. '. . . Was excellent, thank you. Excellent.'

'Tell me.'

'Nothing to tell.'

'*Tell me . . .*'

'A lot of very nice women.'

'A lot?'

'Thousands.'

'Anyone special?

'Each of them was special.'

'Oh.'

'Every single last one of them was special.'

My mouth went dry. For me, everything about him was as if for the first time. For him, apparently, I was only one of a number – a string – of special women. Special for a short while and then he was off. So much for his saying that he wouldn't be able to leave me.

The best way to overcome the suffering was to clothe it in dignity. And one way to find dignity was to get clothed. I stood up. This was it then, I was going to leave, it was all over.

'But none of them – not one of them – was as special as you.' He ran the flat of his warm hand over my chilled stomach. I went on standing there, by the bed, looking down on him.

'How many times have you said that?'

'I have never felt the way I feel about you about anyone else.' He said it solemnly.

'But if they were all special, then I'm no different.'

'If you want me to say that no one before you counted, I can't. But I love you. I'm not in control of it, sometimes I don't like it very much, but I can't do anything about it. And the fucking lousy thing is –' now he looked as miserable as I had looked a moment ago – 'that you are married to someone else.' He pulled me back down to the bed where we sat side by side, straight-backed, staring ahead. 'You are married to someone else and I don't want you to be. I want us to be free and I don't want to cheat in this game any more.'

The conclusion to what he was saying was obvious. And I still wasn't prepared to go down that road. He wanted it all out in the open. Honest. Above board. The way he had always lived his life until now. Just as Francis had been honest when he confessed about his little affair when he did not need to. Oh, yes. If the two of them ever met, they would get on like a house on fire. Both honourable, very, very honourable, men. Except for the little matter of maybe Matthew forgetting himself and slapping Francis on the back and saying how much, how very much, he enjoyed the way I made the rafters ring when I came.

Matthew was forty-two. But, like so many people who have never had children, he was much younger in spirit. I don't know if what we eat is what we are – wholegrain cereal over Coco Pops – but I do think that what we wear reflects how old we see ourselves. Matthew – apart from his little dressing-up spree at the Royal Edward – never wore much other than jeans and T-shirts. Sometimes a denim shirt, sometimes a leather jacket and occasionally a loose black suit. From behind he could have been eighteen or twenty-five or thirty-six. He wore the sort of thing that Francis laughed at: baseball caps, vegetarian footwear; along with close-cropped hair and drinking beer straight from the bottle in a bar. They were, Francis said, phoney statements about being unconventional. I used to nod, sagely, and agree. Now I loved the youthfulness and the freedom of it all. Even those peculiar shoes were exciting because they marked Matthew out as different from everything I knew before. If I ever needed to call up a bathetic explanation for the moment I knew I was lost, it was those Right-On vegetarian shoes.

His way of dressing reflected his nature – easy, youthful,

only himself to think about. What he had done was find my youthfulness for me, too. Fatal seduction. With Matthew I was a girl. Not just because of what the newness of our relationship did to me, but because he was so much younger in every way from my husband. For the first time I felt irresponsible, and I loved every minute of it. The only dampener was – well – that I wasn't . . .

Matthew, like Francis, had been loved as a child. He was good with people. He *liked* people. Like that day on the station when he knew about handing me a handkerchief and what was the best thing to say. 'There is nothing', he said, 'like being there when an old man comes in wet through, blood all over his face, clothes filthy and falling apart, and then seeing the same man the following morning, sitting at a table, eating breakfast, close to feeling normal again.' He shrugged and laughed at himself. 'It makes up for the ones that come at you with a razor when their stash runs out.'

'It sounds like being a Messiah to me.'

'It's exactly like being a Messiah,' he said cheerfully. 'I am the devil's willing temptee. Take me up on the roof of Sheldon Point, tell me that if I proclaim myself Messiah then all the curled up blankets in the doorways below will be mine – and I'll do it . . . What's wrong with doing good and feeling good about it? So what? I'm not going to pretend . . . People being grateful for what you can do for them is *nice* . . . It means you've pleased them . . .'

And I thought, Grandees don't think like that. Grandees do the job for huge amounts of money and as little quiet glory as they can get away with without looking self-serving. And then they get to sit in the House of Lords.

'So why aren't you doing it any more? Being Messiah?'

'Because of you.'

'You were not being Messiah before you met me.'

'Only temporarily.'

'So why aren't you doing it any more Only Temporarily? What happened to *Wunderkind*?'

'Oh, *Wunderkind* will return. He's only temporarily absent. At my last place someone let on that there was heroin in the house. Which there was – no denying that. The people who brought it in broke the rules. No drink. No drugs. On the other hand we had a policy of never searching. So, one day, in came the Old Bill – tip off – and . . .'

'And?'

He looked amused. 'And, if they hadn't dropped it, I might have been consulting a certain Francis Holmes, solicitor, about my impending prosecution for allowing dealing on the premises. How's that for irony?'

Terrifying.

It occurred to me that he might, if Francis *had* represented him over the drugs case, have come to the house. I might have cooked a meal for him, sat down with him, talked charmingly to him, and never thought anything of it. Or would I still have found him – and he me – so unavoidably desirable? God, truly, knows. We certainly didn't. Ah well. As that well-known lady about town, Madame de Stael, was so fond of saying: 'Love: that's self-love *à deux* . . .'

I steered the car into Matthew's road and the excitement grew wild again. Crazy stuff. Oh, there was no sense in it. Nor was there any sense in the way I tempted Providence in its name. Like tonight. Just to see *his* face I had left my husband alone in our house with his own perplexed and slightly hurt one. And he was no doubt wondering why I needed to set off to see an ageing aunt at a time of night when if she wasn't tucked up with her library book she ought to be. I put Francis, his hurt face and My Life as a Gambling Den – everything – out of my mind. None of it bore thinking about. And I didn't have to any more, because here I was.

I pulled up outside his flat, parking behind his old black dish-backed Saab. I even felt emotional about his *car*: the dents, the scratches, the rusty bits, the floppy broken wing mirror, even the leathery smell of the interior – it was all essence of him. Though I never told Matthew. Even he – in his own state of romantic grace – would find it too much. Nor did I tell him that it compounded the strangeness of knowing how well he and Francis would get on if they met. A Saab and the *Guardian* – clear as any Masonic handshake. Only our Saab, of course, was a year old and shiny dark blue. Now, as usual, my heart was racing with anticipation. And I was aware, in a sudden rash of goosebumps, that it was only by chance that I was in the stronger position for the moment. Turn the wheel a few more ratchets and it could just as easily be me up at that window, holding back the curtain, staring down as if my life depended on seeing him arrive. I waved and smiled. Oh, yes – it could all so easily reverse. I could become an Edward Hopper any day.

I tried to make light of everything. I laughed over his appearance at the Royal Edward and asked where he got the clothes – the suit, the crazy blazer – and he said he'd bought them in the Cancer Relief Shop. I told him I'd like him to wear a blazer more often. Just a blazer. Nothing else. But he wasn't laughing. And any sense of power or pleasure in the strength of his feelings soon evaporated. First he apologized for being so selfish in coming to Bath, then he took it all back and said I should never have gone in the first place, then he wanted to know every detail of the weekend because it was better to know than not, then he said he didn't want to hear about any of it. Then he made coffee and while it was brewing he forgot it and poured us each a whisky, then he more or less frog-marched me into the bedroom and when we lay down he sat up again and asked me all over again what Francis and I had done.

'We went for a walk on Saturday afternoon and then saw *The Magic Flute* on Saturday night, and on Sunday morning –'
'What did you do in bed?'
'Slept.'
'You were fucking him when I came into your room.'
'He's my husband,'

'Did you enjoy it?'

'You shouldn't have been there.'

'Did you enjoy it?'

'He's my husband.'

'Does it give it an extra edge because of me? If we do it now, will it be just that little bit more exciting?'

'I'm going.'

'What's it like – with him – now?'

When I refused to answer, he said harshly, 'How can you do it with anyone else?'

'He's my husband,' I repeated, long suffering now, weary of it all.

He asked me if that meant it was all over between us.

'I love you,' I said. 'I've wanted to be here, now, with you, like this, ever since I saw you in bloody Bath. I wish I'd never gone – I wish . . .'

We were both near to tears, in tears, I don't know –

I said, 'I'm not sure I can go on with this.'

'Do you want to finish it?'

I have never seen anyone actually biting their thumb; I've read about it, but Matthew was actually gnawing at the side of his thumb like an angry dog.

'Finishing it', I said, 'is the last thing on my mind. It's how to continue it. You really have no idea what it's like for me – you're harming no one you care for, but He's My Husband.'

'So you said.'

He went on gnawing and looking at me, and then he suddenly bowled the big one. The one I had successfully avoided up until now. The inevitable.

I suppose I was expecting it. But I was always hoping he would hold back. He didn't. The sweet naivety of his thinking Francis and I were somehow only platonic was gone. And with it had gone any pussyfooting about the future. It was obvious really. He just looked down at my hands, touched the palms of them lightly as if to mock the weight of what was coming next.

'Well then,' he said, 'when are you leaving him?'

'I'd like that coffee.'

'Dilys, when are you leaving him?'

'Don't let's –'

'When are you leaving him?'

'Are you saying I have to choose?'

'I'm saying, When are you leaving him?'

You freeze, because there is no right answer.

Now I knew how Michael Howard felt with Jeremy Pax-man's fourteen repeats of 'Did you or didn't you . . .?'

'I don't know –'

'When?'

'I can't . . .'

'When?'

'. . . yet.'

'So?'

'I don't know . . .'

And then I added, without even thinking about it, '. . . if I ever will.'

There's a way of making love, I now know, as if it is for the very last time. And in a way it was. Because whatever else happened to us in the future, we were leaving something behind that night. We were out of the shell. Hatched. No going back. We had to take what the world gave us and sur-vive or die. 'When are you leaving him?' had changed every-thing for ever.

As I drove back, much later than I intended, something extraordinary happened. I pulled up on to the forecourt of a garage and bought a copy of *Hello!* magazine. It was in my hand and I was at the cash desk before I even thought about it. I paid and took it out. It had various colourful pictures of grinning film stars and sports personalities and, as usual, a picture spread of some royal event or other. And when I got home, I took it into Francis, who was in his study, and I said, 'Auntie Liza insisted I bring this back with me.' And we sat there, me on the arm of his chair, leafing through the thing, laughing at its absurdities, until I am sure we *both* believed that my dear old aunt really existed.

The something extraordinary was the deviousness, bubbling up unbidden from my self-conscious. I was in that garage, magazine in hand, before I had any conscious thought of it. That scared me. And it convinced me that I could not go on like this. It was such a clever, convincing thing to do. I was almost beside myself with wonder at my powers of deception. With skills like that I could go on inventing ways to keep the story going for a long, long time. The only problem was, with each new piece of cleverness I perpetrated, I sharpened yet another spike to be driven into Francis's heart when he finally found out the truth.

One day he would sit in a shrivelled heap, probably in this very room, probably alone, and go over each and every one of the lies I had told him. He would remember this moment and the ridiculous magazine – and the image of us sitting here, now, laughing together over it, would break him. And if not that deceit, then the next, or the next, or the next . . . 'Then burst his mighty heart,' says Mark Antony of Brutus's unkindest cut. The treacherous blade of the closest friend. What might he have said if the blade had been plunged into Caesar by Caesar's wife?

9

Fear of Lying

Well, you sit in a heap yourself for a few days. You get a call from Charlotte to babble on about the pleasures of the weekend, and you can barely raise your enthusiasm level back to the level of Marie and her tumbril. She thinks it's hormones again, and you let her. Someone has told her that yam is jolly good. You manage, just, not to tell her where to accommodate a yam in the nether reaches of her own person, and ring off and weep.

You have your grandchildren for the day, Claire and Rosie, whom you have always loved to look after, partly because you can spoil them with non-wholegrain crisps and *infra dig* E numbers, and partly because you can then give the polluted little dears back to their parents again afterwards – and there's old Marie in her tumbril again. Their chatter irks, you have forgotten to buy their treats, you barely smile at their antics.

You go to the theatre with your husband to see a longed-for *Twelfth Night* . . . Tickets that were booked months ago; gold-dust tickets – the critics have gone wild, there are six curtain calls but about the only lines you hear are poor old Olivia's 'I do I know not what; and fear to find / Mine eye too great a flatterer for my mind. / Fate, shew thy force: ourselves we do not owe; / What is decreed must be; and be this so.' Francis claps and claps at curtain down. He calls 'Bravo' – because it is, it appears, worthy of 'Bravo'. And you can hardly . . . etc., etc.

Because it is over. You have, very sensibly, ended it. He wants you to tell your husband; you cannot tell your husband. Not yet and not ever. Stalemate. He says many things, the essence of which being that he cannot live with that shar-

125

ing. And so, buoyed up by the unreality of saying goodbye, you say goodbye. About twelve hours after you very sensibly ended it you feel as if every nerve ending has been cut, every sinew stretched, every muscle gone, clawing its way towards the earth. Indeed, in the circumstances, by about twenty-four hours later, a rattling tumbril could be the height of giddy light relief.

You see the David drawing. A happy queen suddenly tied, defenceless, rattling towards her fate. You pray. Francis comes in on you when you are lying back, eyes closed, in the bath, chanting 'Let him ring', or some such. You just about manage to remember to lie, and through the steam you say it's a new pop song. Francis, at least, will never be able to check.

You feel like drowning yourself.

When you are not being forced to engage with life, you sit with your hands in your lap, by the telephone, waiting for the only call that makes you happy. All the while you both hate yourself and hug yourself. All the while you tell yourself that you are still in control, and all the while you know that you are not. One day this pain will cease, you tell yourself. You imagine the loved one finding solace in another woman's arms. Just like that. One minute he's sitting on his bed with you and you are both in tears as you agree that parting is for the best, and the next you have gone, at which he gets up, has a shower, walks out of his flat into Beeston Gardens, spots a pretty woman coming towards him, asks her out – and that's that. He's happy again. That, approximately, is the scene that you whirl around in your head. In the pursuance of this true agony, a great miracle occurs – you can't eat. A small proportion of you – the tiny amount of brain left functioning – whispers in your ear that losing weight is some compensation. The trouble is, you can drink. So the weight stays.

It was only Francis saying on about Wednesday evening, 'I'm sure I bought a fresh bottle of gin last week . . .' that brought me to my senses. Gin and tonic at half past nine in the morning is not a very good idea. You hate yourself even more when your husband expresses concern for you and you say that it is nothing, that you must still be grieving for your dead friend Carole. Francis is instantly solicitous and the possibility of suspicion dies. The ultimate heart of darkness in this love affair – that you will cheat and betray in any way necessary to sustain it, and that includes the heinous sin of dishonouring the dead.

And then your lover calls because he can't sustain the separation either. He gives you leave to put off any decisions and apologizes for bullying you. By which time you have written him a letter which he receives the following morning. You know this because you are there, in his bed, the following morning, when his post arrives. It is not over at all. It has intensified. It is worse. It has to end. It can't end. It has to have uncrowded thought and clear any-colour water. Forced separation, big space – big enough to house the unthinkable if that is what it comes down to. You agree to separate for a while to let some air into the situation. Your lover therefore goes away to stay with his sister near Bridlington in the unspoken hope that somehow a few days apart will solve everything. It solves nothing. Not for you and not for him. Oh, fuck. Being apart, even in this gentle way, only makes the bond stronger. You say to your husband – dreamily and without thinking – how much you would like to spend a long time in the country; you are thinking of Bridlington. Your husband – who is by now oyster-eyed with weariness at the intensity of your mood swings – tucks the thought away. Your husband, your poor husband, is not, quite obviously, sure *what* to think – but the statement goes in.

Your lover returns and you find ecstatic reunion. Suddenly you are a different person at home. Your husband's oyster-eyes eye you suspiciously. You, who did not wash your hair for days and who barely heated a pizza, are now transformed. You are as exquisite as a supermodel as you serve the slaved-over Sole Veronique to your husband, who was expecting bread and cheese or a takeaway, and you sing while you are doing it.

You love the world again. Energy runs through you like wildfire. You bathe in the light of being loved again. You want to love the world. You therefore suggest having the whole family round for Sunday lunch, including Petra's parents and her brother and his wife, and both sets of neighbours. Just to show God how good you are. Twelve adults, four children, and the neighbours' student lodger from Madras.

It is complete, stilted agony as everyone in your family, being white and middle class, falls over themselves not to say something remotely racist. You remember a conversation with your lover when he pointed out your quasi-liberalism. You try harder to drown out anything said by Petra's family, who are very definitely racist. Petra's father, William, refers to all non-whites as The Coloured People. The meal becomes the same kind of ordeal perpetuated by good debating societies everywhere. As soon as Petra's parents or her brother or his wife open their mouths to address the student from Madras, either you or Francis or *both* immediately talk across them. Perfectly roasted beef does not do much to soothe them for the constant barracking they are given when wanting to say something as innocent as 'Pass the salt.' At one point Petra's mother stands up and is immediately told to sit down again both by you and by her overwrought son-in-law. She is forced to announce, very loudly, to the whole table assembly that she is just going to the lavatory. You wonder if the wide-eyed student from Madras thinks this is a peculiarly English piece of etiquette. Francis glares at you.

William does manage a sentence which begins, 'Did you know that by the year 2030 there'll be more coloured people than us . . .' At which Francis sends you a look as if to say, 'Were you mad?' And then, just as you bring in the Desperate Dan-sized apple crumble, your youngest grandchild asks the student from Madras why he has different coloured skin, and everyone at the table does a kind of seated version of a Navajo war dance. Except, of course, the student from Madras. Hell on earth. You drink.

As was predicted by said husband, you are crippled by the effort of it all. And badly hungover. 'Never do that again,' says your husband very tersely. And you, equally tersely, tell him he's a brute to kick you while you are down. But he looks pretty down too. 'I don't know what's got into you,' he says, like a man in pain.

You spend the whole of the next day, Monday, in bed. Your own bed because your lover has a job interview. You have a sudden awareness that you are old.

Oh, no, you are not. You put on very loud Charlie Parker on the Tuesday and hurl yourself around the sitting room, so that Jess from next door is forced to join in without even leaving her house.

On Wednesday you spend all day with your lover.

With shining eyes, on Thursday, you sit your husband down and you tell him about your plans for a rockery. A *rockery*? Why? Because you have watched an afternoon gardening programme from your lover's bed and suddenly little alpines seem the dearest things on earth.

And on Friday you shop till you drop in pursuit of anything your manic little mind says you might need: eyelash curlers; electric lime-green matching sink set (with toning scourer); book of love poems; more lingerie that is definitely not underwear and definitely lingerie; several hitherto unconsidered CDs, including The Eagles' *Greatest Hits* – within half an hour of getting it home you know all the words to 'Desperado' and you can sing it with all the right inflexions. You demonstrate this so repeatedly that later your husband retreats to his study, slamming the door.

You look up the term 'amenorrhoea' on a women's health website and, as usual, decide you have everything it harbours – cancer, pregnancy, menopause, etc., etc. – and you are cast back down into the glooms. You will bear it bravely and tell no one. Since there is no one you can possibly tell, this is not hard. It occurs to you that if you do have a baby, it will have a niece two years older than itself. You put on the *Brief Encounter* video, and you weep alone.

On Saturday and Sunday things are looking brighter – you have stomach cramps, and you pray they mean you are not pregnant. Rationality tells you it's absurd anyway. But there is no rationality in this. Nothing happens. They simply mean that you have been so tensed up that your muscles have started to complain. 'If you think it's bad for you, you little bastards,' you find yourself telling them as you cook an indifferent Sunday lunch, 'try being me.'

Francis, misreading the sudden glooms and the way you clutch your abdomen, says, 'Period again?'

'No,' you say, and you burst into tears. You burn the gravy, which is, apparently, the culinary equivalent of Armageddon. You weep.

'Come on,' he says persuasively. 'Something's up.'

In that wild moment you tell Francis that you think you might be pregnant. He does the only thing possible. He boggles. Then he looks cautious. Is this a trap? If he says, 'Oh my God, no,' will you have hysterics? If he says, 'Oh my God, yes,' will you also have hysterics? You leave him boggling. But at least you have covered your tracks. And, of course, you want him to know this. Like a thief who returns to his vomit, you want him to know exactly when and *where* you covered them. So – just to make sure – you say, apparently totally irrationally, 'It would have been in Bath,' and he mishears and thinks you mean *in* the bloody bath, which would have been funny had it not been tragic. He laughs at the mistake; he says he always liked you in the bath. You tell him off roundly for being so deeply, deeply insensitive. Pregnant, Francis. This is no time for sexual flippancy. He manages to say something about crossing that bridge when we come to it. He's not at all convinced. Neither are you. But oh those little demons.

'Go to the doctor,' says Francis gently.

'Don't you dare ring Tim,' you say crossly.

Unsurprisingly, Francis, searching around in his mind for some way out of this crazy fandango, picks on something you said earlier and comes home on the following Monday evening to announce that he has rented a cottage in Dorset for four weeks. The whole of July. Somewhere, presumably, to put the mad wife. He says he has done it because he has taken literally something you said – which you vaguely remember saying an aeon ago – which was, 'Oh, I wish I could get away from here and bury myself in the English countryside for a really long spell of time . . .' That was, of course, the Bridlington moment.

It also crosses your mind that he wants to get you as far away from the garden as he can. You have talked about the rockery far too much – not because you really want one, but because each time you talk about it you are back in bed with your lover and preening yourself in the face of your husband with a secret he will never know. It is cruel and vile, but you cannot stop doing it. It is as if you want to tread into the danger zone of discovery. Francis does not know this. To him the idea of a rockery, with itsy-witsy little alpines that you speak of so lovingly, has almost certainly struck some kind of terror in his heart. Hitherto your garden is robust, and designed to be robust. It has a nice large bit of lawn, some easy-care shrubs, a daft pond which Francis and the boys built with great pride, and a York stone patio perfect for sitting out on. That is what the garden is designed for – to be sat out in. Not worked in. And certainly not rockeried . . .

Fandango did I call it? More like a swim around Charybdis.

To me, in my manic state, the Dorset idea was a miracle. At first I sulked and was horrified at the idea of being banished. And then I realized that it meant Matthew and I could spend the weeks together. Francis would come down for weekends, and that could be borne. If I spent Sunday night to Friday morning with my lover, I could be a happy wife for the rest of the time. It was the perfect solution. I could be calm, obliging, relaxed again. Never mind a grain of sand – all I saw was a perfect universe in the renting of Carey House, Woodlynch, for the month of July.

It also meant, so far as I was concerned, that I could put off the answer to the Big Question for a whole month longer. Matthew, on being told about Dorset, backed off, and it was tacitly agreed that any decision about future confessionals would be put on hold. In deference to the greater cause of our pleasure. It was beyond pleasure, actually, the contemplation. It was like waiting for 10,000 Christmasses to arrive all at once. I think Francis was completely thrown by the wildness of my joy.

'If I'd known how badly you wanted to get away, we could have done it much earlier,' he said with bemused irritation.

'I didn't know myself,' I said. And tried not to look like a cat contemplating its cream. But purring seemed to flood my body. We had sex that night, the first since our trip to Bath, and I was like some grateful courtesan whose suitor has brought her something in the region of the Koh-I-Noor. I don't think Francis knew what had hit him.

'Careful,' he said contentedly afterwards, 'or you really will be pregnant . . .' He paused to correct himself. It would have been comical in other circumstances. 'That's if you're not already,' he added cautiously. But I wasn't even going to think of that. Not one cloud would be permitted on the next month's horizon.

There was a bit of thinking on the hoof to be done when he started talking about that part of Dorset only being two and a half hours drive from London, but I was ahead of him. You are always ahead in the throes of deception – every cognisance is honed and poised. I rang the AA (I very nearly rang the drinkers' one by mistake, which was, of course, in our home address book. Now that *would* have been a funny conversation . . .) and they confirmed that it was nearer three hours because of slow-moving traffic, unless you drove after midnight. I was ready with this. When Francis said, as casually as possible and as I knew he would, that maybe he could commute some of the time, I pointed out the three hours minimum each way. When he said that perhaps he would go up on a Monday morning, I had to think quickly. And I did. I said that I thought I would use the time to begin writing again. He looked surprised. As well he might. I had not mentioned writing anything in the nature of a book for ten years.

'Well?' I said, a touch too aggressively. 'What's wrong with that?'

'Nothing,' he wisely said. 'Absolutely nothing.'

'I might even dig out Davina Bentham again.'

'Why not?' he said humouringly.

'Or start a new one.'

'Uh-huh.'

'So if you don't leave until Monday, then I won't be able to settle to it. But if you go on Sunday – you can go *late* on Sunday – I mean, six or seven at the very least –'

He looked surprised. The idea of late, and six or seven, was not, fair enough, really equable, but I was fondling his ear – whoring made easy – and he decided to accept it.

'– then I can wake up and get up and go on Monday morning . . .' At which he looked even more surprised – understandably, since mornings never were my strong point.

'I'll need a lot of energy. Especially if I do start a new one.'

'OK,' he said, 'I'll come down as soon as I can on Friday and go back on Sunday night. Happy?'

'Thank you.'

'What would the new one be about?'

'The nude,' I said promptly. 'Yes – I think I'll probably have a go at that . . .'

He nodded and began tracing my own naked lines. 'The nude', he said, preparing for action again, 'seems highly appropriate.'

All I could think was that Matthew could stay all week – all week, no leaving his warm bed and driving back home and telling lies, living lies. It is the lies you cannot bear. You are

133

not sure if you cannot bear them because they are bad things, or if you cannot bear them because you are afraid you will be found out. What you fear, like the wretched rockery business, is that part of you *wants* to be found out. One thing was certain. I did not want anything to spoil this month – certainly not Francis discovering the truth. I would have to be as nice and normal as I possibly could with him. So that I could be as wicked and abnormal as I possibly could without him.

To your lover you dismiss any possibility of difficulty ahead. 'Weeks and weeks of being together,' you say. 'So let's not spoil it with *truth* . . .' And you just about manage to stop yourself from adding, 'Why ask for the moon, when we have the stars . . .' in case he thinks you were old enough to see it first time around in the cinema and changes his lovely years-younger-than-you mind.

So begins the strangest thirty days of your entire life. You become two women for an entire month. At the end of it you wonder if you will ever feel sane and calm again.

10

Wife in Bath

It *was* like Christmas because I could not sleep for excitement
the night before. Francis was pathetically pleased to have got
something so right. How do we face ourselves when we do
these things? How?

We set off on Friday afternoon, and I have never felt happier. Matthew was coming down on Sunday night. All I had
to do was get through Friday evening, Saturday, Sunday
until – compromise – about eight, and then I would have my
life to myself for nearly five days. With such a blissful
prospect I could afford to be kind.

As we drove, I was singing. Francis was smiling. Out came
the demon again . . .

'Francis,' I simpered, 'this was so clever of you. You really
are the best of husbands.' I watched him smile a pleased smile
without the tiniest qualm of conscience. I was actually thanking my husband for having the consideration to rent a cottage
in which I was planning to enjoy a summer's idyll of sex and
love with my lover. And I was thanking him full-heartedly. I
waited. The earth did not open up in cracks of red hot fire and
swallow me. Instead the sun shone on the green hills and we
caught our breath when the first distant shimmering of the
sea appeared on the horizon. This is the way a marriage ends,
I thought, this is the way a marriage ends – not with a bang
but a simper.

We knew west Dorset fairly well because, when they were
first married, Virginia and Bruce lived just on the outskirts of
Dorchester. True Hardy Country. Francis and I visited them
quite often – the lure of the beauty of the place mixing, later,
with the pleasure of getting out of London and staying with

people who understood about babies. I'll say this for my sister: if you needed help, she was fine. And when I had John, and then James, and then much later the miscarriage, she really came into her own. At least we had moved on from my childhood, when she seemed to relish every opportunity to slap me down. It was only when I climbed back out of the pit and became more like myself again that she went all odd. I turned back to Carole at that point. She held my growing sons, had baked beans dripped all over her, and still managed to talk about art and make me laugh about her own world of lovers in Paris and night flights to New York.

Later, after Virginia and Bruce moved up to Kingston (or Surrey, as Virginia insisted on calling it), and when our boys were growing up, we continued to come down for weekends, staying in Bridport or Eype. It made up for all the holidays I never had, I suppose, and I became a demon with the bucket and spade. Just being with my happy family, on a beach, seemed so good, so easy, so normal, so very much the opposite of my own childhood, that I became a child with them, too. Abroad never really appealed when the boys were small – airports and flying and all that hanging around were just one long stress, and then very hot sun on their tender little skins. So we holidayed in England and loved Dorset best.

It was always a fantasy in those days that we would end up with one of the sandstone, rose-strewn Dorset cottages as our weekend retreat. We used to do those things called 'circular walks' – the only kind of walks to do when you have children, in my opinion, because you end up back at the car. At the end of three miles or so I used to get a warm flush of love as we rounded a bend and saw the old Saab just waiting there to scoop us up. Seems unbelievable now that such simple, silly things could be so pleasurable . . . Given the depths and heights I experienced nowadays, it was as if those times were a mere surface membrane on my life. One good pluck and it was all broken.

I told Virginia when she rang that Francis was taking a cottage in the country for a while, but I was deliberately vague about where and vague about time. Virginia, of course, was both sniffy about the decadence of it and keen to visit, a combination of responses which made her very prickly.

'Francis is overtired,' I told her. 'He needs to wind down. After all, he is knocking on – fifty-eight . . .'

Since Virginia had just seen off her fifty-sixth, this was hardly tactful in ordinary circumstances. In the circumstances of our difficult relationship, it was suicidal.

Her voice went up an octave. 'We're not all in our dribbling dotage just because we've hit mid-fifty, you know. Sometimes I think you live in cloud cuckoo land where other people's feelings are concerned, Dilly, and –'

Francis, who had just come into the room, and to whom I mouthed that I was talking to my sister – as if he needed telling when the decibels were crackling in the air – nearly laughed out loud – with nerves presumably – when, in place of my usual humbleness, I suddenly said, 'Oh, Virginia. Get a life . . .' and put down the phone.

'It'll do her good to stew,' I said crisply. 'Anyway, best to offend her or she'll be coming down to stay for a few days. And I don't want anyone to spoil this idyll.'

Francis looked at me so pleased, and I realized that he, of course, thought the idyll was with him.

Woodlynch was perfect for the fantasy cottage because it was close enough to walk into Bridport, yet it was far enough outside the town to feel part of the country. Now, as we drove along its familiar, winding lane, did I think of my children scampering along to see Champion the Wonderpig in Farmer Hope's pen? Did I remember how Farmer's Wife Hope gave us honey from her bees or how Daughter Hope, not much older than John, made sheep's eyes at him and, to our amusement, followed him everywhere? Did I remember our blackberrying days, our sloe harvests, our walks up and over the hill at the back where we would sit and have our breakfasts sometimes? No. All I thought of was lust and pleasure and illicit acts in this hidden bit of the world. And of showing Matthew how beautiful the area was, and how even more beautiful it was with us together in it. All that family stuff, all those precious memories, counted for nothing any more.

Francis was pleased as we pulled up outside Carey House. 'You haven't stopped smiling since Dorchester,' he said. 'I hope the place is all right.'

Well, of course it was. I ran up the stairs to see. It had a big main bedroom and a vast old pine bed. That, really, was all I saw, or needed to. I sat on the bed and bounced a couple of times, and Francis, coming up with the cases, said something about my being so eager and couldn't I wait until we'd at least had a cup of tea . . .

'You're like Mary,' he laughed, 'when she came back to England with Bill the Orange. A whole country and the throne of England to get excited about, and all she could do was go from room to room bouncing on the palace beds . . .' He put down the cases and came towards me.

'Tea?' I said quickly. 'While I unpack.'

I stayed upstairs, unpacking, trying to calm down, while Francis, equally excited, went from room to room throwing open the doors and the windows and calling me to come and be as pleased with everything as he was. The garden faced west and had apple trees and a swinging seat with a canopy – lovely. The sitting room had an inglenook and a set of French windows out on to an old brick patio. Terrific. The furniture was old and good. Not a hint of bad taste anywhere. Wonderful. I couldn't really give a damn. But the bathroom was big and blessed with a bath generous enough – as I made the mistake of saying idly to my husband – for two. He gave me a cheerful leer that sent me immediately scuttling downstairs for another cup of tea. No wonder we British were said to have won the war on it.

We agreed it was perfect. We hugged. We drank our tea standing at the back door, hip to hip, the picture of perfect unity. But when he asked me if I wanted to try the bath with

him, I said something mind-bogglingly crass, like, 'What –
now?' Instead we went for a walk in the pale late June evening
and watched the sun melt away to the west. And then I
skipped indoors and pulled out my mistress-stroke. I had
remembered to bring the Scrabble.

If Francis was less than thrilled at this, he forgave me,
played well and we ended up enjoying the evening. It crossed
my mind that he and I might become good friends one day . . .
Probably the cruellest thing you can suggest to a man or a
woman who has warmed your bed is, 'I don't want you sexu-
ally any more, but we make a *fantastic* bridge pair, darling . . .'
My sister was probably right – I did live in cloud cuckoo land.

When it was bedtime I genuinely managed to fall asleep
immediately while Francis was still in the bathroom. I hadn't
promised Matthew, because I couldn't, that I would avoid
conjugals, but I did intend to try my hardest to stay away
from having sex with my husband. A task that is a great deal
harder than one might think, given all those old music-hall
jokes about wives and their headaches. How did women
manage to go for months on end without fulfilling their marital duties? I had practically turned myself into mad Mrs
Edward Fairfax Rochester to avoid legitimate sex during the
past fortnight, and I knew that down here it was inevitable.
Just a question of putting it off for a long as I possibly could,
I decided. And I just might get away with it this first weekend, if I was really *clever* . . .

The following morning, Saturday, we were woken by
Julia's telephone call. She had done something silly with her
burglar alarm and hadn't been able to set off from Hove. By
the time Francis had dealt with it I was up, dressed, had made
the coffee and was heating the croissants. If he was disappointed he almost kept it to himself. There was just a very
slight frisson in the air, so slight it was easy to avoid. We had
already decided that we would go and potter round the stalls
in Bridport. And that activity could easily be stretched. Once
we were on the way there I suggested we had lunch at the

Bull. With a bit of luck he'd fall asleep in the afternoon after that.

The stalls consumed a good amount of time. We nodded a hello to Old Farmer Hope and his wife, who recognized us, and later to Daughter Hope and her husband, she now being a full-grown, fair-haired creature who had obviously enjoyed her bacon. They lived on the land that had once been Champion the Pig's, apparently. 'Ah well,' we both sighed when she had gone, 'time moves on.' I bought Francis an old leather box to keep his cufflinks in, because one of the embossed letters on the top was an F. That the other embossed letter was also an F rather than an H did not matter, I said. What I thought was, Nothing matters – nothing at all . . .

He wanted to buy me a little Victorian scent bottle, but I suddenly went very irritable and said I didn't need any more clutter in my life. The man on the stall raised his eyebrows and we walked on. The irritation was nothing to do with the scent bottle, which was very pretty; it was to do with my desperately wanting to buy Matthew a present and having my H for husband apparently glued to my every movement and, like some gaoler, watching every thought and sign and making it difficult. In the end I saw a pair of egg cups shaped like a hen and a cock and bought them. They were fun, but also said something about being a couple and breakfasting together and all that.

'You and me,' said Francis, laughing at their strangeness.

I just about stopped myself from grabbing them out of his hand.

'I'll carry those,' I said.

He gave me a quick, odd look. 'Better get some eggs.' He made for the dairy stall.

'I've already got some,' I lied.

We had lunch at the Bull, and I insisted Francis had another pint. When we got back to Carey House I hid the egg cups for the foolish sentimental reason that I wanted them to be new for Matthew and me. God help me, I thought, as I pushed them to the back of my underwear drawer, if I get run over by a bus and my executors find china fancies hidden in my knickers. And then the chill to the heart. My will? My future? Oh God, there was all *that* to think of . . . Well, I just wouldn't.

Later on Saturday afternoon I was lying on the settee reading a book, with the French windows open. Beyond these, stretched out on a rug on the grass and sound asleep, thanks to the extra pint, was Francis. I was reading an old Agatha Christie, plucked from the shelves, which was just about the only level of concentration I could achieve – anything more and my brain threw a fuse. Even before Matthew I had never worked out whodunnit in any of them. I read them when I was fourteen and re-read them, as if for the very first time, when the boys discovered her in their teens. Third reading and I still couldn't remember any of the plots, nor their *denouements*. Perfect. Floss for the mind. I soaked up the period flavour and the lovely, droning, innocent roll of their stories in which nothing and no one is ever what they appear to be. Clever old Agatha – all she had to do was to put the demons inside of us into a cheap paperback and modern dress, and everyone was a winner. Reading her made the afternoon go by quickly and stopped me thinking . . .

So I was quite absorbed and did not realize that Francis had been awake and standing at the doors watching me for some time. There was now no way out of this. It was a hot day. I was wearing not very much. I had the faintest mocking recollection of Matthew saying, 'You'd better wear a chador . . .' Now I wished I had. I went on reading, trying to pretend I hadn't noticed him, and then he spoke my name in a very unhusbandlike way.

'Oh, hi,' I said, looking up. But he was not about to concern himself with that level of communication. Even with all my wiles I knew this was it. I turned Matthew's face to the wall. 'He is your husband, he is your husband, he is your husband' was all I could remind myself as Francis came over and knelt down and pushed my dress up over my legs. Then, very carefully, very slowly and very gently, he pulled my legs apart and put his head between them.

What was I going to do? Run off screaming?

Afterwards, in the bath, I was soaping his back and thinking it was all right, this duality. I could cope. At least I knew Matthew wasn't going to come bursting through the bathroom door dressed as a yokel and carrying a corn dolly. He need never know the details. So I managed to hum and act like the good wife I was not, while Francis delighted in the size of the bath and I wondered why my pleasant but settled marriage seemed suddenly to have turned into something out of French Art House.

'That was the best it's been for a long time,' he said, reaching behind to stroke my thigh. 'I think I've rediscovered my teenage urges.' He laughed, pleased. And then added cautiously, 'You don't seem – er – pregnant.'

I kept the soaping as inexpressive as possible. 'Um,' I said.

'You know,' he went on, 'I think you were right. About getting away from everything and everyone for a while. I probably need it as much as you. We both need it. I'm glad, now, that you put your foot down about asking John and Petra and the girls.' He slid back and leaned on my knees, full of relaxed gratification. 'I think we deserve a bit of time to ourselves.' I rubbed away very gently and was pleased that the taps were so old and furred up that he couldn't see my reflection.

On the Sunday morning I tried very hard not to seem impatient. Fill your time, fill your time . . . So I suggested we went for a drink at the local pub before lunch. The Watton Arms has a garden very close to where Champion the Pig, or each successive one, used to live, but his sty had gone now and in its place was a big, brazen new house. Presumably Daughter Hope's. Obviously I couldn't get Francis dozy on beer again, not unless I gave him the perfect excuse not to drive back that night, so we had a pint each and wandered back. I was nearly crazy with impatience but managed to saunter as if I had all the time in the world.

'This is heaven,' he said.

'Yes,' I agreed meekly, making sure as we walked past his car that all the tyres were properly inflated.

Back in Carey House we had West Bay crabs for lunch and somehow, by the time we had eaten them, snoozed, washed up and then got Francis sorted out – and narrowly avoided yet another go in the bath, which he seemed to have taken a shine to – it was more or less time for him to leave. And I knew that my lover was already on the road, speeding towards me. Their two cars would pass at some point. At least, I sincerely hoped they would pass. The prospect of starring in the headline WIFE LOSES HUSBAND AND LOVER IN HEAD-ON COLLISION made me weak at the knees. I went even weaker at the knees when Francis, who had just arrived at the bottom of the stairs with his bag, at about a quarter past seven, suddenly dropped it down and said, 'You know, I really *don't* need to leave until Monday morning. If I go early enough . . .'

I froze. Adding to the reality of a chewed thumb, the reality of one's insides going to water. Yes, dears, they really do.

And then I breathed a sigh of relief. 'You can't. You're giving Julia a lift to the station tomorrow morning.'

He picked up his bag again.

'Fuck,' he said irritably.

'Anyway – you could get caught in traffic . . .'

'Not if I leave at five.'

'Or get a puncture . . .'

'Look on the bright side, why don't you?'

'I just wouldn't feel easy if I knew you were driving under pressure . . .' By now impatience was bursting out of me. I was thinking about Matthew so hard it was giving me goosebumps. How could he avoid picking up the vibrations? But he wasn't. Instead he smiled at what it was to be so loved.

'That's true,' he said.

He advanced another couple of steps. Go on, go on, go *on* . . . And then he put his bag down again. This time he put his hands behind my neck and, if I hoped it was going to be a quick goodbye kiss, I was very wrong. You somehow know that a kiss is not going to be a quick goodbye kiss when a hand moves down from your neck, over your breasts, and continues on to where you are already half ready because you've been anticipating your lover's arrival. Francis was far too impressed with what he found to be gainsaid. I kept thinking of the time. Just like deceit, whoredom came quite easily to me. I kept myself happy by imagining Matthew arriving and taking over from Francis, and Francis got the benefit. If it hadn't been cruel, it would have been funny. 'Now put your clothes back on,' I told him at the end of it, 'and no more dallying.' I just about got away with the schoolteacher mode on the vague grounds of S&M, I think.

I tried to sound light-hearted. Inside I was heavy with fear. If he stayed I would – I was sure – die.

As we were walking, or in my case staggering, to the car, he was whistling under his breath and had his arm around my waist.

'I could get to like this life,' he said.

'Safe home,' I said. And went back up the path. I was close to self-combusting.

Just as he was pulling away he said, 'Oh, yes – what shall I do if your aunt phones?'

'My aunt?'

'Auntie Liza?'

'Oh. Well. Tell her I'll write. Anyway, she knows my mobile.'

He nodded and blew a kiss. 'See you Friday,' he said.

There was that leer again. Jeezus H. We had stumbled on his perfect marriage. Me in a state of ever-readiness, in a country cottage with roses round the door and a bathing tub made for two, with, apparently, no other distractions apart from a little desultory dabbling in the writing of a book, and only visited by my Lord at weekends. Verily, all it needed was a chastity belt.

Still shaking from the mention of Auntie Liza and the

recent connubials and a general terror that he would suddenly decide to turn round, I watched the car's tail lights braking at the bends until he was really and truly out of sight. Even as I did so my mobile rang.

'I'm just on the other side of Dorchester,' Matthew said.

'You should have let me call you,' I said, distraught. 'That's what we agreed.'

'I know,' he said, 'but I can't wait.'

That's the other thing about instant whoredom. You can go from one to the other without missing a beat. It is supposed to be one of the ultimately sexy achievements, but, I can tell you, there is nothing remotely sexy about it when your blood pressure has reached the levels of a sixty-five-year-old very unfit businessman being made to run the four-minute mile immediately after a good lunch at the Ritz. And, as I discovered before, you are in danger of swapping names around rather arbitrarily.

When Matthew arrived, with an armful of booze and flowers, I was pink from the fourteen baths I seemed to have had during the day and totally unrelaxed. He must have wondered what he was in for the way I grabbed one of the bottles and took a corkscrew to it immediately, with barely a peck on the cheek for him. Surely there was something wrong with the picture of a woman struggling to get a bottle open, while the man she is supposed to long to see stands behind her trying to make sweet overtures into her neck?

When I had calmed down and we were sitting on the floor of the sitting room together, watching the waning light in the garden, and he was stroking bits of me, and I was stroking bits of him, and my poor jumbled body had begun to mend and want again, he suddenly said, 'And did you?'

'Of course not,' I said, looking up at the moon which had appeared in the dusky blue sky with the fading sun. The moon stared back at me blankly. Enough deceits have been perpetrated beneath her ancient lights to make her think twice before criticizing others.

Matthew breathed a sigh of relief. 'Thank you,' he said. 'It can't have been easy.' And then he was out of his jeans and off with his T-shirt, bare as a babe and gratifyingly ready, before I could dwell on the fact that I was not only lying to my husband now. I was also lying to the one I should be lying to my husband *about* . . . about my husband.

Yo, Tarzan. I had no energy left over for this conundrum. All I knew was that I felt incredibly happy suddenly. A state of mind which was not even dented when Francis rang a few hours later to say he had reached home safely. 'It took two hours fifty,' he said.

'There you are then.'

'And where are you?' he asked playfully.

'In bed,' I could reply. Telling the truth, at last.

11

Not Far Enough from the Madding Crowd

How could I have overlooked the one vital drawback to all this? Part of my brain must have been temporarily missing, because I did overlook it and it wasn't until Matthew was with me that the bit of brain returned – with a vengeance – and I realized. I'm sure it crossed Matthew's mind and he decided to let it be, though I never asked him. No – the fault was mine and mine alone. I had persuaded him and myself that it was all perfection, but of course there was a worm in paradise. Has anyone spotted the undeliberate mistake? It is that nowhere on earth are you able to maintain anonymity. My vision of the two of us walking into an uninhabited sunset was wholly unrealistic. I began to feel that even if we took ourselves off to the Gobi desert for a few days sooner or later some nice chap in a biplane would cruise by and say, 'Mrs Holmes, isn't it?'

After a day or so of staying in and playing all the little domestic games, which included breakfasting in bed on eggs served in the cock and the hen – and very nice too – Matthew and I ventured out. I wandered with him around the lanes of Woodlynch and up over the hill at the back with its ancient furrows and blackthorn, and then, feeling as if we had every right, we went sauntering into Bridport. This was Tuesday lunchtime and there were very few people about. The little museum was closed and we were just coming away from reading the notice about it, when Daughter Hope said in my ear, 'It's only open on Saturday and Thursday now. Can't afford the staff.'

She might have been saying this to me, but she was looking with interest at Matthew.

Matthew, being polite, was about to engage in further

conversation with her when I said a very firm 'Oh well, cheerio . . .' and shoved him in the back.

She said, 'You're doing a book down here then?' And stood her ground.

I nodded. 'Um,' I said, wondering how the rural tom-toms had discovered this, and began moving away.

'What about?'

'Pigs,' I said. God knows why.

'Oh,' she said. 'Well, you've come to the right place. You can ask my dad any time . . .'

'Thanks,' I said, and she moved off.

Matthew looked at me, perplexed. '*Pigs?*'

'Must be association,' I said. 'Her father bred them – in the village. We used to . . .'

He put his fingers over my mouth. 'Don't tell me about the past,' he said. 'Not now.'

So, being together in the heart of the country was not going to be as simple as it seemed. I found this depressing. The joke, that Matthew would have to hide in my bed all week, had worn thin by that afternoon. The weather was wonderful and we wanted to be out in it. Doing normal things together. A short while ago we would have settled for a whole night spent in each other's arms. Now we wanted to be out and about and playing at husband and wife – only there was the difficulty of having a real husband who was also somewhat keen to do likewise.

On Thursday morning Matthew actually had to duck down in the passenger seat as we drove out of Woodlynch and headed towards Dorchester because Daughter Hope always seemed to be doing something in her garden. Probably a rockery. She was, without doubt, a snoop. She was also a woman. And no fool. Matthew might not be the handsome Adonis of fantasy, but he was attractive enough for her to run the possibility through her head that our liaison was not innocent. And, of course, he was not much bothered if she did suspect. So I had to be the one on guard.

At least if we went further afield we would be safe. It was market day in Maiden Bassett. We would go there. We spent a delightful hour poring over things that we would never give a thought to back in London. It was just lovely being together. Finding out how each of us was in the outside world. And then, a voice close by.

'Fancy seeing you two again.' But it was Matthew she stared at with even more curiosity.

She came closer. 'What are you looking for?'

'Raymond needs something for his vintage car.'

Matthew kept his head firmly turned towards a pile of old junk. Suddenly he held up a piece of equipment. 'And, yes, here we are,' he said.

Both she and I stared. He was holding aloft a cobbler's last – circa 1935, as we were told by the cheery stallholder.

'Oh, not the Jaguar '38 model, then?' said Matthew, very convincingly.

The man shook his head, unfazed by idiot Grockles.

'Then alas,' said Matthew, and giving Daughter Hope a dazzling smile, he replaced it on the stall and moved on.

'See you,' I said, following.

I could feel her eyes on us for a very long time.

In the country, market day in any town within reasonable distance is a precious event. We might not be known, but we would be seen. And that was that.

'Dilys,' he said later, as we clambered up over Eggardon Hill, 'we'll just have to risk it. After all, he's going to have to know one day soon.'

'Um,' I said. A useful word, like the sound and the fury, signifying nothing. I had promised myself not to think about that, and I would not think about it. I might have had bits of brain missing, but I was no fool. After this month something devastating would happen. These were the last days of peace.

The best way to ensure that my husband and Daughter Hope did not meet on the village street and fall into a conversation along the lines of 'And how's that nice young man your wife had staying with her . . .' was to keep my Francis busy at the weekend. I could think of only one thing to do. I rang Petra that night and suggested that she and John bring the children down the following Saturday morning. Early.

'Don't tell Francis,' I said. 'Let's surprise him.'

She was pleased to be asked. They were keen to come down and couldn't quite understand our reticence. Usually we were only too happy to include them in whatever we were doing.

'Great,' she said. 'I'll bring some stuff from the shop.'

'Great,' I said. '*Great* . . .'

Then I crept back under the covers for my last night with Matthew before I swapped him for my husband. It was like a very rude version of one of those little weather houses you used to buy. When one pops out, the other pops back in. In more senses than one.

Francis did not arrive until nearly nine the following Friday evening. He brought nice things to eat and a couple of bottles of champagne and apologized for being snarky. 'You were right,' he said. 'They've started roadworks.' I, barely able to keep my eyes open, was warmly uncritical. He began telling me about his week, and what with the champagne and the exhaustion level, I fell soundly asleep while he was in the kitchen making coffee. I just remember him helping me up the stairs and the clothes coming off with a joint effort and then the sweet smell of fresh bedlinen (the illicit stuff thrown to the bottom of the spare-room cupboard) before consciousness fled. Next morning, when I said I was sorry for passing out, he said that he had been tired, too. And what had I been up to, to make me that way?

'Fresh country air,' I said. Feeling sure he could hear my heart.

'How's the – er . . .' He looked at my stomach.

'Same,' I said shortly. Subject closed.

He was standing by the open bedroom window, on his way to make us coffee, looking out over the beautiful morning.

'Don't move,' he said. 'I'll bring a tray.'

I lay there feeling slightly hungover and very miserable, with an ache in my lower belly that convinced me I'd probably got a prolapsed womb. Which would not surprise me given all the activity going on down there. In the past Francis and I had been sporadic lovers – sometimes two or three weeks went by without more than a night-time chaste kiss. But in these last few weeks he had found a new energy from somewhere. Perhaps it was primal instinct. Or perhaps it was my pheromones. But certainly this cottage had bred a new and determined energy in him. If it was a prolapse I'd have some serious lying to do when it came to consulting Dr Rowe. One thing to feel and act like a twenty-year-old, quite another to expect the tender bits to follow suit with impunity. Dr Rowe was no fool. Lies and more lies. And it might yet all founder on the shore of that blowsy blonde who lived where once a rustic pigsty dwelt.

Francis came back with the coffee and an amused expression on his face. There was a spray of scabious and honeysuckle on the tray, which was more moving than a whole array of sapphires. Not for the first time in all this I found myself close to tears. What could I be thinking of? But he was smiling as he put the tray down. 'I'm not surprised you passed out,' he said. 'There are six empty wine bottles down there . . .'

Oh God. Oh *God* – I'd been so careful with the rubbish, packing it up and taking it far away. But the good ecological housewife in me had automatically left the bottles out to take to the recycling bin. It was all too hard. I was worn out with it and I longed to give in – I longed to do what Matthew so clearly wanted and hold out bound hands to Francis and say, 'It's a fair cop, guv.' But I looked at his face as he stood looking out of the window, and at the familiar hand holding his cup, and I couldn't.

'They're not all mine,' I laughed. 'I collected the others. I've been doing a bit of drawing.' Smooth, smooth lies.

He sat down beside me on the bed. 'So, you've abandoned the nudes.'

'Not exactly. I'm drawing as well.'

'Well, you're a lot calmer for it,' he said, relieved. 'Can I see?'

'Not yet. Not ready to show anyone. What about breakfast?'

'I couldn't find the egg cups.'

Unsurprising, since they were washed up and back among the knickers. 'Just toast for me. I'll do it.' I began to get out of bed.

'You won't,' he said, insistent, and came to sit next to me. He put his hand on my arm. 'How's your week been. Missing me?'

And then, like the US Cavalry, there was a sudden and loud insistent tooting of a child's toy trumpet from the lane.

'If I'm not mistaken, that's number two granddaughter making her presence felt,' I said. Saved by the toot.

Francis looked at me.

'John and Petra,' I said.

He stood up immediately and went to the window. 'Yes,' he said, and he waved down at them like a puppet with the strings cut.

'I couldn't say no,' I lied.

He looked at me, amazed, cross, sad, and I looked at him a little apologetically. 'Oh, yes, you could,' he said.

But *fait accompli*.

When we did see Daughter Hope again she was with her hubby Geoff, and it scarcely mattered because we were surrounded by family.

'Can we just not talk to them?' I said to Francis as we sat there in the pub garden on Saturday evening. 'I have a hell of a job shaking them off during the week otherwise.'

Without a backward glance or nod to their greeting, I picked up Rosie and swung her on to the wall and talked to her about the daisies and the dandelions and all the other flowers growing in the field, while behind me I heard a polite exchange and the suggestion that we might like to look over their house. Francis, who would normally have said yes out of politeness, said that we really had to be getting the children back. Then Petra said, 'Oh, that's all right.' And Francis said, 'Dilys?' Which, roughly translated, meant 'Help.'

'We've got a lot of pictures of pigs,' she said.

To which my toads of grandchildren both gave whoops of interest.

'Thanks all the same,' I said, coming back to the bench and my family, 'but I really want to take them up to Golden Cap.'

'Maybe tomorrow.'

Francis, getting into gear, called to the girls to see who could run to the pub gate first. Then he turned and said a very firm goodbye and took my arm.

'Book going OK?' said Daughter Hope. Impossible to know if she meant anything.

'Fine,' I said.

'I told my dad about it. He's got a lot of old photos – unusual ones – you'd find interesting.'

'Thanks,' I said, 'I'll remember that.'

Behind me Francis muttered something, probably the equivalent of Dirty Old Sod. On the other side of the pub garden Old Farmer Hope was waving and smiling away, little knowing he was being branded a pervert.

'Photographs, indeed,' said Francis, who was probably glad to have something to show his suppressed ill-temper over.

'Let's go,' I muttered.

John said, 'What book, Mum?'

I said, 'Oh, nothing.'

Petra, who was into Women Take Your Place In The World as if her lot, and not my lot, had invented it, said, 'Oh, come on – don't put yourself down. What is it?'

'I'm just thinking about doing a book on the nude. That's all.'

There was another exchange of meaningful glances

153

between Petra and Francis. Roughly translated it said, 'Indulge her.' The mother-in-law, the Dilys – with whom something most certainly is *up*.

Francis was out of sorts all weekend. He was not a very concerned father when John wanted his advice on some campaign strategy the Organic Association was planning, and he was not a very happy grandfather either. Indeed, when everyone arrived, pouring out of the space wagon saying, 'Surprise, surprise,' the barely hidden scowl of that moment scarcely changed all weekend. He refused any of Petra's health-food chocolates, declined her bean casserole, and very pointedly poured himself a large scotch while the rest of us sipped our shop-label pear cider.

'I thought we were going to enjoy the space and time to be alone,' he hissed later in bed.

'Don't be so selfish,' I retorted, on my high horse as only a hypocrite can be. 'And remember how thin these walls are.'

It worked. With all of them there, children crammed into the spare room and Petra and John down in the sitting room, the opportunities for togetherness of the more physical kind were scarce. Since we could hear every breath and snort and little cough coming through the wall from the little ones, it did not need saying that the two of us bashing about on the bedsprings would waken the entire house. And no more baths together either. We resumed our marriage-of-long-standing roles and there were no more exploratory kisses. Instead we slept. Which was exactly what I needed. And then, after all my self-congratulation, disaster.

I thought Francis was just the tiniest bit insistent on Saturday evening about whether John and Petra had to get home on Sunday night, and when they said they did, he smiled. I soon knew why. While Petra and I got the children up and dressed on Sunday, and John was sorting out the kitchen, Francis made a phone call. After which he looked worryingly pleased with himself.

'Julia's staying an extra day,' he said. 'I'll go home on

Monday evening instead. I've got a bit of work with me that I can do here.'

Whoever invented briefcases needs shooting, was my first thought. My second was unrepeatable.

I tried to look pleased, but it was as if someone had turned a hose on me. And the nagging in my prolapsed womb grew worse. When I finally got away down the end of the garden to ring Matthew, I got his answerphone. His *answerphone*? This was Sunday morning. So where was he? Maybe he hadn't been home last night? Which meant that now, added to my bubble of fear at the prospect of him turning up on Sunday with a cheery whistle and a whipping off of his clothes as soon as he came through the door only to find Francis staring at his wherewithals, was jealousy. The terrible green-eyed monster that it truly is. I immediately harked back to our conversation in the Oxfordshire motel. Maybe my specialness had worn off? He still saw Jacqueline occasionally. You always choose the worst scenario. I saw myself deserted and pregnant, while he walked off into the sunset with someone new. I left a message.

'Where the hell are you? Francis is staying an extra night. Repeat. Francis is staying an extra night. Come on Tuesday. I'll try and speak to you tomorrow. I hope you're being good . . .'

It sounded so lame for what I felt. I could have killed Francis just at that moment. Really and truly killed him. He was in the bloody *way*.

Oh, I was desperate. Miserable. Where was my lover? Why was he not chained to his telephone? Why didn't he still have a mobile like everyone else? Lovers, particularly covert lovers, *need* mobile telephones. Indeed, half the mobile phones in existence are probably owned by miscreant lovers. It never occurred to me that Matthew might have a life separate from my own, that he might be able to function normally without me. After all, I had to have another life, but he didn't. I realized that I expected him to be always sitting in his flat, waiting for me to ring or arrive, and not have any other existence. As I stood there in the garden, the bells of the village church were ringing the honest to morning prayer.

When I came back indoors my face must have shown how fed up I was.

'What's up?' asked my husband, now sitting, beaming, in the bosom of his family. I looked from him to John to Petra, who all looked enquiringly back.

'I've got a headache,' I said.

A look passed between Petra and Francis.

Magnified, it read as, 'Hello, the old girl's off her nut again . . .'

'Come on,' said Petra, 'I'll massage your feet.'

'It's not in my bloody feet,' I snapped.

She blinked her enormous, wholesome eyes. 'I know,' she said softly, 'but the Chinese know about pressure points. It'll help. Each bit of the foot represents a part of the body, and you can tell from discomfort in the foot which bit of the body needs attention.'

'Go on,' said John. 'It works for me.'

'Tell you what,' I said, 'I'll go and have a bath and you can do it after that.'

And off I went. Irrationally furious with them all. Particularly my loving, caring, thoughtful *existent* husband. As I went up the stairs I thought – just for a moment – that I could understand those Agatha Christie heroines. I'd quite like to do a bit of bumping off myself.

When I undressed for the bath I laughed with sour relief. Well, well – no baby was on the way, that was for sure. And no nice little bit of matrimonial nooky for Francis later tonight, either. It cheered me up. That's how vile and twisted I had suddenly become. I went downstairs later, in my dressing gown, smiling all over.

'No need for the feet,' I said to Petra, and explained why.

Then I caught Francis's enquiring eye, and smiled and nodded and mouthed, 'My period's come.'

Which, from the look on his face, was the next best thing to administering a crack dose of Christie cyanide.

Petra, bless her, cooked the lamb for lunch, even though she was a vegetarian. The rest of us went for a walk along the beach. And I pulled myself together, marginally. I held Francis's hand and hoped Matthew wasn't dug into the cliff face with a pair of binoculars. In any case I was fully prepared for him to miss my message and arrive that evening and blow my world sky high. When we returned from the walk I went out and moved Francis's car off the hidden bit of the drive and on to the road. At least, if he did arrive, Matthew would see it and know. Francis was understandably agog at yet more peculiar behaviour until, brain rehoned by deceit, I said that the gardener needed the space first thing. He accepted this. Of course, I would have to think of something else when no gardener appeared. Unless Matthew did – in which case *he* could be him. Is it any wonder that Francis thought I was going nuts? He should have been inside my head. I was.

We all tucked into Petra's lunch, and after a glass or two of wine I was able to laugh with the rest of them about Dirty Old Farmer Hope and his old photographs of naughty nudes. And cuddle my granddaughters, which was some small fragment of comfort. If things followed their course, one day these simple pleasures would be gone from me.

Francis left at tea-time on Monday. Before he drove off he said, as if to a tiresome infant, 'Please don't ask anyone else down again. We're not getting any younger and we both deserve some rest time.'

'Sorry,' I said, meekly.

'By the way, I spoke to Virginia. She wants to come down.'

I nearly fainted. 'No!' I shouted, forgetting meek and finding furious. 'No, no, no –'

'All right,' he said, laughing. 'I told her we were both a bit strung out and that it was our little hideaway.'

'Good,' I said.

'It is, isn't it?'

I nodded.

'No visitors then?'

I had the distinct feeling I was being played with.

Out at the car we saw Daughter Hope and a sad-eyed beagle coming along the lane. 'See what I mean?' I said under my breath. 'Some hideaway.'

She stopped at our gate.

'Oh, you're going,' she said.

'As you see,' said Francis politely. 'I only manage to get down for weekends.'

'You on your own then?' She looked at me. 'Why don't you come up and have a drink with us one evening?'

'Yes,' said Francis, looking up at me innocently. 'Dilys, why don't you?'

There was definitely a touch of the *touché* about it.

'You know I can't, dear,' I said sweetly, 'I'm practising my yogic meditation all week. Just like Petra said.'

'Ah, yes,' he nodded gravely, and turned on the ignition.

'No need for a cobbler's last there then,' said Daughter Hope.

'Goodbye,' I said.

Francis looked from me to her, obviously thrown by the *non sequitur*.

'Goodbye,' I said, much more positively

She walked off.

'I saw her at the museum,' I said.

'Oh.' He looked relieved. All the same, just as he was about to pull away, he leaned out of the car window and said, 'That's another thing. Don't on any account let that old farmer anywhere *near* this place . . .'

Poor Farmer Hope. His name was besmirched for ever.

When Matthew arrived I forgot all about the gentle art of seduction and the waiting to ask questions until afterwards.

'Where were you?' I said.

'When?'

'On Sunday morning.'

He stopped and looked around as if thinking. My jealousy persuaded me this was a fabulous bit of acting.

'I went to see a movie.'

'What, at ten in the morning?'

'They're doing a Hitchcock season at the Arts Centre. Four a day.'

'Who with?'

He looked puzzled. 'All the usual suspects –'

'I mean, who were you out with?'

'A couple of mates.' Then he added with acid pointedness, 'Maybe you'd like to meet them one day?'

I burst into tears and sobbed and sobbed and got so hysterical that he suddenly became very worried – didn't know what to do with me. It was reaction, of course. Reaction to everything. And those sweet little hormones. But still, it frightened him.

'This has got to end,' he said.

I thought he had stopped loving me. I imagined that the Hitchcock movie was the first date with someone new. Out of sight, out of mind, that was me. I even got them in bed together, and it was no good my voicing all this out loud and asking him if it was so, because he could so easily lie. After all, I did. All the time.

Then he said, 'I love you.' And he repeated, 'This has got to end.'

'I love you,' I said, 'and I know it has.'

The time away had not worked. It was just all the clearer that there was no hiding place. Nowhere for us to be normal. Therefore it had to end. This madness, this strain, this all-round betrayal of so many people just could not go on.

'You fucked him this weekend, didn't you?'

Having had my moment of fear about him, I realized that he was in as much pain as me. 'No,' I could truthfully say.

To which he said, 'Oh, but you will.'

To which I said, 'If only you still had your mobile phone.'

To which he said, 'Not on the dole.'

To which I said, 'I'll buy you one,' as if that would settle everything.

'It won't solve anything,' he said.

In the morning we made a pact. We would keep the rest of this time as our Set Aside. No more difficult questions, no more ultimatums or sulks. No more jealousies. What we had, there and then, we would enjoy. We had three more weeks of it. And when I went back to London, I promised him, then it would be the moment.

Francis and I slipped into a reasonable weekend routine and, if he hadn't been such a nuisance in my life, I might have enjoyed the peace his presence brought. The friendship of thirty years goes deep, and the area itself held many memories. But it was all tainted by the fear of being discovered – and the desperation I felt by the time each Sunday night approached. His distaste at the idea of Farmer Hope's unusual collection of nude photographs kept him away from them – except in the most coolly civil way – so that danger receded. All the same, Matthew and I did very little walking about in the immediate locale and we never went up on the Lytchetts again, or held hands within a ten-mile radius. Fortunately, the weather was good enough to spend a lot of time on the various beaches round about, and this was something the locals tended not to do during the week. We went to Lyme, or east beyond Abbotsbury to the anonymity of Weymouth and Poole. And if we wanted to walk inland there was always Maiden Castle or the long cliff path.

In the evenings the garden was pretty private at the back, so long as we remembered to keep our voices low, and I kept the curtains drawn. Matthew parked his car a quarter of a mile up one of the lanes so that there was no immediate outward sign that he was there. I'm quite sure everyone knew, but nothing was said because I made absolutely no friendly overtures to anyone. This was the strangest change of all –

me, who would always stop and pass the time of day and smile at anyone, had suddenly, easy as winking, become hard and cold towards the world. I didn't need them. Simply that. With Matthew I felt perfectly complete and required no smiles or words from anybody else. It might have been safer that way, but it was also no hardship. I had him all to myself, undiluted, and that suited me perfectly.

Unfortunately, not only did Francis remark on the changing colour of my body as the weeks went by, he was also quite taken with it and liked it spreadeagled against the white of the bed. In the end I ungrudgingly obliged. I was weary with using any more mental energy than I had to for something that now meant so little. Where possible I lied to Matthew; where I couldn't I made the excuse of circumstances beyond my control.

'You promised', I said to him, 'that you would let us have this time without any ultimatums . . .' Which – if not ungrudgingly – he at least accepted.

Francis was also amused by the deepening suntan, which to his mind was the sign of my much needed return to relaxation and – presumably – the return of his good wife. He laughed and said that, judging by the colour, I had not, after all, set myself seriously to any task. Oh, yes I have, I thought cruelly.

If I had ever entertained the vague idea that these few weeks would lessen my love for Matthew – which I think I probably did – it misfired, because it deepened. I told him so on the last weekend. I had never been happier in my life than for those four weeks, nor had I felt so supremely alive, nor so young. Bad news as well as good news. For us both. Yet I couldn't tell you what we talked about, how we filled the hours, what we did and thought while we were never out of each other's company. It just worked. Whatever the chemistry or the mystery of love may be, we had found it.

'What about you?' I asked. 'Have you gone off me?' But I asked from a position of certainty. I knew he hadn't. And that meant that the bomb was still live and still going to detonate when this last weekend was over. When I was with Matthew I had all the courage in the world. If that was the way of it, then that was the way it would be. We even took a walk up behind Carey House that final evening, and looked down on the village and waved in the direction of the Hope homestead, though she wasn't in her garden. It wouldn't have mattered if she was. She could shout it from the rooftops if she wanted to. It didn't matter any more.

On our last morning I gave him the silly egg cups.

He laughed as he packed them. 'Souvenirs,' he said.

'Symbols,' I corrected. 'Keep them safe.'

Since I'd bought them I'd held on to the idea that even if Francis could have me, touch me, he could never have or touch those silly bits of china, and while he never had them, he did not, really, have me.

Matthew shook his head at this explanation. 'The feminine brain,' he said. 'The only way he won't have you, baby, is if you leave.'

As Vonnegut would have it, So It Goes . . .

12

One of Our Aged Aunts Is Missing

I watched the line of the suntan fade from my body like a talisman. When it has gone completely, I told myself, I will be happy again. Or, if not happy, content again. Or if not happy and content, then at least at peace. Things will have changed, answers will have come.

It was now the beginning of August and so far nothing had happened. The lines at the top of my thighs and round my breasts were still quite clear. The skin stood out sharp white in the exact shape of my bikini. I kept my body covered as much as possible from Francis. Partly, I think, it was because Dorset had felt unreal – a dreamscape – that sex with him had scarcely mattered; back in London was the true reality, and I had begun to loathe his touch. It was as if he was saying, 'This is my property: I must get my scent on it again, quick.' It was as if I had no say in what I wanted. Surely, I thought, he can see how I feel? Surely, surely he can read my mind and know that I have begun to hate him?

According to Francis, our month in the country had achieved A Great Leap Forward in our marriage. This seemed to boil down to my behaviour as an exemplary wife in the matter of bathing with him occasionally, making love with him occasionally, and once doing it in a field of corn. According to him, this last reminded him of when we were first married, which was even more Brownie Points. But I couldn't remember. And I could not have cared less. It was easy. That's what respectable and businesslike prostitutes say. It's easy. You just get on with it. I could smile into his eyes and he never guessed that all the time I was somewhere else. It was as irrelevant to me as our games of Scrabble and pints at the pub.

But Francis was entirely pleased. He spoke of the so-called idyll to strangers at dinner parties; no doubt he told his secretary and people he met every day. He was deliberately and uncharacteristically chauvinistic about it, so that I could play the game of squealing objection. 'If you want to recharge the batteries, rent a country cottage for a month and plonk your wife down there. It certainly worked for us . . .'

And he would lean over and squeeze my arm or my knee and leave them in no doubt as to what he was talking about. It disgusted me.

Home became too much of a mockery, and the familiar now jarred. There was too much need for me to be a mother, a grandmother, a mother-in-law, when all I wanted to do in the world was be that near-teenaged chit of a girl that love had suddenly made of me. Pleading a change of scene – at which Francis looked distinctly surprised since I'd only been back in London a few weeks – I went down to stay with Julia for a few days. She, at least, was not going to wish to conduct conversations with me while holding one or other of my tits in her hand. Or both. I felt knocked out by my body. All of it ached from a terrible unhappiness, and all of it felt watched and not private any more. I had been opened up. Now I wanted to shut down. And Francis wouldn't let me. It wasn't that he forced the issue. It was what he didn't do, the muteness of his wishes and the muteness of my refusal. No doubt many marriages totter along or even thrive like this, but *noticing* it was new, and with my added burden of guilt, I could only feel ten times worse. The phrase 'Happy retirement' buzzed around my brain; Francis was looking forward to Happy Retirement, while I suddenly felt as if I had only just been born. Going away was the best option. Julia and bloody Hove would be a good reminder that there are worse fates than having a loving husband who wants to love you and whom you cannot love back. And a lover who wants to love you and whom you cannot imagine ever not loving.

Julia, like everyone else, commented on how young I

looked. How well I looked again. She – sisterly loyalty – put it all down to Francis's cleverness. Not clever enough, I thought, as I lay fucking my lover in the hidden sands near Hove beach. No one was clever enough to outwit me now. 'I'm just going for a long walk to watch the sunset, Julia.' And there was Matthew, waiting by the stumps of old wooden breakers, half hidden in their shadows. Only a short drive from London, after all, Hove. The few days became a week. Francis was impatient for me to come home. Julia was happy for me to stay. But Matthew said something oddly domesticated one evening as we were having a post-coital beer in a not very nice inland pub.

He said, 'The car tax is up next week.'

'Yes?' I said.

'It needs an MOT.'

It wasn't like him to talk cars, but anything to humour my lover. 'How old is it then?'

'Thirteen years.'

'Time to update?'

He gave me a look that said, approximately, What am I going to do with you . . . 'I'll have to get rid of it.'

'What?' I asked.

'I mean, the MOT will show up a lot of things that need doing . . . It'll be expensive.'

'Try our garage – it might be cheaper . . .' I was still in a dream. 'You can't get rid of it. How will we meet?'

He looked at me and shook his head very slightly. 'The dole doesn't exactly include running a car,' he said. 'I think it's probably job time. And just as I'm getting into the midday serial too.'

It didn't take a crystal ball to know that soon there would be no more time to procrastinate. 'I understand,' I said.

Francis threatened, and only half playfully, to come down and get me.

My grandchildren sent little cards saying, in bright crayonned colours, 'Where are you, Granny?'

And I agreed to return to London.

Matthew had now got rid of the car, and for our last beach meeting he arrived, rather gallantly I thought, by train. Since my family were coming down for the following day, I couldn't take him back. I drove him to the station at some impossibly early hour to catch the last connection back to London. A warm, starry night. The station silent, almost ghostly, just one lone adolescent kicking his heels on a bench at the far end, innocuous on his own. Of course, there was no station buffet, nothing like it, but I got that old *Brief Encounter* feeling again. And when the train came in and Matthew got on and the doors slid shut, it all seemed so final, as if he really was going to some far-flung bit of Empire, never to be seen again. As the train pulled out he looked completely astonished at the tears in my eyes and gave little helpless gestures all the way out of sight. I called him and left a message on his answerphone just to say not to worry. It was just that I loved him so much.

When I came back to London a couple of days later I went straight out and bought him a mobile phone. He took it gingerly, but I pushed it firmly into his hand. 'For me,' I said. 'I need you to have one.'

'You may need me to have one a little more than you know,' he said, a touch too grimly.

He had been offered another job.

'When?'

'Beginning of November.'

'Where?'

'Sheffield.'

'*Sheffield?* Will you go?'

'Will you?'

'I thought you were going to kick up your heels,' I said, miserably.

'It'll be nine months since I left Sheldon. Time to get real again.'

And I did understand. Matthew wasn't going to give me *empty* ultimatums – he was going to give me brimful ones.

We were down by the river at Kew. Dangerous ground on a summer's day, so near to home. But I was getting tired of saying, 'Better not . . .' to him, as if he were a naughty child. Anyway, it was August, and the river gave off a slight and welcome breeze – unlike the stagnant fumes of Paddington Green. Here was our contemporary Seurat scene. People were trundling pushchairs, sucking on ice-creams, boats and skiffs rippled past and Japanese cameras clicked all around us. It was just very ordinary. Normality. I craved it.

Around this time I read about a young Jewish girl sent to live on a remote farm in Germany during the war and given a completely new history and persona. She was told that she had to live and breathe this new Aryan identity and forget her other past – she must even dream in Aryan. She managed it for a long time, even the dreams, but one day she got on her bicycle and rode away, as far as she could go, to where not a living soul could be seen in the fields all around, and there she yelled her own name for all her worth, over and over again, before returning to the lie . . . I remembered this acutely as the ordinariness of everybody else went on around us. To be trapped inside a deceit – even a non-life-threatening deceit – is a cruel oppression. In my case it was mine and mine alone no matter how much Matthew thought he was sharing it with me. Judging from what he said next, he had no idea. As if asking me to leave London for Sheffield was not bad enough, he then went on to ice – so to speak – the cake of impossibilities.

Despite the river and the slight breeze, the air was heavy and warm and damp in that particular August way, and it was even heavier now with portent. *Will you come?* indeed. He didn't wait for an answer; he just stopped walking, turned to me, and said, 'Also, before I begin the job, there's something else I want to do – I want *us* to do. Now that I can afford to plunder the savings.'

Savings? What were savings? It sounded so sweet. Like a little boy with a piggy bank.

He looked embarrassed for a moment. 'Can you plunder yours and come with me?'

'Where?'

'You know where. To India.'

Oh my God. I kept my face absolutely still.

'You've never seen the real place – you know how much I want to go back. And I'd like to go there with you. September is a good time to go and we can get cheap flights if we go out through Amsterdam.' He laughed. 'Don't look so stricken,' he said, swinging my hand. 'You're a long time dead.'

The excited part of me was enraptured. Of course I wanted to go. Of course I *would* go. Back to the exoticism of India and this time with *him*. And the unexcited part of me thought, Well, thanks *him* – thanks again – for giving me something so easy to arrange with my husband and family. I could just see myself making the announcement – perhaps one Sunday as we all strolled through Cannizaro Park. 'Well, everyone – wife and mother I may be, but I'm just pissing off to India – on my own – for a couple of weeks . . . Oh, no – not with anyone you know. OK? And, Francis – I'm withdrawing a big chunk of money from the joint account, I don't want you to come, and the pizza's in the freezer . . .'

Instead of saying all this, and speaking as one going for the gold medal in loving not wisely but too well, I just said I'd need a little while to think it through – to hatch a plan. How clever you are, I thought, looking at his smiling face. He could have said, 'Leave him or else,' he could have said, 'If you really loved me . . .' but instead he offered me real pleasures – jewels not paste, irresistible possibilities. This was the future, and I must not shun it this time. Matthew smiled again and looked completely happy. 'What I love about you', he said to the sky and the trees and the world at large, 'is that you are so open to everything. I say, "Shall We?" And she says, "Yes." And then she worries about the difficulties afterwards.'

168

I just about managed to smile – but really I was hand-bound, footbound and back in that tumbril. If he thought that turning the whole of the last thirty and more years on their head was 'difficulties afterwards', I really was in this alone. Well, 'yes,' I had said. And 'yes' did I mean.

Matthew was already talking about travel clinics and the Indian High Commission and Mumbai versus Delhi as if the whole thing was signed and sealed. We were about to run away together – that's what we were about to do. Jeezus, I wondered, what on earth would my sons say? And could you still be emotionally damaged in your twenties if your mother elopes?

However, Fate is a fickle floosie. Even as he addressed me with all this 'Hello, birds, hello, sky' stuff, so death lent a hand. Aunt Cora died. Francis took the call. I came in dazed from the Indian bombshell, only to find he'd come home early.

'You didn't check your phone for messages,' he said. And then told me that my distraught cousin had rung and why.

It was good to be held by him – too much in my life was ephemeral and just at that moment he felt solid and real. It was good, for a change, to want him close since I spent so much of the time nowadays just wishing him away.

'I could do with a gin,' I said. He assumed it was because of the death, rather than because of me trying to juggle notions of funerals, visas, did our black suits need to go to the cleaners, malaria tablets, hepatitis B jabs, *et al.*, and he was kind and solicitous. Which, of course, made me feel much worse.

I did feel sad about Cora, but in the first throes of a love affair you are never seriously touched by anything but that love affair, so I was a little off my guard when I spoke to cousin Lucy. I said all the right things and agreed that a heart could just go at any time and no one was to blame – after all she'd had a good innings, etc., etc. – and it was good that she had been enjoying herself when it happened. She was paddling in the sea at Hunstanton, which was a lovely picture, and then she keeled over and died. 'It's the way you might choose to go, given the chance,' I said, safe in saying so since I had never felt so full of life.

'I suppose so,' said Lucy.

Half my mind was on India and Matthew as we chatted on. There was to be an autopsy, because there was no particular history of a heart condition, which meant that the funeral would be delayed. Then came the mega-bombshell that blew Delhi, Agra, Mumbai *and* the dry-cleaners out of the water completely.

'Oh,' she said, 'and we want Aunt Eliza to come to the funeral. At least she knew Mum – even if they didn't always get on. They were sisters-in-law after all. It's only right . . .'

'Yes,' I said, forgetful in my otherness. 'Do you know where she is?'

There was a slight pause and I felt a shadow pass over the sun.

'No,' said Lucy, 'but I know you do. Francis told me. Go ahead – I've got a pen . . .'

I remember two things. One was that the very air in the sitting room seemed to have been dispatched, leaving a vacuum of silence. And two was Francis's face, looking at me from the settee on the other side of the room, whisky in one hand, papers in the other. What was I supposed to do? Say to Lucy it was all some gigantic practical joke? That Auntie Liza didn't exist at all. Or at least, that she could very well exist, probably did, but that I had no idea where. Perhaps she'd popped her clogs too? But the serpentine lady of lies was to hand.

'Look,' I said, 'she's quite frail and a bit funny about seeing people, so maybe it would be best if you give me the details and I can pass them on and then she can –'

Lucy cut in, and there was that unmistakable touch of offended Virginia about her. 'Are you saying that she won't speak to me?'

'She won't even see Francis. You know how old people can go a bit funny.'

'Francis says she's in Paddington somewhere. That's odd.'

Lucy lived in Bexley Heath, so I suppose Paddington was strangely exotic.

'Ah,' I said, 'she's moving.'

'When?'

I could see Francis put down his papers and sip his drink, listening intently.

'Now,' I said forlornly. 'And she didn't give me the new address. She's very *odd*, Luce.'

'You don't have to tell me – honestly, in the last year Mum did some strange things –' And then her voice went again.

'Sorry,' she said, through the tears.

'Look, don't worry about Auntie Liza. I'll get the new address for you. You concentrate on yourself. It's been a shock.'

She snuffled, but righted herself. 'Well, we won't be able to bury her for a little while. And Frank's going up to town, so if we don't hear from you he can call at Eliza's old address and see if we can trace her that way.'

Resisting the urge to scream at my cousin's apparent metamorphosis from one bowed down with filial grief to one closely resembling Miss Marple, I said that I would see what I could do. It was no trouble. The very least service I could render at this moment of loss. And got off the phone. Francis was still looking interested. I held out my glass. 'I'll have another,' I said.

Mr Merrick's office was entirely fitting for a sleuth. It was at the top of a building at the wrong end of Chelsea, with grimy windows, two desks, both covered in papers, a door that announced the business belonged to Mr and Mrs A. C. Merrick, the latter one of whom there was no sign, and it was full of cigarette smoke. That said, Mr A. C. Merrick was no Chandleresque Robert Mitchum but a man with thin grey hair, brown-rimmed spectacles, a chunky multi-coloured sweater of the variety sold by stallholders at the lower class of market, and stained teeth. He assumed that I wanted to find my old aunt because she might have left me something in her will. Indignation, the indignation of one who is so steeped in guilt that anything offends, rose in me and fell again as Matthew touched my arm. All the way to the Merrick Empire he had reminded me that this man had seen every single aspect of human nature and that sensitivity was not his forte. Results were.

We sat opposite Mr A. C. Merrick while he scribbled down his notes. Beyond him, through the grubby window, was the skyline of Chelsea and St Olaf's spire and assorted familiar buildings, none of which were any comfort to me. I had about a week to track Auntie Liza down – or rather this most unprepossessing man in front of me had – and despite Matthew saying that Merrick was good at his job, had found many a lost child or wayward parent, I very much doubted it. Nor did it help that Matthew found the whole escapade over Auntie Liza incredibly funny, and suggested that, if all else failed, he would dress up for the part. 'I've seen *Charley's Aunt*,' he said. 'A *pince-nez* and a hat with a feather and I'll be fine.'

And a very small part of me, possibly the part called fatalism, thought it just might come to that.

He could afford to be flippant if he thought of my future turmoil as 'difficulties', even more so since he was in no doubt that later, if not sooner, I would tell Francis everything. The immediate situation was just a passing escapade and he was much more concerned with the beautiful vision of the trip to India. I just seemed to spend more and more of my life putting things off.

And as if that was not enough, Francis suddenly said, apropos of the funeral, 'Well, after that's over, maybe we could think about a holiday together? A couple of weeks in the Dordogne would be nice.'

Was that before or after I popped off to Rajasthan, dear?

I had absolutely no faith in our sleuth finding my aunt,

which only goes to show I shall never be so mealy-mouthed about appearances again. Within three days Mr Merrick had found her. And, thank God, she was not living on the moon, but in a private block of wardened flats in Lichfield. I had no idea what I was going to say to her when I got there. Like the family of Darius, I thought, I shall throw myself on her mercy. Anyway, she might be ga-ga. I didn't like to admit – even to myself – that I hoped so.

Francis took a keen interest, and I did my best to seem quite nonchalant about the whole thing.

'I'll probably stay the night,' I said, always mindful of finding a way to spend a whole night with Mattew. 'I'll call you.'

'Shame I can't come,' said Francis. 'I've never seen Lichfield Cathedral. It's got those eighth-century gospels.'

'Well, next time maybe,' I said. I felt the tears brim – frustration, of course, but misread by Francis. He gave me a searching look and then came over and put his arm round me as if to say he was sorry and had forgotten that it was more than just a visit. He squeezed my arm to show his solidarity. The only trouble was that I had visited the travel clinic the day before and it was aching from the jab. I shrieked with pain and jumped about a metre . . .

'Dilys, for goodness sake – what *is* the matter with you?'

'Bee sting,' I said.

That Serpentine Lady of Lies must, I thought, be feeling really tired.

And Francis's credulity was also somewhat stretched. 'Bee sting,' he muttered, and went off to have a bath. Alone.

13

The Hunting of the Aunt

I left Matthew in the town. He was quite content to wander around and have a look at the place and then book a table at our hotel for eight. To give us time for a little preprandial hanky-panky. I said I didn't know whether I would feel like hanky-panky after my ordeal, and he said that of course I would, because I always did.

'Anyway, it's the last time we'll stay in a place as grand as this for a long, long time,' he said. 'So let's make the most of it.'

We kissed and parted, and I told him to light a candle in the cathedral for me.

Auntie Liza's apartment building was privately owned and certainly not council, as my aunt insisted on my knowing before even giving me a kiss of greeting. It clung on to the edge of town by its fingertips, surrounded by dismal shops and dreary dwellings and well away from the grand cathedral, its sound of bells and the mellow attractions of its close. I was disappointed. I had imagined her settled in some little Georgian redbrick cottage in the precincts, and not nestled up to the very last bit of Lichfield's main road. But the grounds were well tended and there was a pretty bit of garden all around with laurels and hydrangea bushes and evenly mowed lawns. Neat and soulless.

Inside the small apartment the air was of that undisturbed variety, the slightly fusty but not unpleasant atmosphere of a place not often left or visited. It had about it the scent of eucalyptus and a smell that I remembered from childhood and the rare occasions when I was allowed into my grandmother's room. It was a combination of rose and lavender water and the vague undersmell of old lady.

Auntie Liza had two rooms, small and square, with a kitch-enette and a bathroom. She was on the second floor with a narrow, useless balcony that barely held a few pots of care-fully tended plants. It looked out over the back. Something that she bemoaned as soon as I arrived. 'They always put me at the back, dear,' she said. 'All my life. Always. Sit down.' She put her face close to mine and peered.

'Well, well,' she said. 'You look younger than your years. I used to look young for my age too . . .' And she added wist-fully, 'So they said.'

The place was as clean as any old person with failing eye-sight might achieve, and cluttered with photographs, bric-a-brac, cheap mementoes from grandchildren's holidays – little straw donkeys, miniature Greek houses, painted wooden boxes, a big and very desirable bronze of Horus, one or two nice pieces of glass and china, and far too many small tables. There was a green and brown checked moquette settee and a matching armchair, both with fawn linen antimacassars probably bought from the Co-op forty years ago. The suite had seen better days, as had the nets at the window – as had everything really. It had the same look about it that I remem-bered from the other houses of my aunts and uncles as they grew old. Everything bordering on the kitsch and all the white things yellowing faintly with age. It made me realize how far I had moved away from my roots. I liked the Horus, though. It was oddly out of place.

Auntie Liza sat upright in the armchair, still showing a good pair of legs and with her fairish, greyish hair obviously recently set. She was small and delicate rather than wizened or shrivelled, and her face was like powdered, pink, plumped-out dough. She had aged well. Only her distant look said that she was dim of sight. When I helped her make coffee, she ran her fingers around each cup rim and judged everything perfectly. 'Only Nescafé, I'm afraid,' she said, putting on posh vowels as she always used to do, 'but I can't do more nowadays.' It was unappetisingly weak. She used to

175

refer to it, I remembered, as 'Coffee with a dash'. When it was offered to my mother, she used to say, 'You mean dash out for another spoonful.' My aunt's tea was famous for being known in the family as gnat's pee.

Once the tray was carried back into the room and set down very carefully, she eased herself back into the armchair and said, 'Now, if you sit there –' she directed me towards the settee with a finger that still twinkled with its engagement and wedding rings – 'it takes full daylight and then I can see you better.' She cocked her head on one side and stared. 'Well, you've grown into a good-looking woman,' she said. 'Nice clothes. What do you do nowadays, dear?'

'Write about art occasionally. Organize exhibitions.'

'Well, that does sound interesting.'

'It is.'

'And are you married?'

'Yes, to a lawyer.'

She leaned back in her chair. 'That's what I should have done,' she said. 'My father would have liked that. But he lost all the family money in the Crash, you know. And I met Arthur.'

'Yes,' I said.

'I had all the skills, you know. I was the one who knew how to make up the commissions. He was the business side.'

'Yes,' I said. 'I remember there were always lovely flower arrangements in your house.'

She leaned towards me, touched my face and looked very sad.

'I'm eighty-five,' she said, 'and I had a man friend until last year. He was seventy-six, dear, and he thought I was the same.' She gave a wicked little smile. 'Anyway, he suddenly went off and married someone else.' A tear trickled down her cheek. 'Fickle lot.'

'I'm sorry,' I said.

'Well, I suppose it's paying me out. You always do get paid out in the end, you know.'

This was said with a deliberate hint of tantalization as she fixed me with her damp eyes, but I was determined to stay on track.

'Auntie Liza,' I said, 'I'm afraid Cora died a few days ago. I've come to ask you if you would like to go to the funeral. Lucy, her daughter –'

'Yes, yes,' she almost snapped. 'I know who Lucy is. Never liked her. No class. Married a greengrocer. So Cora's gone. She was a tartar.' And then, as if to change the subject, she reached for my gift and flowers, clucking and saying that I shouldn't have. But pleased.

'You have come a long way, dear,' she said, fumbling with the wrappings. For a moment I thought she was going to go on, dig a bit of the dirt, but she didn't. Maybe time had taught her a little humility.

She shed a tear at the silk scarf and put it round her shoulders. Then she cooed over the flowers, feeling them with her fingers. 'Very nice Enchantments,' she said. 'And proper Madonnas. Lovely.' I put them, as instructed, in her sink. 'I'll do them later,' she called. 'Come and sit down and talk.'

She made her commands sound like exaggerated elocution exercises. Her voice was so affected it was hard not to laugh. I went and sat down again. I couldn't just plunge in so I asked about her daughter, my snooty cousin.

'Oh, Alison comes when she can,' said Auntie Liza, 'but she lives in Kidderminster now. It's a long way. How much older are you than her, dear?'

'Two or three years,' I said.

She nodded. 'Ally was born in the same year as the Queen was crowned.' Then her hazy eyes held a touch of light. She smiled, as if remembering something, and said, 'It's funny. You were the last thing your mother needed, and I'd waited for years. Ally was a long time coming . . .'

'And how *is* Alison?'

It was hard to sound enthusiastic. I never liked the girl. She was always showing off with her educational toys and piano lessons and pointing out how poor we were. She seemed to think it meant we had no brains as well. Also, she bragged because she had a father, extant, who was so important and respectable.

'He's a misery guts,' I once shouted at her.

'Better than being a drunk,' she shouted back.

'My mother says he acts like he's got piles *permanently* nowadays . . .'

'What's piles?'

Since neither of us knew, we gave up on the insults.

But of all the dads of my acquaintance, Uncle Arthur was the father I least envied. If he had any humour at all, it was sardonic, and his entire conversation with me seemed to comprise 'Be good to your mother.' He doted on Alison, a situation I watched less with envy than with fascination. What was it like to have someone smile like that as soon as you came into a room? Alison never seemed to notice. Often she was rude or cruel to both her parents. But still they lit up for her. It was fascinating to observe. I also thought it was a bit thick that I, who had never been anything but well-behaved towards my mother, should be told how to behave by Uncle Arthur when his own daughter was so horrible.

'I expect', I added mischievously, 'that she has done *very* well for herself.'

A simpering but sly smile stole over my aunt's face and she plucked at her skirt hem. 'Oh, yes. She's very well. She's divorced from that rich young Egyptian royal she married – of course, he adored her but the *cultural* thing was hard for her. She has two lovely children, both grown-up now.' She paused before adding, 'Girl and a boy. They both look very English . . .' she added quickly.

'And are they married? Have you got great-grandchildren?' These politenesses seemed endless.

I waited for the gushing eulogy but none came. Instead her face crumpled, the smile fading, and she looked quite forlorn. 'My granddaughter – she's nineteen now – has a baby on the way. She's not married. All planned and everything, so she said.'

We sat in silence digesting this for a moment. Then my aunt said, in her ordinary voice, 'Marriage doesn't seem to matter to girls nowadays, does it?'

'I think some of them see it as unnecessary in this day and age,' I said carefully. Given what I was about to ask her to do for me, I could hardly side with the connubial angels.

'Yes. Alison's divorce was not very nice. She's taken up with a dead-end chap and moved in with him now. It seems to be the way. Arthur and I were married for over fifty years. Thick and thin. I'm glad your grandmother isn't here to see it. Grandmother Smart, that is. Of course my mother would have been very nice about it. She never really wanted me to leave home. How long have you been married to your lawyer, dear?'

'Over thirty years,' I said.

She slapped her knees, palms opened. 'Really? Your mother would be pleased. You've got all the fortune she never had. Bless Nellie. She was always good to me. Rotten luck with men, she had, rotten.'

She stared at the wall for a moment, as if seeing her. 'Ah, but she had spirit once. Do you know that she was the first one of the whole ten of them to open her own paypacket? She bought herself a pair of silk stockings. Your grandmother never quite forgave her.' My aunt laughed with astonishing vulgarity. 'And Nell and I were the same about that. I kept my first pay rise a secret. I worked in a Very High Class Bookshop and I liked nice things like Nellie, too. Oh, she was a fancy dresser and a half in those days. As was I.' Her eyes were wet again but she took no notice. 'Oh, your *dear* mother. I must say she looked her old self at your wedding, dear. Men were her downfall – plain and simple. Too gullible by half she was. Honest as the day was long.' She paused and then smiled at me. 'Except when it really counted.' Then she fid-dled with the scarf, looked at me again and added, 'She didn't deserve it, you know. When you came along all hell broke loose.'

I felt a sudden surge of sadness for my mother, who was once a fancy dresser and aspired to higher things.

'She was pleased with the way Virginia and I got on in life,' I said. 'And she really enjoyed her grandchildren. They made up for a lot. And she liked the fact that I had a bit of money.'

'Have you, dear?'

'Oh, yes,' I said, suddenly wanting to heal the hurts of my childhood. 'My husband is very successful. We have wealth.'

'Well, that's good,' she said. 'And *quite* unexpected.'

I sipped my coffee and she sipped hers, and the clock ticked and I wondered how I was going to get from this reserved politeness to asking her to lie about my sex life.

'Do you get out much?' I asked

'Well, I did – with my gentleman friend – twice a week. But not now. Wind's gone out of me.'

Here was a possibility. 'I expect you still feel hurt.'

'Stupid at my age.'

'Happens at any age.'

She looked at me for a moment, as if she had recognized the new seriousness of tone, but if she did, she wasn't going to pursue it.

'Oh, you can't beat family as you get older, dear,' she said. 'Don't know where I would have been without my darling Ally.'

She struggled up, her knees cracking. 'Damn things,' she said. 'Used to be my best feature, my legs . . .' She fished about on the table beside her for a photo frame and handed it to me. 'Such a long time she was coming.'

I looked at the picture. There was my cousin, about five years old, standing next to her father. He was wearing foot-baller's kit and behind them was the team – boys of about eleven or twelve. Even at five my cousin had coarse features – a big bump of a nose and eyes too close together. Nothing like the dark, even good looks of her father, or the fair prettiness of her mother. Only the blonde curls were the same. I once heard an aunt call her an ugly little thing and say to my mother, 'Not like your girls, Nell. Pretty as peaches.'

To which my mother replied, 'Fat lot of good that did me.'

But I held on to the idea of being like a peach, all the same.

I handed the photograph back to her and she picked up another. This time it showed her and my Uncle Arthur – considerably younger – sitting on a settee together, he with his arm over her shoulders. Behind them was a Christmas tree.

'I was always a bit shy and a little afraid of him,' I said.

'He liked his football,' my aunt said proudly. 'He was always out with the boys right up until the end. Well, until the cancer got him. He was in the Rotary, too.'

She put the photograph back on the table with a sigh. 'Now,' she said, 'tell me about Cora. Of course I will go to her funeral, but she never liked me, you know. Had her mother's tongue about her. Most of them did where I was concerned. They didn't like the fact that I was from a different class.' She leaned across and touched my knee. 'So was your father, dear. Officer class. He and I got along very well. We understood each other, you know. Oh, yes – you're like him. You've got a bit of class about you, too. I expect your children went to private school? I did, you know.'

She seemed to have forgotten all about Cora. So I told her about my two boys, because she asked, and I told her where I lived. 'We ended up in Finchley,' she said. 'Very Jewish.'

'I remember. It was a long way on the tube.'

'He did his coaching and his Scouts up near Golders Green. You know we went to Ralph Reader's funeral? He was *very* involved with them. Scouts.'

She reached across as if she couldn't help herself and pinched at the hem of my skirt.

'What's that, dear?' she asked.

'Jaeger, I think.'

'Who'd have thought it?' she said, somewhat acidly. Which was much more like the Auntie Liza I remembered.

I nodded. 'I have been very lucky.' There was something of the Marie Antoinette about it again.

'But you are not happy?' she said, sharply. Not surprising, given my expression I suppose.

Which was the moment.

'Auntie Liza,' I said, 'I want to ask you to do something for me.'

'What's that, dear?'

How could I do it? To this respectable old lady who had been over fifty years married and lived, I was sure, despite the carping and gossip of her in-laws, as an exemplary wife.

'If you are going to go to Cora's funeral and you meet my husband Francis, I want you to tell a lie for me.'

Her eyes snapped, brightened for a moment by intrigue.

'Lie?' she said. 'To your husband?' She was more savouring than puzzled – as if she were running the words over her tongue to get the taste of it. I waited, unable to think of what to say next, expecting any minute that she would ask me to leave.

The August air was warm and heavy but all the windows were closed, except the little half window in the bathroom which I had pushed open as far as it would go. I was glad of it now, needing air to circulate. She was guileless in her belief that I had come to see her out of family kindness. Instead I had announced a death and was about to embark on a tale of deceit such as she could not possibly condone nor identify with. Perhaps I should just stop there. My lame excuse was that I did not want to upset the funeral, but Francis had to be told sometime. Blood *was* thicker than water. My sons would forgive me. If not immediately, they would one day. And I couldn't go on living like this for ever. I loved Matthew so much. Already, and despite everything, I was thinking about the hotel and being with him. So it was simple, wasn't it? But unfair to mess up the funeral. Straight after then. Meanwhile, as planned, Auntie Liza must be told.

'What do you want me to say?' she said, very perkily in the circumstances.

I faltered. 'I've changed my mind,' I said. 'I can't possibly ask you.'

'I can tell it's important,' she said.

'Not important enough.'

'You've done well for yourself. I admire that. I wouldn't want you to lose it. Not if I can help.' She was still looking at me enquiringly.

If I could just get through the funeral, I thought. If I could just have some time to think.

'Is it – something to do with your marriage, dear?'

I nodded.

'Well, well. Lies,' she added, shaking her head.

'You really don't have to –'

But she looked quite pleased about something. You could almost say perky. She leaned over and patted my knee, and then she got up from her chair and felt her way across the room. She pulled open the bottom drawer of a very pretty walnut bureau – which I remembered from their house in Finchley – and felt around in the back of it. She took out a brown paper bag, old, scrumpled, with a rubber band around it. The rubber band broke as she tried to remove it, rotten with age.

'Here,' she said, and handed it to me. 'Talking of lies. And marriages.'

I opened it. Inside, rolled up and fixed with yet another rubber band, was an equally crumpled magazine of black-and-white photographs. I smoothed it out on my knee and turned a page. There were two young men, their fair hair cropped in the style of the thirties, one staring out at the camera with a silly grin on his face. Each had his boyish arm around the other's waist, in comradely style. The sun glinted on their perfect golden heads. Behind them was a field of corn and they were leaning back against a white gate, their ruck-sacks carelessly lying by their stoutly shod feet. Apart from their hiking boots and the rough-knit socks neatly turned down and folded over the boot tops, they were both stark staring naked. And the young man who was not engaging the camera with a silly grin was staring just as foolishly at his companion's genitals – which he had obviously been stroking for some time.

'Lies, dear?' she said, as sweetly as if she were showing me her wedding album. 'How about a little bit of truth first?' She went to another cabinet and brought out a bottle of sherry. 'Fetch the glasses, they're in the kitchen,' she said.

I did so.

When I came back, the magazine was nowhere to be seen. I wondered if I had imagined it.

She felt the rims of the glasses and then poured out the sherry. Quite expertly she refixed the top firmly into the bottle with her shaky old hands and then sipped, eyeing me as she did so.

'Lies, dear?' she repeated. 'Oh, your old auntie knows all about them.' She sipped again, put down her glass very carefully, and leaned back in her chair. 'But first, a little story for you. Just between ourselves.'

14

The Importance of Being Dishonest

When Eliza Battle was twelve, her father put a substantial nest egg he had been saving into an assortment of stocks as recommended by his bank. The bank also funded his butchery business, and while he was at it he borrowed a little more and bought another slaughterhouse, in Pinner. Pinner was an expanding area of genteel domestic housing and so while he was at *that* he borrowed on a mortgage to buy a new house there for himself. The Euston Road was no longer a suitable place to live, but they kept the small ground-floor flat and sublet it – just in case.

'Going up in the world,' he said to Mrs Battle, and he patted his daughter's fair, curly head. 'You'll be fit to marry a duke one day,' he joked. Eliza thought it was entirely possible and practised good deportment.

Careful saving and cautious expenditure, combined with a generous wartime income, meat production being a necessary occupation for both the population and the troops, meant that Mr and Mrs Battle had done very well out of those years. Mr Battle now wore a bowler hat and a suit to work. He had five men working for him, the new slaughterhouse looked to be turning a good profit and their daughter was about to reap the rewards. Eliza entered a select little seminary where she was to learn French and piano and the gentler arts. She was not required to walk there every morning to save a penny but to go, with the draper's daughter Molly from a few doors down, all the way by bus.

For the winter term she wore ruffled velvet dresses with white lace collars, covering them with pintucked holland aprons in the classroom. In the summer she wore starched white cotton with lacy yokes. She requested, and was given, a little fur tippet for her winter coat and the very latest in dove-grey flannel for her jacket in spring. She was, as both her parents thought watching her swing off down the road with her arm tucked into her friend Molly's, the bees-knees. And Mr Battle thought how far he had come from the boy who bicycled up and down the streets of Barnsbury and Islington delivering dripping lumps of meat to the back doors of tradespeople's houses.

Eliza was not a brilliant scholar but she developed an astonishing ability for flower arranging and a love of the Latin names, as well as the vulgar names, of as many flowers as anyone could hope to know. In short, by the time she was beginning to develop and wear her fair, curly hair like Marlene Dietrich, she was obviously destined to make a good marriage. Though by no means beautiful, she was pretty in a pink and pale blue way, and she turned delicate ankles beneath her shapely calves. For her fifteenth birthday she wore a mid-calf dress of sky blue crêpe de Chine cut on the bias so that it rippled at the hem when she walked. She was entirely happy with the result.

And then – disaster. In the wake of the Crash of '29 and the ensuing slump, loans were pulled in, bank and mortgage interest soared, the price of everything, including Mr Battle's meat, plummeted, and – a few weeks after Eliza's fifteenth birthday – the house in Pinner had to go. At a loss. Naturally, the seminary closed its doors and suddenly a requirement to find a job became paramount.

Mr Battle kicked out his tenant from Euston Road, and the family moved back there. Eliza found this particularly hard. Her room in the Euston Road looked out over the lightless well at the back. But her nose-wrinkling and her complaints made with rounded vowels cut no ice. When her clothes became too tight – for she developed a decent chest on her – Mrs Battle told her to let out a seam or put in a panel.

'But it will show,' she cried.

'Then wear a cardigan,' said her mother firmly, from

behind a cloud of pheasant feathers. In these straitened times the wearing of a cardigan seemed of little consequence. They were clinging on by their bootstraps, as Mr Battle put it very mournfully over his glass of stout, taken once more in the The Leathern Bottle. 'Bootstraps, matey,' he said to Old Collins, the bookseller, 'and only just at that.'

Mr Battle was back to delivering meat on a domestic scale, and Mrs Battle was back to sitting in her kitchen plucking fowls for the tables of those she had once sought to join. But the business could not sustain Eliza.

'You'll have to support yourself,' said her mother, 'if you're going to stay on here. Molly's got a job with the debt collectors. You could do that.' Eliza was horrified.

Mr Battle asked round about. 'I've got a position she can have,' said Old Collins. 'My eyes are going and you need a good pair for the buying and selling of books.' Books, apparently, still did a reasonable trade, and now you could pick and choose out of the flood of second-hand books from the houses of the boom and busters.

It seemed inconceivable that she would not do something requiring gloves, but the impossible triumphed. Eliza took up a position as bookseller's assistant in the Clerkenwell Road. The ladylike ways instilled in her at the seminary regarding trade and propriety had vanished from her life. She was just like the rest of the young girls in the surrounding shops and offices – her French, her piano and her flowers meant nothing. She served dog-eared books to students and leatherbound books to bespectacled old men, she served threepenny dreadfuls to women with furtive looks about them, and adventure yarns to whistling lads.

Old Collins served the really important customers. In the back of his shop he kept his two most expensive lines: rare antiquarian books and exotica. He alone dealt with the customers for these, and the office door was always closed when they were doing business. The men who came for the exotica stared at the floor as they flitted past her counter and out into the day. She wondered what exotica was, but Old Collins said that it was nothing for her to worry about.

One or two of the young men who came in regularly for adventure yarns were inclined to be kind and pass the time of day with her, and some said she was pretty and others asked her what she was doing on the Saturday night. But she just kept her nose up in the air, served them with civility and no more. She still felt she was destined for better things.

She did accept one assignation. Molly sent a young man from the debt-collection agency into the shop, Harold Binns, and he asked her to join him and Molly and Molly's beau on a spree to the funfair at Battersea. She went. But when he walked her home to her door in the dark and tried to kiss her and a bit more besides – his eyes seemed to change colour, he pulled a very peculiar face and began panting into her neck – she was turned right off. He had slightly grubby nails and his shirt cuffs were not completely clean. Such things betokened a low-class person and she refused to see him again.

Those men who came into the shop with their quality clothing, their soft well-formed voices and their gloves seldom noticed her in any meaningful way. Yet, when her mother mentioned to Eliza the possibilities of the future and marriage, it was those men she envisaged standing next to at the altar. Even shopgirls had standards. She had seen it in the pictures.

When she was eighteen and her wages went up by a few shillings a week she kept it back for herself. She spent it on lace handkerchiefs and gee-gaws and flowers for her gloomy room. One gardenia or a few sprays of freesia to dainty the air with their scent. Sometimes she was given a bit of extra greenery free – eucalyptus, fern, laurel – by the young man who had recently opened a florist's three doors down. His name, she saw from the shop front, was Arthur Smart. He occasionally came and browsed in the bookshop, and once in a while he bought a book – usually on outdoor pursuits or true adventure, scouting techniques or campfire songs. He and Eliza barely spoke, for each was as shy as the other.

Among his large family he was the youngest of the boys, with a mother who brooked no nonsense. Arthur Smart was known within the family to be sensitive and a little secretive, and he did not tell Mrs Smart that he had even a passing acquaintance with Eliza Battle. Mrs Smart also had a passing acquaintance with the Battles: Eliza Battle, whom she called a silly girl who was no better than she ought to be; Mrs Battle was a silly and much put upon woman; Mr Battle was a coarse fool and a bit too big for his boots. Thus the family was dismissed from the proud, industrious air of working-class improvement that fuelled the Smart household.

Arthur Smart managed to buy his flower business in such a decent part of town because of an accident. While on a job for his old employers, delivering flowers to a hotel in Bloomsbury the previous summer, he was toppled off his bike by an omnibus that mysteriously found itself being driven on the wrong side of the road down Southampton Row. It just so happened that one of Arthur's older sisters, Cora, was walking out with a young police officer, and he it was who observed the whole thing, Bloomsbury being his beat. The incident might have been hushed up, the bus company's expertise being more than a match for the average little accident, but Arthur's older sister was a very desirable young lady, and a very indignant one. The young police officer therefore stuck to his guns. On immediate investigation, as he later told the enquiry, he observed the driver to fall out of his cab and to smell strongly of drink. For the shock, the broken arm and the broken finger – the latter being particularly difficult for floral art – Arthur received enough in compensation, when he recovered, to enable him to open the shutters on his new enterprise: Arthur Smart High Class Florist.

He had never been much of a socialiser – particularly with young women, most of whom seemed to take a shine to him. His sisters all teased him for being such a good-looking boy. His brothers despaired of all those charms going to waste. Apart from the Scouts and rambling when the weather was good, for recreation Arthur read his books, supported Arsenal, and attended a woodwork class. 'You'll never meet a girl there, Artie,' said his big brother Dickie. But he paid no heed. He managed the customers tolerably well, but his mother said that he would manage a great deal better with a wife. Arthur just blushed. He asked advice from his favourite sister, Nell, who worked in a baby-linen shop and knew the foibles of customers. 'What you really need', she said, 'isn't a wife, it's an assistant.' Then she laughed. 'Or better still, both!'

Arthur was seen as something of a catch. For over a year he worked so hard at the business, doing everything alone, that he had no time to be embarrassed or harried by his mother and his sisters' constant harping on the subject of marriage. After all, he was only young, there was plenty of time. He was up at four each morning and over at Covent Garden in his little red van by four-thirty. He bought what he needed and stopped off for breakfast, sitting alone in the crowded market café, his nose in the newspaper. Sometimes he stared with longing at the porters, easy in their chatter and jokes and jostling, but he kept himself to himself. When they whistled and joshed him, he looked away.

He employed a lad he met at the Scouts to do the hard graft and the deliveries, but he was too pert and cheeky. Arthur found the insolent stare across the shop while he was making up a particularly difficult spray or bouquet disconcerting. One day he told the lad to go. The lad cocked his thumb at his cap brim and asked for a week in lieu, which he got. Arthur did not want any bad feeling at the Scouts. Another one came, a bit younger – only fourteen – but he was no more respectful and was inclined to lean up against the counter and stare. He tried a girl, but she was vague and what his mother called dozy. He tried another, but she was too bright, too pushy and wore a heavy scent that crowded out the smell of the flowers. Everything she touched, as Arthur told his mother, turned into a dog's breakfast.

'What you want is a wife,' she repeated.

'Maybe,' he said, and this time he did not blush.

And then one day – when he was trying to twist fifty car-
nation stems into button holes and clear the decks to make
the bridal spray – a man ran in and said he must have a corsage for his wife – right away. He had forgotten his wedding
anniversary and she was waiting in the Corner House for
him. And while gesticulating he knocked the box of carnations to the ground. Arthur did not know whether to cry or to
hit him. But he did neither. Because the girl from the bookshop a few doors down had been waiting patiently, and now
she was kneeling and gathering everything up very carefully.

'It's my lunch hour,' she said, in her posh voice. 'Let me
help.'

She knelt among the flowers in a faded blue dress that rippled out around her, and he thought she looked lovely, pure,
like a painting. Gratitude welled up in his heart.

'You were always very kind to me,' she said, very properly.
'This is by way of a thank you.'

Gradually, over the next few months, she started helping
him regularly in her lunch hour. She knew a lot about the
artistic side of the business with flowers and could tot up the
prices in a jiffy, too. Once, when their hands touched, they
both pulled away blushing. The lads at Scouts accused him of
getting spoony, and when they went away to camp there was
a lot of teasing and horseplay. Arthur joined in the song
around the fire more heartily than ever before, just to show he
did not care how much they teased and gloated.

His mother did not like Eliza Battle.

'She's worming her way in,' she said, when he finally told
her about the girl and how helpful she had been over the
months, and how he would like to ask her home for tea.
Arthur's mother liked to be in control, and anyway, she had
her eye on Maudie Harper for him. Maudie was good company and lively, and her father had a quality boot and shoe
business and made a good living. And, as she said to Cora,
'Boots and shoes is *not* butchery . . .' That was what Arthur

needed, a bit of liveliness. Maudie came to tea instead. But whenever Mrs Smart got them together Arthur went all silent and twisted the tablecloth or talked endlessly about the business.

'I hear you're doing woodwork, Arthur,' Maudie said, showing her dimples to best advantage.

'No,' he said lugubriously, 'I've given it up.'

If Maudie was game, she was impatient. She wanted a husband with prospects, but she was getting bored. When they went for a walk and she stopped by a low-hanging branch and peered around it as picturesquely as possible at him and prepared for a kiss, he ducked away and strode off, pointing out the poppies which he said no other flower quite matched for the intensity of redness.

'Oh, don't they,' said Maudie to herself, and ran to catch him up. 'Let's sit in the corn for a while,' she said. But when she took his hand and put it on her shoulder, quite near her breast, it remained there, inert. She let her skirt creep up well over her knee, but that, too, went unexplored. She decided that he was a gentleman, that was all.

Then she came into the shop one lunch time and found him working alongside a slight, fair girl in an unfashionable frock. 'Leave her to it, Arthur,' she said imperiously, 'and let's have a spot of dinner.'

'Will you come?' asked Arthur of the fair girl. Who blushed. Which Maudie found irritating.

'I've already had my lunch,' said the fair girl. 'I'll go on with these for a bit longer. Then I must get back to the shop.'

Maudie mimicked her, there at the counter. Took the rounded vowels and the peg-on-her-nose pronunciation and made a joke of it.

Arthur did not laugh. The fair girl looked upset. Arthur said to Maudie, 'I think you should apologize.'

Maudie, game for a lark, said, 'Make me.'

At which Arthur said he was no longer hungry and Maudie, hissing and spitting, went.

She went straight to see Mrs Smart, who shrugged.

'What can you do?'

'It's my belief that little thing's got her hooks into him,' said Maudie with relish. 'Daft beggar.'

Mrs Smart bridled. 'Leastways, apparently you haven't,' she said.

Maudie was soon engaged to somebody else.

Eliza helped him with the flowers for Maudie's wedding, and he joked that he'd had a near miss. Eliza blushed and giggled. Since she had done so much for this particular wedding, he took her to the dance in the evening. Mrs Smart sat with them. Eliza said her family had come down in the world since the Boom and Bust. Mrs Smart asked very pointedly if she was related to Battle the Butcher, and Eliza said she was, and fell silent. Mrs Smart felt that she had made her point

'She's a butcher's daughter,' she said to Arthur.

'She knows floristry,' he said, obstinately.

And he dug in his heels.

Mrs Smart said he should watch That Little Bookshop Girl because she was no better than she ought to be. He said it was his business. Nell felt sorry for Eliza. She was a bit of a rebel herself and seeing a fellow called Fred, of whom her mother, also, was a little critical. She felt they were both being got at and struck up a unity with Arthur.

'Take Eliza out,' she said. 'Properly.'

'Like what?' he asked nervously.

'Somewhere you can talk a bit – get to know each other – show her you like her . . .' Nell nudged him. 'You do like her, don't you, Arthur?'

Arthur swallowed his fear and thought long and hard. He wanted to do what Nell suggested but he was nervous about being alone with Eliza. In the end he said, 'Come out for a bit of supper with me tonight. My treat. My brother's got a banjo band up at Hampstead, and it's cracking good.'

So she did. It sounded common, but her parents both said, 'Common is as common does,' and he sounded a very decent chap. Eliza was aware that she was becoming something of a burden and it nagged away at her.

He turned up to collect her in a neat suit, clean shirt, discreetly Windsor-knotted tie, proper hat and with a spray each of lily of the valley for herself and her mother, the latter of whom took hers very graciously and thought to herself, He'll do. Arthur's brother Dickie surpassed himself that night – glad to see his younger brother out with a decent girl – and Eliza, though still not quite sure it wasn't too vulgar by half, smiled and clapped and danced and enjoyed it all nonetheless. She looked very pink and pretty while she did so and – well – the rest was history. Arthur brought Eliza home and left her chastely at the door with no more than a fleeting kiss on the cheek. She was so relieved that he didn't try anything on that she decided he might be the one. She said to her mother that he was the first chap she had really enjoyed being with. And Mrs Battle repeated, 'He'll do.'

Arthur was also relieved that *she* didn't try anything on either, or expect him to. The feel of her cheek had been soft and pleasant and, unlike Maudie, she smelled of lemons – fresh and nice. With Nell's support, he stood up to his mother. Mrs Smart said that Nell wasn't worth the candle in matters of judgement, which made Nell cry – and then Arthur was even more determined.

They were married. Eliza upset the Smarts no end by insisting that her dress was made by a woman Up West, not Arthur's sister. And she only had Molly as matron of honour and Nell as a bridesmaid. There was some dispute about this, too, because Molly was six months gone by the time the wedding took place and the Smarts thought it vulgar. But Eliza had read in one of her bride magazines that if your lady-in-waiting was in the family way, it was good luck in that department for you, too. She was sure it was true. She wanted children more than anything.

'No good will come of it,' said Mrs Smart. But it all went off well enough. The wedding breakfast was Mrs Battle's moment of supreme glory. She had plucked enough chickens and ducks to make patties and cold cuts for an army. Mrs Smart sniffed. The apple doesn't fall far from the tree, she thought, given they got everything at cost.

Nell and Dickie looked after the shop while the new Mr and Mrs Arthur Smart took the evening train from Liverpool Street for their long weekend in Lowestoft. She and Arthur sat side by side, brushing the confetti from each other's clothes and being stared at benignly by the other passengers. As they sat there straight-backed, it occurred to her that, apart from at the altar, Arthur had not yet kissed her. Certainly not on the lips. She began to dare to look forward to the night. The mystery of everything would be revealed, was how she put it to herself. On the eve of her wedding, when she asked her mother about *that* – whatever exactly *that* was – her mother simply puckered her mouth and said, obliquely, that Arthur was both a gentleman and a *gentle* man and he would know. She left it at that.

'What about babies?' asked Eliza hopefully.

'They'll come when they want to,' said her mother. And went to check on her pastry cases.

They were booked into a proper hotel, and when she saw the building, with its pale-yellow-painted plaster and its pretty wrought-iron false balconies, the new Mrs Smart was enchanted. It had class. The seagulls wheeled overhead, the air smelled clean and tangy and she was now a properly married woman. She untucked her arm from her husband's, rearranged her expensive little navy hat, and in they went. The smiling owners greeted them with a glass of portwine, it being half past seven, and they were a little late for their supper on account of the train. The supper was, appropriately, a nice bit of local fish and fried potatoes. Neither could eat very much and for most of the meal they avoided each other's eyes. When the plates were cleared the nervous newly-weds were shown up to their room. It overlooked the sea and it had its very own separate WC and wash-hand basin. It was sitting on this WC that Eliza Smart, née Battle, spent much of the night.

She did not know what to expect when she returned from her strip wash wearing the peach satin nightdress and slipped under the covers where Arthur already lay. He wore rough cotton striped pyjamas, so it was remarkably like getting into bed with her father. Then it began. First Arthur turned the light out and they lay as still as effigies for a while. Then they turned towards each other and bumped noses as they attempted kissing. That made them giggle nervously and relax a little. Arthur kept his closed lips pressed against hers for such an age that she thought she might expire from lack of breathing, so she opened her mouth, out came her tongue and without even asking it began to push away at her husband's closed mouth. Very gradually he prised his lips open and they touched tongues, as both had done as a game when they were children. It was not unpleasant.

Eliza rolled more firmly into her husband's front, liking the tingling feeling in her bosoms and her lower bit. Her husband put out a hand and held her lightly across her shoulder blades; she put out a hand and again – quite unexpectedly – found herself saying soft little nonsenses and stroking his cheek, and then he began a rubbing motion up against her and something that she took to be the knot in his pyjama cord pushed into her lower stomach. She put her hand down to move it out of the way, and as she encountered it (most definitely it was no pyjama cord), her husband's eyes opened very wide and stared into hers with an expression she had never seen on him but had once seen on Harold Binns, and then, without a word, he pushed her on to her stomach and rolled on top of her. For a moment, flattened as she was, she thought that the main attribute of a wedding night was to have the breath squashed out of you. And then she felt a searing pain in her back passage and she cried out, 'Stop, stop –' but he didn't. He didn't seem to know how. She twisted her neck and all she could see was his closed eyes receding and advancing, receding and advancing, and then she could bear it no more and she fainted.

When she came to she was still lying face down and there was wetness between her legs. Arthur was lying on his back, and by the lights from the esplanade, she could see his eyes were open, that there were tears on his cheek. She reached out to touch his outflung arm, but he pulled it away and did not look at her. He made a noise like a sob. She eased herself up slowly, and feeling very weak, she dragged herself to the little bathroom. When she rubbed her flannel between her legs and looked at it, it was covered with bright blood. She had heard, somewhere, that new brides shed blood, so that must be it then. How horrible it was. She wondered if she might be pregnant.

They never referred to that night. Not the tears, not the pain, not the weeping of Eliza sitting on the cold WC nor the creeping back into bed in the dawn when Arthur was asleep again. They tried no more of it on their honeymoon and spoke in loud, bright voices of the place and the sights and the nice catering they were getting. When they travelled home in the train she took one last look at the receding town with its sunlit buildings and felt a terrible sadness. It was, she thought privately, as if she had just inherited all the badness in the world. Dickie and Nell greeted them as naturally as if they were the luckiest newly-weds alive, and they played along. Arthur even put his arm around Eliza's shoulders as if to say, 'See what a unit we make' – and Nell was far too busy making tea and chattering on to notice the shadows under Eliza's eyes.

They never kissed in their bed again, only a peck on the cheek before going up, and sometimes, even then, if she lingered over it, she thought that Arthur flinched. She was aware that this state of affairs was shameful and also aware that the shame was hers. Eliza alone faced the constant comments from her mother-in-law about the lack of children and about how Eliza's uppishness might be at fault. She felt miserable, guilty and a failure. Her one ally, her sister-in-law Nell, was sorting out her own wedding plans with Fred, and all Eliza knew was that they hadn't done anything yet, either. Fred wouldn't hear of such a thing, apparently, and Nell was indignant at the thought. Eliza apologized. There was no one to talk to. After a year or so, when she asked Molly – who was about to bring baby number two into the world – Molly said maybe she should be grateful Arthur left her alone. As far as she knew, she said, if there was blood, even if it was just the once, then he'd done it.

Arthur immersed himself in the shop and for recreation continued with his scouting. He was now a respected leader, who, as a successful tradesman, with a wife, could take his place in the world. What with the shop and the Scouts and his football there was little time left over to ponder what his marriage was all about. Eliza, too, found things to occupy her, and they took on more and more fancy work for hotels and restaurants and suchlike. Only occasionally he would look up and catch his wife's sad stare – a questioning, a hurt questioning, for which he had no answers. When Eliza lay in bed beside him, if she ever turned in her sleep and a bosom exposed itself, or touched him, or an arm or a knee, he recoiled. Like Eliza, he said nothing to anyone. He seemed grateful for the peace.

But Eliza felt moments of extreme yearning and wanted to reach out and touch her husband's body and be held by him. But it was not to be. Mrs Smart continued to take her down a peg or two whenever she talked about *lunch* or *Pa's business* or her and Artie being placed on the top table at the Floral Men's dinner. One sure way to shut up Eliza Battle that was, was to remind her that Dora, who got married after her, now had a beautiful bouncing daughter. And that Cora was due next Christmas.

'Nothing wrong with my family,' said Mrs Smart meaningfully.

Oh, yes. That shut her up all right.

And then came the war. Several catalystic things happened to influence Eliza. The first was that Arthur joined the Air Force and went away. The second was that Nell's Fred joined the army and was sent away for training. He contracted TB and died within six months. And the third Nell confessed to Eliza, which was that the last time she saw her husband, not long before his death and although he was very ill, they decided to go for a walk in the woods, away from the sanatorium. It was strictly forbidden to walk with a patient outside the grounds, even if he was your husband, but they paid no attention. They lay together in the ferns and made love to see if they could get a child. Three weeks later he was dead. And sure enough, said Nell, with his death she did not have what she called 'A show'. Nor did she the next month. Nor the next.

'I wondered how you managed to stay so cheerful,' said Eliza.

Arthur, just about to go back again to his training squadron, suggested that Nell might come and help Eliza in the shop for the duration. Eliza was pleased. Nell said that of course she would, thinking to herself that it would only be for a short while, and then she would settle somewhere nice to have her baby – after all, she would have a war widow's pension and something for the child. She moved in and, for so recent a widow, was quite chirpy. If anything, Eliza was the one with low spirits. And then, one morning, a week or so after Nell began helping in the shop, her dreams were dashed. She was bleeding.

The doctor said that it was quite normal for widows to stop menstruating and that she had not been pregnant. Nell, distraught, went back to Eliza and told her, and Eliza wondered how the doctor knew what was and what was not. But Nell was in no shape to be asked.

The women worked together for the next two years, until Nell was asked to join the War Records Department. Something had shifted in her. She was no longer the hopeful fun-loving innocent, but a smartly dressed, almost careless creature – much admired but accepting court from none of the young men who tried it on. She wanted better than that, she told Eliza, and Eliza did not blame her.

Nell started to have a good war. Widow's grief gave way to a sense of living for the moment – and living for the moment included men. Though she drew the line at anything below the waist, as she told Eliza. Eliza tried to look as if she knew what Nell was talking about. Nell used the same phrases that were on everybody's lips. 'We could all be blown to smithereens tomorrow . . .' 'Live now. You're a long time dead . . .' 'Take your happiness while you can . . .' And they were true. People were being blown to bits – going out of the house in the morning and never coming home – or coming home to find there was no house and sometimes no family. Everything could be done away with in the twinkling of an eye. Everything? thought Eliza. What everything?

Only when Mrs Smart came to call did Nell stay in and assume humility. No longer out of fear of her mother, so she said, but because Mrs Smart had been bombed out twice and it was a kindness to be there for her when she visited and to appear to be good. It occurred to Eliza that she had no choice in the matter of being good or not – but she began watching and envying Nell her sparkling eyes and glowing cheeks and the little gifts she sometimes danced home with in the small hours.

And then, when Arthur was due back after his first proper leave and the family gave a little party and all the children were rushing about or crawling on the carpet, or lying so sweetly in their various mothers' arms, Eliza felt a sudden terrible rising anger inside herself for all her dashed hopes. And she thought that if she couldn't have that, she'd have the other.

She asked Nell if she could come up west with her and her friend Dolly from the Records Office. Nell and Dolly bought her a cocktail at the Café Royal, where Dickie's Dance Combo was playing. She hated the cocktail and tipped it into a palm when no one was looking, but she loved the place and the sense of careless fun. She didn't need a cocktail to make her feel reckless. Nell danced. Dolly danced. And, after a little hesitation, Eliza danced too. And this time she felt a different kind of breathlessness as the tall stranger with fair hair and smiling mouth, introduced to her as Rodney, pressed his hand into the small of her back and held her firmly against his moving body. She went from dance partner to dance partner that night – sweet words were whispered, a hand strayed to take her hand, to press her thigh, and no one, including Eliza, was taking anything seriously. She tipped out into the night at half past twelve, her face pink with pleasure, singing the tunes as she and Nell walked home. In the darkness of the night she ran her hands over her body, trying to imagine how it had felt to them. Slender, she thought, but bumps in all the right places, just like one of the men had whispered.

Six months later Nell was seeing a dashing red-haired RAMC officer called Gordon and had, she confessed to Eliza, let things go below the belt. 'And very nice too,' she said firmly, but she put her finger to Eliza's lips and said, 'Not a word to mother.'

And then a big bad thing happened. On one of their dates, when Nell was with Gordon, and Dolly was with a clarinettist, Gordon brought along his brother Johnnie. For Eliza. And she was instantly taken with his jokes and his teasing and his dark, laughing eyes. The very opposite of Arthur's eyes, which were always watchful and sombre.

Johnnie was persistent. She let him hold her a little too close when they danced, and though she removed his hand from areas that were improper, she did so with increasing regret. Johnnie said she had legs as good as Betty Grable's. 'In fact,' he said, 'they're better than Betty Grable's. Know why?'

'Why?' she asked.

He reached down and pulled her skirt up over her knee. 'Because they're here.'

Mrs Smart, of course, knew nothing. Dickie wouldn't say a word. He was the apple of his mother's eye, as well as of half a dozen poppets, and he wanted to keep his nose clean. Arthur came home on leave and went away again, and Eliza was pushed to dangerous fury when her mother-in-law began with her 'Oh dear, oh dear – still no good then?' and repeated that it was certainly nothing to do with her side of the family. As she sat there hearing, yet again, how disappointing she was in her duties as a potential mother, Eliza rebelled and got up and flounced into the kitchen. Picking up the kettle she poured water into her cup. 'Don't mind, do you?' she said boldly to Mrs Smart. 'Only it's strong enough for navvies that brew of yours. And there is a war on.'

Then she sat down again.

Mrs Smart was taken aback but she rallied. No little tuppenny-hapenny butcher's daughter was going to get the better of her in her own kitchen. 'A bit of tea in the water might warm up your blood a bit my girl . . .'

Eliza just smiled. She had made up her mind. Sitting there at the kitchen table with her mother-in-law breathing fire on her, she knew she would let Johnnie have his way. She had been thinking of nothing else, night after night. Tea was not the way to warm herself up. She knew that. The way to warm herself up was to go with Johnnie.

She did not tell him immediately. She decided she would take control this time. She would fall into his arms and let him kiss her all over, as he said he wanted to do, when *she* was ready. There was, she discovered, something sweet in the waiting. Arthur was away, they could have the double bed all to themselves and Nell would wink her eye. All was set. Maybe today, maybe tomorrow – but soon, certainly soon. And then Johnnie was killed in an air raid.

She was shocked at herself for feeling more disappointment than grief. Nell said it was the war that made you tough. But the effect on Eliza was to give her the jitters. She had bad dreams where she saw Johnnie's mangled face and changed it into Arthur's. She began not sleeping, a common occurrence during the war, and then she, too, stopped having her period. At least she knew she wasn't pregnant. Counselled by Nell, she went to the doctor. And what the doctor told her, apart from 'Get more iron into you,' which was a bit thick given the meat rationing, shocked her to the core.

'Mrs Smart,' he said, 'you are still a virgin.'

'A virgin?' she repeated, and then she blushed – both in anger and in shame.

'Mrs Smart, your hymen is still there. All in one piece . . .' He sighed. 'You and your husband have not been doing what you ought to. You are as complete in that department as the day you were born.'

She stared at the doctor, trying to make sense of what he said. He gave her a little sad smile that made her feel worse than all the words in the world. All these years of marriage and she was complete?

'But there was blood,' she said. And she told the doctor that 'indeed he had put – *it* – into her' and – yes – 'indeed there had been blood'. The doctor shook his head and told her, as obliquely as possible, the physical truth. He also said, by way of a little joke, that if her husband could not find the right way home she should, perhaps, draw him a map and show him. And then, more seriously, he said, 'It is for muddled boys and not what civilized – normal – people do.' Then he smiled again. 'Except the Greeks, Mrs Smart, and they were a very long time ago.'

Something began swirling around in Eliza's mind. Something seen twice. Once in one of the exotica books in Old Collins's back office. An incomprehensible close-up image of naked bodies with two sets of privates that looked absolutely nothing like hers and which she now knew to be masculine. The page caption was 'Our Lovely Greek Ganymedes'. The other time seen, more shockingly, in her husband's collar and stud drawer, pushed to the back. Photographs of boys and men, naked among the corn, or standing by a sunlit tree, or lying, as if asleep, legs splayed, in bracken. She had returned the magazine to its hidden place, deciding to think of it as something to do with scouting, and said nothing.

When she left the doctor's surgery she walked home slowly, fists clenched in her pockets, shoes scuffing on the uneven, pot-holed streets. The raids were getting worse – anything could happen, just as it had to Johnnie – and she had a sudden sense that she had not yet lived. The contrast between her and Nell was almost too sharp to bear. She felt deep and painful envy watching her bloom while she withered. Something, she decided, as she picked her way through the streets, something must be done.

Nell's Gordon was going overseas and so they got married. Arthur could not get back for the wedding and Eliza was glad. A few of Dickie's mates came to the evening do, and she let her skirt slip up over her knee as she tapped her foot to the rhythm of the band. It did not escape Mrs Smart that Eliza was showing a lot of leg and that it had attracted the boys. Neither did it escape Eliza. And when she complained of being too hot, though it was early October, she allowed Tommy Wilkins to walk her outside. And she allowed him to do more. Not as much as he wanted, but enough to soothe some of her anger. Enough to prove that she, at least, was firing on all the right cylinders.

She came back bright-eyed and defiantly smoking a cigarette. She gave her mother-in-law a bold stare. Her mother-in-law stared back. Another port and lemon and she just might have said something, but instead Eliza sat down, crossing her legs languorously, giving Tommy a damn good eyeful. Then, when the snow was falling and the emptiness of Christmas made her weep, she took Tommy into her bed. And she understood that a man and a woman could find pleasure together and that there was nothing disgusting about it. Nothing for a man to lie there next to her and cry about. Even though she bled, and even though it did hurt a little, it was nothing like her wedding night. She told a surprised Tommy that it must be her period. That was her real shame. That she was still a virgin. Well, she thought cheerfully the next morning, not any more she wasn't.

Tommy was a coal merchant but what did that matter? All she cared about was that it was a special occupation, that he could not join up, and that what with the disruptions of the war and the Blitz he could always manage an hour or two here or there. It all went off perfectly and Eliza blossomed. She felt herself blooming, just like Nell had, at the attentions she received. After a while, she learned to take her own pleasure, too. She knew that her family and her friends were wondering why the sudden change in her, but she felt free of any guilt, free to indulge herself. She had no intention of doing more than that and, besides, she had overpaid her wifely dues.

Tommy went off home to Hoxton in due course, to marry his fiancée Myra, back from doing her land-girl stint, and there were no hard feelings. Anyway, it was not a good idea to overdo it. Mrs Smart was no fool and she had already commented on how Eliza's body was rounding out at a time when, what with the shortages and all, most people were pulling in their belts. As a reminder of what could happen, Arthur's youngest sister Daff came home in disgrace, pregnant by a married man. So Eliza waved goodbye to Tommy, kept her secret and welcomed her husband home from the war. She was, she assured herself, underneath it all a very respectable woman. In her heart she envied Nell her good marriage, her lovely daughter and her dashing, charming Gordon who looked so dapper and who behaved so charmingly. Eliza got on very well with him, he being officer class.

But Eliza was a different wife – more mature and independent. She employed a young girl in the shop – about whom she did not consult Arthur – and the shopfront had been repainted. It no longer said 'Arthur Smart' above the door, but simply 'Smarts' High Class Florists'. I dare you to say anything, her look said. 'And I needed the girl when Nell left to look after her baby.' She looked him right in the eye with that one. He looked away.

Nell and Mrs Smart were living with Nell's baby girl in the suburbs, Mrs Smart having been, as she put it, bombed to buggery and back. And Mrs Smart had developed a peculiar affection for the baby, Virginia. It was as if, after all her own children, and all her other grandchildren, she had suddenly found time to love one of the little things. She made clothes for her and ribboned up her golden hair and told her she was a beauty and the sweetest little thing. Even Nell was amazed, though she, too, adored her daughter and only ever gave her the best.

Dashing officer Gordon did not behave well for long. Nell had either run through a devil of a lot of her husband's pay and spent it on foolishness – which was his story – or he had run through all his pay drinking and gambling in the officers' mess and blamed her – which was Nell's story. Whatever the truth, Gordon hit her and then waved his pay book at Mrs Smart when she protested, telling her how much her daughter had spent. A tearful Nell denied it. He apologized to Mrs Smart for hitting her daughter but said he was distraught. Everyone put the violence down to the pains of settling back in. Mrs Smart continued to reside there as the rent was useful and she did not want to leave her adorable granddaughter. Indeed, when the violence flared again, Mrs Smart marched little Virginia off to one of her other daughter's and turned the whole thing into an adventure, while Nell and Gordon slogged it out. Or Gordon did.

When it was safe, she brought little Virginia back for her third birthday and life continued fairly smoothly. For a year or two Gordon had a good job, the home was filling nicely with new furniture on the HP, and Nell decided, as she told Eliza, to put the past behind her. Arthur kept his eye on things. Eliza envied her the little girl, but even more she envied her having a husband who put his hand around her waist and smiled into her eyes in a special kind of way. All very well to say that it happened when Gordon had enjoyed a drink or two, but at least it happened.

Nell's happiness resumed for a while. But then Gordon lost it all again. First he told his mother-in-law that she had to leave the house; Mrs Smart put her nose in the air and departed. Then, when Nell complained that none of the bills had been paid and the electricity was about to be cut off, he went down to the pub, came back, and hit her harder than ever. Worse, he had actually dared to cuff the adored Virginia when she cried. Eliza told Arthur, and Arthur had a word. Gordon was icily polite but no longer prepared to bow to his brother-in-law. 'What I do in my own home', he said, 'is no concern of yours.'

What Nell told Eliza next gave her very mixed feelings. She was pregnant again. This was what had really brought on his anger. Another mouth to feed. Another crying baby. Eliza felt her emptiness even more keenly. But it was useless. Every time she tried to even touch her husband – on the arm or on the hand – he froze.

The family, though torn, pulled together over Nell's business. Perhaps Nellie needed to come down a peg or two. She always did think herself a cut above . . . It wouldn't harm her to stop swanning around about her officer husband and buying carpets with a wanton amount of fringing and to start acting normal. All the same – being hit. And then there was that incident with the aspirin bottle. Little Virginia hadn't been the same since she found her. Nellie could always be infuriating with her proud ways, but she didn't deserve *that*. Certainly not now she was in the family way.

Arthur took his mother and his wife and went back to see Gordon about it. Mrs Smart would stay for a week or two to keep the calm and to make sure Virginia was all right. On the drive there Mrs Smart remarked that if Nellie could manage to get herself in the family way again, even with a husband like Gordon, wasn't it about time, really and truly, that Eliza followed suit? Arthur just kept his eyes on the driving. Eliza thought it best not to cause a row. But later, when Nell offered her a second gin and It, she took it. While Mrs Smart and Arthur talked the situation through with Gordon in the front room, Nell and Eliza sat in the back, sipping gin and talking.

Nell lit a cigarette and said, 'When Mum leaves again it'll just be more black eyes.'

'Your mother –' said Eliza, and then stopped herself. 'Oh, forget it, Nellie – you've got enough to deal with.'

'I wish I'd never started this,' she said, patting her stomach. 'If I could get rid of it, I would.'

Eliza found herself crying. Life was not fair.

Nell said, 'Don't let Mum get to you about the babies,' and she patted her stomach again. 'They're not all they're cracked up to be and – well – if it happens, it happens . . .'

But Eliza had had enough. Also, Nell was down on her luck too, so it was easier. She had someone to confide in at last. Not about the photographs, nor about the details of the wedding night, but about Arthur's inability to perform. Eliza confessed to having had 'relations' – she whispered the word – with someone, so that she now knew what it was like to do it properly. 'I enjoyed it, Nellie,' she said defiantly.

'Well, no wonder,' said Nell. 'Just don't let Arthur find out. You couldn't even trust *him* not to hit you. It's not very nice, I can tell you.' She nursed her bruised cheek by way of example.

'Neither's being told by a doctor that you're still a virgin. And married.' Eliza could be bitter, too. She was glad the gin had loosened her tongue. It was like a great stone weight rolling away from her, telling Nellie.

Nell looked at her in astonishment. 'You mean never?' Her jaw dropped.

'Never,' said Eliza firmly.

'Not even on your honeymoon?'

'Never.'

'Well,' said Nell, 'that puts a sock in the jaw in perspective.'

'I just don't think I can stand any more of your mother's digs,' Eliza said.

Nell, still spirited, despite her black eyes and bruises, lit another of her Weights – which used to be Senior Service or Capstan in a tortoiseshell holder – and said, 'I should bloody well think not. Why not just tell her? You ought to let her know that it isn't you at all but her precious Arthur.' Even Arthur, her one-time pet brother, did not escape her scorn now, after delivering a lecture to her along the lines of 'You made your bed, Nellie, and you must lie in it.' She didn't bother to say that she sometimes got turfed out and made to lie in the garden instead.

'I can't,' said Eliza miserably. 'Arthur would never speak to me again. The only reason we have a double bed is because of what your mother would say. Arthur would never forgive me.'

'Well, there won't be any babies unless you get him to play his part,' said Nell. 'You'll have to try a bit harder.'

So Eliza did. She curled her hair, she sang as she moved about the shop and the house, and she became docile again, deferring to him. She did everything she could to please him. If Eliza had learned a thing or two with Tommy, she was ready to apply them to Arthur. She knew, for instance, that baths could get you both going. That you can begin in apparent innocence by soaping his back and then lose the soap, and then, and then . . . She tried this, to the astonished horror of her husband. But she was clever this time. She backed off. She kept her distance completely, good humouredly, for the whole of the following day. Like an animal his hackles returned to normal. But she had learned, through the escapade of the bath, that even a disgusted husband, if handled right, can come up to scratch. He might have looked horrified, this reluctant husband of hers, but the rest of him – the bit beneath the bubbles – had not shown such distaste. It was a useful lesson. And while he still did not touch her in bed, he became a little warmer towards her. Offered her his arm if they walked down the street and let her comb his hair in a new style just for fun. Such little bits of human warmth made Eliza long for more.

At least Arthur was leaving his low origins behind, thanks to her. He liked a bit of elegance too, and their home above the shop was a picture. She had the latest kind of cooker and a new dining suite and proper big carpets with long fringes round the edge (bought from Nellie before the bailiffs came in again). She enjoyed showing off how far she had come up in the world. While Nell held her baby to her breast in the nice warm clean kitchen, Eliza ran her finger over her pristine cream fridge and pointed out the heat adjustments on the new cooker. But it was still no contest.

'You could have this one,' said Nell, half seriously. 'We found Virginia taking her up to the pig-bin the other day. She said it was because none of us really wanted her. They see everything, kids. Mum won't even hold her. Says it's been nothing but trouble since Dilys arrived.' And she added play-fully, 'You sure?'

But that was not what Eliza wanted. She wanted her own.

And then, at the Festival of Britain, where she went with Cora and they took Nell's girls, Eliza met Tommy Wilkins again. With his tired, dowdy wife and three small boys. He looked, Eliza thought, just the same bit of a lad. And while the two of them queued to get the tea, an assignation was made. And this time there was no shilly-shallying. When Arthur went to his Scout meetings, Tommy visited, or they met elsewhere. When Arthur went away to Scout camp, they met every night. The worn-out Mrs Wilkins with her three boys went to bed at eight-thirty each evening, exhausted. Eliza and Tommy made up for lost time. She, who had been feeling old and withered, blossomed again. Tommy, lying next to her, running his hands and his eyes over her body, told her that she could do a lot worse than not have children, that children were the end of a woman.

Arthur's temper improved along with his wife's. If she was

happy, he could be too. And then the unthinkable happened. As if to spite her and her mother-in-law, Eliza became pregnant. She missed A Show and thought nothing of it until a few days later when Tommy came to spend the night and started squeezing and sucking her breasts. She nearly shot across the room with the soreness. Tommy looked at her and he knew instantly.

'You, my old duck, are up the duff.' She stared back at him. He put up his hand and very gently squeezed her nipple. It was too sore to be touched and she moved away. 'And I should know,' he sighed.

Part of her was elated, part of her was sunk in fear. All of her wanted the baby. Tommy suggested an abortion; his wife had had one so he knew how much and where. But Eliza was damned if she would. She wanted this baby and she meant to have it. But Tommy was only a small-time coal merchant with one cart and twenty-five bob a week basic. A one-horse deliverer, that was all. Eliza was used to good things. Nice clothes, nice furniture – decent place in the world. If she left Arthur she would be poor. She would also be the mother of an illegitimate baby if Tommy's divorce didn't come through. All of that didn't bear thinking about. Only the baby counted. And she wanted the best for it. Nell's girls, last time she had them for the night, both had nits and underwear you wouldn't put on a scarecrow. She wasn't going to risk that. But the fact of the matter was that Arthur could not be the father.

She was afraid, suddenly. Arthur had a high moral code and was of some standing in their part of London. She could be divorced, out on the street, with nowhere to go. She fingered her silk underwear as she folded it away, she ran her hands over the piano in the sitting room, she saw how her fair hair danced like a film star's after the hairdresser's art. And, in particular, how her neighbours and fellow tradespeople treated her with respect. She could not, she would not, give it all up.

'Tommy,' she said, 'no hard feelings.'

'It's mine, isn't it?'

'No,' she said firmly. 'It's mine.'

She confided in Nell again. Depressed Nell who was scrimping a hand-to-mouth existence in a factory, looks all but gone, voice coarsened, Gordon suspended from his job and being investigated for embezzlement and Mrs Smart living in the two best rooms at the front of the house, in an aura of righteous disapproval, going off at weekends to the better class of relative and locking her doors behind her.

'Imagine,' said Nell, 'locking the doors in my house and only ten bob a week rent. And she won't have the baby in there. Only Ginny. She acts like it's Buckingham Palace.'

It was a good frame of mind for her to receive Eliza's news.

'Go on,' said Nell. 'You do it the way you want to and you have what you want. Or the other buggers will.'

'But Arthur will know it's not his. He never comes near me.'

'Make him.'

'I've tried.'

'Then get him drunk.'

'But you always said Gordon passed out when he was drunk.'

'Shall we leave my bigamist husband out of this,' said Nell.

'Oh, Nellie, I'm so sorry.'

'Don't be,' said Nell. 'It means the divorce will come through quickly. Hah! Because there won't be one. Anyway he'll be locked up soon and that'll be that.'

'Are you going to tell the children?'

'Good God, no. But I think Ginny's picked up something. She's a sharp one. And some nights he comes home shouting the odds.' She sighed. 'But he'll be gone soon.' She ran her fingers through her now grey hair and Liza saw a string of dark bruises along her arm. She shivered. At least Arthur was kind.

'Anyway, if I think back to before the drink really ruined

him, just the right amount of liquor got him going. But make sure you don't overdo it or he will pass out.' She smiled grimly. 'It's a delicate balance between a cheerful drunk and a violent old sot.'

'Well,' said Eliza, 'that's it then. Because he doesn't drink. Except maybe a beer occasionally. No hard spirits. He likes to keep fit.'

Nell laughed. 'Fit for what?'

Eliza clamped her mouth shut.

'Well, never mind – you can always give him a shot of that Russian stuff in his orangeade.'

'What Russian stuff?'

'It's all the go. Vodka. You can't taste a thing, apparently. How far gone are you?'

'About a week off two months.'

'Better get your skates on. Do it at Christmas when Mum's staying with you. He won't be able to run off yelling when she's in the next room. You can always say it came premature. Like Dilly.'

'Poor little Dilly,' said Eliza.

'Shame she was ever born,' said Nell flatly.

Eliza decided Boxing Day would be best. More relaxed. And she did herself up nicely so that even her mother-in-law said she looked decent. Arthur put his arm round her shoulder on the settee for a photograph, so she knew it was about as good as it got. On Boxing Day night, when they were all tired out and Mrs Smart said she'd get to her bed at nine, Eliza made a little drop of ginger punch just for her and Arthur in front of the fire, experiments having shown that ginger hit the sharpness of the alcohol best. And it worked. They both got the giggles and she somehow manoeuvred him up the stairs, undressed him, and tickled his ribs under the bedclothes, warning him not to laugh or he'd wake his mother. They were like children rolling around and stifling their giggling, and Eliza made sure that every so often, as if by accident, she touched what she knew she had to. It did the

213

job. Up he came and as soon as he did so she slipped it into her – quick as ninepence – and, now that she knew what to do, there was no difficulty with the rest of it.

For just one moment she stared into Arthur's open, half-puzzled eyes, and then he closed them, and groaned, and gave a shudder. But it was done. She let him roll over, but before she let him fall asleep she said in his ear that it had been *lovely* . . . Just *lovely* . . . And left it at that. Arthur went out for the morning and when he came back it was as if nothing had happened between them. Eliza was quite content.

'Well, I'm jiggered,' said Mrs Smart. 'So – she's done it at last.'

They brought out the portwine, and Mrs Smart broke her rule and had one. And even Arthur was persuaded, though, as he said to the assembled few members of his family round his table, he never usually took strong drink.

'You should try, Arthur,' said Eliza, beaming. 'I think it's very manly in a man.'

Nell, who laughed seldom nowadays, dived under the table to retrieve her paper serviette and did not come up for quite a long time. When she did she winked at Eliza and smiled.

'Well, isn't that nice,' she said, raising her glass. 'Another baby on the way.'

Arthur looked pleased as punch. 'It'll be a boy,' he said. Clearly he was already planning the football and camping trips.

'Well, here's to the first of many,' said Mrs Smart.

Eliza kept silent.

A girl was born at the beginning of August and nobody had any ideas about counting up the dates, especially not Arthur, who was totally and completely enraptured as soon as he held the child in his arms. She had a screwed-up, plain little face, a big nose even then, and fair hair. The fair hair was her mother's, and the face, as Eliza whispered to Nell, was most definitely her father's. This did not stop Mrs Smart from seeing her own family shining out like a beacon.

'Just like our Arthur,' she said at the christening. 'And it'll be a boy next time. Which is what, I'm sure, he would like.'

She fixed Eliza with her basilisk's eye.

Eliza smiled, very sweetly.

And all honour was saved.

What the eye doesn't see, she thought, the heart doesn't weep over. And anyway, she was a great deal more aware of things nowadays and she knew now what the things she had seen among her husband's private papers meant.

Tommy died in 1976, of a bad liver and complications. The Smarts went to visit him in King Alfred's – Eliza's suggestion – and he was not a pretty sight. As they left the hospital, Eliza put her arm through her husband's and thought that a respectable woman of her age could put all that sort of thing down anyway. She'd had a good run. And she had a lovely, grown-up daughter upon whom Arthur doted. She hooked her hand more tightly into the crook of her husband's arm. In his good tweed coat and Church's shoes he was Smart by name and Smart by nature. And unlike Tommy, he never touched a drop. They rubbed along tolerably well.

Just coming up the steps was Myra Wilkins and two of her sons. Good job Alison isn't here, thought Eliza, for the similarity between her and her half-brothers was almost shocking. Myra still lived in a council house. Eliza shivered and thought that it could have been her. They stopped on the steps for a little chat, two women comforting each other while the men stood around looking awkward. Tommy was, as Myra said, going to go at any minute. Nothing they could do. So she was taking him in a half bottle of whisky, which he had asked for, and she wondered what Eliza thought. If the doctors found out . . . Eliza said that she could see no harm in it. Why shouldn't he have a little of what he fancied – it'd probably do him good.

'Too late now to do him any harm at any rate,' sniffed Myra.

When it was all over for Tommy, Eliza, who no longer worked in the shop, went in especially and made him a beautiful wreath. It was, she decided, the very least she could do. Arthur was a bit surprised at the lavishness of the gesture but, as Eliza said to him, if it hadn't been for Coalman Tommy after the war, goodness knew how she would have kept herself warm.

With my mother Nell's death, so died the secret of Eliza's sex life. Until the day that I drove into Lichfield and found her and asked her to lie for me. And if ever the truth about age bringing a poor short-term memory and an excellent long-term one needed confirmation, my Auntie Liza's telling of it proved the rule. She had obviously waited a very long time to do so.

'I feel better for telling you all that,' she said. And placing her hands on her knees she looked me firmly in the eye and said, 'Lie for you, dear? I'm a dab hand at that.'

So I told her what I had done and what she had to do. She didn't say much but she nodded and agreed.

'Yes, yes,' she said neutrally. 'You're Nellie's daughter after all. Family is family. We all need our families. How's that prickle-backed sister of yours?'

'Impossible,' I said.

'Ah, well – she saw some sights, that one.'

'I don't know anything about that.'

'I'd let sleeping dogs lie.'

'She wouldn't talk about it anyway.'

'You'll talk about anything as you get older. Look at me.' She smiled with those vague old eyes. 'It's been good to let the burden down,' she said. 'You keep quiet about me. And I'll keep quiet about you . . .' She stood up. 'Though I think you're a fool.'

She showed me out and stood at her mean little doorway, her half-sightless eyes blinking in the bright evening sunlight, and she put her hand on my arm.

'Twenty-five bob a week,' she said. 'I just couldn't do it, you see.'

'Not if you didn't love him enough.'

'Love?' she said, squeezing my arm. 'Love? Do you know where Myra Wilkins ended up?'

I shook my head.

'In a filthy old home in Lewisham. I went to see her once. "Get me out of here," was what she said. Of course I couldn't. Don't the boys visit? "No," she said, "the one's in Australia, the other's in drink and the third nobody knows . . . " I never went to see her again. So you see – I was right. You need your family at the end.'

She fingered my jacket, then rubbed it with the palm of her hand. For a moment she was my old, snobby Aunt Eliza again. 'Good quality,' she said. 'Who'd have expected it of a grubby little thing like you?'

I kissed her and walked over to the car.

'Make no mistake,' she called as she waved, 'it was worth it all. Staying put.' Then she put her finger to her mouth. 'Mum's the word,' she called, and went in.

15

Not a Time to Dance . . .

When I'd finished telling him the whole story, Matthew lay quite still, propped up on a pillow, hands behind the back of his head. I was lying on my side, foetal-like, tucked into him for comfort. It felt as if a giant, cold shadow had passed across me.

'You women are amazing,' he said. 'Not only what you can do with your bodies but how it directs your minds. A man wouldn't think of anything halfway so devious.' He laughed. 'Thank God I never had children. What a brilliant piece of theatre.'

'Real enough,' I said. 'Shocking in fact. Some families have dainty little skeletons in their cupboards and some have Woolly Mammoths.'

I did not add that I was about to add another one to the endless cycle of family betrayals and deceits. It was too depressing. I was also trying to digest the story of my mother and father, my sister and myself. It was as if I had been living in a pencil sketch and now I'd found the finished oil. I put it all away to deal with later. Whenever I was with Matthew there was no left-over space for anything else. Not even the quaint idea of one's sister attempting to dump one in a pig bin.

'Pragmatists, you lot are,' said Matthew wonderingly. 'Realists.'

'I suppose we are. After she finished telling me, she just tutted to herself and said, "Well, you just had to get on with it. Besides, what would I have done on a coalman's wages of twenty-five bob a week?" And that was that.'

'Poor fucker,' said Matthew eventually.

'Who?' I said indignantly. 'My aunt?'

'Not your aunt,' he said, equally indignantly, and sitting up. 'Your uncle. Imagine being gay and not being able to express yourself.'

For a moment I was stunned. All I saw was her suffering, for which she had no choice. Not his, for which, even if difficult, he did.

'But he should never have got married, knowing what he knew . . .'

'Ah – but did he know it? I've had lads of sixteen and seventeen at the centre who had no idea what was *wrong* with them – and that's sixty years on.'

'Well, he must have known that getting horny over pictures of naked boys wasn't exactly acceptable.'

'He probably thought getting married would *cure* him. That's another fantasy still around today. Anyway, in the end no harm done. Women are such good manipulators.'

I bridled. 'That's not a very nice thing to say.'

'What?'

'That we are manipulative.'

'Reclaim the gender in the language,' he laughed. 'Good at handling things into place? What's wrong with that? I'm not so sure I want to be involved with you any more – not with the blood of your aunt flowing in your veins . . .'

'Only an aunt by marriage,' I said, and tried to laugh it off. But the chill left by that shadow remained. I had walked through the Looking Glass into someone's life – a life that looked absolutely dull and perfect from the other side of the mirror, but which was neither. As mine had once looked.

'Come on,' he said. 'Let's eat.'

Who's the pragmatist now? I wondered.

While Matthew was showering I rang Francis. There was something very comforting in the sound of his voice. Something that made everything ordinary and straightforward for a moment.

'How was it?' he asked.

'Oh, fine. She's agreed to come.'

'I'll look forward to meeting her at last. You sound a bit tired.'

'It was a long day. She decided to open up to me and talked for hours. It was quite draining really.'

'Skeletons in cupboards?'

I thought how intuitive we had become over the years.

'Many skeletons,' I said.

'We've all got them.'

The words hung there while my heart began beating a little too swiftly for comfort.

'Have we?' I said eventually.

Francis laughed. 'I'll show you mine if you'll show me yours.'

'Careful,' I said lightly.

But I knew he didn't have any. At least, not in any meaningful way. He thought the same about me. He said it from a position of absolute trust. Guilt reared again. But also a sudden sense of intimacy. I suddenly felt like talking. 'Five minutes then,' I laughed. I told him as much of the story as I could – about my uncle probably being gay and how she just got on with her life – sparing him the details of how she had accomplished this. The great thing about being married to someone involved in the law is that they have seen and heard just about everything. If I had told Francis that Auntie Liza liked biting the heads off ferrets, he would have registered some surprise but his heart wouldn't have stopped for it.

At the end of the telling he said, 'You women are the pragmatists – it's us poor mutts who are the romantics.'

'That's just what M–.' I very nearly said it.

'Just what?' asked Francis.

I really wanted to say Matthew's name to Francis. I really wanted to say, 'That's just what Matthew said,' because it was so extraordinary – the parallels between the two of them helped the guilt, I suppose.

The shower stopped, the lavatory flushed, I yawned again.

'My aunt,' I said, alert again. 'That's just what she said.' Which was true in a way.

'I wonder why she chose to tell you about it all now?' he said. 'She's seen enough of you in the past.'

'Must be the effect of Cora's death, I suppose.' How could I have forgotten that I was supposed to know her very well indeed! 'Also,' I said quickly, 'she's fond of me. The snob in her thinks I'm the icing on the family cake – having married such a successful lawyer.'

'Quite right,' he said

The bathroom door opened.

Matthew stepped into the room, naked and damp. 'Talk to you tomorrow,' I said and put down the phone. The guilt vanished, the blood pulsed in its place, and that was everything that mattered.

In the morning, as we were packing, Matthew said he thought I had been very clever to have persuaded my aunt not to blow my cover. I was about to preen myself, when I detected the faintest whiff of rebuke about the way he said it. And there was.

'But after the funeral, when we go away, you have to make up your mind. Not if, but when. We're just wasting precious time. I'm fed up to the back teeth with subterfuge.'

'I'm not enjoying it,' I said.

'No?' he asked sharply.

'No,' I said.

His expression suggested Well You Could Have Fooled Me, but all he said was, 'Then don't prolong it. *Why* are you prolonging it?'

It reminded me of the olden days of girls and men, when Evelyn Home had her problem page in *Woman*. How simple morality was then. When He put the pressure on and said, '. . . If you loved me you would Do It . . .' Evelyn's blanket advice was to Get Rid Of This Man. To turn on your stockinged heel and walk away. Because if he loved you, he'd respect you; if he loved you, he'd jolly well wait until you were married to Do It. So said Evelyn then. Now Matthew's version was the world turned upside down. Traditional female role usurped in a post-modernist masculine variant. He was saying, 'If you loved me you would stop fornicating with me in secret and legitimize our relationship.' Whatever happened to men wanting to have their wicked way with you, their cake and eat it, another notch on the gold-handled cane? I'd stumbled into the arms of a man wanting everything made proper when all I needed was an Archetypal Male. No wonder blokes were confused. I certainly was.

In the end we agreed that I should concentrate on getting through Cora's funeral, while he did all the planning and made all the necessary travel arrangements. It seemed a fair bargain. I was excited at the prospect of surprise. Of not having to be capable and organized. Francis liked to sit and look at guidebooks and maps and brochures and talk about what would and would not please us both, so that wherever we went we were always prepared. Up until now I always liked this. Now, listening to Matthew and the way he liked to travel, mine seemed a very old-fashioned, cautious method. I was looking forward to just getting on a plane and flying away.

I looked at Matthew. How confidently he smiled back. The smile of one who has no hesitation about facing the world. Nothing sneaky about him. He had a face as honest and open as a bright new flower. A little irritation scattered its grit.

'Couldn't you be a bit more like Tommy Wilkins?' I asked.

He misunderstood. His eyes widened with absolute incredulity. 'You want a child?' he said.

I shook my head, gripped by a great pain, thinking of my sons, my grandchildren, their lives.

'India?' he said, calling me back.

I nodded. He was my happiness, just as I was his. There was no retreat from that. I would have to tell Francis. If I couldn't go to Lichfield easily for one night, I certainly couldn't go to India. And I wanted to go with him more than I knew it was possible to want something. Francis must be told. But not yet. With the more immediately pressing item of a funeral and an aunt to attend to, in that time-honoured way of my friend the ostrich, I carefully reburied my head in the coarsest of procrastination's sand.

16

Alison in Wonderland

When I picked her up at the station, Auntie Liza said that if things got difficult with Francis she would just play the dotty old lady. 'Which I more or less am anyway, dear.' She then went on to ask me if there would be any single men at the ceremony. 'Suitable single men,' she then added. 'Distinguished.' I said that I thought not.

'Pity,' she said. 'It'd be one in the eye for that blackguard.'

We're a game bunch, I thought. Eighty-something and still up for it. Though part of me had a sudden yearning for a time when I might be beyond such urges. A very far-off land that seemed at the moment. I was in for another few days without tripping off to Paddington and already I was missing him.

I clicked her into the seat belt and we set off.

She looked all around her as we turned into traffic. 'Shall I take you through the centre?' I asked.

'Yes, please,' she said, without a second's hesitation. 'Take me up to Park Lane. I like that drive.' She settled back. 'This is a nice car,' she said. 'Expensive.'

We drove for a while with her exclaiming over this and that – the changes, the things that were the same, the memories – 'Well, *that* was a pub, and *that* was a dress shop where your mother and I used to go sometimes – it's all electrical now. Oh, your mother. If she'd only been sensible.'

So she was back on form. Something to do with bringing her back to her old stomping grounds, I suppose. Well, two could play at that game. I offered to stop at the Dorchester and buy her some lunch. 'I took my mother there', I said, 'for her sixtieth birthday. She was quite at home.'

My aunt raised an eyebrow and pursed her lips. 'Best get

home,' she said. I thought she sounded slightly miffed but perhaps that was wishful thinking.

It was inevitably nerve-racking when we arrived at the house. Francis treated her as if she was made of Crown Derby after all my assertions about her delicacies and sensitivities and fears about men, and she, with no notion of being nervous or modest or inclined to reclusiveness, handed him her walking stick and swaggered into the house ahead of him, having given him quite a twinkling – no other word for it – *leer*. He looked back over his shoulder at me with great surprise. And then, to make matters worse, she was totally outspoken on the subject of the great wealth involved in the value of our house, and the abundance of expensive things within it.

'Oh,' she said, 'when you think of what Dilly came from . . .'

Another look from Francis.

'Your mother never had a fitted carpet in her life, dear. As for that chandelier – well, it isn't a shilling in the meter for you nowadays, is it?'

'No,' I said wanly.

Francis gave me a smile. Then, with his own brand of charm, mixed with an irony she failed to notice, he said, 'She costs me a pretty penny to run, Eliza.'

She nodded knowingly. 'Those who've never had always overdo it,' she said.

She walked on slowly, admiring everything. Then she stopped by the mirror, also from Venice. She ran her fingers around its gilded edges. 'How can you ever think of leaving all this, dear?' she said over her shoulder.

Francis looked back at me with even more confusion. I just shrugged and rolled my eyes. I would have given him the sign for 'She's a little unhinged', but she was peering into the mirror and could probably just about see me.

The important thing was to keep her occupied so that Francis didn't trip her up in his innocence. It would be quite difficult to put everything down to elderly dottiness, and I broke out in a sweat imagining her leaning forward and saying conversationally to Francis that the last time she saw me before Lichfield I was wearing school uniform . . . Which would certainly open a whole new window for him on what I got up to when visiting aged aunts. Or I could hear him offering her a White Lady, 'Because I know you like them,' and her saying, which happened to be true, that she couldn't stand spirits in any way, shape or form and only ever took a little sherry.

Visiting the health-food shop seemed a safe option. We introduced John to his great-aunt, and Petra was enormously pleased when she stood leaning on her stick at the entrance, sniffed once or twice appreciatively, and said with her *grande dame* vowels, 'Ah – this smells like how good quality shops used to smell.'

She was taken back to their house for tea, and Petra made the right kind – high-class gnat's pee, and much approved of.

'Quality,' said my aunt, with an expression of bliss. 'Quality.'

She delighted her great-nieces, showing them how to make a floral tiara with a few roses and some leaves from the garden and a bit of wire. They were ecstatic. And I was exhausted.

It was all very gentle and genteel but, with Francis around, I found it hard going. At any moment he could discover the truth. After all, it was his job. Her 'Well, dear, if she doesn't want you she can always pass you on to me . . .' brought an interesting light into his eyes and had me leaping up and ricocheting around the room like my schoolfriends' fathers used to do when something vaguely sexual broke out on the telly.

He was staring at me. 'Are you all right?' he asked.

Oh, that concerned and loving look of his. How I wanted to knock it out of existence.

The telephone was our lifeline. Matthew was finding it hard. Not surprisingly, I suppose. Always a useful exercise to put yourself in another's shoes before criticizing. If I'd been him I'd have been beside myself. So he was understandably thin-lipped. 'We love each other,' he said, for the umpteenth time, 'so why aren't we together? I'm going to a wedding next week. You can't come. It's lonely living this half life.'

'This is the very last time,' I promised. My heart was thumping with fear. Weddings were also parties, and parties at which people usually drank too much and flirted. Matthew standing around, on his own, looking available, feeling lonely . . . Apart from that, I was shaken by how much I missed him. No going back to the marital vale of health.

'Once all this is over,' I added. 'I promise.'

'Good,' he said, full of confidence. 'Because there's a life to be lived out there. For both of us.'

I was standing at the top of the garden, telephone still clamped to my ear, riveted by this parting shot, when Francis came out. He said that I looked as if I had just seen a ghost.

Two of Aunt Cora's friends from Norfolk, both women and both in their early eighties, insisted on coming to pay their last respects. Francis and I played host to them the evening before the ceremony – what was another pair of old ducks in the maelstrom that was currently my life? Besides, it stopped the conversation going anywhere dangerous. Would that I will be able to talk so much and so fast in thirty years or so. Naturally the manner of the death was ground to be raked over. It happened when they were on a group trip to the seaside: Cora just keeled over. The two women seemed slightly peeved, despite being in mourning. One of them, Susannah, said that it was the way they *all* wanted to go. The implication was that Cora had pinched the last opportunity and that the only thing left to them was a long and lingering death.

'It's marvellous to be in your eighties and still paddling,' I said.

'Never turn anything down,' said Susannah. 'When you get to our age you remember your lost opportunities and you wonder where it all went.'

Not what I wanted to hear.

Francis, whom they adored, said that was why he intended to retire while he was still hale.

Nor was that.

'We lost our husbands, but we found each other,' they agreed.

'Still time to find a sweetheart,' he said.

'Oh, *no*,' they said, affecting to be shocked.

He looked at me and winked.

'Oh, yes,' I said wildly.

'Not if you're happily married!' Susannah said, genuinely shocked this time.

'Of course not,' I said in a strange, high voice that was not, as far as I knew, mine. But I avoided Francis's eyes.

'Some people', he said teasingly, 'say it's having a sweetheart that keeps their marriages going.'

The old ladies looked even more shocked – and loved it. I just looked like an old lady.

It was all very skittish and girlish. They told him not to say such things and then led him on some more.

'Love keeps you young and pretty,' he said. And winked at them. Rather horribly, I thought. But I was amazed. They loved it even more. He had judged them just right. Given his profession I suppose it was hardly surprising.

We assembled the following day. There were few close relations. Some family feud involving money and the scattering of Smart descendants reduced the numbers. I was grateful. The fewer I had to deal with, the better. Cora's daughters, Lucy and Pauline, were there, of course, with their husbands Frank and Kenneth, and Lucy's son George and his wife and children. John and Petra could not come because they were away hosting something for the Organic Soil Association. Just as well, as I felt uneasy around them nowadays. There were a few other cousins whom I vaguely recognized and the two or three others were unknown friends and acquaintances from

Cora's past. And then, just as we were about to begin and the music of 'I Vow to Thee My Country' was fading away, there was a shuffling in the back. I turned round to see a short, fair woman, a little younger than me, wearing a very chic black hat with a veil. She began to roll the veil down over her face ostentatiously as she slid into a pew. I thought it all looked a touch overdone and I wondered who she could be. Not family, certainly. There was not a hint of the Smarts about her.

A few tears were shed, the coffin slid away, and while we sang the last hymn, 'All Things Bright and Beautiful', Auntie Liza leaned towards me and whispered that the flowers were *extremely* vulgar.

And then we shuffled out. First to look at the extremely vulgar flowers which were set out in neat rows – an odd thing to do, I have always thought, encouraging competitiveness – and then to hug each other and mop tears, and finally to gather ourselves up to go back to Pauline's for the funeral baked meats. My aunt hooked an arm into first Francis's, then mine, and we were just making our sedate way to the car, when – in a flurry of veils and black leather gloves and perfume – the late arrival came running over and scooped my aunt into her arms.

'Mummy,' she said, in a piercing rendition of Auntie Liza's own curious vowels. 'Only just made it. And these dear people must be my cousin Dilys –' she gave a very theatrical pause and, in the exact manner of her mother, added – 'and this must be her husband.'

'Darling,' said Auntie Liza, in a voice I had not heard since I was a child. 'Darling Alison.' Auntie Liza was back in superior mode.

They embraced as if on stage and then, with a slight stagger, Darling Alison stood back, let her mother go, and re-adjusted her veil. It looked slightly skew-whiff and drunken. I realized – as we now took our turn to kiss on each cheek – that so was its owner. Apparently she decided that she could make it all the way from Kettering after all, getting as far as

Streatham Hill station on various trains, then flagging down a surprised motorist whom she hijacked to the church. Now she assumed she had a lift.

'I don't drive nowadays,' she said grandly.

I thought I probably knew why.

'Mummy,' she gushed, 'are they looking after you?'

Immediately I felt myself bridling. That word 'they'. It was as if the past had never gone away, as if I was some kind of ignorant alien with neither money nor place in their kind of world. It implied the impossibility of the very idea.

I was about to say something quite brisk on the subject, when my aunt said, 'Oh, yes. Just like royalty, Ally,' in that strangely strangled voice I remembered from childhood – the one that my grandmother called coming from her arse and taking the long way round. 'Your cousin Dilys *has* come on in the world.'

Cousin Dilys kept her mouth shut for fear of saying something very rude. All I could think was, Thank God Virginia isn't here, or there might have been two old ladies on the funeral pyre. Every time those early Broadcasts to the Nation are replayed, I can hear Auntie Liza saying, 'Ai Cin Only Teke Mey Tea in a Bowne China Cup.' At least Celia Johnson and the dear Queen saw fit to ditch their accents and use the language of the twenty-first century . . . Something darling Ally hadn't even managed to do, apparently.

'Good,' trilled Alison. 'Jolly good, Mums.'

My cousin then proceeded to take Francis's outer arm, and together we made our way to the car.

'Very nice,' said my cousin in a tone of amazement as we prepared to get in. She said it either of the car, or of my husband, or of my coat, I couldn't be sure. And then I knew. She slipped off her thin, leather glove, reached out and clutched at my sleeve, just as her mother had done with my skirt. 'Who would have thought it of you, Dilys?' And then she let out a gutsy, braying laugh. 'Remember that raincoat. God, you did look a sight in those days . . .'

I froze for a moment. I just could not move. Not backwards, not forwards. All I knew was that I was suddenly eight years old again, and experiencing condescension without even knowing that the word existed. I was back to being poor, wearing Ginny's old raincoat, which reached my ankles and had lost its proper belt so that my mother had attached a blue plastic one, and a pair of shoes that were too tight. I was at Finsbury Park Station, I was being collected, and Alison, in her sweet little coat and velvet collar, was laughing at my mackintosh. Old habits die hard. To cover my pain at the memory, and as my cousin made no move, I began settling Auntie Liza into the back. When I looked up I saw that Alison was about to slide herself into the front seat, next to Francis. My eyes met his. What he read in mine put him on his guard.

'OK?' he asked, lightly.

With an extraordinary rise of fury, I took hold of Alison's wrist and pulled her away and shoved her, very firmly, towards the back, where she got in, in some dishevelment, next to her mother. She seemed not to notice the force of the shove. I retrieved her dropped glove from the pathway, just about stopped myself from slapping her round the chops with it, and slid into my rightful seat. After which I managed to calm myself down.

'OK?' he said again, as I slammed the door.

'Fine,' I said, very loudly. And then I added, even more loudly, 'I'll just slip off this wool and cashmere mix coat and put it over the back of my seat, then I shall be *fine* . . .'

I don't think Darling Ally registered any of it. But my husband did. No fool my husband, as I have said. 'Oh, Dilys,' he said affectionately, 'you haven't said what the lining is made from.'

The car moved forward, carrying us all to who knew where.

'And what do you do, Frank?' said my cousin, leaning forward so that she was practically licking his ear.

'Francis,' we both said in unison. He mildly. Me angrily.

'Remember how Carole tried calling me Frankie?' he said smoothly. Then, addressing my cousin over his shoulder, he said, 'Even Dilys's best friend wasn't allowed to call me that.'

'Oh,' said Alison, silenced either from confusion or remorse.

Meanwhile, I was feeling that old feeling again, the one of inferiority, the one that said that anything I had could not be worth having, and if it was worth having, they (the mysterious haves) had a right to it because they were superior. It was the peasant coming out in me again, the deep-scored feudal psyche in which nothing was really mine and everything was the Rich Person's. By talking to my husband so familiarly, my cousin demeaned me. And worse, I was still vulnerable to it.

Francis, of course, read it like a seer reads the runes. He said the only thing necessary. 'What do I do, cousin Alison? Why – I earn buckets and buckets of money,' he smiled at her in the mirror. 'Which I then lavish on my beloved wife.'

She sat back again looking wonderfully put out, if a little mystified. Oh, yes. She heard that all right.

'And you?' he asked. I realized, suddenly, that he was enjoying this – if only on my behalf.

'Oh, I inherited from my father. He was a businessman,' she said.

'And what line of business was he in?'

'Floral interior design,' she said promptly.

My aunt, I saw in the wing mirror, did not even blink.

'So I don't actually have to *do* anything?' continued Alison happily.

Or can't, I thought, but out of deference to present company, I kept the suggestion to myself.

My aunt looked up at me, and I looked back at my aunt. She was very lucky that Alison had some of her looks. For she sure as hell had none of my Uncle Arthur's.

Secrets, I thought. Ours were *certainly* safe with each other. All the same, the memory of that raincoat rankled. Well – more than rankled really. Downright hurt. Crystallizing everything. Shame, insecurity, Dilys alone. I think if she had mentioned the shoes as well, I would have hurled myself at her neck. Those tight, tight shoes. The agony. I managed to wear them all day and every day and I never once told anyone for the whole four-day visit that they had rubbed blisters on the ends of my big toe. Had I known anything about it I would have thought of myself as a little saint with so much silent suffering. But children have instincts and my instinct was that, if I told on the shoes, I was really letting my mother down. To her being poor was a very great shame. Shame made her angry. 'It's them or nothing,' she said crossly as she shoved them on my feet. Why complain when there was no alternative?

It was always feet among the women in my family. Maybe trainers (what Francis's mother damned in a single breath years ago when we took her to New York by referring to them scathingly as 'surgical shoes') have changed the way feet used to suffer, but not for my generation. At the end of a life, if any particular part of the body tells of a woman's poverty, it is her feet, which are supposed to be dainty and arched and rosy pink, with not much of a spread. Lady's feet. Mine, in pale imitation of my mother's and her mother's before her, are broad, a little calloused, a little bunioned, a little corned; throughout my formative years they were pushed into ill-made, ill-fitting hand-me-down footwear. Not so bad as my mother's or my grandmother's because they were saved from too many years of bad treatment by affluence. But they are a reminder. As much a social indicator in their way as the bound foot indicated wealth in pre-Mao China. My Aunt Eliza's feet were in reasonable condition since she was brought up in comparative comfort, but they were not beautiful. Alison's feet were elegant, long, thin, rosy, and each toe pressed out perfectly when she walked with them naked, not a corn or a bunion to be seen. I knew because I remembered them from childhood. They were princess's feet. Mine were the pauper's.

'You'll stay with us, then?' I asked her.

'You don't mind putting me up?'

'On the contrary,' I answered, and meant it. 'It will repay you for all those times you looked after me as a child.'

'Yes,' she said happily. 'And didn't you need it. Remember how you always arrived with nits?'

Auntie Liza fell asleep. Deeply. Alison made a little cushion for her mother's head in the angle of the window and the seat, and she looked comfortable enough. Occasionally she gave a genteel little snore.

'Out like a light,' said my cousin, who was remarkably lively now.

We chatted about this and that and then – when the subject of her marriage came up – I said I was very sorry to hear about her divorce.

'Oh,' she said airily, 'better that than stuck with someone you don't want to be stuck with. I waited until Daddy had gone. He wouldn't have been able to stand it. He believed that once married you stuck to it, thick or thin.'

'Did he now?' I said. Francis gave me a little warning nudge.

'Oh, yes. One thing for me to marry a foreigner, quite another to get divorced from him. It took him years to adjust *to* the ruddy man, just to be able to go shopping with the children, so the idea of divorcing him . . . Well, anyway . . . Farouk never liked my father. He said there was something shifty about him. Which, of course, is what my father said about Farouk when I first brought him home. Honestly, men.'

'What did your mother say when you brought him home?'

Alison gave a very enviable cackle. 'Oh, she just started telling everyone he was a prince. And very rich – which he was. Trouble is he had the same failing your father had.'

I sat up very straight. Francis put his hand on my arm.

'Which particular failing was that, Ally?' I said, quite softly.

'Oh, gambling,' she said, adding lightly, 'don't worry – he never drank or hit me. And he was certainly never married to anybody else.' She shrieked at this.

'Oh, good,' I said evenly. 'Fathers can be quite a millstone, can't they?'

There was that little touch from Francis again. I wanted to shriek just like she did, and tell him that I was a big girl, leave me alone. But I just moved away from him very slightly. Let her go on like that, I thought, just let her . . . Mercifully, she didn't.

'By the time the divorce came through there wasn't a lot left I'm afraid.' She flopped back in the seat.

'So you were hard up?'

'Oh, no,' she said comfortably. 'I'd got all Dad's. But money isn't everything, is it?'

Try living without it, I thought.

We drove for a while. Alison had dozed off. I thought about Matthew. Perpetual fear – how long would he wait while I dawdled in my marriage? Not Much Longer. He had already said, 'Why not just reverse it? Why not imagine that I'm the woman and you're the man. Would you find it so unacceptable then that I want you to leave?' He, too, had spotted the Evelyn Home reversal. And he was right. How many married men had I seen Carole go through, knowing that the only valid proof of their love was to leave their marriages for her? A lot.

If I had just met someone less intelligent and less sensitive. Someone I could just screw and walk away from and meet again when I felt hot. Not Matthew, who stood his ground like a moral Colossus. Between him and Francis I was like some squeezed out, dried up old hag of moral turpitude, while they were all honour and chivalry. I was a woman just dying to be as black as history has painted us, and no one would let me.

Alison rallied suddenly and leaned forward and said to the space between me and Francis, 'Anyway, I've got a lovely manfriend now. He came to do my central heating for me and – well – one thing led to another . . .'

'How did you know it was love? The manly way he gripped your U-bend?'

'Dilys,' said Francis warningly.

'Oh, *love* . . .' she said as if it was yesterday's custard. 'No – he just moved in. Lovely body. *Now* I understand why Ginny chose Bruce. Plumbers are very sexy . . .'

All I could think was that even she, even Darling Ally and her damaged liver, could just meet someone across a crowded central-heating system and move him in without all this subterfuge, all this fuss – all this unrequited *wanting*. Not fair, not fair, not fair.

Alison was laughing. 'My son fancies him, too,' she said. 'He's gay by the way . . . Dad used to get furious with him when he was little. Tried to get him to play football and join in the healthy outdoor life. But all he wanted to do was dress up. You know Dad. A man's man.'

Both Francis and I swallowed hard. 'Dilys,' he said again.

'And – er – did your father accept it in the end?'

'Oh, no. Never expected him to. But my boy will be a great fashion designer one day. He's got talent just *pouring* out of him.'

And then she dozed off again. 'Frightening woman,' whispered Francis.

'Her father's daughter I'd say.'

He laughed. 'And her mother's.'

When we reached the house Alison was bright-eyed and bushy-tailed once more. We woke my aunt very carefully and got her up to bed without fuss. She scarcely came to, she was so tired.

'Lovely of you to look after us, Dilys,' she said. 'If only your poor mother could see you now –'

Her last words, as she perched on the bed while I pulled off her shoes, were, 'Hmm. Nice table lamp. You're surely not going to leave him, dear?'

I kissed her goodnight. Thank God she was going tomorrow and the danger would be past.

Downstairs Francis offered Alison a nightcap. And then another. From the size of the brandies I thought he might have set out to kill her. An idea not entirely anathema to me. Eventually she went again. Just went. Mid-sentence. One minute she was upright and managing discernible, if slow, enunciation, something to the effect that she thought Francis was trying to get her drunk – a highly enviable bit of transference – and the next she had sunk sideways like a rag doll. I felt no pity for her. She had had her chances. There was something altogether hard about her – something unconcerned about the rest of the world – and it wasn't to do with the drink. It was selfishness, seeing herself at the centre of things. In her blood it was. Until she re-entered my life I had no idea how much harm she and her mother had done.

As we plopped her on to the bed, her hat made its comical way down over her eyes, the veil rumpling and catching untidily round one of her ears. I pulled it off her head, dropped it to the floor and trod on it, grinding it with my toe. Francis bent down, picked it up and put it neatly on the dressing table. 'Better now?' he said.

Alison snored gently on.

My aunt's ability to overlook her daughter's interesting take on social drinking had become wonderfully apparent after the ceremony, back at Pauline's house. She apparently failed to notice the amount that Darling Ally consumed in the matter of the wake's popped corks and was quite unperturbed by her falling asleep on my cousin's settee.

'She was up very early to get here,' said Auntie Liza, 'so she's taking a little rest.'

Later, when I woke her because it was time to leave, she asked if I could give her a little dab of perfume. I handed her my Arpège, and as she took it and looked at the name, she gave such a smirk of surprise that I was momentarily near to tears with rage.

237

'She was firing on all guns, never mind the drink,' I said to Francis as we undressed. 'I'm still picking out the shrapnel.'

'Listen,' said Francis, 'all that is over. You are here and you are not that child any more. Don't let Darling Ally get to you.'

I found myself thinking, with a newfound bitterness, What does he know? And wishing, oddly, that my sister had been there. She would have understood. I might have inured myself from any real depth of feeling as a child, but it was sure coming out in me now. I began to see why Virginia was so unforgiving.

I climbed into bed feeling as if I had spent the day on the Somme. Francis moved closer. He smelled of soap and comfort and home. 'Don't let her get to you,' he repeated.

'I won't,' I said. He wanted to hold me, but I rolled away and lay with my back to his. I wanted Matthew, who smelled of everything dangerous, desirable and free, and I feigned sleep.

17

The Ideal Husband

I was irritable the next morning. I had hoped to deliver both our guests to their respective stations, and then go on to see Matthew. But Francis was determinedly supportive. 'Of course I'll come with you,' he said. And that was that. I felt defeated, too tired, too emotionally charged, to argue coherently. Besides – what could I say? Here was my husband doing the kind of things that women who *don't* get such treatment tell their therapists they want, so I could hardly tell him to leave me alone, which is all I wanted. Ironical, life. Highly ironical.

The two of them might have left before lunch, which was Francis's whispered suggestion, but I decided to take them on the slow and detailed guided tour of Holmes Towers. Childish I suppose, but the raincoat, the shoes, the nits needed to be exorcised. Material goods were the best way to do it, and it really did make me feel better. Especially when I pulled the wardrobe door right back and saw my cousin's somewhat dull-eyed, but nevertheless impressed, expression. I ran my hand along the tweed and wool and the jersey and the satin and saw it all as if for the first time. 'Well, we all collect far too many clothes,' I said, 'don't we? I just can't stop buying them.'

Francis walked away.

I even made her look at the en suite so that I could point out the amber taps and fittings from an old twenties hotel in Perugia. Balm on that old wound. The bathroom of my childhood was a grimy, scabrous affair with a decaying monster of a geyser that scarcely produced enough for a footbath. I wondered if she remembered that. It was also on the tip of my tongue to ask her if she remembered my last visit, the one of the Poor Relation, when I turned up without a toothbrush. Because, as I innocently announced to my aunt and cousin on arrival, we could afford either the train ticket, or the toothbrush, but not both. I told them we had had to feel down the backs of the chairs and the old settee with its spilling horsehair – a job I hated, always imagining I would find mice. There we found the required sixpence to make up the cost of the half-price tube ticket. Oh my, didn't they snigger. I remembered the snigger particularly. And my aunt immediately marched me off to their bathroom – clean and sweet and lovely – to wash my hands. I was also bought a toothbrush, which I loved, but was made to leave it behind 'for next time'. Old Meanies.

After the amber taps and the clothes, I took her to Francis's study with its massive old desk and booklined walls.

'Ooh,' said Alison. 'He does read a lot.'

'A lot of those are mine,' I said airily. 'All the art books.'

She looked impressed. But then I blew it by descending to the kitchen and becoming no better than an advert for fitted domesticity.

'Here's the extractor – see how it pops out at a switch – and these window seats are storage as well –' On and on I went. By the time I had finished the extended tour they were in no doubt that I had everything my heart desired. And that what my heart desired were the things that money could buy. Particularly, it seemed, a wardrobe full of clothes, fitted Wilton and white goods. I did manage to stop short of plunging them into the cellar to see our wine. I thought darling Ally might never leave if I did that. Throughout it all my aunt tottered along in the background, peering and touching and cooing and occasionally nudging me as if she were Redemption Incarnate.

Finally we set them on their journeys and began driving home. A miserable fog descended. One visit from my aunt and my cousin and the whole perfect mirror world shattered. I began crying great big tears of both rage and self-pity.

Where was Carole, who would have understood? And why didn't I have a proper sister to share it all with? As soon as we got home Francis insisted that I went straight to bed. Making no suggestion of joining me there. I was too tired to even make a phone call. And I did sleep. I'd done it. Got through the Big Lie all in one piece. But as Matthew would say, For What?

When I woke up I felt better. There was a message on my mobile asking how it had all gone, and I was suddenly desperate to get over to Paddington that night. But I was unlucky. Downstairs I made tea and chatted fairly perkily, so that Francis – who I hoped might go to his chambers and catch up on some papers – booked us a table at our old favourite restaurant instead. He was interestingly confused when he came back and announced this, and I went from perkily chatting wifey to glowering spoiled baby. Of course, he could unbook it if I wasn't up to it. But I could hardly say that I didn't want to go, and then say I was going out. In any case, to where? My aunt no longer lived in Paddington and Lichfield was just a bit too far away for a quick round of cocktails. I was stuck. I felt stuck. I felt thoroughly miserable again, actually. So much so that, perhaps out of envy for the obvious blunting it provided Alison, I drank far too much. At least a bottle and a half of wine with the dinner. Francis stoically refused to say anything critical. Which made me go at it all the more, like a defiant child. Thank God it was good wine.

'Like cousin, like cousin,' I hiccupped as he slid me out of the restaurant with a firm, slightly peeved, grip.

In the end he was amused more than anything. 'He's too good to be true,' racketed around in my head. Not fair – why can't he be a bit bad to me? Give me some justification? Hit me or something?

I was silent in the car. Which made it better for me and worse for him. The screw turning. As it was, when we got back home, and fresh from having slept all afternoon, the devil gnawed and I put on the Bryan Ferry CD. Francis sat slumped in a chair, sipping brandy, looking like a defeated man. He seemed to be close to tears.

'I just can't get it right,' he said, and got up to leave.

For one small moment I sensed a victory, instantly followed by deep shame. This was my husband whom I once loved – still did, in a way. The better side of my nature struggled and won.

'Don't go,' I said. 'Not yet.'

He looked at me with a sickening light of hope in his eyes. For some reason, the drink and the music I suppose, I remembered Elvis and Old Shep. Not a very nice thought. Not a very nice sense of power, either.

'Come on,' I insisted. 'Let's dance.'

It was a comfort, being held.

'There is no right,' I said. 'And you are not wrong. I'm just a bitch.'

'No,' he said, and sighed. 'You've had a lot to handle just recently. This funeral business, going back into your past. All sorts of difficult things. It's bound to get to you. I was lucky. You weren't.'

A certain little well of anger bubbled up. A surprising spring of resentment. Yes, he'd had everything. So didn't he deserve –?

'We should just get away,' he said. 'Right away somewhere.'

'Somewhere that feeds the soul,' I said dreamily, remembering Matthew's words.

'Or maybe you need some time on your own?' he said sadly.

There was the moment. Perfect opportunity. I could hear Matthew saying, 'Tell him.' And I failed.

'We'll see,' I murmured into his shoulder.

'Anywhere you like,' he said, at ease again, warm breath against my hair. 'Anywhere at all.' And then he added lightly, 'Money no object.'

The music went on. Here we were, two people, married to each other, nice meal, good wine, house to ourselves – inevitable really. High on drink and the power of my own body, I enjoyed the joke and ignored Matthew and his admonishments. This was my husband after all, my husband who did, indeed, lavish beautiful things upon me. Who did, indeed, provide cupboards of beautiful things for me to drape over my body, slip my feet into, wash my naked, well-fed body in. The devil that was in me gnawed deeper. It was the very least I could do . . . He had bought me, so he could have me, if only for a while.

'Where shall we go?' he said later.

'How about India?' I said, half asleep.

'Lovely,' he said.

'Lovely,' I agreed.

That was the night I called my husband Matthew. But by then he was asleep, breathing deeply and contentedly, and I just ran my fingertips lightly over his back and whispered the name, as if to get inside my own skin again. Then, like that first time all those nights ago, I padded off downstairs on my Doris feet and poured myself a brandy. This time I didn't need the directory – I knew the number to ring.

'What have you been doing?' said my lover sleepily.

'Thinking about you.'

'Come over and get into bed with me.'

'I've drunk too much.'

'Then I'll come over to your bed.'

Silence.

'When?'

'Soon,' I promised.

'Have you told him yet?'

'Soon.'

When I went back to bed, Francis was sleeping. I studied his face for a long time in the moonlight. Peaceful, familiar, benign. I hated every single line of it.

18

A Taste of Money

There was no logic to it. When I woke up the following morning, headache and all, I wanted, suddenly, to see my sister. I wanted to talk to her about all that childhood past. That murky sludge of my mother's life stirred up by Auntie Liza's heedless spoon and Darling Cousin Ally's careless observations. It was something Virginia and I never did talk about, the early days. She refused. In psychobabble, she was in denial – and I couldn't really remember. What I knew was apocryphal, it was hearsay, it was surmising. Now the sketch had become the full-blown painting and I wanted to share that discovery with the only other survivor.

When I told Francis I wanted to go down and see my sister, he thought that I had really blown a mental gasket. The age-old belief that women are eternally borderline mad is an amusing one to observe in men who consider themselves enlightened. A couple of millennia of prejudice are not overcome in a couple of decades, it seems. But I suppose Francis had some justification. I'd spent my life with him trying to avoid such a tectonic confrontation and now, at the point in our marriage when all was potentially secure and serene, I was not only going peculiar in my own domestic right, but I was about – in sisterly terms – to go to war.

He pointed this out. Wearily he suggested that it might, just, be a good idea to go for the quiet life. 'Couldn't we drop the complications and go to India? See how everything is when we get back?'

'It's got to be done,' I said firmly. 'For me.'

'Well, it certainly won't be for *her*,' he said, eyeing me beadily. But he relented. 'What will you do? Go down there to her or –' slight pause, almost indistinguishable had I not known my husband – 'invite her up here?'

'Oh, God,' I groaned. 'Don't ask . . .'

'Poor you,' he said. 'I did say it might be better to wait.' He sounded suspiciously smug. And then he just chuckled. 'Oh, Dilys,' he said. 'Whatever you do will be wrong.'

'So?'

'So do what you want. At least that way someone is happy.'

My turn to look beady. 'I do realize that all Tragedy is supposed to be very close to Comedy,' I said. '*And* that it's no coincidence how all the big agonized Greek stuff – the Medeas, the Agamemnons, the Antigones – is to do with families. But this is not funny.'

'Oh, lighten up, Dilys,' he snapped, suddenly irritated. 'And don't exaggerate. Life is good, isn't it?'

I stared at him. I hadn't heard him use that tone of voice since James, gated for bunking off school, suggested that he would ring Childline. He suddenly looked very angry and there was ice in the stare he returned. 'And you and your sister are hardly the stuff of Greek Tragedy. You've had a bad time. You've put it all behind you. Why do you suddenly have to turn it upside down now? What, for God's sake, is *wrong* with you?'

This was just what I wanted. Francis behaving badly. About time. He left the house scowling and slamming doors, and as I watched the car pull away I vowed to tell him about me and Matthew just as soon as I had talked to my sister. Then, with the past set down, I could walk towards the future clean and whole again. To the place I should have stayed in, beyond the willow trees. This was what I thought, with great relief and feeling fully vindicated, as I watched him crash the gears as the car lurched away up the street. No more lies. And no more ancient, badly buried secrets. That one little bit of Francis's rebellion crystallized everything. Nice was hard to bear. Since the moment I met Matthew, I wanted my husband to stop being nice to me so that I could leave him. And now he had.

245

*

The trouble with my sister is that, not being able to do anything right, I still have to go through the agonizing ritual of
trying – and usually failing – to choose the lesser wrong. In
this case it was quite simple: did I ring her up and say I'd like
to have lunch with her and

(a) wait for her to say that I should go to her house and she
would give me lunch;
(b) suggest that she come up to town to a restaurant for
lunch and that I would pay;
(c) suggest that she come up to town to a restaurant for
lunch and not suggest that I would pay;
(d) suggest that she come up to my house for lunch;
(e) suggest she come up to town to a restaurant and we go
dutch;
(f) suggest I went down there to a restaurant and we went
dutch;
(g) suggest we had lunch down there and I paid;
(h) suggest we take sandwiches somewhere;
(i) suggest we skip lunch, both bring hip flasks and have
vodka slammers instead;
(j) suggest she could do with losing a bit of weight and forget the whole thing?

All of these would be wrong. Francis was quite right. But
which would be the most wrong? I went through the possibilities with him later, when we had both eaten our humble
pie and apologized to each other. He was upset at having
gone off the deep end, I was indifferent. Truce.

At the end of the list he said, stone-faced, that there was
one other possibility.

'What?' I asked eagerly.

'Suggesting inviting her to our house for lunch and then
asking her to pay for it,' at which he fell about laughing.
Another nail in your coffin, oh my husband, I thought sourly.
Nobody has normal families. But there is a wonderful sense

246

of *Schadenfreude*, no doubt, when you spot one that is so much worse than your own.

The absurdity put everything in perspective. I rang Virginia and I said, 'Look, I've got to go to Kingston. Can I buy you lunch? You'd be doing me a real favour.'

'What are you going to Kingston for?' she asked, very nicely.

'Don't ask,' I said, thinking that I'd cobble up something by the time I saw her. Not easy. If I said it was to buy something specific, something that was mysteriously available only in Kingston, I lost on both counts – one for being so snobbishly eclectic, and one for having the money to indulge it.

In the end I asked Petra to give me the name of a good vegetarian restaurant in the vicinity, and then to give her blessing by telling the whopping lie that she wanted me to do some market research by visiting it. I thought this was remarkably clever – the mind becomes infantile in such situations – but Petra, like most vegetarians, is not given to lying – it goes with the territory. In the end she nodded grudgingly and pursed her lips much as she did when her children stepped out of line.

Francis was highly amused at my delight in the plan. Insensitive bastard, I thought, hungry for such failures.

'One – Love,' he said, wielding an imaginary racquet. He shook his head, his mouth showing the trace of a smile. 'I had no idea you were such a consummate liar.'

'Must have got it from my aunt,' I said sharply. But he ignored the irony.

'Only by marriage, dear. Oh yes . . . I thank my stars that I'll never have to cross-examine you in court.'

Was there an edge to it? Who cared. I was nearly free. I just smiled all sweet and dovelike and hoped it hid my black, black heart. He returned the smile, relieved, I suppose. The mad wife in the attic returns, docile, to the kitchen.

'If it all gets too much, just hang on to the idea of India and spiritual solace,' he said, half amused. 'Recommend it to your sister. She could do with a bit of soul soothing . . .'

On the morning of the day in question, as we breakfasted, he spread out some brochures and a couple of new, inches-thick guidebooks on the table. 'Don't forget,' he said, 'we'll need shots and stuff.'

'Oh, but I've had them.'

He gave me a sharp look.

Bugger: wrong man, wrong holiday.

'Last time we went,' tripped smoothly off my tongue. I smiled. 'But I'll check if they're out of date.'

Then he, thank God, set off for chambers, and I, thank God, set off for Paddington . . . An interesting route to take to get to Kingston but needs must.

Of course, all my good intentions about sitting Matthew down and having a good talk and sorting a few things out and all those other platitudes melted away in the hot fire of not having seen each other for nearly a week. He, too, had all *his* Indian stuff spread out over the bed, though none of the same glossy brochures or books.

'I've done an itinerary, a list of everything you'll need to pack, and all the stuff about health. You can look at it all later,' he said, shoving it into my bag. 'You'll see the real India but we won't be staying in the Holiday Inns of this world and you have to be careful.'

'I've never stayed in a Holiday Inn in my life,' I said with mock indignation. 'We only ever stayed in Maharajahs' Palaces.'

'Well, an Indian three-star is a *little* different.'

His eyes were bright as stars and his smile had nothing to do with indigenous diseases. He reminded me of a child in a sweetie shop and I laughed. I was already pulling his shirt over his head. 'I don't care as long as I'm there with you.' I went to kiss him, but he pulled back.

'Have you talked to –'

But India, Francis, everything, could wait.

'Tonight.'

'I mean it,' he said.

'So do I.'

I had forgotten how I became so young again, with that sense of being exactly where I wanted to be. Matthew was right. As I always knew he was right when we were together. This could not go on; there was no point in living and not being with the one person who made me feel alive.

'We are both in suspension,' he said afterwards. 'I exist only in a tiny corner of your life – the rest of it, most of your days and nights, are a complete mystery to me, and me to them. None of the people who are important to you know about me, and none of the people I know – my friends and my family – really know about you, except in a half-hinted way. They don't know if you're married, if you're halfway through a terminal illness, if you've got three heads . . . Some of them think you are under-age, some of them think you must be about ninety, some of them think you are famous – they all speculate on the wildest possibilities and I just want them to meet you and to know who you are . . . Like normal – you remember normal?'

'I live normal. Too bloody normal.'

'Well, we're going to have to spend some time finding our own normal and that won't be easy. We're not exactly rushing,' he said. 'It is six months.'

'Nearly.'

'Are you sure you can abandon your middle-class trappings?' He gave me a teasing look. We'd played this game before. 'Can She Live Without Them.'

'Not only can she, but she will – this very night. I just want to square the circle with Virginia. If I don't settle the past I can't begin all over again. In my heart I'm ready.'

He looked at me sceptically. But it was true. Things had begun to mock me since my aunt's visit. The well-kept exterior of the house, the neat front path. The comfortable, quietly stylish chairs and couches. Bookcases and cabinets for drink, for the hi-fi, for the television. The carpets and the heavy, last-for-ever curtains. The wallpapers and the paint finishes, the number of Italian lamps that gave out their discreet evening glow. The picture frames of happy families scattered throughout the house. The Ivon Hitchens and the early Hodgkin prints. The rugs from who knew where, those amber taps, the glass, the china, the cutlery for daily use and the canteen of cutlery for high days. The polished, polished furniture . . .

I looked around Matthew's bedroom. I could see it in the paucity of his clothes, the impromptu nature of posters just tacked up on the backs of doors, the lack of personal effects, the way the books were stacked against the walls since Jacqueline took the bookcases and they were not replaced – it was space ready to move on from at any time, and he was ready to do it, one of those enviable aliens you sometimes see with only a rucksack and a few bulging pockets to denote their homestead. On the dusty window ledge were our egg cups. The only symbols of future joint possessions. Right to be there because they had meaning, resonance. They were not like all that lifetime-of-living stuff Francis and I displayed in our house like a discreet version of Hindu marriage gold. It was my youth I was looking at – uncluttered first love – the youth and first love I turned my back on when I said 'Yes' at Henley.

I might have understood love texts before, but I never knew until Matthew and that spare, unencumbered bedroom how well Shakespeare knew his lovers – always wanting it to be the nightingale and never the lark . . . But one thing I will say for the tyrant that is my sister: even the urgent needs of love bent their trembling knee before her. Despite a very strong desire to close the skimpy curtains, unplug the telephone, and stay in bed together all day, I had to get up. I washed every last bit of the scent of our illicit liaison from my body, bestowed a promise upon my unenlightened lover to enlighten him, and set off for Kingston attempting to remove the smirk from my face, pushing all the brochures and general stuff about India as far down in my bag as it would go.

All I needed was my sister to find out I was having yet another exotic holiday and that'd kill all conversation until Christmas.

'Tell her about me,' was his highly amused parting shot. 'She can be the first to know. She'd like that . . .'

I gave him a queenly wave and drove off. I had a sudden icicle thrust right through my spine at the thought of what she would say if I told her about him. Or rather, of course, when.

As we sat opposite each other amid the pine-panelling, country feelgood checked tablecloths, scrubbed waitresses and yoga music and sipped our cranberry juices, Virginia said, 'Have you lost weight?'

Coming from her this was not an expression of anxiety; it was a gauntlet thrown down.

'Perhaps just a little,' I mumbled into the juice-that-dare-not-speak-its-aim – cranberry being the *woman's* drink – and I almost added that I'd try harder not to in future. Instead I fired a shot. Dangerous but I felt like danger. 'You'd have lost weight if you'd been running around with Francis and three old ducks and Darling Cousin Ally.'

'Well, you did volunteer,' she said sharply.

'That's not a criticism of you, Ginny,' I said, putting the fun away and remembering to tiptoe on eggshells.

'I should hope not.'

Then she seemed to retract, not that you could ever tell if my sister was retracting, saying sorry or having a seizure – they all looked the same on her face where I was concerned. Nevertheless, a shadow of remorse crossed her face.

'We don't do this enough,' she said.

'We don't,' I agreed.

'Mind you . . .' she said.

Here we go, I thought.

'. . . there's never been much room left over in your life for me – what with the career and the family and –'

'You have family, too. Just as much as I do.'

'But you had Carole,' she added. 'I always envied you that friendship . . . You must miss her.'

She said this with uncustomary sympathy. Suddenly I was back in that bleak Bristol station again, staring at the railway lines, feeling that huge cold hollow inside. It was just six months, half a year, nothing in terms of grief. Matthew was the only warm thing I had now. I wanted to tell her, bring down the barriers. She was my sister. Why not? And then she beeped, blushed and started rooting around in her bag.

'Virginia!' I couldn't help crowing, 'You've got a *mobile* . . . You always said they were pretentious. Oh, how the mighty have fallen –'

She had the grace to look half amused, half exasperated. 'I needed it to get in touch with Bruce, and it was free with my new washing machine.'

I couldn't resist it. 'Glad you've got a new washing machine.'

'Well, the other one was –'

'A million years old. Bruce has a lot of dungarees to wash, it isn't a luxury . . .'

She debated which way to go at that piece of sisterly piss-taking and then – there was that seizure again – she gave up and laughed too.

I took out my phone and asked her to tell me her number so that I could key it in. She looked pleased and did so. And then she keyed in mine. We were equals.

'Oh –' I said excitedly, 'we can send each other text messages. And you can look up John and Petra's web page on it and –'

I realized she was looking at me very stonily. I had cracked a thousand shells. Around my ankles ran all the yellow and white of all the yolks and albumen in our fragile world. Virginia's mobile phone was not state-of-the-art anything. Free with a washing machine did not entitle you to the Philippe Starck of hi-tech. What on earth were we doing

252

unravelling ourselves over something so stupid as a mobile phone when I was about to turn my whole world – and to some extent hers – inside out, upside down and sideways? Bugger it, I thought, in a mad and very dangerous moment. If my sister was at her best with me when I was in trouble, she could cop hold of this lot. Matthew, I wanted to scream. I'm in love with Matthew. That was so big and dark and frightening that she'd be my friend for life. I needed to tell someone so badly it made me ache, and surely, surely this was what sisters were put on the planet for.

I said, 'Virginia, I've met a man –'

But she put up her hand.

'Don't even begin to tell me how you know someone who can get it adjusted for me – attach this, put in that, twiddle this, change my sodding life with a flick of his wrist . . .'

It did occur to me that, quite without knowing it, she was making a pretty good summation of Matthew. But then, abruptly, it was all over. She leaned across the table, pointed her finger at my telephone, and jabbed the air. 'You just tell me how often you've needed three-quarters of the stuff those things can do . . .'

And she sat back, folded her arms, and looked triumphant.

I shook my head. 'You're right.'

She smiled. 'I know I am.'

We put our phones away. She leaned across the table and rested her chin on her hands. 'Now,' she said, 'tell me all about Auntie Liza. And dear poisonous cousin Alison. No doubt she's made a great success of her life – as indeed she ought to given the money and effort that went into it, if I –'

'Dear poisonous cousin Alison drinks.'

'*Drinks?*' Virginia looked delighted. 'What, you mean –?'

'Uh-huh – like a fish. And Auntie Liza manages to call it tiredness, or getting a little over-excited or just plain ignores it. Oh – and she married an Egyptian. Auntie Liza refers to him as a prince, of course.'

'Of course.'

'Anyway, Alison is now divorced from him – and one of her sons is gay . . .'

Safe ground at last.

'Gay?' said Virginia, smiling with tremendous satisfaction. 'Crikey Moses.'

I took her reverting to the Bunty lexicon of swearing to mean she was much moved. And then, in one of her penetrating, and very occasional, shafts of wisdom, she added, 'Well, by the law of averages someone in the family was bound to be –'

I let that one lie.

'And Eliza is just the same old snobbish Eliza – smokescreens to disguise life's reality, everything is for the best and in the best of possible taste. And she lives in such a little flat in such a dismal part of town now. It's a far cry from the gabled semi with garage.'

'Is she happy?'

I hadn't thought about it before but now I remembered those parting words called from that shabby doorstep. If you live a lie for long enough, presumably it loses its sting.

'Yes,' I said. 'I think she really is.'

'Well, not many people can say they're happy come the end, now can they?' said Virginia bitterly. 'Look at Mum.'

We looked at each other. There was the past, suddenly, lying between us like a great dark stain. I opened my mouth to speak, but she was too quick for me.

'Lichfield though,' said Virginia, wrinkling her nose. 'Lichfield?'

'Oh, Lichfield is very nice,' I said. 'The cathedral is stunning and it's got a lovely close –'

Mistake. Already Virginia was bridling.

'Yes, well,' she said, 'I've never been . . .'

As usual the implication was that some of us were filthy rich hedonists who did nothing but – in this case – travel around from cathedral town to cathedral town just to be able to show off our knowledge to our sisters . . .

I smiled humbly and said, 'But Liza's nowhere near the centre. Stuck out on the edge – dumped really – well, that was the feeling I got. Alison seems to have inherited what wealth there was.'

'How are the mighty fallen, Grandma would have said.'

Just for once we were bonding. I began to think that it might, after all, be the right thing to do.

'Dear old Grandma. I really miss her.'

'She was a cow to me,' I said.

Virginia ignored this as she always did. 'Well, Liza deserves it. Talk about humiliations . . . When I think how she treated us. How our mother stood it, I don't know. I'd have given her what-for if she tried it on with me.'

'Liza was very . . . interesting about Mum. They were very good friends apparently – shared secrets . . .'

I saw Virginia's eyes cloud just as they always did when the past was mentioned. 'She couldn't stand her. Nobody in the family could.'

'I don't think it was always like that.'

'No?' Virginia's eyes were hard.

'Anyway, everyone has their own hidden reasons for the way they turn out.' I tried to make it sound as light as possible. 'After all, look at us . . .'

'Us? What do you mean? Nothing secret about you and me. You've done very well for yourself and left me standing.'

'And for reasons I don't understand it gets up your nose –'

The eyes remained stony but Virginia said nothing.

'Why?' I asked.

'What do you mean, why?'

'Well, why should me doing very well get up your nose? Usually families enjoy each other's successes.'

'In your dreams. Anyway, it wouldn't if you didn't flaunt it.'

'I don't.'

'You use money like some people use bog roll.'

That was too much. Even she saw that. 'Sorry,' she said. 'That's not fair.'

'You must think it if you say it. *Why?*'

'Oh, because –'

'Yes –'

'How are *yew* . . .? And today's specials are Parmesan Tabouleh with Chillied Olives, Aubergine and Crisped Almond Bruschetta, Fresh Green Pea Soup –'

In a relieved voice Virginia said, 'Soup please.'

I, absently, longing to get back to the interesting point, also opted for the soup. At which point my sister said, 'You can't,' and kicked me. At which point something in my rabbit humility broke. Bog roll indeed. I wasn't ten years old, for heaven's sake, and despite Bunty and the Crikey Moses, we were *both* grown-ups.

'Soup,' I said again, more loudly.

When Virginia said, warningly, 'Dilys, you must not have the same as me –' I saw red.

'Why the bloody hell not?' I said, my voice rising. 'I'm sick and tired of watching my step with you and if I bloody well want green sodding pea soup, I'll have green sodding pea soup.'

Up came my jaw, out went my chin. I *was* ten years old after all, and this was my moment. That it had to centre on a bowl of organic green pea soup was, I grant you, something of a bathos, but the blood was up at last. After all, I was about to blow up my entire family, metaphorically speaking, and run off to India with my freewheeling lover – why not go for broke and blow up the chance of sisterly union as well? Soup or not.

Virginia looked down at her place setting very, very meekly. 'Well, I think the whole restaurant got that, Dilly . . . All right, I'll have the bruschetta.'

Crikey Moses, I thought, I've won.

'Anything to drink with that?' asked the nervous waitress.

'Yes,' I snapped. 'We'll have a bottle of something really good – and I will pay for it.'

I defied Virginia to say anything, but she was still looking at her place setting. The waitress backed away to get the wine list. Then I saw that Virginia's shoulders were moving. Oh my God, I'd made her cry. Well, no going back now. 'Ginny?' I said sternly.

'Yes?' she mumbled.

'I *needed* to assert myself. You can't always be in control, you know. It's not good for you.' Even to me, from up on my high horse, this sounded pretty prissy.

The shoulders went on shaking, the head remained downcast. But of course, she wasn't crying at all. She was laughing.

'You Complete Dope,' she said, selecting from the Famous Five this time. 'I wasn't telling you what to eat – I was thinking of Petra and John's market research. It's no use both of us reporting back on sodding green pea soup, now is it?'

Later, the soup and bruschetta dispatched, and a conversation of disproportionately fine detail regarding the merits of either dish being finished, and, I suppose, emboldened by the wine, I tried to steer us towards a more meaningful conversation. Virginia slipped right into it, smooth as soap in the bath. She watched me sip at my second glass of wine and then said, very typically, 'I suppose if you get done for drink-driving all Francis has to do is have a word with the local magistrate . . .'

Perfect opening. I put down my glass, took a deep breath, and said, 'Virginia, why do you always have to put me down?'

She blinked.

'And why do you think of me and money as some kind of wicked confederacy?'

'Because you've got it and you know how to use it – and bloody hell you do . . .'

I was shocked at the anger. 'Virginia, what have I ever done to you?'

She raised equally shocked eyebrows in return as if to say, '*Moi?*'

'Yes, you! I've had one glass of wine and about a tablespoon of my next glass and you've already got me bang to rights on drunk-driving and my husband slipping the

authorities a greasy tenner . . . Helluva stretch of the imagina-
tion, that.'

'Oh, don't exaggerate. Money speaks.'

'Virginia, you're the one who exaggerates. It's as if you
can't find any good in me –'

She looked at me with her '*Moi?*' again. 'You don't need me
to find any good in you. You've done very well for yourself.'

'There you go again – making a compliment into a criticism . . .'

'Well, do you think you deserve all the luck?' Her voice had
risen. Whatever well she drew that up from was very deep
and very, very murky. 'I mean – I was – it was always me –
and then you –'

'What does that mean?'

'You make of it what you will . . .'

'No – I'd like you to explain. It couldn't be anything as simple as jealousy – could it?'

Virginia sat bolt upright and looked absolutely outraged.
Also close to tears. But we were saved by the Spanish
omelette which was placed before me. The cautious waitress
gave Virginia her seared peppers tagliatelle with a little look
of sympathy. It was quite odd to seem to be on the reverse
side of sane when out with my sister. The opposite was usually true – even to her stalking off and shouting that I was a
patronizing little pig and leaving a Kentish publican gaping,
when the four of us went away for a weekend (the only time)
and I attempted to explain a point of travel procedure. In
short, she had directed us down the wrong country lane and
was banging on about how she just couldn't understand it . . .
The map had to be wrong. It was, of course, my map.

The trouble with people like Virginia is that people like me
try so hard not to offend that those fragile eggshells are very,
very old. When they do finally crack, and they always do,
they send up a real stink. I went through hoops of linguistic
nicety in that Kentish pub as I tried to point out that east was
– er, well now – usually to be found somewhere around the

opposite of west. Bruce, after giving me a guilty but sympathetic smile, went scurrying after her like a frightened rabbit. Francis groaned in commiseration, and we didn't see them again – in any meaningful sense – until the Sunday we were due back. But at least then I knew that the others knew that it was *her* behaviour that was nuts. Not mine.

This time the waitress had cast me in the role of villain, an unfairness that only made me more determined to get to the bottom of all this pent-up whatever it was. Being with my aunt and having my horrible past stirred up, and hearing how she dealt with her own, greased my determination. That and a sudden memory of a conversation I had some years ago, shortly after the 'east is west' debacle, with a psychoanalyst I met at a party. I was so desperate that I did that unforgivable thing of collaring him in front of the cheeseboard. He was kind and summed the situation up pretty accurately.

'Totally insecure people think the world is trying to get at them and – more often than not – this boils down to a sense of being patronized.'

'Well, I don't know why she should feel so insecure,' I said crisply, 'when I don't . . .'

He raised an eyebrow at that.

'Have you tried asking her?' he said, quite firmly.

'Well, we both had the same upbringing.'

'Nobody has the same upbringing,' he said, even more firmly.

'She doesn't want to talk about it.'

'People who don't want to talk about things are usually frightened or unhappy about those things. Why not try?'

Twenty years on from his suggestion, here we were. Why not? What did my sister have in her cupboard that was so different from mine? I looked at my omelette. Then, looking up quickly, I saw Virginia's eyes flick from my plate to hers. She was *comparing bloody dishes* . . . This was ridiculous. Oh, well – in for a penny, in for a greasy tenner. I took a defiant swig of the Pinot, and began.

259

'Ginny,' I said, 'when I was with Auntie Liza and Alison it didn't half stir up some reminders. All that stuff about our being the poor relations and being patronized –'

I saw her wince. Why, I wondered, does the idea of being patronized nearly kill my sister and only slightly graze me?

'And it made me wonder about us – you and me – and why there is the . . . gulf between us.'

She went on eating and did not look up.

'Why you always seemed so angry with me, and with the world, when you were such a star – everybody liked you, you were beautiful, you were clever, you were everything you could want – and I was just a squidgy lump of nothingness by comparison . . .'

She dug into her tagliatelle as if she were gouging out eyes, and then threw down her fork. The clatter made everyone nearby look up.

'That's just it,' she hissed, grabbing her glass and clenching her fist around it so that her knuckles were white. 'You *were* just a, well, nonentity really – a nuisance – nobody thought you were much to be reckoned with – and now look at you . . .'

'You mean *money*?'

'I mean everything. The complete chameleon. All the trappings that go with absolute success. You'll never have to want for a thing – you never have to wonder if your husband loves you, or if your children and your grandchildren want to be with you, or if you ought to go on that holiday, or have that meal . . . You've overtaken me – everyone – and all without pain or shame. I was brought up to believe I was somebody. I had expectations – you had none. That Nirvana of the Psyche that we are all supposed to aim for –'

'Hey, hey,' I almost shouted. 'Where did you pick all that stuff up from? Nirvana of the Psyche?'

Virginia was pleased. 'I read it in a book,' she said. 'You don't know everything.' She had the upper fist now. 'Unlike me, you had no expectations as you grew up and therefore nothing fazes you – you can speak to a duke or you can speak to a –'

'Dyke?'

She had the grace to smile. 'You don't see it because you're living it. You can afford to laugh at it because you've got it. But I'd like to see you cope with what I have to cope with. To meet someone at a party who says to Bruce, "And what do you do for a living?"'

'That's a very ill-bred thing to do –'

'There you go again, pretending to be the Duchess . . . And then, when Bruce says he's a plumber, I have to watch their eyes glaze, or they start talking about a leak they've got or something – you become tradesman class.'

'Virginia, you can't expect me to take this seriously. Bruce is an artist among –'

'He's a fucking *plumber*, Dilly. So stop turning it into art . . .'

'Fucking plumber' also drew the eyes of our co-lunchers. We were certainly giving good value. I buttoned my lip. Nothing for it but to let my sister have her say. I didn't like it. But at least she was saying *something* at last.

She took another swig of her wine. 'Oh, nothing is real for you because you've never had to go through that kind of humiliation. Having no expectations is easy. It's when you've got them and they're taken away from you. Even when we were little and the very worst stuff was going on at home, you were too young to know any better . . . Whereas *I* lost something wonderful . . . A mother who doted on me, a home that was full of nice things and pretty clothes . . . Cuddles, warm fires. And then That Man came home, and Mum was pregnant and tried to kill herself, and there was nothing in the house to eat, and he was raging around. Grandma, who adored me, had to go and live somewhere else. I'd never been hit in my life, never been punished, but he hit me – for looking at him, for spilling his beer when I poured it, for breathing. He never hit you. He called you his one, true own. "At least this one's mine for sure," he said. Then, when he finally went away for good and we were left in the cold and the dark, you never stopped crying. You were always there – in the bed, on her lap, sucking at her – she didn't want you but she had to look after you, which meant she couldn't look after me. And the aunts and cousins all gloated because I had been a little princess and I wasn't ever going to be like that any more. I should never have married Bruce. When I saw what you got, it made me feel ill –'

She stopped and drained her glass.

I had to stop myself from saying, 'Well now, Virginia, don't pussyfoot – if you've got something to say you just come right on out and say it . . .' But I didn't, thank God. I just sat there, waiting, with all the happiness leaking out of me, draining away. To be hated that much? Virginia had waited a lifetime to say all this and I had invited it. I thought I was so strong. Invincible, me. I could scarcely tell her to put a sock in it now and walk away.

I refilled her glass. She didn't even notice.

'Oh, yes, little sister. Something hardened in my heart – I must have been six or so and I thought, Oh God, now I'm going to have to look after my mother . . . And that fool of a baby that nobody wants. I'll never be happy again. At the age of *six*, Dilys, I thought that and – do you know – I never was. It was all your fault. Oh, what on earth did you have to go and get born for? Did you know that? Is that what made you so – so –' she searched for the word – 'unmoved. That's what you were. Unmoved by it all. Immune. For God's sake, didn't being unwanted hurt?'

Virginia's pain was so palpable and shocking that I could only hide my fear of it and concentrate on the practical. I had no idea what being unwanted as a child felt like – because to feel unwanted you had to know what it was to feel wanted.

She was waiting, breathing through her nose like a dragon, eyes hard and bright as polished glass.

'I don't think so,' I said carefully. 'I just . . . well . . . got on with it – I just lived. Got up in the morning, took a breath and the day was what the day was – I don't think I ever asked for anything to be better, I just floated through it all, took the knocks as well as the pleasures and carried on. I remember when I took what I could find – what we could afford – to harvest festival at school and it was three potatoes and two oranges, and the bag burst and Mr and Mrs Corbett and the Corbett girls from number nine laughed – I expected nothing either worse or better. I just picked them up from the floor and put them on the school platform and went back to my seat . . . walking past their whispering as if it didn't belong to me.'

'Didn't you want revenge?'

'Never crossed my mind. They had what they had, and I had what I had, and that was the pecking order. It could be home-grown marrows and baskets of beautifully polished fruit, or affection, or clothes. When I had no shoes until Mum's pay day I just stayed away from school until I got some. It was all the same to me –'

'You coped with those years – all that – very well,' she said grudgingly. 'I mean before you met Francis and *you* became the golden princess.'

'I don't remember much of it.'

'That's how you coped. Immune. Unmoved. I remember every living moment. Mum's black eyes, the bruised arms, her missing tooth, the tears – and worse – the silence, the ambulance, the tipped over bottle of pills and whisky, being thrown down the stairs by my father, the night the bailiffs came and took everything away . . . everything except you. They left only the bed you were born in where you lay with my mother, and my bed which was on the other side of the room. You lay wailing and being comforted and sucking on that breast while I was banished, to the thorns, to the thicket, to the tower. I grew up being the golden princess. And my father, the rich and fabled king, was away on the high seas – and my mother was queen of her little palace, and we had fine clothes and held our heads high and there was a wonderful fairy godmother who looked after me and adored me and one day I would marry a prince –'

'Ginny,' I said. 'Have you gone raving mad?'

But there was no stopping her. Half the tables were listening, too.

'. . . And along came a changeling – thin, unhappy, wailing, unwelcome – and it – this changeling – brought the whole palace down on everyone's head . . . All the good fairies surrounding this unhappy newcomer immediately recognized that she was the evil-bringer, the ne'er-do-well, but the thirteenth fairy, the one who had not been invited along with all the others, whispered over her cot and said – though nobody heard it – that one day she should have luck, she should have money, fulfilment, a good husband of high standing, and love and affection and a beautiful family to compensate her for her life as a poor little changeling child. These things, said the thirteenth fairy, will sustain her through her life. The rest of you may think you have it all, but she will show you eventually that you have *nothing*. She will have the riches of the pocket and the riches of the heart, and she will never lose them.'

Ginny laughed, raised her glass, smiled her halfway bitter little smile and said, 'And of course, you will never do that, little sister, will you? You may be sweet and generous-natured as everyone says, but you are not a fool. That's the sand you are built on. Mine is Bruce. I chose him because he was a good, quiet, reliable man who I thought would be kind.'

'He is kind. Very kind.'

'With a decent job – plumbing – that would never go out of fashion . . .'

'But you loved him?' I said.

'I loved him loving me. That felt safe . . . He was never going to turn my world upside down and break my heart – or my neck. But I hadn't lived, Dilly. I hadn't lived.'

Those scullers, that willow, a decision that It Would Do.

'Me, too,' I said.

But Virginia wasn't hearing that.

264

'Oh, you. You got the lot. Jackpot. All the things I didn't know about and suddenly wanted. And you didn't even have to wait. Not even twenty and along comes Francis and it's the love match of the decade, golden coach and all –'

'Oh now, Ginny – that's going a bit far –'

'Oh now, Dilly – you were barely nineteen and the throne of life was handed to you on a plate.'

'I grabbed it too, just like you did, and probably for the same reasons.'

She looked at me sceptically. 'You always were a patronizing little runt,' she said.

Quite warmly I thought, in the circumstances. I was only glad, given the wiggling ears all around us, that she hadn't substituted a 'c' for the 'r'.

'Thank you,' I said.

'Don't mention it. Anyway, you've got your insurance policy against whatever lies hidden inside. What's that thing somebody said – about the centre will not hold?'

'Yeats,' I said. 'Irish poet.'

'I bloody well know who Yeats is,' she said. 'I just couldn't remember who said it. I'll remind you that I got to grammar school and you didn't.'

'And I'll remind you that I didn't know enough to care about that, either. And you did.'

'*Touché*,' she said. 'Anyway, nothing is going to fall apart for Mr and Mrs Perfect One, now is it? Whereas over here, in the black corner, representing the three ugly sisters and assorted wicked Queens –'

I should have thought before I spoke. I should have but I was so mesmerized by what I'd heard, so caught up in the whole drama of it – of the *truth* at last, after all these years of blankness or innuendo – that I forgot to tiptoe and crashed mightily on.

'Ginny?' I said, all cosy and conversationally. 'Have you ever thought about having therapy?'

Of that moment I think I shall probably remember most the

waitress's eyes goggling like a frog's as she watched my sister push back her seat much too sharpish, stand up, and then be immediately accosted by the man behind her into whose soup-drinking back she had just thrust her chair and who, as a consequence, had upended his plate all over the table so that its contents spread, like a pool of green algae, towards his lunch companion – a pretty young woman – now a surprised and pretty young woman – who was not, it seemed, best pleased to find pea soup – organic or otherwise – dripping into her neat little lap.

I ran after my sister, who, on reaching the door, turned, raised her finger and said in a voice so venomous that I had to take a step back lest the spit of it kill me, 'Don't come after me and *don't* ever, ever try to get in touch with me again. *You* – the very thought that *you*, who started all this mess, should suggest I'm mentally deranged – *I* need psychiatry – well, it just shows – it just shows – that You Are Off Your Trolley –'

And then she went.

Somewhere in the ether I heard Francis's voice, guide and mentor, saying, 'Oh, *Dilys* – how could you?'

And Matthew's amused one saying, 'Tell her – she'll be pleased.'

I returned to the other, more immediate, mess and apologized to everyone. I gave the waitress a healthy tip, I gave the pretty young lunching companion over and above the odds to pay her dry-cleaning bill and I paid for their meal. All without blinking. I came out into the beautiful September afternoon having put that bit of the world to rights, and I realized, with a sudden resounding clanging in the area of the skull, that – as my sister said – I had just been passing around the greasy tenner. I saw it. In a flash of reversal. She Who Had Nothing Now Has It All. There, on the pavement, with the sun shining down and the old market town awash with shops and banks and credit facilities, I was the goddess of the mountain top. This was my world. A chocolate box ready to be raided. A world of ease and pleasure and indulgence and happiness . . . I had succumbed to temptation, cast myself down into it, and the angels had not saved me. It was a world in which I could go to a bank and order any amount of travellers' cheques for my cost-any-amount holiday. A world in which, after doing that, and given that Kingston has some decent shops, I'd probably buy myself some nice lightweight clothes for the trip, and then go home and book a hairdressing appointment, have a leg wax, maybe a facial. I would drive myself to and from these places in my nice new car. Waiting for me, at the end of the day, there would be a comfortable, unostentatiously well-furnished house in a wealthy part of London. In it would be a kind, good, loving husband, father to my two happy, loving sons and their happy, loving families. None of us would ever want. Virginia was right. These were the blessings, the thoughtless blessings, the structure and foundations of my life. They had grown from rocky ground, a miracle. And I was about to cut them all down, pull up their roots, with someone called Matthew, whom I loved more than I had ever loved anyone, even my children.

'Fuck,' I said to a pair of swans passing by under the bridge. But they floated on, blissfully unaware and naturally without any sympathy, of course. In their world, too, you mate for life.

I went to sit by the river and think – and to wonder where that thirteenth fairy might be lurking now and what she might be thinking – and, given the powder keg I was about to put under her generous little christening gift, whether she had any more offerings to give. Ungrateful little chameleon, she'd be thinking, Stupid, ungrateful little chameleon. I give her all the happiness in the world and she does *this*.

Idly, almost without thinking, I checked my phone for messages. There was one from Matthew. It said, 'Don't forget to buy a good, stout rucksack.' My heart turned over at the sight of his name. I wiped the message and then punched out a number.

*

Francis was standing drop-mouthed by the fireplace, the back of his head reflected in the mirror. For the first time I noticed, with great tenderness, that his hair was beginning to go a little thin. Having just dropped The Bombshell I did not feel it was quite the appropriate time to point this out. After saying, 'I'm going to India, Francis, but I'm not going with you . . .' it would have been interesting to see his response if I had added, 'Oh, and by the way, darling, your hair's going a little thin at the back . . .'

Beyond his reflection was that Perfect Looking-Glass World, in which everything looked solid and real yet was fragile illusion. Break the glass and that world would end. Through there was where the good fairies lived. Only the thirteenth fairy lived on this side, my side.

Francis looked scared rather than angry, which fleetingly I thought was odd. The face that confronted him, my face, could not be read clearly, even by me.

'Going alone then?' he said.

'No.'

19

Love in a Warm Climate

The driver parked the little cream-coloured car as close to the level-crossing as he could and then began batting cheerfully at the faces gathering at his open window. They were peering at us and talking excitedly as we sat in the back – young, old, in between, males only at the front, some of them just boys. They were dusty because there had been no rain and the car churned at the unmade road. Some of the dust caught in my throat and I coughed while the spectators looked in, nodding their approval. Coughing and hawking was one of the less seductive pastimes in this vast and beautiful land. Nod, nod, they went, white-teethed, with huge grins, eyes alive with merriment as they encouraged me to really let it go. I drained my little bottle of water and managed to stop. They were still smiling. Mostly their clothes were old, faded and western. One of them pointed to a logo on his chest which said 'Levis'.

'Hello, hello,' they waved at us. 'British, British . . .'

I waved back, suddenly feeling like Princess Diana. The smiling of strangers is infectious. Their smiles broadened, the waving became more frenetic, the press on the car more acute. Now a few little girls dared wriggle their way to the window, washed-out print dresses slipping off their shoulders, gold in their ears. Their mothers and sisters held back, holding their saris up to their faces, smiling and self-conscious, in their pinks and oranges and yellows, as bright as birds of paradise. More men arrived, jostling and laughing, hands coming in to try to shake ours. We were in the middle of nowhere – some-where between Bharatpur and Jaipur – and it was stiflingly hot. I coughed again but the water bottle was empty.

'Come to my house,' said one.

'And mine,' said another.

269

'You can have drink. Nice beer, nice Coca-Cola.'

A tall old man with a long white beard and tattered dhoti made his way to the front of the crowd. They parted to let him come forward, and he put his hands together in *namaste* and held them up at us through the window in a beseeching manner. Then he bowed his head to us three times.

'Come back, British,' he said. 'Come back to save us from this very terrible corruption.'

Everybody nodded. The smiles became broader.

'England. Lovely,' laughed one.

'Lords,' said another, elbowing through. 'Very good cricket.'

'Manchester United,' said a third, nodding and smiling.

'Come back British,' said the old man again. And he slipped back into the crowd.

'Well, that's very heartening,' said my sister. 'Nice to find we're wanted somewhere for a change.' And she bestowed a queenly wave.

'I'd give my eye teeth for a drink,' I said.

The train roared past and the gates went up. She turned and gave another regal wave as the car pulled away. Behind us the smiling and jostling ceased.

'Stop,' I said to our driver.

He pulled into the side. Behind us the crowd surged forward again, excited, chattering.

'Mr Singh,' I said, 'would it be all right to go to one of their houses?'

Mr Singh looked at his watch. We were due in Karauli for dinner with the Maharajah at his palace hotel. Mr Singh did not like saying no to us, so he always did that peculiarly Indian thing of saying yes and moving his head negatively at the same time. We'd learned how to interpret this over the past few days and not to ask for what was hard to give, but this time I decided to stand my ground.

'How many hours to Karauli?' I asked.

He looked uncomfortable. 'Two,' he said, 'maybe three.'

'That means four,' said Virginia. Indian time went with Indian miles. We had already been driving for two hours.

'Oh, go on,' I said. 'Why not? It's an adventure.'

'Go on then,' said Virginia.

Mr Singh shrugged and looked pained.

Outside there was a laughing frenzy. 'Yes, come, welcome,' the crowd shouted. 'See my house, it's a very nice house.'

Mr Singh sighed. Virginia laughed nervously. 'OK,' she said. 'After all, it's polite.'

Our host was a young man, perhaps twenty-five, small and barefoot and wearing a western shirt and dusty blue dhoti. He was very pleased to be chosen and kept turning round to smile at us and encourage us as he led the way through the rutted, dusty pathways. The air was not quite bad but not quite sweet, and the houses that flanked the road were eyeless patchworks of all manner of bits and pieces. The nearest things I'd ever seen to them were the sheds old men used to build on their garden allotments. We arrived at a one-storey construction made from basic concrete, bits of wood and corrugated iron, with a faded orange curtain draped across its door.

Virginia looked at me, and I looked at her, and she crossed her eyes in a sympathetic grimace of togetherness as the curtain was pulled aside. The man called into the darkness – something to do with British and something to do with bread – I heard the words 'roti, roti'. Then out came a very young, very pretty, very shy woman, holding a baby and with another child of two or so clinging to her hand. She cast down her eyes as she sidled past and then went swiftly up the rutted track, her yellow sari fluttering as she slipped out of sight, pulling the reluctant child behind her.

'Soon, soon,' said our host. 'Come in, come in.' He hooked the curtain up and we bent our heads to enter.

Light came from a small opening at the back – a brilliant streak of it, full of motes and specks and blinding in the rest of the gloom. But it was cool inside and smelled of damp earth and paraffin. Our host showed us to a stool and a chair

271

by a small, square table – the stool local and rough-fashioned, the chair – clearly his great pride – a straightback with a plush seat, looking much as if it had just come out of a boarding-house dining room in Brighton. Virginia sat on this, I took the stool. We folded our hands in our laps and waited while our host beamed and beamed at us, nodding with pleasure. There was only one room, only one doorway. People came to the curtained entrance, but he shooed them away and went on standing in front of us with profound gestures of welcome and honour.

He gave the *namaste*, which we returned, and then said, 'I am Sunil.'

'I am Virginia,' said my perfectly composed sister. 'And this is my sister, Dilys.'

'Ah,' he said, 'I also have a sister. Sisters are good things.'

There was the slightest of pauses.

'They are,' I said.

'They are,' added Virginia quickly, as if not to be outdone.

We all three nodded our accord.

It had taken a long journey – longer than a flight to Delhi and our various tourings by road – to get me to the point of thinking that they might be. At any moment Virginia could revert to her own impossible ways and flare up. Or I might revert to my – apparently – impossible ways and make her. I was responsible for whatever happened on this journey – between her and me, between her and India – because I had practically forced her to come. An experiment, I told myself privately. Expediency, was what I told her.

'Please,' I had said. 'It's planned and paid for, and now Francis can't do it after all. It'd be such a waste.'

That got her, as I knew it would. I was learning, slowly, to adapt to her extreme sensitivities.

Francis gave the final appeal. 'For God's sake, do please go with her, Ginny,' he said, very convincingly. 'You'll be doing us all a favour. Otherwise she'll set off alone and you know better than most what that could mean.'

'Oh, what?' I asked, quite intrigued, but he just gave me a quelling look.

She liked the sense of conspiracy. Lunatic little sister having a strange mid-life whatsit. And Bruce dared to stand up to her and told her she would always regret it if she didn't go . . . So she did. I suppose the dangled jewel was too desirable, even for her to turn down. India – in luxury, and all paid for. Even a discarded golden princess has her price.

So far, with a few little difficulties – like finding ourselves in a double bed together, an experience which scotched any sisterly yearning I ever had for Austenesque boudoir togetherness – we were doing well. Sisters might be A Good Thing – but some of them had bloody big elbows.

Sunil waited, anxiously looking from us to the door and back again. It didn't seem polite to do too much staring, but as our eyes became accustomed to the dimness we could see a small wooden box used as a cradle and woven mats on the floor which evidently made up their bed. There were a few bowls and jugs on a bench along one wall, and an enormous metal cauldron from which he helped himself to an enamel mug of water. He held up his finger to us as he drank, as if to say, 'Your turn soon.' And it was. Within a few minutes his wife returned with two tins of Coca-Cola and – unbelievably – a small packet of cut white bread wrapped in waxed paper.

'Special roti,' said our host. His wife moved shyly to the far corner of the room, folding the children into her sari with her. We were solemnly given the tins, which he opened for us first, and then the waxed paper was pulled back from the cousin to Mother's Pride. We each took a piece. And then we nodded and sipped and munched.

'Very special roti,' he said, pleased. 'From Britain.'

Mr Singh peered in around the curtain nervously and looked at his watch. He was also given a piece.

'And how is the Queen?' asked our host.

'Very well,' said Virginia.

'Beautiful lady,' he said, making an eloquent gesture with

273

his hands. And then he gave a dramatic sigh. 'And Princess Diana,' he added, and nodded sadly.

'Ah, yes,' I said.

We all paused to give the sadness its proper due.

'And you have husbands?'

We agreed that we had.

'With good jobs?'

We agreed that this was so.

'And you, Sunil? What is your job?' asked Virginia.

'Oh, I am very lucky, very lucky. I make –' He got up and went to another corner of the room, returning with a half-finished sandal.

'Sandals,' I said. And took it from him and inspected it as it seemed polite to do. I saw him slide a quick look at my feet and then away again sharpish. Virginia's were hidden beneath her skirt and she kept them there. We all looked from the sandal to my feet again and even the two-year-old laughed. His wife immediately hushed her, but her eyes still danced with both amazement and amusement. Even barefoot in this most basic of communities, her feet was considerably smaller and daintier than mine. I knew she was the one who carried that immense water cauldron on her head. How many times a day? Two? Three? Four?

'Peasant feet,' I said.

Sunil looked embarrassed and did that negative/positive head movement again. There was an awkward silence. The children dug themselves even further into their mother, peeking out from her with big eyes.

'It is a very nice house,' I said.

Virginia nodded. 'And you are very kind.'

'Thank you, thank you,' he said, bowing again. His wife beamed through a fold of her sari and the children giggled with delight.

We were both near to tears at the generosity of it all.

'Mem?' called Mr Singh. He woggled his wristwatch at us through the open doorway. We got up and bowed.

274

'Time to go. Thank you, thank you,' we both said.

Virginia put her hands together and bowed a blessing. Everybody stood up and bowed back. I opened my bag. Virginia looked at me uncertainly. Then she looked away, tickling the baby's chin, cooing to it. Just typical of her, I thought peevishly, to leave the decision to me. I shrugged, not sure at all how much would be right. Given the cost of the Coca-Cola and the bread and how poor they clearly were, it should be generous. I indicated to Virginia that I would do the honours. She looked at me even more uncertainly and gave a little shake of her head. I shrugged again and gestured at the empty drink cans and the loaf. I looked at Mr Singh, but he wasn't giving anything out except impatience to go. The man and his wife and his children were all staring at us, unsure, half smiling. I dipped into my bag and brought out a couple of large rupee notes – about five pounds' worth – and handed them to Sunil.

Instantly his smile froze – he stepped back as if I held out poison. When I gestured that he should take them, he stepped back even further. Behind me I heard Mr Singh draw in his breath. In front of me the wife retreated back into the shadows. For a moment nothing moved – and then Virginia darted forward, took the notes and began chattering to the man about children and how it was the custom in our country to give money to each child you meet.

'It is the British custom, Sunil,' she said, firmly.

The man looked troubled – Mr Singh joined in and nodded encouragingly – then Virginia stepped over to the children and tucked a rupee note into each hand. The toddler looked at her fist in wonder, while the baby, universal gesture, began to bring the money up to its mouth to suck. Virginia quickly took it from the baby's tight grasp and tucked it out of sight in the folds of the mother's sari. Everybody laughed, except the baby, which – universal reaction – screamed. The tension had gone. It was a gift for the children, nothing more. Face, pride, honour – all were saved by Virginia. As we said our

275

final goodbye she shot me a look that I hadn't seen since Snow White was revived in front of the wicked Queen.

'Sorry,' I mouthed.

'You and your Lady Bountiful act,' she said. And pushed me out of the doorway.

We trudged back to the car, waving over our shoulders with false, bright smiles. 'Would you invite someone into your house for lunch and then take money off them?'

I remembered Francis's jokey suggestion of doing just that to her. Only now it wasn't funny and I didn't laugh. I winced. I also thought, for the umpteenth time, that if my friend Carole were with me, instead of this difficult bit of bloodkin called a sister, the trip would have been so much easier. But then, easy was not the point of it. I was here to find redemption. And to learn to love my sister. And hope that she might one day learn to love me.

I was also thinking as I sank back into the car and returned my purse to safekeeping, *bugger, bugger, bugger,* she's *right.*

'Sorry,' I said, as our much relieved driver started the engine.

He gave that Indian headshake again. 'Do not worry,' he said. Meaning do.

As we drove along the dusty road to Karauli, I remembered standing in front of the looking glass and telling Francis that I had decided to go to India with my sister because if she saw the other side it might help her not to be so envious of me. To be aware of how much she possessed.

I also remembered what he said in reply.

'And how about you?' he asked mildly.

'I already know,' I said.

At which he looked at me a little strangely.

'I wonder,' he said. But at least the fear had gone from his face.

20

Long Day's Journey into Right

Years ago, when I first met Francis, he told me that he still had nightmares about his school. Would he get his homework – he called it prep – in on time? Would he pass muster with the worst of the teachers and avoid sarcasm and singling out? Would he fail on the sports field? Would he pass his exams?

I listened and looked sympathetic but I understood nothing about childhood trauma. Virginia was right. Oh, I had suffered from those shoes, that raincoat, the bag of potatoes and oranges, but none of it went very deep. My life had never been turned upside down because there was nothing to turn. I had known no other way. There never had been a golden time in my life, there never had been a mother who laughed or a sister who smiled nicely and shared; I had never lost carpet on the floor, toys and treats, soft new clothes bought specially for me, the adoration of two women and the petting of a mini-goddess. Other people lived in different ways, that was all, I thought.

Looking back to that childhood, this may have been happiness. Certainly I never had a dream about any of it, never stayed awake at night churning it over and over like Francis and his school, or felt it gnawing at me, like my sister had been gnawed at from the night the wailing harbinger of ill arrived. By comparison my growing up had been like walking a flat plain going absolutely nowhere. Without disappointment. And before I ever came to the age when slings and arrows might have found their mark, I was happily protected by my cocoon of a marriage. I understood Virginia's anger. I who asked for, who needed, so little, had been given so much. Apparently quite painlessly.

Well, now I knew it in buckets, in spades, in ocean upon

ocean. Every night, Delhi to Agra, Agra to Jaisalmer, Jaisalmer to Dungarpur, there was the pain and there was Matthew, so real I could feel him lying next to me, so real he spoke things in my ear, seductive things that made me wake sweating with desire, and then lie there, weak with tears and longing, disgusted with myself.

Or he would call me awake to see some new sight – a Jain temple, a wedding procession, an ancient, decaying palace with mirrored ceilings and glass walls, a room of exuberantly erotic frescoes. I would open my eyes and be halfway out of bed before I remembered. And then I would bite my thumb, understanding at last, while the pain made me want to cry out. Virginia slept through it all. It was my secret. If I could relate anything of Aunt Eliza's tale to myself, it was that I should keep my secret, too. As with hers, there were only three people in the world who knew mine, and that was risky enough. I had already destroyed a life. Oh, not in the real world – it was my father who had done that, and a system in which women were second-class and whose value as mothers was negligible without men beside them to push the pram and pay the rent. No – what I had destroyed for my sister was that beautiful looking-glass world, which to her had been real enough and into which she could never enter again. There was no point in my denying it to her when she was six years old, just as there was no point in my denying it to her when she was fifty-six years old. She had seen it with her own eyes, and she knew it was real and out of reach.

I don't suppose Virginia had ever considered herself an Existentialist or a disciple of Sartre, but she sure did believe that I was responsible for what I had done to her and that I should judge myself accordingly. I had. I could not hurt my family again. Neither my husband, my children nor my sister. And then there was the good fortune. Haunting me, alongside dreams of Matthew, were my aunt's words: 'I couldn't live on twenty-five bob . . .' and 'Love, dear? It doesn't keep the bailiff away.'

When I told Matthew that I was going to India without him and that I was never going to see him again, he was not surprised. Enraged yes, hurt yes, but not surprised. 'I never thought you would,' he said. 'I hoped. But I never believed it.'

'I did.'

'Why now?'

'It was the rucksack,' I said, almost hysterically. 'I just couldn't see myself with a rucksack.'

He sat on the end of the bed, amid that half-emptied space, with the peeling posters and sagging curtain and those futile egg cups as his backdrop, and he looked even younger. His eyes were that penetrating blue again, Titian's sky, the exotic sapphires of fidelity.

'How did you always know?'

He spoke in a voice I had not heard before. A detached voice, as if he wasn't really there any more.

'From the moment I walked into that private view and saw you in a white dress, with your hair just so and yourself so poised, I knew. You had far, far too much to lose. You had no idea how much. Nothing to judge it on. But I had a sixth sense – the same one that I got when you talked to me about replacing my car, about buying a phone, about five-star hotels in India. It's the rock you've built on. That's how you love yourself, that's how you let others love you. So you would have gone eventually. Too much to lose.'

That stung. It was the sort of thing my sister would say. 'Well, I didn't think it would end like this. I never *knew*, as you put it. So why go on with it? Why Dorset? Why any of it?'

'Never heard of Bastard Hope?'

'Too much to lose wasn't just dresses, Matthew, or cars. It's other people's happiness, too.'

'There was a dead place in you when we met. It will be a dead place again.'

'I know that,' I said. It was, of course, the Royal Chamber.

His detachment slipped, just for a moment, and his voice

was hard. 'You know that we'll never be happy again, don't you? Not you and not me. Those waking up in the morning wondering why you are smiling days are gone for good. From now on at best we'll be getting through, propped up by whatever we find. But we'll never know complete happiness ever again.'

He was right, of course.

Six-year-old Virginia's voice: I'll never be happy again.

Well, sister of mine. Now I have joined your ranks.

Francis met us at Heathrow. Bruce couldn't be there because he had hurt his back. I saw Virginia's mouth pull down at this bit of news. 'Typical –' she began.

I said warningly, 'Ginny . . .'

I felt, rather than saw, Francis freeze. He was waiting for the explosion. Instead my sister took a deep breath – you could actually see her counting – and said, 'Sorry. It's been a long flight. Poor Bruce.'

Francis looked at me and raised an eyebrow.

I looked back at him with an expression of deep smugness. Inside, my heart was breaking into a thousand pieces – pain in every bit of me – but I kept that archly smug look on my face. I must be just as I was before. The Perfect One. It's a cold thing, perfection, as the poets say.

I suddenly thought of Davina Bentham. How much had really changed in 200 years? Who remembered or cared about her and the sacrifices she made? There's still a mountain of wives and women who come out crashing those cymbals and end up lotus-eating in Jaeger and Harvey Nicks. This is, indeed, a little life and it is rounded by a long, long sleep. Even the airport, bloody old Heathrow, had the power to hurt. I should have been standing there with Matthew, not linking my arm through my husband's and acting his perfect wife.

I thought I might work on the book again – something to do. I understood now what it was to have a passionate nature, I understood now what it was to know pain, and I also understood the enormity of her bravery in defying all the odds to stay with what she loved. That was the piece of the jigsaw that evaded me. Even if it never got published, she, too, was a sister and she might be a way back to health. If I couldn't be like her, I could honour her. It would be something to do to keep my fingers from being idle . . .

We dropped Virginia home, paid our respects to the injured Bruce; our husbands listened while we told our tales and agreed that one way or another everyone becomes born anew in the soul of India. They with so little, us with so much. And vice versa.

Then Francis and I went home ourselves. On the doorstep my sister and I embraced. It was what Hollywood calls a movie moment. And then we were on our own in the car. Small talk. I could only manage small talk. We were taking the exact route back into town that I took from Kingston the last time I saw Matthew.

I said, 'Poor them. If Bruce's back doesn't mend quickly he won't be able to work – which means he can't earn.'

Francis nodded. And then said, 'Lucky you married me then.'

The assault of his words was physical. So the knife could be twisted anytime, anyplace, anywhere. I wondered when the pain would become manageable. *When?*

Indoors he made some tea and we sat drinking it on the settee in the old companionable way. I felt so tired. I leaned back and closed my eyes and heard Matthew sighing, felt him breathing in my ear. I sat up quickly. Opened my eyes again. It was Francis. He was saying something to me. I shook myself alive. 'Sorry,' I said, 'I was miles away –'

He pulled my head on to his shoulder and he nodded. 'You've been on a very long journey,' he said. 'For a very long time –'

'Only two weeks –' I began.

'For a *very* long time. But now you've come back to me.'

There was just something in the timbre of his voice, something underneath the ordinariness of it.

I turned to look at him.

He looked back at me.

So he always knew, too.